THE AFTER MIDNIGHT GHOST BOOK

ALSO EDITED BY JAMES HALE

The Thirteenth Ghost Book
The Midnight Ghost Book

The
After Midnight
Ghost Book

Edited by
JAMES HALE

Hutchinson
London Melbourne Sydney Auckland Johannesburg

Hutchinson & Co. (Publishers) Ltd

An imprint of the Hutchinson Publishing Group
3 Fitzroy Square, London WIP 6JD

Hutchinson Group (Australia) Pty Ltd
30–32 Cremorne Street, Richmond South, Victoria 3121
PO Box 151, Broadway, New South Wales 2007

Hutchinson Group (NZ) Ltd
32–34 View Road, PO Box 40–086, Glenfield, Auckland 10

Hutchinson Group (SA) (Pty) Ltd
PO Box 337, Bergvlei 2012, South Africa

First published 1980
© in this collection Hutchinson & Co. (Publishers) Ltd 1980
The individual copyright in each story remains with its author

Set in Intertype Baskerville

Printed in Great Britain by The Anchor Press Ltd
and bound by Wm Brendon & Son Ltd
both of Tiptree, Essex

ISBN 0 09 140600 5

Contents

Contents

Introduction

When you ask writers to write a ghost story for a collection such as this, they say that they've never written one before, and it's not their kind of thing. They are thinking of the invisible-coach-and-horses-rattling-and-neighing-up-the-gravelled-drive-at-midnight variety of ghost story. No, no, you say; *any* kind of ghost story will do as long as it's good. *Any* kind? they ask dubiously. At this point you are expansive and confident in the breadth of their imagination. Take your pick, you say: historical, romantic, fantastic, modern, experimental, conventional, real, whatever you like. They go away and brood. A few months later the stories begin to arrive, and they have taken you at your word! It's extremely unnerving.

The variety of the stories in this collection is to my mind extraordinary. Take first, for instance, Robert Nye's brooding and superb story 'Glendower'; move from there to Steve Stern's present-day American tragi-comedy; go on to the pseudonymous H. H. Washbrook's disturbing German experience; travel a few continents to James Aldridge's Australian aborigine's trial; return to Fay Weldon's modern lives in an English stately home. The stories cross seas and centuries with the ease of a phantom passing briskly through a brick wall.

I don't know, in fact, of any recorded cases of *ghosts* crossing continents. If a family emigrates to Australia in order to flee a British poltergeist, does the pet kookaburra get flung across the living room? Ghosts have been known to haunt aeroplanes; the Bermuda Triangle isn't too safe for sailing vessels; the beasts clearly like hanging around the *means* of travel. But do they travel well? I don't think so. Traditionally, they are house-bound. They haunt places, not people. So just remember, if there's a ghost where you live : you are the intruder. Be kind to your invisible friend. You may become one in time.

James Hale

ROBERT NYE

Glendower

That night he was born there was a storm. The rain came down thick and cold. Wolves howled in the woods above Sycharth, and the brook Cynllaith burst its banks. It was so dark that you couldn't see your hand if you held it up in front of your face. Then, about midnight, the storm ceased. The downpour softened to a steady drum, drum, drum. After a while the moon rode out. The wind dropped and the stars stood still. But there was something stormy even in this new calm. The mountains to the west and north looked on fire with moonlight. The river Tanat ran red. Suddenly the sky was full of birds. A swan, drifting low over the water, shed feathers as it flew. Cocks began to crow, as if the day had come.

In the big brocaded bed, in the highest tower of the house called Sycharth, the woman lay back and smiled at the child which the midwife was holding up by its heels. She hummed, tired and pleased, as she listened to the child's first crying.

'Owain,' she said.

The woman was beautiful. She had long black hair and blue eyes. Her name was Helen. She was descended from the princes of Deheubarth, one of the three families which had once ruled all Wales between them.

'Owain,' she said again.

The midwife nodded. The midwife had red hair and a long nose. 'The right name,' she said. She took up the dagger she

9

had used to cut the birth cord, and plunged it into a bowl of water.

'A name for a prince,' the mother said softly. The child had stopped crying now. She held him in her arms but his head was turned away from her. The child's eyes were wide open. It was as if he was already staring with some kind of understanding at the dagger in the midwife's hand.

'The firelight on the blade,' said Helen. She shivered. 'Oh put it away, do! I can see it reflected in his eyes.'

The midwife said nothing. She picked up the dagger's sheath, which was made of snakeskin, and tried to slip the shining blade into it. The sheath swelled and burst. Then there was red all over her fingers.

'You've cut yourself,' said Helen.

The midwife shook her head. Her hair was the same colour as her hands, and that hair seemed to drip red too as the firelight licked at it. She held up the broken sheath. 'I'm not cut at all,' she said. 'The sheath was full of blood.'

Helen frowned, dabbing at her forehead with a square of wine-soaked silk. She had lost quite a lot of blood in giving birth, and now she was beginning to feel dizzy and confused. She kept staring at the midwife's crimson fingers. She hugged the child tight to her breasts. Then her puzzled blue eyes turned away to the wall, and she noticed another sheath, a bigger one, a richly embroidered one, a sheath with a long sword in it.

Helen hesitated for only a heartbeat. She took a deep breath. Her knuckles were white where her hands tightened about the child.

'Go on,' she whispered.

'My lady?'

'Draw that sword,' Helen said.

The midwife drew the sword from the long sheath.

The sword came out dripping with blood. More blood flowed from the open mouth of the sheath. It was like a wound that could not be staunched.

'No,' said Helen weakly. 'No, no, no,'

She put her hands over the child's eyes, so that the child should not see what she was seeing. But the child began to cry again when she did that, and it cried and it cried, and it would not stop crying until its mother took her hands away and let those bright little eyes get their fill of the bloody sword and the bleeding sheath on the wall.

Outside the house, but within the moonlit circle of its moat, was a chapel built in the shape of a cross. A man was kneeling on the flagged floor of the chapel. The man had not paid any heed to the storm and now he remained equally unmoved by the strange peace that had followed it. The man was not praying. His eyes were open. They were dazzled with tears that did not fall. He cupped a swan's egg in his hands.

The man's name was Gruffydd. He was master of Sycharth, and Helen's husband. Royal blood flowed in Gruffydd's veins also, and showed in the way he raised his head proudly to gaze at the altar. He was descended from the princes of Powys, another of the kingdoms of ancient Wales. Hence his right to keep swans at Sycharth.

The swan, Gruffydd thought sourly, the royal swan. No subject could possess a game of swans without licence from the Crown. Once his family would have granted that licence to others. Now they were supposed to be grateful that a foreign king granted such right to them on account of their royal descent.

Tall, tapering beeswax candles burned on either side of the crucifix. The Christ looked angry. A trick of the darkness, no doubt. But the candle flames themselves looked angry to Gruffydd's eyes.

While he waited for news from the tower where his wife was, Gruffydd kept his mind busy with indignation. His eyes never moved from the nailed hands. His thoughts dwelt especially on the way in which Wales had been tricked into slavery, a hundred years before, when the English King Edward had promised the Welsh people that they should have their own prince to rule over them, a prince born in Wales and speaking no English. How stupidly a man's heart could be invaded by old insults at such moments as these! For Edward had kept his promise. Of course. Edward had kept his promise by sending his queen to the newly built castle at Caernarvon for the birth of his own son, Edward the Second, who being a baby could indeed speak no English. . . .

Gruffydd sought to calm his mind, to stay it on some gentler image. The crucifix was all there was. The Christ was like a swan. Spotless white plumage of the flesh. The wound in the side, like the orange-red bill. What was it you called the black knob on the end of a swan's bill?

The berry. That was it. That was what you called the black knob on the end of a swan's bill.

Gruffydd tried to pray.

'*Libera nos, quaesumus, Domine,*' he said aloud.

He stopped. He gave up. His lips set back in a bitter line. *Libera nos.* . . . Deliver us. Lord, once. Yes, once upon a time, he supposed, as in a story for children, Wales had indeed been free. But what did that mean? Free? A word you said quickly, unless you were thinking about it. Free. Freedom. Would the wind before the English came have blown more wildly on these same hills? Would the rain before the English came have tasted sweeter to the tongue? It was not impossible. The wind and the rain were free and they let you know it. Freedom. What it meant to be free. The wind and the rain were free and if you were not they let you know that. To be a slave meant to think about words like free and freedom all the time. Ach, the wind and the rain must have been *different*, that was certain, in the old days.

Libera nos. Besides which. Besides which, had not the Welsh themselves once been the masters? The rulers of all Britain, after the Romans went. So it was said. But then there had been trouble with the Picts and the Scots, and Vortigern had let the Saxons in. Hengest and Horsa. Gruffydd had seen a history by a monk called Gildas. *De Excidio et Conquestu Britanniae.* If you could believe it, the English had been called in to help put down the Picts and the Scots. They had done this, but then overcome the original Britons through treachery, tricking Vortigern into letting them send home to Saxony for great contingents of their own countrymen. With a result that Gruffydd's forefathers had been driven into these western mountains by pagan barbarians, and lost their name of Britons and their kingdoms. They had lost everything, as their poets said, except wild Wales. And, for such as Gruffydd, the right to keep the merest token of kinghood. Allowed to keep a royal bird. Allowed to be reminded by a foreign king that his fathers had once been kings here.

Gruffydd stroked the swan's egg and remembered his wife in labour. He held the egg against his cheek. It was of a greyish-olive colour. He fancied he could hear the beginnings of movement inside it. He closed his eyes and touched his eyelids to the shell. Yes, there it was again. A brittle, uncertain shiver of life.

The moonlight, falling through a narrow window, cast Gruffydd's shadow across the altar. He got up and rubbed his knees. For the first time, he heard the crowing of the cocks. A frown furrowed his forehead. The night beyond the thick stone walls of the chapel sounded all at once full of unlikely noises. He could distinguish the neighing of horses, the clash of hooves, and over these sounds the crying of birds of many kinds and the whirr as of a great host of wings. He hurried to the door and opened it. He drew his cloak about him, and stepped into the dark.

He had not taken more than a dozen strides when his left elbow was seized from behind. His sword was in his right fist and the offending fingers almost chopped off before he realized that his assailant was a woman.

'The swan flew against the wind!'

The woman's voice was shrill and ugly and urgent. Gruffydd could not make out her face in the shadow of what looked like a blue hood, but her body was bent as if with extreme age.

He found himself shouting, for no apparent reason, save that this night was unsettling, what with the neighing of the horses, and he was worried about his wife in labour in the tower room above.

'What the hell are you talking about?'

The woman seemed to ignore his question. She muttered to herself, in a low broken tone, some words of a language Gruffydd could not understand. Then she went on in the same chanting tone she had used at first:

'The swan. Your swan. The cob. His feathers were pieces of moon, master, patches and bits of the plague-improved flesh. They fell as he flew. His black legs trailing. It was beautiful.'

She is mad for certain, Gruffydd thought. She has the Black Death on her. Her manner suggested a mixture of disease and second childishness and the patronizing authority of someone suffering from the delusion that they are God. Gruffydd could cope with such things. But the word *plague* was one which he did not care to hear spoken. Half the people living on his own lands had died of it, at Glyndyfrdwy on the far side of the Berwyn mountains, and here at Sycharth.

'If you do not let go of my arm,' he said, 'I shall cut off your hands at the wrist.'

The woman relinquished her hold on his elbow. But then her fingers were scrabbling at him again. Gruffydd raised his sword. The woman's thin yellow fingers like claws were seeking and then touching the swan's egg he held wrapped in the fold of his cloak. Her nails and knuckles were stained with blood. All this he saw in a sudden stab of the moonlight. He had intended to kill her. But now the sword fell from his hand.

'None but the swan should hatch the swan's egg,' the woman said gently. 'Why do you carry it, master?'

'Because the pen is dead,' said Gruffydd.

A horse screamed in the stables.

The woman said, 'Not dead, master. Asleep.'

Gruffydd tried to break away. 'You speak in riddles,' he complained.

The hag held fast to his cloak with the egg under it. The claw-like fingers of her free hand were fondling and stroking the shell where he guarded it in the cloak's velvet lining from the cold of the night.

'I speak of Wales,' she said.

And then:

'Will you offend the Tylwyth Teg?' she whispered.

Gruffydd shrugged. He looked back over his shoulder to the chapel. The dim blue votive lamps that flickeringly illuminated its windows from the inside were good to see. Its outward shape also. Solid in the moonlight. 'You're crazed or possessed,' he said. 'The Tylwyth Teg are no more than shadows on the wall to frighten children, and you know it.' He glanced down at his sword where it lay on the ground and felt suddenly ridiculous. 'Look,' he said, 'there was a swan dead on her nest in the moat. The pen, dead, and the dead weight of her had crushed all her eggs save one. The cob had flown. I took up the one remaining egg. Foolish, no doubt. But my wife Helen –'

'A son,' said the hag.

The neighing of the horses was now terrible to hear. It sounded to Gruffydd as though they were trying to kick their way out of the stables.

'A son,' the woman said again. 'A son with eyes that see. A wolf from the west. An Owain indeed.'

Gruffydd stared at her. The face was all shadows, there seemed nothing else to it. 'You were with Helen?' he said. 'But how? You are not the woman I appointed. How do you know I have a son?'

'I know what I know,' said the woman. 'I know your two swans were marked with the mark of kings. Five nicks in the beak. Two lengthwise. Three across the bill.' She nodded. 'Remember to your wife the midwife who came, with the red hair and the long nose.' She laughed. 'And now you will give me the swan's egg,' she said.

Gruffydd was full all at once of blind, unreasoning fury.

'I will not!' he shouted.

He leapt back sharply, leaving his cloak in the old woman's grasp. He clutched the egg tight to his breast.

The hag turned away from him. Her body unbent in the moonlight. As he looked upon her from the back she was old

15

no longer, but young and tall, and with a gait like a queen.

'Gruffydd Vychan,' she said in a soft voice, 'tonight your immortality was born. But you will die before the swan flies that will one day be hatched from the egg you hold so dear!'

Birds wheeled above her in the night sky. She stretched out her arms to them, as if to bless or curse, and she was gone.

Gruffydd was a brave man, but now he shook with fear. He passed his hand through the space where the woman had stood. It was mere air. He took up his sword. It was covered with blood. Again there came a terrible screaming of horses. Gruffydd shuddered. He hurried towards the stables.

His grooms were nowhere to be seen. Gruffydd could not understand it. The grooms should have been sleeping in the loft, ready to calm and comfort his horses on such a night as this. As it was, the horses, unattended, had lashed themselves into a frenzy. Many had broken free of their tetherings, and run about, up and down the long low barn. Their polished sides were dripping with blood where they had kicked at each other and torn themselves in their blind turnings. The moonlight, streaming through a slit in the wall, picked out one horse, a giant black stallion, standing slightly apart from the others. His nostrils were distended, his neck blood-flecked, his fetlocks hacked and red. Unlike the other horses, the black stallion stood quite still.

From outside, shrill on the night air, came the crowing of a cock.

And, simultaneously, the crying of the child in the high tower.

The black stallion's eyes were looking at the man.

'No,' said Gruffydd as strongly as he could. *'No!'*

The cock crowed again.

The door was too far away.

The cock crowed for a third time.

'Helen,' said Gruffydd quietly.

The swan's egg smashed as the horse hit him. The yellow part of it ran everywhere.

AGNES SHORT

Intercom

The Chanonry is a tranquil street of high walls, trees and quiet, professorial houses. Four hundred and fifty years ago this same Chanonry contained within its high walls and dykes (for defence in troublous times) not only the grand cathedral church with its tower and sonorous bells, but also the bishop's palace, the prebends' lodgings with their yards and glebes, the chaplains' court (or chambers) and a hospital for twelve poor men.

But the great tower fell. The Reformation stripped the ancient cathedral of its statuary and gold and reduced it to the gaunt, grey proportions of a parish church. The houses of the prebends were demolished and the houses of the gentry sold, pulled stone from stone to build up different, democratic houses for the Presbyterian middle classes. The chaplain's passageway is lost and there is a students' hall of residence where the bishop's palace stood, but somewhere under the vaulted pre-cast concrete of the modern dining hall the old-town draw-well still holds its secret and the buried bodies of men. The hospital, too, has disappeared and what remains of the chaplains' court is an ordinary private house.

Or so Margaret Ford believed until she stood on the doorstep in a night of drenching rain and looked up at the great, blank wall above her. It was a wall of dead windows: the larger blinded by shutters, the smaller by stones and cement. Bricked up how many years ago? By whom? And why? The rain glistened on the pitted quarters of a heraldic crest set into the wall above a small, barred window. The girl made out beyond the darkness the crude outline of a boar's head, castles and Latin, picked out in scraps of scarlet and gold. *'Spe – '*

'Hope, lingering hopelessly on,' she thought, with unexpected sadness.

Beneath the crest there was the bricked-in crescent of what must once have been an arch, and a window embrasure at ankle level told her the walls were four feet thick. The raindrops which clung to the rough stone of the walls were dark and moist, like blood, except where the gleam from a street lamp rounded them briefly with light. The glistening street stretched on either side of her, silent and empty, between high, crenellated walls.

The only sound was the steady drip, drip of moisture from the overhanging trees and somewhere, in a far-away street, an echoing footstep which receded deliberately into silence. The girl shivered, pulled her cloak more tightly around her and rang the bell again.

The door opened and light flooded the steps.

'I'm so sorry. I hope you haven't been ringing for ages, but we can't hear the bell upstairs. Or downstairs, come to that. One of the penalties of living in a big house.'

The man was thin, with the nervous thinness of the ascetic. He was good-looking in a famished way, especially now, in dinner jacket and black tie. The girl stepped over the threshold and shook herself like a timid animal. Rain showered the hall with diamonds.

'Let me take your coat.'

Professor Adams lifted the dark cloak from her shoulders. His wife, descending the stair in her sensible black dress with the beading at the neck, felt an uncomfortable jolt of the heart when she rounded the last landing and saw them standing there. Her husband dark, thin, intense. And the girl . . . she could find no words to describe the girl. In her simple, timeless gown of crimson wool, belted loosely at the waist, and her black, straight hair she was at the same time innocence and danger. Joan Adams shook away the fear and stepped briskly down the last few steps.

'I'll show you where everything is, dear,' she said with a professional smile. She opened a door and they descended below street level to a low-beamed room of oak and brass and rough stone walls.

'We like the bare stone,' she explained. 'It's the original structure down here, all sixteenth-century. The floor's intact, too, but I'm afraid I drew the line at stone flags, even for history's sake. This is the intercom,' she went on, indicating a small box on the dresser. 'The walls are so thick it's impossible to hear them without it, so keep it switched on. Then you'll hear if one of them wakes. The kitchen is this way.'

She led the girl out of the beamed room by a second door, into an arched scullery.

'This is the old coach entrance,' Mrs Adams explained. 'They used to drive in this way to the courtyard. I expect you saw the crest on the wall outside. It really was a court in the old days, you see. Four sides of a square and four towers, one at each corner. The piece we live in is all that's left.'

'Who lived here?' asked the girl.

'Here? Originally twenty chaplains from the cathedral and a hard time they must have had, too. All sorts of rigid rules. Doors barred at eight o'clock and no women, of course. They still went in for celibacy in those days, though I expect some of them managed to get round it just the same, don't you?'

The girl didn't answer. She was looking upwards to the arched dimness of the ceiling where there was a huge iron hook.

'That's where they hung the lantern,' said Mrs Adams. 'And men too, I wouldn't wonder. Here's the kitchen,' she went on, going up three steps to the next room. 'I've left everything ready. There's coffee and sandwiches and so on when you want them. I think that's about all. I've locked the back door. In a house like this where everything is so spread out you have to be careful. You'd never hear if anyone came in uninvited. Not that they ever would,' she continued hastily – good baby-sitters were rare and precious – 'but it's best to be careful. Now I'll just show you where the children are.'

They passed back through the arch of the scullery and the low-beamed living room, up narrow stairs to the front hall and upwards again to the open doorway of a shuttered room. The girl looked quickly into the darkness – shadows, two beds, two sleeping shapes, more shadows.

'What do I do if they wake?' she whispered.

'They won't. They never do. But if by any chance something should disturb them, give them a drink of orange juice and tell them a little story. Reassure them that we'll be back soon. I've left a note of where we're going.'

As Margaret nodded, something made her glance over her shoulder. A movement? Or a stir of cold air? Behind her a shadowed corridor stretched to a short flight of steps; more doors. Stairs climbed upwards into narrow, creaking darkness. The uncurtained window of the landing showed her nothing but her own outline, a small, slim girl with flowing hair and a long dress. The dim landing lamp flickered back from the glass like candle flame against the night. Somewhere on the floor above them a board creaked, a window rattled softly in its frame.

'Is the rest of the house empty?' asked the girl, timidly.

'There's no one else in, if that's what you mean,' said Mrs Adams. 'Only you and the children. But there's nothing to worry about.'

'Joan!' called a voice from the hall. 'We'll be late!'

'Coming!' They descended to the front hall. 'I was just showing Margaret the ropes. Now,' she added, turning to the girl, 'are you sure you'll be all right?'

'There's television and so on,' said John Adams vaguely. 'Books. Help yourself. Make yourself at home.'

'Thank you, but I'm going to try and get some work done. It's so noisy in my digs and I've that essay of yours to finish.'

'Good girl,' said Adams. 'You'll find it quiet enough here and you can use any of my reference books you like. Oh and if you do hear noises, don't worry. It's only the central heating.'

Outside in the car Mrs Adams turned worriedly to her husband. 'Are you sure she's all right? She hardly spoke a word and she looks so frail. Almost unreal. That ridiculous dress and all that hair. And her eyes! She looks as if she lives in a different world.'

'She's all right. A bit tense, perhaps, but sensible enough. Things have been getting too much for her lately, that's all. Overwork, depression, end-of-term nerves, you know the sort of thing. And her digs sound pretty grim. She jumped at the chance of an evening on her own.'

'Yes, but the children ... you do think ... ?'

'For Christ's sake, Joan, stop fussing. You want to go to the party, don't you? I thought that was the whole point and you said yourself there was no one else.'

'Yes, I know, and you did very well to find anyone at all. But she gives me the creeps. You don't think she's on drugs, do you?'

'I have not the slightest idea. Would you like me to go back and ask her?'

His wife ignored the sarcasm. 'It's her eyes, I think. When I saw her standing on the doorstep in the rain with that cloak to her feet and the hood, I had the ridiculous idea that she'd found her way into the wrong century.'

'She's certainly brilliant on sixteenth-century poetry,' agreed Adams. 'Especially the love poems, which is odd because I gather she has no time for boys.'

'Oh?' Mrs Adams pricked up her ears. 'Not girls instead?'

'Of course not!' John Adams felt unreasonably angry on the girl's behalf. 'There's nothing at all abnormal about her. In fact, she's a particularly feminine and attractive girl. I had the impression that her fellow students just don't interest her.'

'Perhaps it's you she's after?' said Joan Adams with a laugh, but her voice had an edge which made her husband jam his foot down hard on the accelerator and set his teeth. The party had better be good.

The girl stood in the middle of the room and waited until the car engine disappeared into the distance. She stood a moment longer, listening to the silence, then she began to move slowly round the room, touching the rough stone of the walls with reverent fingers, tracing the outline of the ancient beams. There was a Jacobean chest, a refectory table, and a row of leather-bound books. Campion. Lyly. Sir Philip Sidney. She took one out, opened it and read aloud at random.

' "Joy to the person of my love".' Her voice moved like velvet in the silence. Suddenly her heart swelled and she laughed softly. She spread her skirts, dipped to the carpeted floor in a sweeping curtsy and began to pace the first stately steps of a galliard. Somewhere, far away and faint, she heard a lute pluck sweetly in time to her dance.

The girl paused, listened, but there was nothing.

'Wishful thinking,' she said aloud and sighed. 'And this won't get that essay written.'

She opened her bag and took out papers, a clip file and a sheaf of notes which she spread out in front of her on the refectory table. She turned off the main light and sat down at the table in the small golden pool of the reading lamp. She wrote a careful headline 'The Sacred and the Profane in Sixteenth-Century Poetry' and began to work.

It was some time before she noticed the music. But gradually she became aware that somewhere beyond the black and white clarity of the written word there was sound and light. Somewhere the soft, plucking beauty of a lute was stringing the darkness with gold. The girl's hand stopped and she looked up. Her eyes probed the shadows of the room, listening. The lamplight splashed the surface of the polished wood with gold but on the edge of that light the shadows held only shapes, formless and unknown. The notes dropped on, like needles now, into the silence. They were the same measured notes of the galliard. The girl's heart beat painfully fast until the crimson wool trembled over her breasts. Then a draught knifed under the ill-fitting door and the floor beneath her feet struck cold as stone. She pushed back her chair and stood up, holding her body rigid and tensing slender fingers against the oak of the table.

But the music had stopped. She listened for an endless minute until the room seemed to fill with the patter of rain on leaves and the creak of silence. But there was nothing else. Only against her cheek a puff of cold air like a dead kiss.

The girl shuddered. She straightened her papers with nervous, unseeing hands while her eyes searched the shadows.

At last she sat down and deliberately forced herself to concentrate on the carefully written page. 'The conflict of divine and human love . . . Woman on the one hand as Mary, on the other as Eve the temptress . . . the fleeting nature of beauty and human love contrasted with the permanence of heaven . . .'

Heaven in those days, she thought, was an unquestioned and coveted goal. Damnation must have seemed a very real danger, with one's own eternity at stake. Men might well have been driven to monstrous deeds to preserve that hope intact. She had made a marginal note to remind herself to follow up the point and decided to strengthen her spirits with coffee and something to eat.

She opened the second door, stepped quickly out under the vaulted arch and the hook, then up the three short steps to the kitchen.

While she waited for the kettle to boil, the girl went over and over the essay as she had written it so far. There was still, she knew, something that evaded her, but it would come. Professor Adams was good – some said brilliant – but there was an aspect of sixteenth-century literature which the girl felt had escaped even him. It was not a question of intellect or understanding or even of research. It was something more nebulous than that, something she could only describe as feeling. As she stirred the milky liquid in her cup, the girl realized with a strange sense of loneliness that she was more in tune with the period than he was.

It was then that she heard the voices. They came from the room she had left and seemed to be arguing. One pleading, the other, younger, protesting.

'It must be the intercom! The children have woken up.'

She left her cup on the dresser and hurried out of the kitchen, back to the living room. Sure enough, faint, blurred voices were coming from the intercom on the dresser. She flicked the switch to make sure and the voices stopped. She flicked it on again and the indistinguishable murmur resumed. She scurried out of the room and upstairs, but at the door of the children's room she stopped, listening, wondering how she was going to deal with these two unknowns. But she heard nothing. Until, as she stood tense and receptive, straining to hear, the sound of steady, peaceful breathing reached her ears from beyond the darkness.

'Someone talking in his sleep,' she decided and tiptoed quietly downstairs.

But she had scarcely regained the kitchen and picked up her cup when the voices resumed. Then the music. It was the same tune, but this time there were words, in a soft tenor voice which caressed the silence with persuasive sweetness.

> *Joy to the persone of my love although she me disdain*
> *Fixt are my thoughts and may not move*
> *And yet I love in vain.*

The lute played unmistakably in the background. The girl stood immobile, listening, while her eyes grew larger and darker in the pale oval of her face. She put down the cup with trembling deliberation and moved slowly towards the door. The skirts of her crimson gown brushed softly over the stone flags of the floor and her breath was like mist in the cold air.

But the beamed room was empty. She crossed to the dresser and put out a hand. The small grid of the intercom was warm to the touch. With fumbling fingers, the girl switched it off.

She stood a long moment with her hand on the set, waiting, while the silence taunted her with shadows.

'I'll leave it switched off,' she decided. 'That will stop them.' Then Mrs Adams' voice came back to her, competent and firm. 'Keep the set switched on. Otherwise you'll never hear them.' At last, submissively, the girl's fingers moved to the switch.

This time the result was instant and unmistakable. Margaret ran into the kitchen, snatched up the phone with hands which trembled uncontrollably, and fumbled at the dial. As she waited for someone to answer she glanced over her shoulder through the open door, across the gloom of the vaulted scullery to the low-beamed silence of that other room. And the intercom . . .

'Mary? Mary, listen . . .'

'Is that you, Margaret?' The voice sounded aggrieved. 'What on earth's the matter? I was just washing my hair.'

'There's something odd,' began Margaret anxiously, glancing over her shoulder to those alien shadows.

'How do you mean, *odd*? Look, I'm dripping all over the carpet. Hang on a sec while I get a towel.'

In the waiting silence the music came clearly across the distance, but as soon as Mary spoke again, it stopped. 'Okay now. What's going on?'

'I'm not sure, but I keep hearing music that isn't there.'

There was a snort from the other end. 'You've been at the Prof's whisky!'

'No, honestly, Mary. It's true. It's coming over the intercom. A man, singing.'

'It's probably the next door neighbour in his bath.'

'With a lute accompaniment?'

'His wife, playing to him as he soaks. Who lives next door anyway?'

'But it's not that kind of music, Mary. It's personal, as if he is singing to . . . *me*.' She paused, tense and waiting. 'Yes! There it is again. Can't you hear it?'

'Not a thing,' said Mary cheerfully. 'Look, Meg. You can pick up all sorts of things on an intercom. Radio transmissions. Other people's TV. Voices in the road. Just forget it. Haven't you a book to read?'

'Yes, but . . .'

'Then why not make yourself some coffee, put your feet up and enjoy it? I'd come round to keep you company, only I'm in the middle of setting my hair.'

The girl didn't answer.

'Are you still there, Meg? You're not having one of your moods again, are you?'

'I don't think so, but . . .'

'Look, Meg. Don't worry. It's somebody's record, that's all. But if you really want me to come over, I will.'

'No, of course not,' said Margaret humbly. 'You finish your hair. I'll be all right.'

Slowly she replaced the receiver and stood, listening. Now there was nothing. Nothing at all but the huge, silken silence of the night. She picked up the cup of coffee and walked deliberately back into the living room. She put the cup carefully on the table and sat down. But she made no attempt to work. Instead she sat wary and rigid, waiting.

Five long minutes passed. At last, when nothing happened, she picked up her pen and began to read over what she had written.

She read through almost five pages before she heard the weeping; soft, insistent, heartbroken. The poor little things! They must be having a nightmare and she'd been so absorbed she hadn't even heard them. She flung back her chair and sped upstairs.

But at the door of the children's room she stopped dead. There was no sound except the steady rise and fall of breathing. Carefully she tiptoed into the room and stood looking down at the two sleeping shapes.

'A bad dream,' she told herself. 'It must have been.' She slipped out of the room and moved reluctantly downstairs.

At the door of the living room she stopped. From inside the room came the same unmistakable sound of a woman weeping. 'I can bear it no longer!' followed by a heartbroken sob.

Then a man's voice, loving, anguished. 'Do not tempt me.'

The girl's heart flipped painfully. She leaned gasping against the wall while her trembling fingers plucked at the stone for support. She must be going mad. Mad. The wooden door at her face seemed an entrance to a different world and she was incapable of moving away. A cold draught stirred the folds of her skirt and she felt the hair on the nape of her neck rise. On either side of her stretched stone-flagged floors, stone walls and silent shadows. Here stood the common hall of the chaplains four hundred years ago. Here twenty priests had eaten together in candlelight and celibacy, night after night until death. Until eternity. Margaret felt terror rising like a scream in her throat. She pressed back against the rough wall, while her eyes searched the darkness fearfully, probing, probing . . .

Shadows stirred. A draught lifted the hem of her skirt and passed coldly on. Somewhere a window rattled. From the depths of the ancient passageway came a whisper like the breath of time. 'My deireste . . .'

The girl broke away from the wall and fled. Through the living room, through the scullery, to the telephone on the kitchen wall. She clutched the instrument with wild hands and dialled the number that Mrs Adams had left her.

She heard the phone shrill on and on, regular and strident like the beat of her own heart. But there was no reply. At a successful party records and conviviality drown all sounds except their own.

After five endless minutes the girl gave in. She dropped the phone back on to its hook and stood with head and shoulders bowed while tears of despair beaded her cheeks. She could fight alone no longer. If no one would help her there was nothing for her but to give in. She moved slowly back into the living room and stood submissively beside the intercom, waiting . . .

The small rectangle quivered soundlessly in the silence. The girl listened. And waited, while her fingers twisted restlessly in the strands of her belt. She heard breathing, the tiny creak of an infant turning over in bed, a childish mumble. Then, faint at first, but growing steadily closer came the swish of cloth on stone, of sandalled feet. The breathing grew louder and louder.

'Deireste . . .'

'No,' gasped the girl as she felt cold breath brush her cheek, her breast. 'Please, no . . . I can't bear it!'

She backed away across the room, her hands outstretched,

pleading. The voice strengthened until it filled the stone-flagged hall. 'Do not tempt me!'

Later, softly, came the song.

> *Oh woe is me that ever I did see*
> *The beauty that did me bewitch . . .*

The notes of the lute swelled and reverberated through the room until they seemed to soak into the very stone.

'Funny,' said Mrs Adams. 'She's not here.' They had let themselves into the house in the small hours with a careful key. 'I'll see if she's upstairs.'

Professor Adams drifted vaguely in a haze of alcoholic good humour towards the table, where his fuddled brain had recognized something he knew. An essay.

'Good girl. She's been busy. A sweet child. "Here woman is seen as the temptress who must be . . ." ' His smile became puzzled. The essay ended in mid-sentence. And at the foot of the page were three scrawled words, in different ink. 'Farewell my deireste . . .'

His wife appeared in the doorway.

'She's not upstairs either,' she said worriedly. She pushed past him towards the kitchen. But as she opened the door to the scullery something soft brushed against her face.

'John!' she screamed. 'She's here!'

Together they looked upwards, appalled, at the crimson gown, the pale dead face and flowing hair which hung from the lantern hook by a twisted cord – a tasselled, silken cord such as was worn in olden times by a novice priest.

FAY WELDON

Spirit of the House

Some time after the trouble with Jenny began, Christine wrote off to a professor of psychical research in California, whose name she had discovered in a magazine article. 'Whenever Jenny comes into the room,' Christine wrote, 'I feel cold. So I know there's something wrong with her. But what is it?' She had an answer sooner than she expected, and more alarming, too. The professor wrote that the presence of evil was often registered, by sensitives, in this manner; and was there a bad smell as well?

Now Jenny did indeed quite often smell strongly of carbolic but Christine felt that this was not in itself significant. The soap provided for employees up at the Big House was a job-lot of hard, orange, carbolic tablets, bought cheap from an army surplus store, and Jenny washed herself with it, hard and often. Christine always took Mornay's Lavender to work with her, the more sweetly to wash her pretty hands. She liked to smell nice, and her husband Luke liked her to smell nice, and how he could put up with Jenny smelling of carbolic, Christine could not tell. Let alone love her.

But carbolic was not, in itself, a bad smell. Nothing, after all, like the stench of sulphur and decomposition associated with the presence of the devil. True enough, though, and bad enough, that the feeling of cold wafted around Jenny like an

Fay Weldon

odour. She could be said to smell cold. Christine discontinued her correspondence with the Californian professor for fear of discovering worse. She prayed instead.

'Dear God, let him get over her. Dear God, let her not harm the baby. Dear God, let them believe me.'

But God seemed not to be listening. Luke went on loving Jenny, Jenny went on looking after Baby Emmy, and no one believed Christine when she said that Jenny was not to be trusted.

Christine had been married to Luke for nineteen years. She loved her husband with an energetic and consuming passion well able to withstand his occasional lapses into the adoration of passing girls. She would treat him, when he was thus enamoured, with a fond indulgence, saying, 'Well, men are like that, aren't they?' and waiting for common sense and reason to return, and uxorious content to shine once again from his gentle eyes. But Jenny was different – she had suspected something unwholesome about her from the very first. In retrospect it was hard to tell, of course, quite when she had begun to think it – before Luke started mooning after Jenny, or after. But surely it was before – a sickly, chilly menace, a sudden shiver down the spine? Evil, the professor had written. Or perhaps he only wrote that, knowing what she wanted to hear? Americans were strange.

Jenny was stranger. Now Christine feared for Luke, body and soul, and feared for Emmy, Lord Mader's baby daughter, even more. Jenny was Emmy's nanny. Little, pretty, safe words, adding up to something monstrous.

And of course if Christine murmured against Jenny, the other members of the staff assumed that Christine was jealous, and discredited what she said. Jenny was quiet, gentle, pale and young. Christine was noisy and volatile and ruddy and in her middle years. And Christine's husband, everyone knew, was in love with Jenny, trailing after her, gazing after her.

'But look,' Christine felt like saying, 'he's been in love a dozen times in as many years. It's just the way he is. I don't mind.

He's a genius, you see. A mathematical genius, not one of your artistic geniuses, but a genius all the same. My feeling about Jenny is nothing to do with what Luke feels or doesn't feel for her.'

But the rest of the staff were dull, if good-hearted, and had their preconceptions about the world, which nothing now would shake: it was almost as if the chilly presence of Jenny had cemented in these preconceptions, where once they had stood free, able to change and move. Their vision narrowed to what they already knew. Christine concluded that Jenny had a strange deadening power over everyone, excepting only, for some reason, herself.

Jenny had a white, dead face and large, pale eyes which she magnified with round owl spectacles, and short plain hair and a child's body. The face was thirty, the body was thirteen. Perhaps that was her power – the desire of the grown man for the pre-pubertal girl? A sickly and insidious love! And did the women perhaps remember themselves at thirteen and set Jenny free now, to do what they would have liked then?

Christine herself, at forty, was plump and maternal and pretty and busy. There could be nothing unhealthy in anyone's desire for her, and many did desire her, but she seldom noticed. She loved Luke.

Christine, the Doris Day of Maderley House! Wonderful Maderley House, Stately Home, giving the lucky villagers of Maderley full employment! With its Elizabethan chimneys, and Jacobean mullions, Georgian casements and Victorian tiles, it still remained imposing, if hardly gracious. Its lands and gardens, its ancient oaks, its Disneyland and zoo, its Sunday lunches (£50 a place-setting) with Lord and Lady Mader, made it popular with millions. Lord Mader was often indisposed and his young brother Martin sent in his place, but the third Lady Mader was always there. She was young and did as she was told, as did the villagers.

The latest, newest Lady Mader had, it is true, given birth to little Emmy instead of to a son, but as Lord Mader observed,

coming to terms with his disappointment, if any Lady Mader's
first-born was male the child was doomed to die before the age
of twenty-one. There was a family tradition that it was so.
Take for example Lucien, eldest son by his second wife. Lucien
was on hard drugs and wouldn't make twenty, let alone twenty-
one. Said Lord Mader, peering myopically at Emmy, bending
over the family cradle, hands clasped firmly behind his back.
He never touched his offspring, if he could help it.

The Maders, their disparagers murmured, had fallen from
being a powerful and wealthy family to a handful of publicity-
seeking degenerates. Even Christine, who loved to be loyal,
increasingly saw truth in this observation. Yves, the present
Lord, was thrice married. His first wife had been barren, and
for that reason divorced. Lucien, son by his second wife, was a
junkie, and Lucien's little sister Deborah now played the lead
in skin-flicks. Yet these seemed matters of mirth rather than
shame to Yves. A further son, Piers, was in real estate, and
considered too boring for discussion. Left a widower by his
second wife's suicide, Yves promptly married Mara, a twenty-
year-old Greek heiress, and sired little Emmy.

Yves had selected Jenny from over two hundred applicants
for the post of Nanny. He prided himself on being a good judge
of character.

'Does he love the baby?' people would ask Christine. 'Oh
yes,' she'd reply, adding in her heart, 'as much as he loves
anything, which isn't very much.' The pressure of the words
grew and grew and she was frightened that one day she would
say them aloud.

'And the mother?'

'She's not very much at home, but I'm sure she does.'
Christine was nice. She wanted to think well of everyone.

Mara loved treats and outings and hunting, and occasions
on which she could wear a tiara, and the Mader family jewels
– or, rather, replicas of same. The originals had been sold in
the thirties; and Maderley House itself would have followed
in the fifties, had not Yves discovered that the people's fas-
cination with their aristocracy could be turned to excellent fin-

ancial account; whereupon he flung open the gates, and filled up the moat, and turned the stables into restaurants, and himself into a public show.

The show business side of Maderley was in Christine's charge – it was she who organized the guides, the cleaners, the caterers, even the vets for sick animals. She saw to brochures, catalogues and souvenirs. She took the takings to the bank. She had the status in the household of someone dedicated, who is despised for their dedication. She was underpaid, and mocked for being so by those who underpaid her, and did not notice.

Christine's husband Luke sat in the Great Library and worked out efficient mathematical formulae for the winning of the pools. Yves had once met, over dinner, a Nobel Prize winner, a mathematician, who had convinced him of the practicality of working out such formulae, computer-aided. Yves promptly had a computer-terminal installed in the Great Library, and Luke installed likewise. Visitors gawped at both between two and three on Wednesdays. Luke had a first-class honours degree in mathematics from Oxford. He had been a Maderley child with a peculiar gift for numbers and few social skills. He had returned to the village, married to Christine, a girl from far away, to write textbooks for graduates, which he did slowly, with difficulty, and for very little money.

The Great Library! There Christine fed the computer with data about visitors, gate takings, capital costs and so forth. And here Luke puzzled over his formulae, and here Jenny liked to sit in the winter sun beneath the mullioned windows, and rock the baby's pram, and watch Luke at work. The baby never cried. Sometimes it whimpered. The cover was pulled up well over its face.

Christine had tried to say something to Yves about Jenny and the baby.

'Yves – ' his employees were instructed to call him by his Christian name – 'can I talk to you about Jenny?'

'What do you want to say?' He was unfriendly. She knew he did not like trouble. It was her function, after all, to keep it away from him. She had once asked for a rise in her wages, and the same shuttered, cold look had fallen across his face, as it now did, when she wanted to talk about Jenny.

'I don't think she's very good with the baby,' said Christine, tentatively, and wanted to go on and say, 'My Lord, I have seen bruises on the baby's arm. I don't like the way the baby whimpers instead of crying. I don't like the thinness of the baby's wrists. A baby's wrists should be chubby and creased, not bony.' But she didn't speak. She hesitated, looking at his cold face, and was lost.

'You mean she's too good with your husband, Christine,' was all Yves said. 'You sort out your own problems, don't come running to me.'

Christine, later that day, came across Yves with Jenny. They were together in the library. He had his hands on her thin shoulders: he, who seldom touched anyone. What were they saying?

Christine heard the baby make its little mewling cry, but Yves did not even glance into the pram.

Christine said to Mrs Scott the housekeeper. 'I'm worried about that baby. I don't think she gets enough to eat.'

Mrs Scott said, 'You don't know anything about babies. You've never had one. Jenny's a trained Norland nanny. She knows what she's doing.'

Jenny sat next to Mrs Scott at the staff lunch that day. They seemed very companionable.

Christine watched Luke watching Jenny being companionable with Mrs Scott, and the staff watched Christine watching Luke watching Jenny, and sniggered.

Christine telephoned the Norland nanny organization, and they had no record of a Jenny Whitstone on their books.

Christine watched Jenny hold the baby's bottle an inch or so from the baby's mouth, so that the baby stopped whimpering and rooted with its mouth towards the warm, sweet smell and found it, and Christine watched Jenny tug out the bottle after the first few mouthfuls and put it back on the shelf. The baby moaned.

'What did you do that for?' asked Christine.

'I don't want the baby getting too fat,' said Jenny. 'It's a terrible thing to be fat.'

And Jenny eyed Christine's plump form with cold distaste. Luke stopped making love to Christine altogether.

'It wouldn't be fair to you,' said Luke. 'How can I make love to you when I'm thinking of her? I wish I could, but I can't.'

'Why, why do you love her?' begged Christine.

But he didn't know, couldn't say.

It seemed to Christine that Luke felt cold in bed, as if his flesh was dying.

She spoke to the guides about Jenny, at their Monday morning meeting, where such things were discussed as meal breaks and the positioning of the silken ropes which guarded certain rooms and passages from the touch and view of ordinary people. 'Where did she come from?' Christine asked. 'Does anyone know?'

No one seemed to. It was as if she had always been there, along with the house itself, along with the family: the worm, or whatever it was, that nibbled away at the souls of the rich, so that born angels, they grew up devils.

For what could become of them but this? Generation succeeding generation: heartless mothers, distant fathers, and the distress of this made light of, by a surfeit of manners and money?

'The scale's all wrong,' Christine said in her heart. 'The house is just too big for people.'

Life's battles, life's events, triumphs and disasters – all were rendered puny by the lofty ceilings. Words of love and grief alike, hate and joy, all were muted beneath the arching vaults of the great hall, were sopped up and made one by ancient panelling. The stair was too high for the child to climb, or the old woman to descend. Marriages were lost in a bed so big it made passion trivial: the sexual act ridiculous under the cold eyes of ceiling cherubs. And animals! The love of dumb beasts put before the love of people; the death of a horse marking the year more than the death of a child; kennels always warmer than the nurseries. Manners replacing morals.

'They're born like anyone else,' Christine said in her heart, never aloud. 'And then I don't know what happens, but they end up monsters.'

So, now, it seemed to Christine, the damage which little Emmy could expect in the course of the next twenty years was being, at the hands of Jenny, inflicted upon her in as many months.

'I know why you love her,' she said presently to Luke, 'it's because she's the spirit of the House. And it's sickening and disgusting, and everyone loves it. Except me.'

'That isn't why I love her,' said Luke. 'And if you feel like that about the House, why go on working here?'

'What else could I do round here? There's no employment except at Maderley.'

So in spite of what she said, she stayed and she knew she stayed because she too, like Luke, was still under the spell of the Big House, and felt honoured by the company of Yves, whom she was privileged to call by his Christian name, and because she did not want to leave Emmy and Luke to the mercies of Jenny.

Lady Mara was due back from the Bahamas. The whole house gleamed with polish and glowed with flowers.

But Emmy was listless, and blinked a good deal, and flinched and grizzled the day Lady Mara came back.

'She isn't very pretty,' said Mara, disappointed, peering into the pram, and after that seldom asked to see the child at all. She rode to hounds a good deal, along with farmers and carpet manufacturers.

'I wish you wouldn't,' complained Yves. 'Only the bourgeoisie go hunting these days.' But Mara was regaining her spirit, and learning how to do not what she was told, and she persisted, slashing at grasses with her riding crop, as if she'd like to slash at life itself.

Presently Christine came across Jenny in the Great Library. Jenny had taken Emmy, for once, out of her pram. Jenny stood there, among ten thousand books, which were beautifully bound but never read, turning her owl eyes up to where the sunlight glanced through the windows, so that her spectacles dazzled, and seemed to retain the blinding shine even when she turned her head out of the sunlight to face Christine. Jenny, with her child's thighs in their tight, faded jeans, and budding breasts beneath a white T-shirt, and a dazzle where her face should be.

Jenny, with her soft, flat, slightly nasal voice, which could turn sharp and cruel and hard. Christine had often heard it. 'Christ, you little monster!' And slap, slap, thump, and then the weary grizzle again from Emmy.

Christine had never managed to get pregnant.

'Well,' the doctor had said, 'I daresay you have a child already, in your husband.'

Christine, cooking, nurturing, caring, worrying, had agreed with the doctor and not minded too much about their lack of children. Christine, after all, was the breadwinner. Perhaps what Luke saw in Jenny, suggested Christine, trying again, was his own unborn daughter? An incestuous love, given permission to live and thrive.

It was Yves who had given permission. Yes, he had. 'We all love Jenny,' Yves had said. 'Jenny saves us from our children.' Everyone except Christine, everyone's look said, watching Christine watching Luke watching Jenny, everyone loves Jenny.

Christine tried Yves' younger brother Martin, born by Caesarean while his mother lay dying from an overdose of sleeping pills and whisky, self-inflicted. Martin was the estate manager at Maderley, and kind and reliable, by virtue of an inborn insensitivity to the world about him. When Yves spoke to Martin it was in the same way he spoke to the upper servants – with a derisive politeness. Martin stuttered, so that Christine's conversation with him took a long time, and she was busy, needed at the toll gate with new parking tickets.

'Sir, I don't think Jenny is what she says. She isn't a Norland nurse at all. I checked up.'

'No one round here is what they claim to be,' said Martin, sadly. 'And the baby is Lady Mara's business, not ours.'

'Couldn't you say something to Yves?'

'Not really,' said Martin. 'If you feel strongly about it, say something yourself.'

'I have, but he just got angry and wouldn't listen.'

'The baby looks like any other baby to me,' said Martin. 'Not that I know much about them, of course.' Martin was commonly known to be impotent and one of his eyes turned inwards – a squint which had been left untreated in infancy, and so remained. 'Yves is a very good judge of character,' said Martin. 'If he employed Jenny she must be all right.'

The next day Christine saw Jenny wheeling the baby in the grounds, and Martin was with her. Even Martin! Martin, saying good-bye to Jenny, pecked her on the cheek, and she turned her face so that once again her glasses glinted and dazzled and the space beneath the pram hood seemed black, like the mouth of hell.

When Jenny wheeled the baby into the kitchen that day Christine bent to pick the baby up.

'Don't pick up the baby,' said Jenny sharply. 'She's sleeping quietly.' But to Christine the baby looked not so much asleep, as dead. And then an eyelash fluttered against the white cheek and Christine knew she was wrong. She went on counting sandwiches – two hundred ham, one hundred cheese – for the special Maderley tea, £4 a head, served in the converted stable block.

'But *how* do you love her, *why* do you love her?'

She knew that she was nagging: she couldn't help it. She kept Luke awake at night now, working away at the truth. It was only while he slept that his body grew cold, and the pain of his answers was preferable to the chilly numbness of his sleep; she knew that, sleeping, he drifted off somewhere away from her, over the safe, surrounding walls of her love and, moth-like, floated towards the chilly, blinding light which used Jenny as its beacon.

It was at that time that she wrote to the Professor of

Psychical Research, and had confirmation of her fears. Jenny was evil.

'Lady Mara?'

'What is it, Christine?'

Lady Mara, broken arm in a sling – her horse had lurched and reared at nothing in particular, a sudden bright light in the grounds was all she could think of – was lately very much the grande dame. She would have bathed in asses' milk if she could.

'Lady Mara, I'm worried about the baby.'

'The baby is nothing to do with you. You look after the visitors and let Jenny look after the baby.'

Lady Mara was only twenty-one. The same age as Yves' daughter, the one who presented her body at rude, amazing angles for the benefit of the camera, a publisher and a million wistful men. But a title and wealth, and the assumption of power, of the right to tell other people what to do and what to say, add up to more than years. Mara stared coldly. Christine fumbled. Christine was impertinent. If she didn't stop meddling she might have to go. There were more than enough only too ready to take her place. Mara said nothing. There was no need to. Christine fell silent.

Yves and Mara went away to attend a wedding. Five thousand pounds, they had heard, were to be spent on flowers for the marquees alone. Who would miss a wedding like that?

Christine found her husband Luke weeping in the conservatory. 'What's the matter, Luke?'

But he was frozen into silence. Presently he thawed, as if warmed by Christine's presence, her arm round his shaking shoulders, and spoke.

'I asked her. I plucked up courage and asked her. I said I wanted to sleep with her more than anything in the world.'

'And?' How cold the pit of the stomach, where words strike their message home.

'She laughed at me. She told me I was old and flabby. She said I was weak. She said I was a failure. Am I these things, Christine?'

'Of course not.' But he was.

'I have no right to do this to you, Christine.' He cried **again** in her maternal arms. 'But I love her more than ever.'

Christine went to see Jenny in her bedroom. 'You leave my husband alone,' said Christine, 'or I'll kill you.'

'Get him to leave me alone,' said Jenny, laughing, a cold, dead laugh. How could you kill what was already dead?

The baby murmured in its cot. Christine looked at little Emmy. Her eyes were black, and swollen. Christine lifted the baby out of its cot.

'You leave that baby alone,' snapped Jenny. 'You poor jealous frustrated barren old bitch.'

It was the cry of the world, but it was not true. Christine's spirit was warm, loving and fecund.

Christine unwrapped little Emmy from her soft blankets and found that her back was bruised and her right leg hung oddly. Christine cradled the baby carefully in her arms and ran down long, long corridors, hung with family portraits, and down the great staircase, and into the reception area, where the tickets were taken, and rang all the bells she could, and Martin came, and Luke and three of the guides and Mrs Scott the house-keeper, and a cleaner; and Jenny followed after but stopped halfway down the stairs, in a little patch where the sun shone in, so she glowed all over, the source and not the reflection of light.

'Look,' said Christine, showing what was in her arms. 'Look! See what she's done to the baby?'

'It was an accident,' called Jenny, in her soft, nasal voice. 'You're all my friends. You know I wouldn't do it on purpose.'

But the sun had shone in upon the wrong stair. She was just too far away, her voice just a little too faint. Jenny's words meant nothing to the cluster of people gazing at the baby, Lord Mader's baby, with its swollen eyes and its blue-black back.

'I'll get an ambulance,' said Christine.

'Think of the publicity,' said Martin, but he spoke without much conviction. 'Yves won't like it.'

'Perhaps we'd better telephone him and get permission,' said Mrs Scott.

'Let me take the baby,' called Jenny. 'It's me Emmy loves. You're all strangers to her. She'll get better if I hold her.'

And what Jenny said was true, but she couldn't make up her mind to lose the sun and step another stair down into the hall, and she faltered and was lost.

Martin rang Yves. Christine had his number : flicked through her efficient files and found it at once.

'Yves,' said Martin, stuttering his message out. 'You'd better come back here. The baby's got a bruise on its back.'

'How big a bruise ? Big as a sixpence ?'

'Bigger.'

'Big as half a crown ?'

'A fiver wouldn't cover it,' said Martin. 'Christine thinks we should call an ambulance.'

'Christine would,' said Yves, sourly. 'Well, stop her. We'll be right back.'

But Christine called the ambulance all the same. They took the baby away and just as well, because Yves and Mara didn't return until the next day.

Emmy had a fractured skull, two broken ribs, a broken thigh and a damaged kidney, but they patched her up quite well, and returned her after eight weeks looking quite pretty, so that her mother picked her up and murmured endearments and nuzzled into her baby neck, and fortunately Emmy smiled at that moment and didn't cry, which would have spoiled everything.

Christine lost her job, and Yves abandoned his hopes of breaking the Great Proletariat Pools Swindle and fired Luke too.

'You'd think they'd be grateful for my saving their baby,' said Christine. 'But the upper classes are just plain twisted.'

'The Greeks used to kill the bearer of bad news,' said Luke, 'so think yourself lucky.'

The sight of the damaged baby had made him fall out of love with Jenny, and now he slept warm at night, and Christine beside him. Jenny did not lose her job, but she was no longer allowed to look after the baby. For a time she did what Christine had been doing, for twice the money and with the help of an assistant.

'What a great judge of character Yves is!' said Christine sourly. Everyone she asked, and ask she did, everyone, agreed with her. The Maders were degenerate and decadent. She could say the words aloud now, not just in her heart.

Later she heard that Jenny had taken another post as nanny to two little boys whose mother had died, and that Yves had written her an excellent reference.

'Your employees reflect back on you,' said Luke. 'That's what it is.'

Christine wondered whether to telephone the father of the two little boys and warn him, but knew she would never be believed. And perhaps, who was to say, there was someone like her in every little pocket of the world? Someone to save while others destroyed, or looked away. Wherever Jenny went, there would be someone like Christine.

'I loved her because she was evil,' said Luke, at last, explaining. 'She anaesthetized my moral nerve endings and that was wonderful. And you were right : she was the spirit of the house.'

PETER DICKINSON

Mink

That coat was a nice gesture but a bloody nuisance – I expect you are lumbered with something of the sort in most marriages. I gave it to Gillian when Jacynth was born, but I don't suppose she'd worn it a dozen times since then. It just turned out we don't live that kind of life. I get by all right, mark you, but somehow we aren't mink people.

So there it was hanging in its polythene bag in the built-in cupboard, year after year. I can't remember how we noticed it was moulting – it was during that hot spell in '76 – but I do know it fussed me a bit. Capital depreciation is part of my stock-in-trade, sort of, but I'm not used to it happening in the form of little dark brown hairs inside my bedroom slippers. In the end I went on about it enough to make Gillian ring up somebody who knew.

'Nicky says keep it in the fridge,' she told me.

'Is there room?' I said.

'Of course not,' she said. 'And I'm not having it in the deep freeze, either. I've got half a pig coming Monday morning.'

It must have been the word 'pig' that caught Jacynth's attention. She doesn't notice people much, even her parents. We had to explain the whole thing over to her again.

'Why don't you put it in Dr Sperry's box?' she said.

'But, darling, the whole point is to keep it cool,' said Gillian.

'That's what I mean,' said Jacynth. 'It's always cool in Dr Sperry's box. He said it was something to do with the wood.'

(Dr Sperry had been an animal collector – used to hire his beasts out to TV studios and so on. He lived in a house just like ours a hundred yards up the road. Soon as we moved up here Jacynth chummed up with him because of the animals. She was seven, then. Proper little zoo he had, and she spent more time at No. 23 than she did with us, to be honest. Well, he died. Nasty sort of death. One of the animals bit him and he got blood poisoning. The three of us went to the sale to see if we could pick up a memento for Jacynth to remember him by. Soon as she found there weren't any of the animals in the sale (thank God) all she wanted was a ratty little stuffed gerbil, which she keeps in her room. It was part of a lot with a set of fire irons and 'one dog kennel'. We gave the fire irons to Gillian's niece as a wedding present. And we could have had the auctioneer under the Trade Descriptions Act about the so-called dog kennel, which was nothing more than a rather posh crate for transporting animals in. Teak, I think, with iron clasps and air holes. We got to calling it 'Dr Sperry's box'.)

You don't say 'rubbish' to a kid who normally doesn't speak to you at all, not once you've got a bit of a conversation going, so it ended up with me fetching the greenhouse thermometer and taking the bloody box's temperature, which meant turfing out all the dressing-up clothes and . . . oh, well, we persuaded ourselves that the reading *was* a couple of degrees lower inside the box than out. It certainly felt colder. So we put the mink in the bottom of the box – more to be shot of the problem than anything else – and piled the dressing-up clothes back on top because we hadn't anywhere else to put them.

It may seem a bit crazy of us to keep a boxful of dressing-up clothes when we've got just the one kid, but Gillian's always tried to see that Jacynth had friends to play with. Got precious little encouragement from Jacynth, mark you. In fact the last few years it's pretty well come down to a yearly beano on Jacynth's birthday. We really lay that on, twenty kids or more, conjurer, film, charades, sardines, all that. Last year Gillian said to Jacynth, 'Aren't you getting a bit old for all this? I mean, won't they expect a disco and purple lights?'

'I like it like it always is,' said Jacynth. 'Honestly. I mean, they think they've got to act teenage, but really they're only twelve and they sort of like acting younger some of the time.'

That's a long speech for Jacynth.

'Okay,' I said. 'We'll hold the teenybopping over for another year.'

So there we were with the house squealing with kids like a piggery at feeding time, racing all over the shop in fancy gear. I got a bit of a shock when I saw Jacynth swanning downstairs in eight-hundred quids' worth of Gillian's mink, but she looked so stunning, so *alive* for once, that I hadn't the heart to make her go and put it back. Honestly, as I said to Gillian afterwards, seeing her come down the stairs looking like that made it suddenly worth all the trouble and responsibility of having a kid at all. The conjurer had been pretty awful – judged the age-range wrong and they'd resented it – so I took it into my head to lace the orange squash with a dash of whisky, which may be why the party had really picked up by the time they got round to playing sardines. A fat little boy called Bobby Todd drew the straw to hide and we set the kitchen timer for two minutes. When it pinged we turned off all the lights and told the rest of them to sniff him out. Somebody managed a really devastating hound-snuffle and away they went.

The trouble with having twenty pretty-near unknown kids in is that you can't guarantee their behaviour. The Todd boy was really upset, and I don't blame him – in fact I thought his mother under-reacted, coming to fetch him and finding him almost in coma with shock, blood all down his T-shirt and a raw hole in his shoulder. Just a chilly upper-class titter and 'Please don't worry, Mr Davis. He's always doing this sort of thing. I'm sure he'll be right as rain in a day or two.' As Gillian said when we were talking it over in bed, Bobby was probably a born victim, and his mother liked it that way. Poor kid.

Anyway, we didn't feel like holding an inquest to find out which of the little brutes had done it. There'd been a dozen of them in the airing cupboard before anyone cottoned on that something was wrong with Bobby, and by then most of them had a bit of blood on their party best. It cost me twenty quid to get the mink cleaned, but at least I was relieved when the furrier told me it was in tip-top condition. 'Couldn't have been better if the original owners were still wearing it,' were his actual words. 'You keep it like you've been doing, and you won't be far wrong.' And when he brushed it down and squeezed it between his fingers, the way they do, even to my eyes it still looked pretty good.

Naturally enough in the circs we popped it straight back into Dr Sperry's box, and didn't have it out for a couple of months, when I was conned into buying some tickets for a snob charity concert, a genuinely boring evening of the sort that only we moneyed provincials can achieve. A lot of our female friends oohed and aahed over Gillian's coat, though one bitch did manage to spice our pleasure by pointing out that the cleaners hadn't managed to get quite all the blood off.

You'll have realized by now what was up – I wouldn't be telling the story this way unless I was leading up to that. So I needn't go into all the details about the fox that got in among Sir Jack Penny's ornamental pheasants, or the other animal – an escaped leopard the local rag suggested – that made such a mess in Mr Tebesco's weaning pen, and so on. But you're looking at this from outside, seeing it as a story that's working towards a particular end. It was quite different being on the inside. Things don't have any particular shape from there, not until it's all over and you can look back on it.

It was the hound-snuffle that woke me. I suppose I do have dreams because everybody does, but the only ones I remember are the nightmares, because I wake up in the middle of them when the fear reaches a particular pitch, like the musical note that breaks the wineglass – snap! sudden as that, and you're awake. This time I'd run into a Cotswold beechwood to escape the line of Japs who were coming across the common with fixed bayonets, and I'd found a perfect hiding place inside a dead tree with a bit of loose bark which I could pull shut behind me like a door, and I heard them tramping past and I knew I was okay, and then I heard this hound-snuffle. 'They've got dogs,' I thought. 'They can sniff me out like they did Bobby Todd.' By that time I thought that I was awake.

When you wake up in the middle of a nightmare you are sort of paralysed. You have to work up a lot of willpower to move the first muscle. I suppose it might be an evolutionary left-over from when man might find himself hunted as much as hunting and the final defence was for fear to freeze him absolutely still. Anyway, there I was, lying in the dark, locked rigid with fright. It wasn't fright about myself hiding in a dead tree from the Japs, it was fright about myself hiding in an airing cupboard with children's footsteps tiptoeing about outside and then the door opening in the dark and something coming snuffling in.

After a bit I began to be awake enough to work up the will to move. Come on, Davis, I said. Move or you'll get cramp. There's nothing waiting in the dark by the bed. You'll have to start thinking how yellow you are if you don't put out your arm soon and prove it.

Carefully, not to wake Gillian, I put out an arm and touched warm fur. The snarl and the savage pain in my wrist came on top of each other. I yelled and tried to pull away, but my arm was jerked fiercely in the other direction and that hurt so much that I had to go with it. I fell half out of bed, so that I was upside down with my legs all tangled in the bedclothes. The light went on, but I didn't see much because the thing that was attacking me at once let go of my wrist and leaped for my throat, coming at me from above so that my face was all smothered in rank, urine-smelling fur. I managed to get my good arm across my throat in time and it bit into that while its claws raked through my pyjamas at my ribs. That all hurt like fury, but the worst thing was being smothered in that loose, warm pelt, smelling of kennels and musky meat-eater's breath, and no real body inside it, nothing to hit at or push away, just fur, and teeth, and claws. Then there was a shock of cold all round me. The creature gave a violent jerk and lay

47

still. It really didn't weigh much, and once it had stopped attacking me I had no trouble wriggling myself out from under it.

When I was the right way up the first thing I saw was Gillian standing at the end of the bed with the yellow plastic bathroom bucket in her hand. She was looking down at the floor, so I did too and saw Jacynth lying there, very pale, fast asleep, wearing the mink coat. Jacynth and I and the bed were drenched. Gillian had done the most extraordinary thing – I mean, I couldn't imagine myself reacting like that, that's all. My yell had woken her up, so she'd switched on the light and seen me fighting with what she thought, half-asleep, was a mad dog. You stop dogs fighting by throwing water over them, so she'd dashed into our bathroom, got the bucket and heaved. The bucket happened to be full of water because she'd just started the curse, got her panties a bit bloody and put them to soak. I've read quite a few books since then, and now I think perhaps it wasn't the water that did the trick, it was the menstrual blood. It doesn't matter.

Gillian was on the edge of hysterics, but I made her bandage my arms and rub Savlon into the scratches round my ribs, which calmed her down a bit. Then I took the mink off Jacynth and carried her back to her bed. I only had to dry her head. She didn't wake up. I made Gillian take a couple of valium and move into the spare room, where she went out like a light. The mink was sopping, but I relit the fire in the lounge and spent the rest of the night hacking off bits of coat with the kitchen scissors and burning them. As I did so I kept thinking eight hundred quid, all for my wife to wear a dozen times and one flash of my daughter on the stairs.

Gillian slept through breakfast, but Jacynth was up at half past seven saying she had a bit of a funny feeling in her throat but not enough to miss school. She didn't notice the bandages. As soon as she was out of the house I rang up the office and cried off for the day, then I went haring down to the hospital for all the injections they could think of because I kept remembering how Dr Sperry had died. I told them I'd been out for a walk in the small hours and a dog had attacked me. That meant telling a lot of lies to the police, which took most of the morning. I got back to find Gillian absolutely furious about what I'd done with the mink, and saying I should have gone straight to a trick-cyclist to ask what we ought to do about Jacynth. I didn't say much.

That afternoon I built a bloody great bonfire, hacked up Dr Sperry's box and burnt it. It was almost as difficult to get going as the wet mink had been. I kept wishing I'd paid a bit more attention to old Sperry, because that might have given me a better chance of finding out what he'd imported in the box in the first place, and where from. Once or twice I saw the beginnings of a sort of shape moving away in the smoke, but I'm fairly sure now that was just nerves.

Next morning I went out to rake through the ashes and make sure there weren't any unburnt bits left. It had rained in the night, giving the ashes a sort of crust which was marked all round by large paw-prints with long claws, more spreading than a dog's or cat's. I raked them out at once. When I told Gillian, though, she asked me in a tired, pitying, almost sneery voice why I hadn't taken a photograph of them. But they weren't anything like a child's hand-print or footprint, I'll swear they weren't.

KATHRINE TALBOT

Amongst the British Soldiers

She agreed to marry him at the point of the road where the bay opened out on their left. Jake stopped the car and took her into his arms. She thought how simple it was to give so much pleasure, then retracted the thought: she had just promised to make him happy for the rest of his life.

'Eve, darling,' he said, letting her go, looking at her as if after asking her so often he couldn't believe she'd said yes. Then his expression changed, he grinned widely: of course he'd been sure, he'd *known* she'd capitulate.

Eve was not displeased. Perhaps he was right and it had been a foregone conclusion. Anything was better than the vacillation that had beset her ever since they had become lovers in the spring. He had wanted to marry her from the first, and she had wanted marriage, wanted to settle down, yet could not bring herself to say this final 'yes'. She had used the fashionable excuses: her career, her freedom, the irrelevance, nowadays, of marriage. Had he believed her? She had known well enough that her reluctance had another cause, that she was still expecting a different kind of love, that she felt she had been promised some greater emotion, some overwhelming happiness.

That wasn't Jake's fault, she had told herself. He was a perfect lover, considerate, gentle, handsome. She found his foreignness attractive, an American straight out of a film. He was wealthy, would spoil her, and he had told her from the start that she wouldn't have to give up her life in England. They would have two homes, his business took him to London as much as to New York.

Now, as he started the car once more, she promised herself that she wouldn't ever again allow herself to listen to that subversive inner voice nor look round every street corner for that promised husband whose face she could not imagine.

'Darling Jake,' she said, and put her hand over his on the steering wheel.

'Has the island persuaded you?' he asked.

'Yes . . . no,' she said, and didn't know. She had certainly not anticipated her capitulation, not planned it on the jumbo from England or the smaller plane from Boston or on the ferry afloat between mainland and misty islands, sea, and blue sky.

He let it go at that. He had hoped that this place which he considered perfect would work its magic on her. That it should have done so so quickly just proved how right he had been. When he had caught sight of her across the auction room he had recognized her as the ideal wife he had been looking for. He had been in London for a series of big art sales, and that first day had felt as if the treasure he had come to bid for had been unveiled for him. He had pursued her subtly but firmly. He was not surprised that he had succeeded.

'Great-aunt will be pleased,' he said. He was the senior of his own generation in that big family. One day he would be its head. Eve had soon learned that his family was of great importance to him. He spoke of them often, and when Eve had asked questions, he had overwhelmed her with answers. When Jake began on genealogy she was lost. At home there had been mother and father and a sister, grandparents in the north of England, an auntie or two, all long shed. Jake had shed nothing. His grandparents and great-grandparents, all long dead, were real people in his real world. His uncles and aunts, his cousins and their husbands and wives, their children, all were part of a private universe, a family network throughout the United States. They lived, she had learned, 'all over'.

But every summer they came to the island, their earthly paradise. That her own children would one day be part of this tribe
was attractive. She had never felt that she belonged to anything much.

They turned off the road up a curved drive. The house
stood, long as an ocean liner, on the flat land facing the wide
view of the sea. Here Jake had spent all his childhood summers
and it seemed right that the porch should be full of children
now. They came running to surround the car, opened the
doors, took Jake's hands and pulled him out, and when Eve
stood beside the car a little girl put her arms around her knees
and looked up at her. Jake laughed, bounced one of the small
boys up in his arms, threw a ball for another, introduced Eve.

'Did you come on Concorde?' one of the boys asked.

'My dad bought a Jaguar in London last year,' another said,
and one of the girls came over and touched her necklace, leaning on her in easy intimacy. They all looked at her with interest
and curiosity, vocal and uninhibited in the American manner.
Friendly.

'Scat,' Jake finally said. 'We'll see you at the beach. We're
going in to see Great-aunt Susan.'

'I want to come,' one of the children whined, hanging on to
Jake's arm.

'I was born in this house, Uncle Jake,' a little girl said, as
if this gave her a right.

'And me, and me,' the others shouted.

'Nonsense,' Jake said, and laughed at them. 'Scram now,'
and they scattered, making for the road and the beach, others
vanishing through a stand of pines beyond the house.

'Do they all live here?'

'They're here for the summer,' Jake said, 'and they don't stay
in this house.'

Indeed it was very quiet when they got indoors, cool after
the heat outside. An old lady got up from the sofa and came towards them, walking with a stick. She was small, and Jake
stooped to kiss her. Eve took her hand, then, as if compelled,
bent to kiss her too. The old lady smiled up at her.

'Welcome to the island,' she said, and might have meant welcome to the family.

Later Eve and Jake crossed the road they had come on and followed a track through grass and low-growing blueberry bushes towards the sea. The sun filtered through a white veil of mist and wrapped Eve in delicious warmth. She could see the thin mist lying just above the water which was very calm. Far away, on the other side of the island, a foghorn boomed, but here on the side facing the distant mainland shore there was no fog, just this mysterious vapour which made the far-away hills look like the faint outlines, later to be rubbed out, of a pencil sketch for a watercolour.

Eve stretched out her arms to catch all the sun and heat she could absorb and made a little sound of contentment. Then she bent to the blueberry bushes and looked at them closely.

'We have plants like that in England,' she said, 'on sandy soil. But I've never seen berries on them.'

Jake stooped and picked her a handful. They were very small but grew close together on the stem so that he quickly stripped them from the plant. The little miniature bushes were greener than the surrounding grass which looked poor and parched. On the rocks, grey and rough between the tussocks, lichen grew.

'Look,' Jake said, and, stooping, showed her a patch of lichen, grey as the stone but with little individual red tips on each tiny plant. 'We call them "British Soldiers".'

Eve laughed, strutted ahead of him straightbacked and high-stepping, imagining the Redcoats as she had seen them in films, fighting in this country: Indians or French or the early Americans.

'Did they come as far as this?'

'From Nova Scotia,' he instructed. 'There was a battle in this bay.'

'Now I've come to invade you.' She felt suddenly completely happy.

Now the path began to slope down and they could see the crescent beach with spruce, pine and silver birch growing on

54

the two points which reached into the sea. Each side of the path was waist-high in purple willow herb which Jake called fireweed, wild raspberry bushes bearing fruit, juniper and wild roses. She reached for, but did not pick, a cluster of the flat, perfect pink roses.

She could see a beach house on her left, a picnic table among the trees, and groups of grown-ups and children on the beach, a solitary figure in the water.

'Will it be cold?' she asked Jake.

'It'll be okay today,' he said. 'We've had hot settled weather and no high winds. Early in the summer it's like ice.'

As they stepped on the pebbly beach she looked at Jake's family, felt suddenly shy and wished she'd stayed in the cool house, so private, with the old lady. She had not even been given time to look around before being taken to the beach.

'It's no good trying to swim unless the water is right up,' Jake had said, and Great-aunt Susan had nodded and supplied the time for high tide.

Couldn't she see the house first? Eve had asked.

Plenty of time for that later. Jake had taken her to her room to rummage for her bathing suit, and change. Everything else would have to wait. She had just had time to look around the living room which had a fireplace and many books, large paintings of sailing ships which looked nice in the dim corners but rather crude when viewed from nearer. Great-aunt Susan had explained that these had been painted by her grandfather. Eve, professionally interested, tried to fix a date to them, glancing speculatively at Great-aunt Susan to find the old lady smiling at her, quite capable of reading her thoughts.

There was a row of boats lined up on a shelf: a galleon carved in other people's lifetime, a beautiful model of a man-of-war, and at the end the plastic model some grandchild had made from a kit.

'You can look at everything later,' Jake told her, impatient for a swim, or perhaps for a chance to show her off to the assembled family on the beach now that she had said she would marry him.

It seemed only too likely. She looked askance at all the people and wished she had turned back into the room where the old lady had already been engaged in a book.

Jake made the introductions. If he did not quite say, 'This is *my* Eve,' he implied it. Eve remembered just such a look on his face when he had claimed, after that first auction, the paintings he had bought.

The men got up politely, the girls smiled and waved from prone positions. Some sat with babies on their laps or kept an anxious eye on naked toddlers. Eve smiled and nodded, but the names floated past her memory. 'This is my Aunt Libba and her her sons Gene and Chester, and you've met two of their children ...'

There was Uncle Dan, swarthy and obviously an uncle by marriage among all those fair-haired relations, cousins called Jody and Susan, Tom and his wife and children.

'I shan't be able to remember,' Eve said, 'but I'll try.'

'Never mind,' Uncle Dan said. 'We'll help you, Eve,' as if to demonstrate how easy it was for them to remember her name.

Eve looked towards the beach hut, but it seemed boarded up, and by the careless heaps of towels and clothes she guessed that one just stripped off there on the beach. She pulled her dress over her head and stood in her bikini, ready to go into the water.

But Tom and his family, who had only just arrived, had captured Jake for an immediate gossip. Jake squatted on his haunches to talk to Tom's wife.

'I'll have a quick swim on my own,' Eve said, turning from them.

'I'll be right with you,' Jake called, 'I'll catch up with you.'

'Fine,' Eve said, glancing back at the group, girls in bikinis exposing their bronzed bodies to the misty sun, the boys in brightly coloured trunks, fair curly hair to their shoulders, the noisy children playing among the pebbles, a group of older ones with a basketball bat and softball, a teenage girl, long hair trailing, walking alone searching the pebbles for beachglass or sand dollars, and Jake already getting up, about to follow her.

The water was icy cold. With the mist floating above it she had expected it to be gently steaming, like bathwater in a cool bathroom. She went in slowly, shivers running up her spine, savouring the contrast of the heat and intense cold, submerging herself until her chin touched the water. Then she struck out strongly, a good swimmer from schooldays and holidays at the seaside. This was what she had wanted, a moment alone out here. She swam slowly, breast stroke, enjoying the cold water, the dazzle, sailing boats far out like ghost ships in the mist, their sails shimmering. Then, perhaps because of the tiring journey or some chemistry of heat and cold sea, she felt cramp in her legs. It paralysed her so instantly her heart seemed to have stopped beating. She needed firm ground to stamp on to unknot the muscles in her calves and thighs, something other than water to tread. She turned towards the beach where they all moved about or sat, shouted frantically without a sound, and as she went under thought that even if Jake were already in the water, not far behind her, in this dazzle and haze he wouldn't see her. Down and down she went into blackness until unconsciousness took the pain away.

Then the pain left her quite suddenly, she rose sharply towards the surface and came up spluttering and splashing, took deep breaths into her aching lungs and floated for a moment, wheezing and heaving, before she struck out for the shore.

The family was dispersed about the beach. Swimming rather jerkily, her legs still sore from the cramp, Emma looked for Alden, found him playing ball with the two little boys, her brother Tad joining in now and again from a sitting position. On the balustrade of the beach hut Susan's pink bathing dress was drying. It looked very bright in the sun and had shocked the aunts with its low back and its print of huge black roses, and the fact that Arnold had bought it for his bride-to-be. In their day such intimate presents had been left until after marriage.

The wedding was fixed for late September, and Emma told herself that it was just as well she hadn't drowned just then. She had brought up her brother and sister since their parents' early death, and the arrangements, from the guest list to the bride's bouquet, were in her hands. She had often dreaded that day and imagined in advance the heartbreak of their parting. Now it seemed suddenly ordinary, bearable. She too would marry, and as married sisters they would extend their love into a delightful new relationship.

Nobody knew as yet that she loved Alden, that he had proposed. She would keep that secret, she thought, until after Susan's wedding, allow that girl her deserved glory. After that she and Alden would marry quietly and settle down to their happy family life. They would have children, cousins to Susan's, and would all come here summer after summer, grow old, please God, as her grandmother had who, until a few years ago, had been pushed down to the beach in a bath chair by her maid.

'Happiness,' she thought, her face transformed by her smile.

Walking across the beach from the hut, Susan noticed the change, astonished to find her sister suddenly pretty. She had been prepared to feel both pity and self-reproach to be leaving Emma who had done so much for her and who, until recently, had been so close to her she had thought it difficult to tell where Susan stopped and Emma began. But this had changed since her engagement. She had ceased to confide, had allowed the distance between them to grow so that the final gulf, her marriage, might not be more painful by being sudden. Now she hoped that Emma's unexpected happiness might add to her own good fortune, that they might even find a different intimacy in their adjacent marriages. She would like Alden as a brother-in-law. She thought of him as a very solid and deliberate person, a little reticent as she imagined the British among whom he had fought in the recent war. She suspected him, secretly, of a little too much idealism: how else could one explain that he had gone to England to volunteer for that war long before the United States had thought it their business to involve themselves in it?

'Hi, Alden,' she said, as she passed him, stooping once more to throw the ball.

He grinned at her, his future sister-in-law, fully aware of her feeling of astonished relief, then saw Emma coming across the beach, went to join her. She took off her bathing cap, shook out her short fair hair, smiled. For the first time she recognized a wish to touch him. She blushed.

'Good swim?' She nodded, would not admit to the cramp which had frightened her. It would take some years of marriage before she would get used to confessing her own weaknesses and worries.

'I don't know how you youngsters can go into that water,' Aunt Clarissa said from her deck chair. 'Before the war I reckon there wasn't a man, woman or child in the whole of Maine who'd venture into the ocean.'

'Do you think we've grown tougher since the war, Mrs Ellis?' Alden asked.

'Just a whole lot more foolhardy,' Aunt Clarissa said. 'The world's changed.' She gave a deep sigh. Emma thought that it was the prohibition her aunt most deplored, she'd complained at lunch about the bootleg liquor, nasty stuff. That Alden had brought her, the senior aunt, a decent bottle had endeared him to her from the first.

'The world's changed, all right,' Uncle Ned said. He'd been intransigent in his opposition to the States' involvement in a conflict he considered none of their business, and showed a deep antipathy to those who had fought and returned and had, he thought, been made too much of, especially by the women. 'Never should have interfered in that war,' he grumbled. 'Wouldn't have found me going over there fighting with the British army. They're our natural enemies.'

'Rubbish, Ned,' Clarissa said. 'Couldn't have let the Kaiser get away with it!'

'I think it was very brave to go and fight,' Emma said, and felt as if she had announced her love or engagement to the assembled family. 'I guess I'd better go and change,' she said, and made her way to the bathing hut.

Later she walked with Alden up the path. Out of sight of the others he picked a pink rose and stuck it in the top buttonhole of her dress.

'Will you marry me soon, Emma?' he asked, taking her hand.

'I love you,' she said, and the blush which enveloped her seemed to be part of this hot afternoon, so that the feeling of blood in her cheeks and heat in her arms wouldn't go away. She turned back towards the glittering sea where Aunt Clarissa could just be seen topping the rise from the beach, Uncle Ned in her wake. Far away two sailing boats stood still and shimmering as if the accumulation of light amid the mist had conjured a hallucination of white sails.

She disengaged herself and bent down out of reach of his kiss and touched the cool blueberry bushes.

'I've never seen so many berries,' Alden said. 'We'll come back here every summer,' he told her firmly. 'We'll build ourselves a house.' He looked about him as if already considering its location. 'It'll be great for the kids.'

She looked down and saw the grey lichen with its red tips and thought of the name they gave it and how she would tell him some day in that happy future stretching as widely as the immense view, and she smiled secretly to think of him 'over there' where he had fought.

The house felt wonderfully cool when they walked in. The smell of kerosene from the lamps hung faintly in the air. A tray of lemonade stood on the table before the empty fireplace, newly poured and with chunky ice in each glass.

'Did you swim, Emma?' her grandmother asked from the sofa, and Emma bent and kissed the old lady.

'It was very cold, Grandma,' she said and shivered suddenly, remembering the fright she had had. The old lady put up her hand and ruffled the fair hair.

'Convenient to have your hair so short,' she said to Emma, and to the young man, 'In my day nobody went into the ocean around here.'

'Grandma could sit on her hair when she was young,' Emma told Alden. 'Help yourself to lemonade.' Then she went towards the kitchen to hang up her bathing dress and towel in the back garden. She smiled back at Alden, and the smile stayed on her face as if to salute all the familiar things around her, the bookcases as she passed them, the shelf with the old galleon and the man-of-war and the two sailing boats the little boys had made of last night's walnut shells with visiting cards for sails, smiled at the schooner grandfather had painted just before he died, and at the cook as she passed through the kitchen.

'Did you go into that cold sea, Miss Emma?' the big black cook said. 'Don't you go catching your death.' Emma went out of the back door where a line was strung between two stunted apple trees which never bore fruit. She touched the stout cord as if it were some lifeline that held her to her world. Don't let it ever go away, she thought in sudden panic, twin to what she had felt out there in the water, don't let me ever not come back, holding on hard, tears in her eyes.

'Did you get cramp?'

Eve was holding on hard to some object which she imagined a lifeline but found to be Jake's finger.

'Let me tow you.'

But she let go of his hand and swam strongly towards the shore.

Nobody seemed to have moved, yet the bikinied girls and the naked children appeared strange to her. She shook her head as if to get water out of her ears.

'Were you in trouble?' Jake looked concerned enough. She got to her feet on the rough pebbles and staggered a little on her way up the beach.

'I'm only a little tired,' she said in a strange and stiff voice, and the others noticed that she looked pale.

She sat down on a large stone and hid her face in her striped towel. She knew well enough who these people were, she thought suddenly that she could even remember their unmemorable names. But it was the others she wanted. She wished and wished that she should lift her face from the towel and see the little boys play ball with Tad . . . and Alden. But it was Jake who sat down beside her, Jake her lover, her future husband. She shivered.

'You're cold,' Tom said, 'You stayed in too long.'

'I'm not used . . .' she said. The water was so calm, and the gentle mist still made it look as if it were just off the boil. From the other side of the island the foghorn sounded very far away and muffled.

'Perhaps it's the heat,' Jake said. 'Shall we go back?'

'That would be nice.' Eve got up and looked about her, thought of the cool house up there.

'Give the girl a strong drink when you get back,' Uncle Dan advised, smiling. 'She looks peaky.'

Eve thought of the bootleg whisky Alden had brought, and in her memory she would reproduce its fiery taste. She looked at Jake with great surprise, and he was astonished at the coldness of her glance.

Walking into the house she thought again that Alden would be there, that the old lady on the sofa would be Grandma, not Great-aunt Susan, that *her* Susan would walk through a door, the bride-to-be. She felt an ache of longing. When she saw the schooner in full sail on the canvas, the galleon on the shelf, she felt hope. But the plastic warships at the end of the line, the television box on the low table dashed all happy expectations. She sniffed the air, but no oil lamps had been lit in this house for years.

Great-aunt Susan sent her to lie down upstairs where she drew thin curtains against the glare, and where the sound of the foghorn hardly reached her, and Eve, falling asleep, thought that it might be Emma who awoke.

Later all the family came to dinner. They sat at the big round table where the dishes each household had provided made a varied feast of the meal. A large flask of red wine circulated, there were candles, faces became flushed from this double heat. They talked about the island, *their* island, and it might have been their ancestors who had colonized it and defended it in that long-ago war against the British, kept sheep on it last century, built the lighthouse, anchored schooners in the roads, started the lobster fishing. They talked about the bay, dark now and free of mist, luminous under the three-quarter moon.

'Did you swim here when you were young?' Eve asked Great-aunt Susan.

'Why, certainly,' the old lady said, 'though the fashion didn't start until after the First World War. Before that nobody thought of it.'

'Ah, the twenties,' Uncle Dan said. 'I remember my first summers here. I don't think your aunts ever liked all that stripping and bathing,' to Great-aunt Susan.

'No bikinis,' one of the young girls said sagely.

'The year we were married, my husband-to-be brought me a pink bathing dress from Paris,' Great-aunt Susan reminisced. 'It had a little skirt, hitched up one side, and big black roses printed all over it. The aunts considered it "fast".' She laughed.

'They wouldn't have thought much of the Johnsons all swimming in the raw.'

Eve leaned across the table, catching Great-aunt Susan's eye. 'The year you were married . . .' she prompted.

'We waited until almost Christmas,' Great-aunt Susan said quietly.

'It wasn't a very happy summer,' Uncle Dan added as if to quench further questions. 'Of course it was before my time. I didn't come into the family until your Bobby was a year old,' speaking of Jake's uncle.

Great-aunt Susan smiled. 'There's no sense in not speaking of it after all this time. Arnold was here for the first time, staying with my aunt Clarissa who was a great one for the bootleg whisky. But that summer my sister died, and after that everything was sad for a while.'

'She drowned,' the youngest of Jake's cousins said, eyes wide.

'It was a terrible tragedy,' Great-aunt Susan said, sighing. 'Now it's part of family lore and you shouldn't forget her, though I'm the last who'll remember what she was like. After our parents died she brought up my brother Tad and I. Tad was Jake's grandfather,' she explained to Eve. 'It was a day like today. Calm. There wasn't any cause ever found for her drowning, vanishing like that before our eyes, though none of us saw her go.' She was silent, as if that great puzzle was as fresh now as on the day it happened.

'Could she have wanted . . . to drown?' one of the young men asked.

'No. She was happy too, in love. She went in to swim and simply didn't come back. Nobody noticed at first, the children were playing ball, then the young man said, "Where is Emma?" and we missed her. We looked for her in the bathing hut, then we took the boat out. Her body was never found.'

And though all except Eve had heard the story before, there was a deep silence, as if they were stunned again, unbelieving. All the knives and forks were still. Then one of the girls picked up the flask of wine and filled everyone's glass, resting her hand for a moment on the old lady's shoulder.

'It's a long time ago,' Great-aunt Susan said. 'I never thought she'd marry, now I can't even remember the young man's name.'

Alden, Eve thought. I remember your name, Alden. I shan't forget.

'What a sad story,' one of the girls said, and Jake took Eve's hand and squeezed it as if to promise her all the happiness Emma had missed. But she knew that she would leave the island next day, that she wouldn't see Jake again, wouldn't marry, not him nor any man who wasn't Alden.

PETER TINNISWOOD

Summer, New York, 1978 – That's All

Eyam is a village in Derbyshire.
In 1665 it was hit by the Plague.
Within weeks 80 per cent of the villagers died.
Panic raged.
The rector alone remained calm.
'We have a duty to mankind,' he preached.
'We must not flee our village and carry the plague abroad. We must remain in our homes in our dear little village of Eyam. We must be prepared to sacrifice ourselves for the good of others.'
Calmness returned.
The villagers bowed their heads, stayed in their plague-stricken village and threw themselves on the mercy of their God.
One man did not.
In the dead of night he crept out of the village.
He carried the plague deep inside him.
His name was Hallam Brandon.

New York in the summer of 1978.
Hallam Brandon woke up quickly.
Uneasily.
The morning was early.

The hotel slumbered.

Uneasily.

The voice whispered into his ear:

'You are sick, friend. You are desperately sick. This is it, friend. This is it.'

He tried to sit up in bed.

He could not.

The mind was active. The body would not obey it.

The voice took on an urgent tone.

'You are dying, friend. No chance. There is no way out for you now, my friend.'

He struggled with his body.

No movement came to it.

Only the eyes flickered and focussed briefly on a blue-and-white check sports jacket with a pink carnation in the lapel and beside it the crumple of a woman's skirt in Indian cotton.

A snicker. A cackle.

'I told you, friend,' said the voice. 'You are dead. You are really dead.'

I am that voice.

I am the voice of the plague carried out of that Derbyshire village centuries ago.

I am the voice of the ghost that has lived in the bodies of the countless Hallam Brandons who have travelled to the farthest corners of the globe.

I am the voice of the ghost that has at long last come alive.

At eleven o'clock that morning the maid came to clean room 487.

She had seven kids, and her man worked the barges on the Erie Canal.

Sometimes he came home. More often he did not.

New York she loathed and despised.

She was frightened of it, too.

She put the pass key into the lock of room 487.

She turned it.

She hummed softly to herself as backside first she entered the room, pulling in her trolley of fresh sheets and cleaning things.

When she turned and saw the body on the bed, she screamed.

She screamed at the top of her voice, bending double and clutching her stomach.

She retched.

Hallam Brandon heard the key turn in the lock of room 487.

He tried to move his head.

No go.

But he could see everything in the room.

It was sharp and clear.

He saw the plump backside of the maid flubber into the room.

He smelled starch and tart disinfectant.

He heard her voice humming. It was a low, tuneless growl.

She turned to him.

He saw heavy jowls, pink plastic spectacle frames and a stubble of moustache above a smeared red upper lip.

He heard her scream.

When he looked down on his body, he screamed, too.

But no sound came.

I am the voice of the plague.

I am the voice of the ghost come alive.

I see a body stretched out on a slab.

It is the body of Hallam Brandon.

I see three men in dark rubber smocks, dark green rubber boots, dark green rubber skull caps and taut white face masks.

Incisions are made in the body.

Organs are removed.

'Jesus.'

'Sweet Jesus.'

I am free to go, where I please.

I am free of my host, the last in a mournful line of mournful men.

67

I see laboratories shrouded in plum-red light.

I see culture plates and coils of tubing.

An office now and a smug, cunning face with powdered jowls and calm-clipped sideburns.

It smiles slowly.

'I have no doubts at all. Our tests have been exhaustive. They prove conclusively that the man, Hallam Brandon, died from the plague.'

'The plague? In New York? In 1978?'

'Sure.'

'How many people know of this?'

'You. Me. Himmelweit.'

'No one else must ever get to know of this. Those are my orders. You understand? You are absolutely clear on this?'

'Sure.'

Freedom at last.

I can go where I please.

The whole of the city of New York is open to me.

I am the plague, and I am free to choose my next victim.

Hallam Brandon had flown into New York one day previously.

His mission was to terminate a love affair.

This he had promised to his wife.

Unhappy man.

At 30,000 feet high above the storm clouds in mid-Atlantic the giant jet had retched and heaved.

An hour and fifteen minutes he had been, passing through immigration.

The yelping heat bounded at him, smacked him in the guts and then sensuously and surely sucked the energy from every tired fibre of his body.

In the cab from Kennedy Airport his limbs began to ache and a slow, corrupting throb came to his temples.

More queues in the lobby of the hotel.

The wrinkled bell boy in a wrinkled lime-green jacket limped up to the desk and picked up the slip of paper.

He frowned as he read it painfully.

'Bardon?' he croaked. 'Any guy here answer to the name of Bardon?'

'Brandon,' said Hallam Brandon. 'My name is Brandon. Is that who you are looking for?'

The wrinkled bell boy ran his wrinkled forefinger listlessly across the slip of paper.

'Bardon. Brandon. Who cares?' he said. 'Room 487. You follow me. Okay?'

Once in the room he hung up his blue-and-white check sports jacket in the closet.

He took off his pants and his shoes and his socks and his navy blue silk shirt.

He flopped on to the bed and in an instant was asleep.

His dreams were troubled and once he awoke in the darkness, every single sense alert and jangling.

He thought he heard a voice whispering in his ear.

But he could not be sure.

I am the ghost of the plague.

The killer.

I am alive and free.

I am in New York in the late summer of 1978.

Ten hours is all I have to live.

Without a body to act as host I shall die.

No panic.

The whole of teeming, searing, throbbing, snarling, singing, yelping, crooning New York is at my mercy.

I have ten hours to choose my victim.

Jesus, what fun.

When Hallam Brandon awoke from his troubled, whispering sleep, he straightway took his pocket book from his blue-and-white check sports jacket, looked up a telephone number and dialled it.

'Hi,' he said. 'Marie?'

'Who is this, please?'

'Hallam.'

'Hallam! For goodness sakes, how are you?'

'Grand.'

'Where are you?'

'New York.'

'New York? For goodness sakes, Hallam, what are you doing in New York?'

'I've come to see you.'

'To see me?'

'I can meet you for lunch.'

'Oh, Hallam, my darling, no. I have to go out of town today. Business. How about this evening?'

'Fine.'

'Nine o'clock? Usual place?'

'Fine.'

'Oh Hallam, what a really swell start to the day. Hallam, my sweet, I love you. I really do.'

'Fine.'

He put down the phone.

And this time he heard the voice whispering into his ear and once more his limbs began to ache.

Eight hours to go.

How shall I choose my victim?

An aimless whim?

Why not?

This wisp of a girl with sad shoulders and drab ankles here on the concourse of Grand Central Station.

She books a ticket for Poughkeepsie.

No. Not her.

Poughkeepsie has plague enough of its own.

What about this jogger here on East River Park?

Yellow track suit, knotted hairy chest, heaving plates of feet, the look of love in his eyes.

No.

Love is plague enough in itself.

And what about here in the flea markets on Canal Street?

70

The fat woman there, running chapped fingers over a bake-lite radio?

Heavy jowls, pink plastic spectacle frames and a stubble of moustache above a smeared red lip.

Follow the plump backside as it flubbers into Mulberry Street.

Follow it as it turns into Kenmare Street.

Follow it up the aching stairs of the apartment block.

Follow it through the lobby to the peeling, leaking kitchen, where a parched man in black vest and denim pants lounges askew in a stiff-backed wooden chair.

'What in hell are you doing here?'

'They threw me off the barges.'

'What?'

'I ain't got no job.'

'What?'

'And there ain't no beer in the fridge.'

'Sonofabitch.'

She attacks him with her beaten-down slipper.

'Sonofabitch. You know what I seen this morning in Room 487? You know? You know? I seen a body. That's what I seen in Room 487 and you're telling me you ain't got no job. Sonofabitch. Pig.'

She belabours him with her slipper.

No.

The plague is already on this room and deep within this family.

Seven hours to go.

All through the long summer afternoon Hallam Brandon sat by the Sheep Meadow in Central Park.

There was pain in his body, but he could not locate its source.

There was unease in his mind.

The source of that he knew.

The voice whispered to him:

'Remember? Do you remember?'

He nodded. He remembered.

He remembered the basement of a brownstone mansion in Greenwich Village.

He remembered a divan bed and a girl stretched out on her back, nut-firm breasts and pear-smooth thighs.

'I love you, Hallam, I love you,' she groaned as her head thrashed from side to side.

'I love you, too, Marie.'

The voice whispered to him again :

'Remember? Do you remember?'

He nodded. He remembered.

He remembered the garden of a house overlooking a sullen reach of the River Thames.

He remembered the laughter of children in a tree house and the steady gaze of eyes set in a puffed and ageing face.

'It's not for me, Hallam. It's for the children. You must break with this woman. You have to promise me that.'

'I promise.'

Dusk came loitering through the park.

Hallam Brandon shivered.

He stood up and brushed the sleeves of his blue-and-white check sports jacket.

An hour to go before his meeting with Marie.

The slow, corrupting throb returned to his temples and he began to shiver violently.

What fun.

What sport.

All the livelong day I have had this city and the people in it at my mercy.

Hither and thither I have flitted.

Coughing subway trains, a deep-chested bar on the Bowery, the Catholic church on Lexington and 66th, the foyer of Radio City, the broken-backed drugstore in Yorkville.

And the people!

An Irish priest with bloodshot tongue, a fat cop with blue-bruised elbows, a parched lady selling towels in Maceys, a thin-jawed college boy on Coenties Slip, a fat-arsed matron on Madison.

Whom shall I choose as my host?

How about this sloe-soled gigolo in the lobby of the Waldorf Astoria?

His date approaches.

A gold-rinsed hag with doddering arms and pouched neck. She holds out her hand.

He takes it and presses it to his lips.

He winks at the pianist and raises his eyebrows.

No. Not worth the bother.

And what about this mohair-suit, striped-shirt, floral-tie, stubby-socks, inserting his key into the lock of an apartment door on Washington Heights?

Smug, cunning-faced with powdered jowls and calm-clipped sideburns.

'And what sort of a day have you had, my dear?'

'So so,' he says, and he accepts the tumbler of cold malt whisky from his wife with scarcely a glance.

'Busy?'

'So so,' he says. 'Some guy died in his room. That's all.'

Oh, the temptation.

So strong.

I move forward towards him.

Yes, this is it.

But then in an instant I am whisked away, whirled across the city and then softly and silently deposited in Washington Square.

Now I know.

Now I know where I must go and whom I must meet.

The bar had a mahogany door inlaid with the bases of ancient flat irons.

The Flat Iron Bar. No less.

Hallam Brandon entered.

Cramped mahogany booths with bottle-glass windows. A

springy floor bewhiskered with sawdust. Dusty ancient flat irons hanging from hooks on the ceiling.

She was waiting for him in a booth halfway down the room. She gave him a pink carnation.

'Hallam.'

'Marie.'

They kissed.

'My God, Hallam. For goodness' sakes, do you look ill.'

He nodded.

They sat side by side, and she held his hand.

He drank his bottle of Miller's beer in three easy gulps.

He did not speak.

'Why, Hallam? Why have you come all this way to New York?'

He leaned towards her and placed both his hands on her nut-firm breasts.

Two hours to go.

Now I know who is to be my host.

Here in this bar I shall find my victim.

Springy, bewhiskered floor, bottle-glass windows, ancient flat irons.

There she is.

I spot her in a booth halfway down the room.

She wears a long skirt of Indian cotton, and her breasts are free beneath a thin black sweater.

She talks intently to a man hunched inside a blue-and-white check sports jacket with a pink carnation in the lapel.

Two hours to go.

Two hours to savour.

Two hours of freedom.

And then I am the dead ghost once more.

Listen.

Listen carefully.

'You don't love her, Hallam.'

'No.'

'You don't need her, Hallam.'

'No.'

'She's destroying you, eating you alive, cracking your balls.'

'Yes.'

'You need me. I need you. For goodness' sakes, my sweet, darling, Hallam, you love me, don't you?'

'Yes.'

'You're here now in New York with me for ever?'

'Yes.'

'Promise.'

'I promise.'

He takes her by the hand, and they leave the bar.

I follow.

Already I feel the warmth and passion of the body that will be my host.

I feel a surge and a thrill.

A taxi is hailed. They enter. They embrace. The taxi draws up outside the hotel. They get out. They enter the lobby of the hotel. A wrinkled bell boy in a wrinkled lime-green jacket weaves a wrinkled trail towards the lift. They enter the lift. Four floors up. They get out of the lift. They walk hand in hand along the corridor. They pause outside a door. He takes out his key. He inserts it into the lock. He opens the door.

They enter room 487.

An hour to go.

They made love fiercely.

Then they made love gently.

Hallam Brandon raised himself on one elbow and looked down on her as she slept by his side.

On the floor at the foot of the bed he saw a blue-and-white check sports jacket with a pink carnation in its lapel and the crumple of a woman's skirt in Indian cotton.

'I love you, Marie,' he whispered. 'I shall never leave you. Never.'

I see her stir in her sleep.

I see her open her eyes.

75

I see her turn to him and open her arms.

I see her hoist herself on top of him, and I see her hips move and her breasts sway.

Now.

Now is the time to enter her.

Softly. Carefully.

What a body to be my host.

What juices to feed on.

What passion to feast on.

Carefully now as her breasts swing faster and her cries get louder.

Careful.

Ready.

Ready, ready.

Now.

Jesus.

I missed.

At eleven o'clock that morning the maid came to clean room 487.

When she turned and saw the body on the bed, she screamed.

She screamed at the top of her voice, bending double and clutching her stomach.

She retched.

WILLIS HALL

The Victorian
Leather Hat-Box

There was something about the crumbling early nineteenth-century building that appealed to Timothy from the very moment he pushed open the creaking wooden gate. Perhaps it was the delicate tracery of the leaded windows, or it might have been the latent possibilities of the overgrown and weed-infested garden. Whatever it was, Timothy was quite sure that Flint Cottage was just the place that he and his new wife were looking for.

Susan was not so sure. In fact, she shivered slightly as they made their way towards the front door.

'I don't like this one half as much as that thirties property we looked at in Thirlton Drive,' she said.

'Give it a chance,' said Timothy. 'You haven't even seen inside this one yet.' He thumped the cast-iron knocker hard, on the flaking green-painted door.

'I'm talking about the *outside*,' said his wife.

'Never judge a sausage by its skin,' snapped Timothy. 'Besides, the Thirlton Drive stucco monstrosity was almost twice the price of this place.'

'I *know*. But what they're asking for this dump will be almost doubled by the cost of doing it up. It's in a dreadful state. And in any case, it's miles from the nearest – '

She broke off as the front door half-opened and a scruffy

77

middle-aged man in a collarless shirt peered out at them.

'My name's Hampson,' said Timothy. 'This is my wife – we've called about the house.'

'Oh.' The man showed not the slightest enthusiasm at their arrival, but at least he opened wide the door. 'You might as well come in,' he said.

Timothy and Susan stepped into the bleak and panelled dark-wood hallway that was badly in need of repair and decorating.

The scruffy man smiled, blandly. 'I won't apologize for the state it's in,' he said, waving an expansive arm to take in the cracked and filthy linoleum on the hallway floor and the stained and scruffy Victorian wallpaper above the panelling that led up to the shadowy half-landing beyond which lay the bedrooms. 'I'm only trying to get it off my hands. My name's Harrison. This place belonged to a cousin of mine who died. Funny old bugger. Eighty-nine years old he was, when he went, and never let a woman inside this house in his entire life.'

'I can believe you,' said Susan, shuddering at the oh so many years of accumulated dust and grime.

The man grinned and continued brightly : 'You're the umpteenth ones I've had this week. They've all turned it down.' He spoke quite cheerfully; his inability to unload the property did not appear to daunt him. 'I had a whole family of Sikhs went over it on Tuesday – from top to bottom – and even *they* turned their noses up at it.'

'May we have a look round?' said Timothy, anxious to get on with things.

'Feel free,' said Harrison. 'Take all day. Only you won't mind if I don't accompany you? It's been six months since the old sod was cremated, and I'm *still* trying to sort out his bits and pieces.' As he spoke, he pointed into a room that was jam-packed with cracked vases, pendulum clocks and decaying furniture. 'I've got a van coming next Wednesday morning – I've got to get that mess sorted out and packed and parcelled.' With which, he shuffled off into the room full of the deceased owner's bric-à-brac.

Susan pulled a face. 'Shall we make an excuse and push off now?' she said.

'No. I'd like to have a look round.'

'Whatever for? It's hideous. It's *awful*.'

'Not at all,' said Timothy, defensively. 'All it wants is a bit of cash lashed out on it. A wall down here, a door up there, a lick of paint. It's not what it *is*, Sue – it's what we can make it. Good Lord above, it's *miles* ahead of Thirlton Drive – at least it's got a bit of *character*.'

Susan sighed, and followed her husband, dutifully, from room to room. Her spirits fell as Timothy grew more and more enthusiastic. Their tastes in living accommodation, she had realized, were diametrically opposed.

But Timothy Hampson had spoken the truth when he said that Flint Cottage had 'got a bit of character'. It was not the inglenook-and-exposed-beam type of architecture that Timothy secretly hankered after, it was true – but at least the old house was full of interesting nooks, intriguing crannies and odd-shaped alcoves.

'Dust-collectors,' Susan told herself, gloomily. Her unspoken dreams were of clinical utility rooms that came already plumbed for the latest line in dishwashers and tumble-driers.

The longer the time they spent inspecting the bare, empty rooms, the more Timothy waxed enthusiastic, 'oohing' or 'aahing' as he discovered an odd-shaped window or an unexpected cupboard. And it was becoming more and more apparent to Susan that her husband had set his heart on acquiring the dated property.

'It's so out-of-the-way,' she said, attempting to throw one last spoke in her husband's wheel. 'It would take you *ages* to drive up to the office.'

'I am planning to spend more time working at home in future,' he said, neatly parrying her argument. They were standing in the attic bedroom at that moment and Timothy beamed as he gazed around. 'In fact,' he said, 'this'd make an ideal upstairs study. It's quiet. It's just the right size. It'd be easy and cheap to heat.'

'There's not enough light.'

'That sloping roof,' he said, 'would stand another window, no bother.'

Susan sighed again, and gave up trying. She had only been married to Timothy for a matter of weeks. Their acquaintance-ship before the wedding had been no longer than a couple of months. She had known that he was an only child, born of a couple of doting and over-indulgent parents. She was only now beginning to realize the full implications of her husband's up-bringing. Timothy's voice broke in on her despondent thoughts.

'Come here,' he said. 'Take a look at this.'

She crossed to the attic-cupboard he had just discovered and opened. At first sight, the cupboard was bare, but then, tucked away on the top shelf and at the very back, she could see a worn, leather, cylindrical container.

'It's an old hat-box,' she said.

'I know that,' said Timothy. 'But what's it doing up here? He's cleared out everything else. Why leave a hat-box? And, what's more to the point – what do you think is inside it?'

Susan shrugged. 'How about a hat?' she said.

'The trouble with you, Susan,' observed Timothy, with only the slightest hint of censure, 'is that you've got no sense of imagination whatsoever.'

'I don't see that imagination's got anything to do with it,' said Susan. 'It's a hat-box – open most hat-boxes and tucked away inside them you're pretty sure to find a hat.'

'Not in old houses,' quibbled Timothy. 'And certainly not when they're tucked away at the back of attic cupboards. In all the best horror stories I've ever read, hat-boxes contain severed heads, usually ones that are dripping gore.'

'Oh,' said Susan, with distinct disinterest. She was not a horror story buff. Neither was she in any sort of mood for play-ful argument. She had a sorry presentiment that if any head was destined for the chopping block – speaking metaphorically, of course – then it was to be her own, certainly as far as living in this tumble-down decrepit property.

*

Credit where credit was due, Susan was forced to admit to herself. When Timothy got down to things, he blistered into the attack and didn't hold back any punches.

Within a fortnight of their deciding to purchase Flint Cottage, contracts had been exchanged between their own and Mr Harrison's solicitors. Before a month was out, Susan's competent husband had organized what had seemed like a regiment of builders, plumbers and interior decorators, all scurrying hither and thither. Walls were knocked down. Walls were put up. Windows were put in. Ugly alcoves were subtly rearranged into tasteful display shelves for family ornaments. And, while all of this was taking place, a slick salesman had called upon them in their temporary abode and vast quantities of carpeting were in the pipeline – before the concrete had even begun to set in the old back kitchen at Flint Cottage which was being speedily converted into a brand-new utility room, fully plumbed for dishwasher, washing machine and tumble-drier.

'I'm sorry, darling,' Susan murmured one afternoon, when they were visiting the house at about the halfway stage in its renovation.

'What for?' said Timothy, surprised.

'For ever wanting to buy that dreadful place in Thirlton Drive. This house is going to be *ideal* for us.'

'I always said it would. I do know best,' said Timothy, who was not a great believer in false modesty. He patted his wife, fondly, on the head. 'You must always be guided by me in future.'

Susan smiled back at him but, somehow, a little of the edge had been taken off her appreciation.

They had officially acquired the property in March. They moved in, lock, stock and utility room, in August of that same year. They both agreed that it was a total triumph for Timothy's powers of perception and organization.

From the outside, Flint Cottage had not changed. There was the same early nineteenth-century architectural structure;

the same creaking wooden gate; the same flaking green-painted
door with the same cast-iron knocker. But once inside – ah! –
what alterations met the eye. The entire interior had been
skilfully converted into an eminently desirable residence, fully
equipped throughout with oil-fired central heating with two
recep, modern fully-automatic kitchen/bkfst rm, utility room,
two bdrms, one with *en suite* bthrm with shower attachment.
And there was also the attic room which, as any estate agent
worth his salt would print in his brochure, 'was suitable for use
as third bedroom or children's playroom'.

Timothy, as has been previously stated, had chosen to use
the attic room as his study. But the hectic business of moving
house had eaten into his working days and, for some weeks
after they had settled in, Timothy had been forced to spend
more time than usual at the office.

The attic/bedroom/playroom/study remained unexplored.
Susan had no call to go up there. She was far too busy during
those early days investigating and then experimenting with the
whole range of gleaming gadgetry that was contained in her
authentic Italian-ceramic-tiled kitchen. During the early days,
Susan Hampson was as happy as any lark – well almost.

They were well into the second month of their new domest-
icity before Timothy decided to go upstairs and poke around
on the second floor of their little nest.

'Shan't be long,' he said.

'Don't you dare,' said Susan, with mock severity. 'Dinner
will be on the table in half a minute.' And as Timothy disappeared up the open pinewood staircase, she peeked in at
her cheese soufflé which, even now, was rising steadily inside
the glass door of her built-in, fully automatic, eye-level electric
oven. She hummed to herself cheerfully as she laid out the
wedding-present table mats embossed with faithful reproductions of English castles.

'Come up here, Sue.' It was Her Master's Voice.

'I can't!' she called back, a trifle flustered. 'You come down
here! The soufflé's ready!'

'*Do* come on! It won't take a second!' Timothy was putting

on his peevish voice which Susan had learned it was best not to quarrel with.

She sighed, switched off the oven, leaving the soufflé to fend for itself, and made her way up to the attic room study.

'Look there!' Timothy was pointing, slightly dramatically, into the cupboard. The inside of the cupboard had been stripped of its faded Victorian wallpaper, its shelves had been re-decorated, and now all of its interior gleamed with new-white-paint all-over brightness.

On the uppermost shelf, pushed back as it had been before, stood the scuffed leather hat-box.

'Oh,' said Susan. 'It's the hat-box.' For some odd reason which she could not explain, she felt a vague sense of uneasiness. 'He didn't take it with him.'

'Of course he didn't take it with him,' said Timothy. 'How could he? He had to leave it here, didn't he? Because he knew its grim and grisly secret.'

'What grim and grisly secret?' Susan's thoughts were fixed on the soufflé which, she felt, was fast deflating in the cooling oven.

'You *know*!' said Timothy. 'What's inside it. The gory severed head, dripping blood.'

'Don't be silly, Timothy. Let's go downstairs. Dinner's ready.'

'We'll open the hat-box first.'

'The soufflé's ready.'

'The soufflé can wait.'

'Soufflés *don't* wait.'

'Let it wait! We'll open the hat-box first. It'll only take a moment.'

There was that peevish note in his voice again. Better, she felt, a spoiled dinner than a whole evening of recriminating silence while her husband sulked. 'Oh, all right,' she said. 'Go on, if that's what you want. Satisfy your morbid curiosity. Get it down. Open it. But I'll bet you what you like that it's empty – or it's only got a hat in it.'

'You get it down and open it.'

'I *beg* your pardon?' she said, surprised – shocked.

'You heard – you get it down and open it.'

She had never heard him speak like that before. He was often peevish; sometimes even taciturn. But the voice he was using now was authoritative – commanding – dictatorial – harsh. Cruel? She almost felt afraid of him. No, that would be silly. All the same, it was even sillier to stand there playing out the stupid charade. She decided she would obey his order – once the wretched box was open, at least he might agree to go downstairs for dinner.

Susan had to stand on tiptoe in order to reach the leather box, and that with difficulty, but once it was in her hands she was relieved to discover that it wasn't heavy. Well – not *that* heavy. 'Severed head my right boot!' she murmured to herself as she placed the hat-box on the reproduction Georgian table that Timothy intended using as his desk.

'Now open it,' said Timothy.

Certainly she would. Why not? Nothing would suit her better. The lightness of the box had proved to her already that she need fear nothing for its contents. The leather strap that secured the lid caused her some slight difficulty. The buckle that held it secure had rusted with the passing of many years. Her fingers fumbled with the fastening for several seconds before she was able to loose the stiff, cracked leather strap and throw back the lid.

They looked inside.

'There,' she said, 'it *is* a hat – now are you satisfied?'

Nestling snugly within the hat-box was a brown bowler hat that shone as if it had been placed in there the day before but the musty smell that rose up from the interior of the leather box suggested otherwise. Judging by the 'old-clothes' odour that came out of the hat-box, the bowler hat must have lain inside the container for a hundred years, perhaps more.

Timothy lifted out the bowler, held it up and turned it over in his hands. The nap was soft and smooth and sleek. It was a hat that begged to be worn with a rakish tilt.

Susan stared at the bowler as though mesmerized. It nudged

at her memory of Victorian literature. Like something out of a Cruikshank illustration. The archetypal hat for a Dickens villain . . . It reminded her of a past and gloomy gaslit Thames embankment . . . of the clip-clop of horses' hooves on cobblestones and the clatter of the wheels of a hansom cab . . . of a unidentified maniacal fiend who roamed the foggy East End streets and mutilated women . . .

'Put it back in the box,' said Susan.

Timothy looked at her, laughed oddly, and made as if to put the bowler on his head.

'Put it back in the box,' she said again, and added : '*Please*.'

He shrugged, his mood of petulance and anger evaporating as he pushed the bowler back into the leather hat-box and closed the lid.

They went downstairs together.

Susan paused, her back to Timothy, as she lifted the totally deflated soufflé from the eye-level, fully automatic oven and spooned it out on to a couple of plates. 'Put it in the dustbin tomorrow, Timothy,' she said.

There was a pause. 'Put what in the dustbin tomorrow,' he said.

'You know what. The leather hat-box. And the hat.'

'What for?'

'To please me.'

'Oh, all right.' He made no complaint about the sogginess of the soufflé, almost as though silently admitting that its failure was due entirely to himself. He chewed reflectively on a mouthful, swallowed it, and then : 'On the other hand though, y'know I *might* just hang on to it.'

'That awful smelly hat? What for?'

'Oh, I dunno. You never can tell. It *might* just come in useful. For somebody.'

'I don't see how,' she said, trying to sound as if she didn't care. 'I don't know who.'

'Local amateur dramatic society type-of-thing,' he said. 'In any case, it might be valuable.'

'*Valuable?*'

'Mmm. Genuine antique. Might even interest the Victoria and Albert.' He paused, then: 'It *might* even have a history, you never know, you know – do you?'

Susan made no answer. She had a feeling that he was trying to infuriate her; she didn't know why but she wasn't going to let him. She ate the remainder of her portion of the unfortunate soufflé without so much as another word.

He did the same with his. He pushed his empty plate away from him, and smiled. 'Well then,' he said, 'what's for pud?'

Several days passed without any reference being made by either party to the leather hat-box. About a month later, while Timothy was up at his city office, and while two boiler-suited workmen were busy in her kitchen installing a waste-disposal unit, Susan went upstairs and into the attic/bedroom/play-room/study. It was a visit she made but rarely. Timothy's study was the one room in the renovated house that she had never quite taken to – strange how the addition of such a *large* window seemed to let in so little light? Strange too, that on such a bright day this particular room should feel so chilly? But she had come up here with a purpose. She crossed to the cupboard and, after only the barest moment of indecision, she opened wide the door. The uppermost shelf was empty. He had got rid of the hat-box and its contents after all. Odd, how it seemed as if that musty smell from inside the box was lingering still inside the room. Very soon, she told herself, she would come up here armed with the vacuum cleaner, some dusters and some polish, and give this room a thorough going-over. She would throw open the double-glazed window too, and let in a generous quantity of God's good air. Then, having made this resolve, Susan went downstairs and made coffee for the boiler-suited workmen with her electric percolator.

It was shortly after the installation of the waste-disposal unit that Timothy started spending less time at his London office. Not that his spending more time at home had anything to do with the waste-disposal unit. No, it had always been his intention, once he and Susan were comfortably settled in at Flint Cottage, to do as much of his business as was possible in the comfort of his own home. His profession as a consultant accountant enabled Timothy to pursue such an agreeable life-style.

Not that Susan saw any the more of her husband under the new regime – if anything, the reverse applied. For Timothy took to spending many of his evening hours shut away in the attic-study, as well as most of his daylight ones.

'It baffles me what you find to *do* up there all that time,' she said to him one evening, over a beef casserole she had prepared in her slow-cooking electric crock-pot.

'Consultant-accountancy,' Timothy replied, favouring his wife with a disarming smile.

A couple of nights later, under the pretext of taking up a cup of electrically percolated coffee, Susan made one of her rare trips to the attic-study. She opened the door quietly, carefully. Timothy was sitting with his feet up, his hands in his pockets. There was no sign of any documents referring to consultant-accountancy on Timothy's reproduction Georgian desk. In fact, the only thing on Timothy's desk, besides Timothy's feet was the open, empty, leather hat-box. The brown bowler hat was on Timothy's head. It was set back at a rakish angle. His eyes seemed curiously narrow. He was whistling, soundlessly, through his teeth.

'I thought you'd got rid of that thing,' said Susan, once she had recovered her composure.

'You thought wrong then, didn't you?' he snapped.

'You promised me you would.'

'I did nothing of the kind. I told you I was going to keep it.'

'Give it to the amateur dramatic people, or else the V & A, you said.'

'I told you, quite distinctly I recollect, that I was going to keep the bloody thing! For Christ's sake, what the hell are you doing in here, anyway?'

'I came up, Timothy,' she said, stiffly, 'to bring you a cup of coffee.'

87

'In which case, you can put it down, get out, and, in future, you will never enter this room again without having been given my prior permission – and even then not without knocking first – now then, is that clearly understood?'

'Timothy!' she gasped, horrified.

'You heard me, woman – bugger off!'

Susan's cheeks were wet with tears as she fled down the open pinewood staircase to take refuge in her ultra-modern kitchen-breakfast room from the brute of a man who was her husband.

Following the *contretemps* in the attic-study, the marriage of Timothy and Susan Hampson began speedily to go further downhill.

For one thing, Timothy took to wearing the Victorian bowler hat, openly, about the house. Even at mealtimes, and when she had gone to some particular lengths in order to prepare some favourite delicacy for him. No sooner would the fully automatic, eye-level electric oven make its warning *ping!*, announcing that the meal was ready, than there he'd be, standing in the doorway, wearing that idiotic hat at an idiotic angle. Shouting at her. Swearing at her. Even, on occasion, raising his fist at her. Then, at the table, stuffing food into his mouth, eschewing the use of knife and fork.

There was a point at which Susan gave serious consideration towards consulting the marriage guidance people. But she dismissed the notion. After all, how would it look if she were to try to explain to a total stranger that her husband seemed to be acting under the influence of a Victorian bowler hat? And that his character changed totally as soon as he put it on his head – came close to it even – not that he often took it off these days. 'Goodness,' she murmured to herself, 'they'd probably think I was stark, raving bonkers!' 'Or else,' – she paused as another frightening thought passed through her head, briefly, for she refused to countenance the possibility but momentarily – 'perhaps *he* is – *yes*! – perhaps it's him that's stark, raving bonkers!'

The situation regarding their relationship reached boiling point one sunny, autumnal Sunday afternoon. Susan had come out of the back door for a moment – merely to pop into the dustbin a paper package of bones that were indigestible by the waste-disposal unit. She had come across Timothy, brown bowler perched perkily as usual on one side of his head. He was chopping firewood.

The wood, when chopped, was earmarked for use in the mock-inglenook fireplace which Timothy had had built during the renovations into the pseudo-beamed sitting room. Susan had opted, in the balmier days of their marriage and also in the Electricity Board showroom, for an expensive heater that glowed rich and red from realistic-looking simulated logs. But her husband had insisted on having real flames, at least, in his fake-period fireplace.

And now, here he was, chopping real firewood for that very fire. But it was not the fact that Timothy was hacking at logs that disturbed his wife. It was the manner in which he chose to do it. Timothy Hampson swung the axe as if his very life depended on it – or, perhaps, not *his life* – someone else's death. His face was flushed. His breath came hard. His eyes blazed anger in his head. Time after time, without pause, the axe rose and flashed down, passionately, hard. There was a look on his face which suggested that, in his head, it wasn't wood that he was hacking away at all. There was a fury in his action that said that in his mind he was not attacking an inanimate object. It was as if he was chopping . . . as if he was chopping away at . . . not something . . . someone.

Susan felt that, above all, she had to keep calm.

She held her breath, staring at him, unable to speak, unable to look away, and all the time he swung and hewed wildly at the hunk of timber. At last, she found her tongue. 'Timothy? *Timothy!*' she said, brusquely, attempting to bring him back to reality. But it was as if he did not hear her. He just went on, insanely, the axe rising and falling – *crash!* – *smash!* – *crash!* – on the splintering wood.

Susan backed away from him, towards the house. 'You *are*

mad,' she said, horrified. 'Absolutely mad! You want putting away! You do – you want locking up!'

And then, although she had not raised her voice, it became apparent that he had heard her words. The axe faltered in mid-stroke as he raised his head and his eyes found hers. He stood, gazing at her, like a maniac, as if he wanted to murder *her*. And all the time, the thing that seemed to hold her petrified was not the fury that blazed in his eyes but the Victorian brown bowler hat that sat, raffishly, on top of his head.

Fear gave her feet at last. She turned and fairly burst through the back door and into the kitchen. Her feet clattered across the Italian ceramic tiles as she made for the hallway where she snatched up her coat and her bag. The flaking green-painted door slammed shut behind her. The wooden garden gate creaked on its rusty hinges as she pushed it open, sped through it, and then on down the lane.

Looking back, she saw that Timothy had made no attempt to follow her. Only then did Susan relax her pace.

Stirring her teaspoon in her cup of tea, she gazed around at the ordinary people sitting at the ordinary plastic-topped tables in the slightly garish, brightly lit, coffee shop. Once again, she was close to tears. What could she do? Go to the police? And tell them what? She acted out the scene in her head:

'*Excuse me, sergeant, can you help me, please?*' '*Certainly, madam, what seems to be the trouble?*' '*It's my husband. I think he wants to kill me.*' '*Oh yes, madam, and what makes you think a thing like that?*' '*Well – there was this look in his eyes while he was chopping wood – and then there's this awful old hat that he insists on wearing . . .*' '*I shouldn't worry, madam. You should see some of the gear my old woman wears – and the look in her eyes when she stuffs a chicken!*' And in her imagination, Susan saw her make-believe police sergeant exchange a wink with a make-believe constable.

No, she couldn't go to the police. After all, Timothy had not actually attacked her physically – yet. She sipped at her tea, nervously. Then, across the coffee shop, her eyes fixed upon a familiar figure. She rose, and carrying her tea cup, crossed to where the man was sitting.

'Excuse me,' she said, 'but it is Mr Harrison, isn't it?'

The man, who was wearing a scruffy gaberdine raincoat, glanced up, surprised. 'Don't tell me,' he said, 'it's on the tip of my tongue – *Hampson*, that's it. You're the young woman that's married to the chap that bought old Sumner's place. How is it suiting you?'

'May I sit down?'

'Take a pew, Mrs Hampson,' but the smile faded from his face as he caught on to her anxiety. 'Look here,' he continued, 'if it's about that bottom garden wall, I got my surveyor to have a look at that most . . .'

'It's got nothing to do with the garden wall, Mr Harrison.' She paused, took a deep breath, and bravely broached her subject: 'There was an old Victorian leather hat-box in the attic when you went.'

Harrison swallowed, awkwardly. 'That bit of rubbish?' he said. 'Yes – well – you don't have to worry about sending it on. I don't want it. You can sling it out.'

'I need to know about it, Mr Harrison.' Her voice was calm.

He looked down at the table, avoiding her eyes, and several seconds went by before he lifted his head, and spoke: 'I suppose you have a right to know the facts.'

Flint Cottage, it was said, was haunted. The story concerned a middle-aged Victorian roué and his wife, a woman with a frail body but a waspish tongue. There had always been arguments between the pair, and always about money. The woman had wanted more for house-keeping; the man preferred to spend his earnings on other women and drink. On one particular occasion, he had struck lucky with a wager he had had on a horse. The woman had heard about his good fortune and had set her heart on a lace-trimmed blouse. But the man had come home, eventually, late at night, the worse for drink, his pockets empty. The argument that night was vicious and brutal: the woman accusing the man of drunken debauchery; the man taunting the woman, sneering at her skinny unattractiveness.

Legend did not say who struck the first blow: whether she laid into him with the flat-iron, whether he caught her first with the back of his hand. One thing is certain, the argument ended with the man murdering his wife. He had subsequently gone to his own death on the gallows. It was the man's restless spirit, it was said, that still roamed Flint Cottage. Oh yes – one other thing: on the fatal night at the cottage, the man had not come home having got rid of all his winnings on women and drink. He had spent some portion of it on an expensive brown bowler hat for himself. He was wearing that bowler hat when he took up the carving knife and slashed open his wife's throat.

Harrison paused, embarrassed. 'Mind you,' he said, 'I never paid much heed to the tale myself. He was twenty-odd years older than me, my cousin. I was no more than a lad when he first told me the story – and showed me that hat-box – I always reckoned that the silly old sod was trying to put the wind up me.'

Susan said nothing.

Harrison looked at her, curious, his eyebrows raised. 'Anyway, why do you want to know?' he said. 'You haven't been having any funny goings-on at the cottage, have you?'

Susan Hampson walked up the lane purposefully towards her home. She was not afraid. She knew exactly what she had to do. She had to destroy the brown bowler hat, that was all. It was as simple as that. And, if Timothy happened to be wearing it – well – she would just have to snatch it from his head. She would toss it on to the flames in the inglenook fireplace. It had turned out for the best, really, that Timothy had insisted on a real fire in his fireplace. 'All's well that end's well,' she said to herself, smiling.

She pushed open the wooden gate and walked up towards the flaking green-painted door. What she had not seen was the face beneath the brown bowler hat that was peering out at her from behind the lace-curtained, leaded window.

The moment that Susan opened the front door and stepped

into the hallway, Timothy leaped upon her. She fought back, hard – scratching, biting, beating with her fists. But her womanly strength was no match for his maniacal fury. He dragged her, kicking and screaming by the hair into the kitchen, across the Italian ceramic tiles – towards the plastic work-surface where the three-year-guaranteed electric carving knife stood plugged into the wall socket.

Detective Inspector Stephen Gravesend did not believe in ghosts. He never had; bowler-hatted or any other variety. In his considered opinion, Timothy Hampson was no more nor less than your dyed-in-the-wool, twenty-four carat genuine nutter. It was, as the Detective Inspector always said himself, one of the simplest cases he had ever had to wrap up. Within twenty-four hours of his being assigned to the job, the maniac had been apprehended. Not that Gravesend found much to boast about in this achievement. After all, Hampson had practically given himself up. He had been arrested on the forecourt at Euston Station. The railway police had had no difficulty in recognizing the suspect. At the time of his arrest, Hampson was wearing a Victorian brown bowler on his head. In his right hand he was carrying a scuffed leather Victorian hat-box. On inspection, the hat-box was found to contain a woman's severed head, dripping gore.

PHILIP EVANS

The Gold Medallion

On the day he received his nomination to play for England, Graham Hadfield decided to keep a diary.

Wednesday 7 November

For weeks the newspapers have said that I should play for England. I knew I was in with a good chance when the new England manager, Brian Keyes, came up to watch our team play several games during the past two months; but when it actually happens, when you're picked to go into the pool of players, it's still nice. But as I've just started this notebook maybe I should fill in a few points about myself.

I've always been very aware of death. All my grandparents had died by the time I was six; my elder brother, Gregory, died from a rare illness – a brain tumour – when I was eight and he two years older; I lost another brother, Stephen, when he was only a few days old; my father named us after some of his friends who had died in a disaster at some pit; but it was his own death, when I was only ten, that most affected me.

He was a miner; one who worked at a colliery in Dodworth, just to the west of Barnsley. Several times in the previous years he had come home with a long face, having heard news about disasters at other collieries nearby. But although the risks of a stroke of bad fortune in mining are high you never believe it will happen to you. So with my father. He worked at a colliery whose coal was used to feed power stations. One morning he said good-bye to my mother and me, and it was at about eleven o'clock that my mother opened the door to an official from the

95

Coal Board who told her that the cage carrying the men to work had run loose and had crashed to the bottom of the shaft. All the men aboard had been killed. Dad had been one.

Of course you get over these things in time. My mother re-married soon afterwards – married a schoolmaster, a teacher of languages who she had met at church. We moved to live in Silkstone, a village just outside Barnsley. I was lonely at first, cut off from all my friends of the past few years; but I gradually made some new ones in our new neighbourhood. And then there was our football. Dad had always encouraged me when we had lived just to the south of Oakwell, the ground at which Barnsley played. He had taken me to see game after game; had played football with me for hours after he'd come home from work – even when he was tired out; and in our new home in Silkstone I made sure of using the wide spaces in which to practise running and ball control.

As time went by I found that I was doing fairly well at the game. Barnsley is one of those centres that breeds many gifted players but has been unable to hold on to them when they grow older. And there were always those pessimists who com-pared you to players of the past and always unfavourably. Things were going well for me – I played for the school team and found myself chosen to represent Barnsley Schoolboys. But there was this old codger who drove me mad. He used to turn up to all our games and make a point of talking to me as I was on my way home after the game. He would mention some previous player who'd become an international, poke me in the chest with a grimy forefinger and say things such as, 'Thee, lad, tha's not good enough to polish his boots and tha' nivver will be,' and fix me with a firm stare. 'Nivver. Tha's just a big bit of puff-pastry when compared to him.' If he made remarks like that once, he made them a million times. But when I got home my stepfather would calm me down and say I must be *some* good else the old man wouldn't bother to talk to me.

Sure enough, in time I came to be signed by Manchester United – and the idea of death came close again. The night before I was supposed to make the trip my mother came over to me while I was watching the television, pressed something into my hand and said, 'Here, love, take this.' It was the gold medallion my father had worn every day, ever since I could remember. It was the size of a fivepenny piece and I learned then that it had been given to my father as a present by a friend who'd won money on the pools : my father had worn it to work every day and come to think of it as being a good-luck charm. One day, some years later, he had taken it into a jeweller's and asked for a motif to be engraved on it – the motif of a wink, as if to say to bad luck, 'Sod off. You can't affect me.' Good luck it certainly brought him for, in the following years, several friends were injured or killed at work. But one day he had to take it into the same jeweller to have the chain mended; they asked to keep it for twenty-four hours; and it was on the following day that my father died. That was the charm my mother gave me to take to Manchester.

So, naturally, I thought of the medallion as being a good-luck charm for myself. I went to Old Trafford as an apprentice, turned professional when I was seventeen and made my League début a year later. But those three years were a rough, tough, hard time. In schoolboy football I had grown used to having lots of time and space to play with, but as I grew up I became used to receiving the odd tackle that was brutal, had to get used to playing with and against people who had more determination than skill and were eager to put you out of games, had to get used to tackling with much more severity. And all the time there were those reminders; reminders of that crash in February 1958 when more than half of the passengers aboard the plane trying to take off at Munich airport died. The Manchester United team was on its way back from Belgrade, where the players had just drawn 3–3 with Red Star in the European Cup quarter-final leg. Among the dead had been Tommy Taylor, who had himself come from Barnsley, had been signed for almost £30,000. I remembered hearing his name spoken around Barnsley, remembered hearing it spoken with awe; and I would find it impossible to forget that crash with so many memorials of that tragic day peppered around the club premises.

Which brings us up to the present. In the past six years I've gained much more skill, much more flair, much more stamina. There was a turnabout in international football in England in July with a new manager, Brian Keyes, being brought in to organize things and make sure that we got good results. His first objective is to get us into the World Cup final tournament.

Tuesday 13 November

I've been training hard all these past three days and the great delight is that I've been chosen to play against Yugoslavia. I saw the programme for tomorrow's game. It listed many other players, then came to me :

> GRAHAM HADFIELD (Manchester United): Winger who has been developed by the club and has been capped at youth and Under-21 levels. Born Barnsley. Uncapped. Aged 21. A young player whose sureness of touch and speed with the ball have often made their mark.

That's a programme that I'll make sure to keep until my dying day.

We'd been drawn inside a qualifying group with Northern Ireland and Yugoslavia and got off to a bright start with a victory in Belfast. But when the Ulstermen came to Wembley they held us to a goalless draw. Yugoslavia had also made a bright start defeating both England and Northern Ireland in Belgrade. But they tend to play far more effectively at home than abroad; lost by two goals when they went to Belfast; and are now about to play us at Wembley to make sure of qualifying for the final stages of the competition proper. But there is always this in their favour : a draw would suit them fine but we, on our side, would have to win to be sure of going through.

Wednesday 14 November

Not surprisingly, we were all keyed up for the game. We knew we had the determination, the will to win; we had three fine players, almost world-class, in our side; but would we have the luck that makes results go our way? Or would we have the bad luck that makes you wish you were dead, that makes all your attempts at goal go just outside, rather than inside, the goal posts?

It was a mild night for mid-November – but the game was hectic from the first whistle until the last. I remember groaning inwardly when one of the Yugoslav defenders crashed into our main striker, Neville Smith, who had only played a couple of games since being out of action for a few weeks with a strained groin. He lay writhing on the floor for a time grasping his right knee where he had been kicked savagely. The referee took the name of the defender, which made him feature in less forth-right a manner for fear of being caught again and risking expulsion. But you can imagine our joy and the fury of the Yugoslavs to discover that we'd been given a penalty! A decision that would have gone the other way if we were playing the match in Belgrade. And we scored.

I became increasingly glad we'd been fully briefed about the Yugoslav team. We went further ahead by another goal; they got one back soon afterwards; and the last ten minutes were all blood, sweat and tears, trying to keep the pressure up front in order to keep their defence stretched and making sure that we didn't let in any more goals. Our goalkeeper, Kevin Durkin, made an astonishing save from one of their forwards when he was clean through, leaping to his left to turn the ball round the post; our tall centre-back, Tom Kennedy, made a series of superb interceptions when some of their players appeared to be straight through; and I swear that many of us fell to the ground in a mixture of both exhaustion and relief when the final whistle went.

Saturday 17 November

Stuart Patterson gave a party to celebrate our victory. He played alongside me in the United forward line; but his country, Scotland, had been eliminated from the World Cup. It was the same old story : they had played magnificently against West

Philip Evans

Germany but pitifully against Finland and Switzerland. Their low point was reached when they lost at Hampden to Switzerland – a game they should have won by a handful of goals.

'The usual thing, Gra',' Stu said when I met him at training later that week. 'We murder the big boys. *Murder them.* But we can't play agin the trash.' And he joined me in a jog along The Cliff – the United training area.

He jumped on me the night of the party and told me that there was an Italian girl coming and he'd make sure to introduce me because I could speak Italian, couldn't I? When I explained that I only knew a few words, a few words that I'd learned from my stepfather, he waved my protestations aside and said that no one else in the room spoke her language, but I did and I'd have to talk to her. Okay? Okay. And with that he walked quickly away to make sure the record player was working all right.

About ten minutes later he came up to me with this girl, made the introductions very quickly and then left us. It helped to break the ice and I could see her eyes still smiling as I found out a bit about her. Her name was Jane Piatti; her father was Italian – he ran a restaurant in Manchester – and her mother English. Her father came from a village just outside Florence, a village called Impruneta; had met Jane's mother when she was visiting Florence about twenty years ago; had pursued her to Manchester – which was where she lived – and began learning the language and customs. They married almost straight away and began a family soon after.

Fairly tall, Jane was an intriguing amalgam of looks. She had inherited some from her father – the olive complexion and hair the colour of sable; and some from her mother – she had the full mouth that was similar and also the most riveting pair of eyes, the colour of cornflower blue. It was those eyes that I came to find most intriguing and magnetic as we got to know each other better. I felt as though they were seeing right through me, almost as though they were X-raying me, whenever I looked into them. As though they were almost ghost-like. During that evening we danced a fair amount, talked about our tastes

100

in books, in films, in television – you know, the type of conversation you have with someone you meet for the first time. Stuart had been thankfully wrong about her inability to speak English; for she spoke it very well, with a nevertheless personal and quixotic mannerism. And as we left I made sure of taking down her address and telephone number.

But I have found that the demands made on my time even greater after that England game. I have been forced to spend increasing amounts of time at training sessions for the England squad, lured on by the prospect of doing well in the tournament in the summer. The new manager likes to make us train in small groups, urges us to do this wholeheartedly and with enthusiasm; and takes us aside from time to time in order to discuss our particular playing problems, our strengths and weaknesses. It is a far cry from those days when, as an apprentice, I'd spend as much time washing out the training rooms and cleaning the boots – doing things like that – as well as training.

Wednesday 9 January

The draw for the World Cup was made yesterday. We had hoped for an easy draw and are delighted to find ourselves drawn in a group with Kuwait, France and Hungary. Of our group games three are to be played in Florence and three in Bologna. Other games are being staged in Genoa, in Milan, in Turin, in Naples and in Rome – which is where the Final is due to be held. And all this gives us a five-month time-span in which to prepare – to study the strengths and defects of the other teams who have qualified, and polish up minor features in our own play.

Luck has played its part again. The manager believed very firmly in watching as much Continental football as possible and this took him off to a series of games in France, in Hungary and in Kuwait. He has come back with first-hand information as to what progress our first opponents in the tournament are making – information he has been able to pass on to us at our regular squad meetings. Thoughts about who were the speedier players in the teams he had watched, which players had the best ball control, facts even about the goal-keepers. For example we have learned that the Kuwaiti goal-keeper, Saad, is left-handed – a point that may come in useful if a penalty is ever awarded against his side.

He has also encouraged us to feel part of a squad by making sure that the same players are invited to his squad get-togethers, despite the fact that sometimes some of them are injured. It's done wonders for the morale of the team, being sure of meeting up with your friends on a regular basis, and it certainly helps to damp down the feeling of disappointment when someone is left out of a team.

Wednesday 20 February

We played against, and beat, West Germany in the stadium at Munich. Our team included ten players who had been present when we had beaten Yugoslavia three months ago. And during that period we had played together four times in practice sessions – working with the ball on each occasion, working to improve our skill. We played sessions of keep ball, sessions in which we practised one-twos, sessions in which we tested both our heading and tackling abilities, sessions in which we practised our volleying. Then we spent some time working without the ball, working on our acceleration, turning around quickly and stopping.

We won that game against West Germany by three goals to two, our scores coming from Neville Smith – who scored twice, once with his head and once with a glorious volley from my centre when he was fifteen yards out – and Jim Noble. I felt quite pleased with my performance although I was helped by the fact that the defender opposite me, Klaus Fluegge, had a wretched game. But we had been blessed with luck – luck that their superbly gifted player in midfield, Manfred Haggan, had been injured and was unable to play. On top form he is capable of doing anything. I'd seen some film of him and been most impressed: he had wonderful acceleration, marvellous ball control, the knowledge of the exact moment in which to make a pass or when to slow the play down and, above all, a cool temperament. You would never see him being disconcerted. I left Munich the following morning being absolutely sure that we would hear much of him during the World Cup finals.

Sunday 31 March

I was woken up late this morning by Jane. She began playing with the necklace around my throat, turning it over and over, asking questions about it, propped up on one elbow and staring gravely at me. She kept turning it over while I answered her questions and told her the story about my father, about how he had believed it to be a good luck charm, about the wink carved on to it and about how my mother had given it to me when I had come from Barnsley.

She lay back and snuggled up to me. 'I have to go away for a time,' she said suddenly.

That statement woke me up a lot. 'Where to?' I asked.

'To Impruneta,' she said. 'My aunt has been taken ill and I have to go and look after my uncle.' She paused. 'But it will only be for a few weeks, until she comes out of hospital. I'll write to you and tell you how things are.'

I lay back and tried to relax. If she had to go, then she had to go.

And, in any case, I hope to be very caught up in football for the following few weeks.

Wednesday 3 April

I hate farewells, and I was silent as I drove Jane to the airport. She was booked on a flight to Milan, and would go from there by train to Florence where she would be met by her uncle.

She was quiet also. We made small talk when we reached the airport and she watched me sign a couple of autographs for schoolboys; then, with about ten minutes before her plane was due to be boarded, she burst into tears and cuddled up to me.

'Could I beg something from you?' she asked.

'Of course,' I replied.

'Could I take that medallion? Please, Graham, please.' She pronounced my Christian name as though it was two words, with a very heavy stress on the 'h'. And she looked directly at me with those ghostly-blue eyes.

I took the thing off, pressed it into her hand and walked swiftly away. By then it was my turn to be crying.

Wednesday 17 April

We played a friendly against Brazil, who were over on a long tour of Europe before the competition proper started. They had recently had a change of coach, a man who was prepared to try and build in some of the harsher features of the European game, prepared to sacrifice some of their native skills at ball control. They had a masterful player in midfield called Machado but for the most part the rest of the team played as if they were involved in a wrestling contest. The match ended in a 2–2 draw; I was taken off halfway through the second half covered in a mass of bruises and small cuts.

I was very depressed. Depressed not because of my injuries but because I had not been playing at all well for the previous ten days. You can get used to high tackles, trips, when opponents try to gouge your eyes out or spit at you. But you can never get used to having lost form.

Sunday 28 April

I was left out of the club side for yesterday's match; and I wasn't even named as substitute. Since the reserve side was playing very well, it was decided to keep it playing together. So I spent the afternoon away from the world of football. If they don't want me – okay, stuff them. I began to want Jane back.

Sunday 5 May

I was left out of the team again on Wednesday in the match in the UEFA Cup, and again yesterday. I did go to the game on Wednesday since we were playing against AC Milan and in their team was a midfield player who played for Italy – Dino

Lanati. He played with a great sense of calm and authority and seemed to have all the time in the world when he passed the ball with great precision over distances both long and short.

We lost at home yesterday by the odd goal in five: but I didn't go, nor even play for the reserves. I was so pissed off with being off form that I pretended to have injured my back. But it was during the night that I had become most upset.

It happened first on one night when my father paid a visit to my room. I slept alone then and had done ever since Jane had gone away during the previous month. Dad just came in, sat down on my bed and began talking in a low voice. He looked exactly like he'd looked when he was just going to work.

'Now then, lad,' he said, 'I know and tha' knows tha's just been playing silly buggers.' He pointed at my chest with his forefinger. 'Get on that pitch and show 'em what you can do. That there medallion brought me luck and it will do to you.' Another jab in my chest. 'Get a move on.' And with that he disappeared.

I woke up to find myself covered in sweat. Of course, of course, of course. Why hadn't I realized it before? *That* was why I'd been playing so wretchedly for the past month – my divorce from the good-luck charm. I *had* to get the thing back.

So I rang Jane in Italy; begged her to return the medallion as soon as possible; and promised to send her another, replacement, token.

Sunday 19 May

I may have been dropped by the club side but I was still part of the England squad and chosen for the Home International Championship. I played against Wales in Cardiff, where we won by the one goal, despite a superb performance by the Welsh goalkeeper, John Watkins; and I also played in the second game, against Northern Ireland at Wembley. So we were putting things together neatly in time for the World Cup, building up a close understanding.

But on the night following that game, on the night of the 15th, I had a very depressing nightmare. I had received several more nightly visits from my father; on several occasions had woken up screaming with terror; and so they had found a room for me to sleep alone and not disturb anyone else. That night I was visited by Jane, who appeared wearing a dress of midnight blue – a dress that set off acutely those cornflower-blue eyes of hers. She was walking towards me slowly, but when she was about ten metres away her eyes opened wide, suddenly she screamed, 'No, no, no' and pushed her hands out ahead of her. At the next moment she fell and began to bleed across her front.

I woke up shrieking, sitting up in bed with my arms out in front of me. And then I heard myself repeating for several moments, '*Carissima*, why didn't you tell me?' – repeating that over and over again.

This dream stayed with me the following day. And as I had been playing so ineptly it came as no surprise to me to learn that I had been dropped for the game at Hampden Park against Scotland. To be truthful it was a very good game to miss. Those Scots! They're always inclined to treat the game against England as though it is the last moment on earth; and, since they'd not qualified to take a team to the World Cup finals, they'd go into tackles with animal ferocity. On our side the list of players who'd been slightly wounded grew longer and longer; and Geoff Hardy, a key player in midfield, received a tackle brutal enough to have him carried off the field on a stretcher. I was very pleased when the game finished as a 1–1 draw without further serious injury to our team.

I woke up after another horrendous nightmare, again about Jane, that night. And by that time I was prepared to blame all my troubles on the medallion – which had not yet arrived. Or so I thought. But when I returned to Manchester to collect some clothes before setting off for a month, I found the medallion waiting for me. It must have arrived while I was down south with the England squad. I unwrapped the parcel as gently as if it contained a breakable object; kissed the medallion; and then put it around my neck. Now I would be all right, if I was given the chance to prove myself. If. If. If.

Wednesday 22 May

It all came together on the night and we beat Portugal 3–0 in Lisbon. We scored once in the first half, from a diving header by Jim Noble; and at half-time I received the stroke of good fortune for which I'd been hoping and praying – I was brought on as a substitute. *That* was the piece of luck I needed, and I made a resolve to put the following forty-five minutes to good use.

Good luck, good luck, good luck. Everything I tried came off, and I ran through my repertoire of tricks. I was playing a bit deeper, more in the midfield than usual – Geoff Hardy was still away through injury – but I managed to score the second goal myself, jinking my way through from inside our own half. And I laid on the pass from which Bob Horton scored the final goal – making a neat volley from ten yards out. As we left the pitch at the end of the game it was good to hear the crowd cheering us. As I went into the dressing rooms I gave the gold medallion a tacit vote of thanks. I felt confident I'd won back my place in the team.

But I still experienced nights of restlessness, nights in which I'd wake up from dreams and nightmares. Always they involved Jane; always they concerned her dying; always I woke up covered in sweat, feeling weak and strangely experiencing some form of foreboding; always they served to keep me awake for the rest of the night. But I'd got the medallion back – and all other things counted for nothing when set against that fact.

Thursday 23 May

We flew from Lisbon to Linate Airport in Milan, and from there continued our journey southwards on the motorway to the south. As two of our first three games were due to be played at Florence we made our way to a hotel just outside Prato, about fifteen miles to the north-west of Florence itself. With our first game, which was against Kuwait, due to take place the following Thursday, we settled down to do some relaxed training, concentrating on practising over and again movements that were aimed to make us play more collectively. And to guide us we had those notes made by the manager. I rang Jane, but there was no reply from her phone.

Friday 24 May

Again I rang Jane; and again there was no reply. In fact I rang her three times without getting an answer.

Wednesday 29 May

Still no reply from Jane's phone.

Tuesday 4 June

I can't believe it; or, at least, I don't want to. This time, when I rang, the phone was answered by a man, a man whom I presumed to be her uncle. I spoke one of the few phrases that I'd learnt from Jane, had been practising it for some weeks. '*Posso parlare con la signorina Jane?*' But that only served to send him off speaking a torrent of Italian which I couldn't understand. So I merely said that I didn't understand – '*non capito*' murmured over and over again – and went to look for the interpreter. When he came and made the call to Jane's uncle I noticed that his face grew grimmer and grimmer every second. Suddenly he said a few quick, sharp words into the phone, nodded several times and hung up.

He came over to me, took my elbow and walked me away several yards – as though we were going to somewhere more private. Suddenly he stopped, turned his face to me and said in a low voice, 'That was a relation of Jane's.'

'Yes,' I said. 'Her uncle.'

He nodded, and looked at the floor for a long time before he said in a soft voice, 'He told me that three weeks ago she was killed in a car accident.' He looked straight at me then.

Three weeks ago. The 15th of May, the night when I'd had the terrible nightmare. The night when I'd imagined Jane was bearing my child and had wanted to keep that fact a secret to herself.

And he comforted me as I burst out crying.

The Gold Medallion

Sunday 16 June

The competition is half-completed and we have won our Group. In fact, we were determined not to undervalue the Kuwaitis and scored five good goals, and against France we ran in three more. Both of those games were played in the open stadium at Florence. But against Hungary we had to travel up the motorway to Bologna and found ourselves playing a very well-organized team which gave our defence, superbly marshalled by Tom Kennedy, quite a handful of work to get through. At the final whistle we ran out victors but it was only by the odd goal in three, and one of our goals had come from a penalty.

The stadium, which lies to the west of the city, resembles a bowl – a stadium that gives you a very strong impression of being hedged in. Before the game we were given the grim news that Geoff Hardy would be out through injury. He struck me as never having quite recovered from the savagery he received when we played against the Scots. Once or twice he had pulled up in training, an expression of pain in his eyes, and slowed down markedly. And although he played in our first two games, his left leg had received a further strain in the match against France. When I met him in the hotel corridor two days before the Hungary game he was still limping slightly.

'No go, Geoff?' I asked.

He shook his head, and slowly walked past.

But in our attack both Jim Noble and Neville Smith had been on superbly sharp form – the former using his great strength and wonderful sense of balance to carve out openings, and the latter making swift, determined bursts forward and using his skilful footwork and ball control to score on many occasions.

That first game against Kuwait took place only two days after I'd heard the news of Jane's death, and during the first half, I'd given the defender marking me, Salim, no trouble at all. But during the second half of the game I found myself able to switch my mind completely on to football. And the same thing in that game against France : I found myself going through periods during which I was able to concentrate completely on the football and periods when the image of Jane came close to me. Jane – with that blood across her front; Jane – with those cornflower-blue eyes opened wide as they registered her state of shock; Jane – with that scream at the back of her throat. Even during the game against Hungary those images cropped up frequently.

Wednesday 26 June

We played and beat West Germany this evening; won 3–1, all of our goals coming during the first half. Neville Smith scored twice with neat play and thunderous shots from twenty yards out. And Jim Noble got the third with a spectacular overhead bicycle kick. But during the second half, Geoff Hardy, the key person in our midfield, wrenched his left knee and had to hobble off. And in the midfield of the opposition Haggan played his big heart out, clearly surrounded by players much less clever than himself; but the crowd at San Siro stadium in Milan admired his play and gave him a big hand of applause whenever he touched the ball.

As for me, I had to go off after being caught in a 'sandwich'; and when I came to be taken to the dressing room to receive some treatment I was still a bit woozy. I didn't take much notice as the doctor asked for my jersey to be taken off so he could clean up some small scratches. But in doing this they completely stripped my top half – medallion, chain and all; and in the ensuing rumpus it completely disappeared.

I was too sleepy to pay much notice, and still a bit drugged as I left the stadium. But during the following night I kept dreaming about the ghosts of people who'd been near to me and I became certain that the medallion was missing. Of course, I had experienced dreams about Jane while wearing the medallion but these dreams now were more frightening – nightmares about people being killed over and over again; about pints of blood; about fearful noises while they were going down.

Sunday 30 June

We were beaten in the Final by Italy – backed by that maniac crowd in Rome, knowing that they couldn't lose, aware that they would each receive millions of *lire* for winning and a near-pillorying for losing. They always say that if you want to win the World Cup you have to be blessed with four or five great players in your side – but you also have to be blessed by luck. Italy had a stroke of luck in playing all their games in the tournament at the Stadio Olimpico in Rome; and they had this superbly gifted central attacker, Roberto Cianfanelli. We had been told of his prowess at our team-talks with regard to the other countries taking part in the competition, but on the day there was nothing, absolutely nothing, that our defence could do to slow him down. I could see Tom Kennedy patiently trying all the skills he knew to hold the centre of the defence tight and he seemed to cover acres of territory giving help to his colleagues. But Cianfanelli seemed to be blessed with all the attributes you could name – he had pace, courage, flair, an exceptional sense of balance, superb reflexes along with the gift of lightning acceleration and an explosive left-foot shot. His courage helped him climb so high when the ball was in the air – and Kevin Durkin in our goal knew absolutely nothing about a header that flew past his right shoulder in the second half. That made the score 3–1 in their favour, and it stayed like that until the final whistle. In fact, both Neville Smith and Jim Noble became so fed up with receiving little ball from midfield – where Mick Bish had taken the place of Geoff Hardy that they fell back hungrily and tried to win the ball around the halfway line. Neville did have the minor satisfaction of finishing the tournament as the leading scorer.

As for me, every time I touched the ball I felt uneasy and was prone to make crass mistakes. Those words of my father's kept running through my mind – *'Now then, I know and tha' knows tha's just playing silly buggers. Get on and show 'em.'* And at one moment when the ball went out of play near my part of the touchline I looked up and saw them standing there, saw them as clearly as though metres had been converted to centimetres – both my father and Jane, both staring at me, Dad with his soft brown eyes and Jane with those eyes of hers that were cornflower blue. They were both shouting: Dad, pointing his forefinger at me and telling me 'to get stuck in', 'to fight, lad, fight', and Jane in that dress of midnight blue just kept shouting my name in that particular, peculiar way of hers, 'Grah-ham', trying to pronounce letters such as the 'h' that she found difficult. But try as I might to make it up to them, I always came back to feeling guilty about Jane's death, the knowledge that when she had her fatal accident the medallion was sitting in a state of solitary confinement in my flat in Manchester. And I swear it – I did play my heart out to try and redeem myself in their eyes. But as the match went on I noticed that I was being starved of the ball, even when I fell back to playing in midfield. It must have been no surprise to the crowd when I came to be substituted twenty minutes before the final whistle. And when I looked up at both Jane and Dad from the bench I saw they weren't following the play but just staring at me coldly.

Extract from *The Manchester Courier*, Thursday 4 July:

'. . . *Enrico Piatti, aged 45, was taken into custody yesterday and is helping police with their inquiries into the death of the United international footballer, Graham Hadfield, who received two shots through the heart from a .32 Beretta pistol. Piatti, a local restaurant owner, is the father of Hadfield's late fiancée who died tragically in a motorway accident in Italy in the middle of May . . .*'

MICHAEL LEVEY

Unsettled, with Outbreaks of Rain

Mr Carter slipped his tightly rolled umbrella into the narrow, darkly polished shaft of the umbrella stand deftly and with his customary satisfaction, as if replacing some precision tool in its protective case. Despite the forecast, he had not needed to open it during the day.

But his satisfaction lay deeper. In that first action of replacement every evening was symbolized his own slipping back into the perfect fit of his environment. It never ceased to give him a combined sense of relief and pleasure; and though there no longer came the gentle, cheerful, unquestioning query of 'Is that you, Herbert?' from the bedroom at the end of the corridor, he still felt the flat exuding a positive welcome as he paused in the hall on his return.

It was four months since his mother had died. Over the period sporadic letters had continued to arrive from widely scattered, dwindling members of the once large family, some of whom he scarcely recalled from his childhood and who only just had the news passed on to them : '. . . sad she was bedridden so long . . . so devoted to you . . . hard at your age, though always a blow . . . naturally thinking of you . . . must be years since we met . . . ever this way, do visit us . . .'

To each letter he scrupulously and truthfully replied, avoiding any commitment to seeing the writers and extending no invitations, however vague, to them. He thanked cousin Doris and the rest at Ruislip, but silently declined to share her amazement at Philip being now nineteen and employed in a bank. To Louise in Canada ('I think you knew I married again after Sam's death') he simply included respects to her husband. Young Arthur and Hazel had written to him as Uncle Herbert, which was not strictly accurate, but he felt it right to sign himself similarly when replying.

Sunday was the day he set aside for answering letters and paying bills. He liked to sit at his desk in the living room of the quiet Battersea flat. He thought carefully before composing the accounts of what his feelings were, increasingly reassured at finding that his state of mind did not fluctuate. 'Mother's death,' he wrote, 'has grieved me deeply, but it did not come as a shock. We were very close, though she never attempted to run my life. I always went abroad each year for holidays on my own, and though she always enjoyed seeing my photographs, photography was never an interest of hers. Fortunately, she suffered little pain and kept her good spirits up to the end. I believe hers, like mine, could be called a contented life. Nellie (whom you may recall from when we lived in Streatham) came in to look after her and is only too anxious to go on being of what help she can.'

He thought he had told them enough. And if it all sounded a little remote, that was not because of him but because his correspondents were remote, emotionally at least as much as physically. Privately, some of them had probably smiled – as he knew colleagues at the office did – at the son who remained in middle age unmarried and living with his mother. Unpleasant things might nowadays be said or hinted. And if the bedridden woman hadn't turned into a querulous, nagging tyrant, the son ought nevertheless to experience at her death a tremendous sense of either relief or loneliness.

He felt neither. Being alone was something he was well used to, and savoured; even at the office he had, after twenty-seven years, not made any particular friends, though he had plenty of friendly acquaintances. The flat was inevitably emptier now.

Of course he missed going down the corridor every evening in response to the clear call that greeted him. Yet he had told his mother about his day to please her rather than himself. In that way he saluted her sense and courage in saying nothing about how time passed for her or about the condition of her body which seemed oddly to bulk larger in the bed as daily she grew progressively weaker. It was true that he had secretly dreaded her actual death – as perhaps she guessed – and it was their one-time maid Nellie who was present when she died quietly in mid-morning on a weekday.

He had decided to remain in the flat and leave it largely unaltered, with the furniture and pictures he had been familiar with since his childhood: the then already old-fashioned mahogany chairs, the blue-enamel and glass-domed clock and some framed sepia reproductions of such subjects as *King Cophetua and the Beggar-maid* and *Hope*. The only change he planned was in his mother's narrow bedroom, abruptly confronting him now almost as a threat, to become the spare room. Yet although he had never envisaged a use for it, he rapidly realized how suitable it was to accommodate all his photographic equipment, including his projector and the cabinets of his slides.

Tonight he looked forward to mounting a batch of dramatically fiery sky studies taken by him recently from the bathroom window, as it faced west and the weekend autumnal weather happened to be unusually brilliant. He could imagine mingling them with some of his best Alpine studies and defying anyone to believe they were not taken from the lower slopes of the Matterhorn.

As he paused in the hall, he was irritated faintly to notice three letters lying on the mat. Until recently there had seldom been any post for him except bills. Although he would not deal with them until Sunday, he resented tonight even having to read letters. It was a relief to find that two were in fact no more than demands for the telephone service and the water rate. The third envelope was pink – 'cheap' was the word which occurred as he fingered its flimsy exterior – and he did not recognize the childish handwriting. He kept it unopened, incurious and uneager as he changed his shoes for slippers, took off his jacket, but kept on his waistcoat and then went to the corner cupboard in the sitting room to pour out a glass of medium sherry. Once it had been an evening routine for mother and son to take a glass together, but Mrs Carter's years of illness had long ago eroded it. He had resumed only on the evening of her funeral.

As he sipped he slowly opened the envelope and unfolded the sheet of pink writing paper decorated on one side at the top with a spray of lily-of-the-valley.

'Dear Mr Carter,' he read. 'You may not remember me but I used to work at the office before I got married. I've kept up a bit with Mrs Neale and she told me of your sad loss and I just wanted to write and send you my sincere condolences. Your mother must have been wonderful, I knew you thought a lot of her. Please forgive this letter in haste and believe me, Yours truly, Joan (of Archway). P.S. I am a mother now – two boys and a little girl!'

He remembered it all instantly, even while he scanned the letter again, realizing that she had, accidentally or not, omitted her address.

On learning that the new, rough-spoken, red-headed girl in the typing pool was called Joan and travelled home on the Underground from Archway, some would-be wit (Dickinson in Accounts, probably) had christened her in a style that had stuck. That by itself would hardly have interested him, but the girl did. Or rather, to be precise, it was she who first unexpectedly showed an interest in him. It was ten, or even twelve, years ago. He could recall the day she left, after a party and a whip-round organized by the other typists. He had wished to stay away, but she had worked for him – quite apart from going out with him several times. It had been awkward, slightly humiliating, furtive. Nobody, he felt, must know. He had said nothing to his already ailing mother, but to Joan of Archway he had implied her shock if she were ever to learn of it.

With an effort he checked his memory from running on,

vividly, effortlessly, on and back. He got up, as though by moving he might halt the process. And it seemed temporarily effective. If only he had her address, and could, when calmer, send her a reciprocal bulletin which briefly, though firmly, showed where he stood. Or if only, he thought as he went into the kitchen, she had not disturbed him by writing at all.

But after supper the effect of her letter had worn off. Absorbed in the tedious, finicky process of mounting and labelling slides, he grew soothed again and the spell of the flat around him reasserted itself. It was good too to feel that it was entirely his. The extra room could always be used to show slides in, should he decide to invite somebody to come and admire them. Perhaps he never would, but the idea was strangely pleasant to consider and it sent him to bed in his usual tranquil mood.

He woke once suddenly in the night, wondering what had woken him and then hearing the soft insistent sweep of rain on his bedroom window. Normally, rain made the traffic noises louder in the room, but this night they seemed infrequent, virtually inaudible, and only the steady downpour against the glass filled his ears.

The street looked dry enough the next morning as he made his way to the bus stop, carrying his rolled umbrella. The surprisingly warm sun had perhaps dried them early, and untypically he had missed the weather forecast.

'Wonderful for the time of year, isn't it?' a middle-aged woman in the queue burst out enthusiastically as they waited. 'I do hope it lasts.'

He nodded politely. By lunchtime he half expected it to have clouded over, but in fact by then there was a glass-like glitter about the streets and an almost Edwardian leisured look to the parks, where the trees had barely begun to turn and formally-suited figures like himself strolled before going back to their offices.

Three days later the weather changed, just as he had foreseen. The mornings and evenings were misty and the atmosphere damply autumnal. The forecast had spoken of it becoming unsettled (with some sunny periods), but even so he was startled, even mildly alarmed, to find himself woken once again at night by the increasingly heavy murmur of the rain. When he woke there was a pause; he lay there in total, puzzled silence, and then – as though turned on by a switch – the sighing, trickling sound penetrated to him. Soon it was pouring outside, rustling in the gutters and streaming noisily over the window pane with a force suggesting pails of water persistently flung at the glass.

No windows in the flat were open, he felt sure, reluctant to move and yet thinking he ought to check. The rain beat down with vehemence, seeming uncannily close at hand, and he had a sense of the thinness and ultimate frailness of brick and stone to exclude the elements. The block was early post-war modern and, he suspected, poorly built. Twice he had had to write to the landlord, an openly indifferent property company, about drainage problems. Such torrential rain as this might easily overflow a blocked pipe or gutter, and he felt thankful that at least on the first floor his flat was well away from the roof.

Rain at night was conventionally soothing. He could recall listening to it, drizzling down lightly on a summer evening in his childhood, as he dozed in a half-darkened bedroom and heard his parents hurrying and calling, half-laughing, in the garden below. 'Those cushions will get soaked!' his mother cried, and he had known she was smiling. He too had smiled into his pillow, pressing deeper into the bed, under the thin sheet, feeling intense happiness at his drowsy yet god-like awareness of the rain, his parents out there alone, almost playing together, and the house extending shelter to them all.

The rain falling now was dense, increasing, flooding his ears oppressively and somehow washing his mind into unwelcome activity. It could rain hard enough in the Alps, he knew, but he had never much minded – feeling rather contemptuous of tourists who expected every day to be of serene, picture-postcard blueness. Tonight, the rain seemed positively tropical in its steadiness and inevitability, as though setting in for weeks or even months. He suddenly felt he could not sleep until it stopped, yet some sort of pride made him hesitate to put on the bedside lamp and read. He never suffered from insomnia. He could hear himself curtly saying as much to Mrs Neale of the typing pool when she feebly attempted to 'explain' some erratic typing he had sent back. 'Sylvia's been sleeping badly, I believe,' she had confided. 'Worried over something domestic. Her grandmother lives with them,' she added inconsequently, irritating him out of his usual calm demeanour.

Sylvia was a blonde who always looked to him pert, healthy and cheerfully indifferent about her office work. She was a cartoonist's idea of the sexy typist, though she was by no means as young as she appeared and strangely remained unmarried. She must have been quite junior when Joan of Archway arrived, he thought, annoyed to be thinking at all of life at the office. He had been planning to work late one evening when Joan of Archway tapped on his door.

'Some of us are going across the road for a drink, Mr Carter,' she said boldly. 'We wondered if you'd like to come.'

He had glanced up at her bright green blouse, her red hair and her big, rather inexpressive, almost peasant-like face.

'Thank you,' he began declining stiffly, seeking for words to indicate without actually snubbing her that it was not correct for a typist to approach an official in this way.

'Oh, goody,' she replied, disappearing and leaving his door open.

'You *were* funny,' she told him, weeks later. 'In a way, you still are. Are you afraid of me?'

'We are both afraid,' he ought to have said. It was one of many things he had thought but failed to say. Her apparently easy, confident air vanished as soon as they were alone together. She became serious and unsure, nervous in restaurants and even more when once he took her to the theatre. She listened solemnly when he spoke of his mother. She had never called him anything but Mr Carter, and he had hesitated to tell her his first name.

In the darkness of the bedroom, lying there as if exposed to the ceaseless impact of the pelting rain, he felt a shameful longing to see her again. Mrs Neale would be only too glad to provide her address, but he knew that in fact he would never ask for it. Besides, she was married: a mother, with three children of her own. He was beginning to wonder what those children looked like – did they have their mother's red hair? – when he woke again. It was a dark morning. He was much later than usual in getting up. But at least there was no sound of rain.

As he hurried down the stairs, he found himself awkwardly overtaking crippled Miss Dee, limping slowly from step to step, clutching the banisters as she descended, with her stick crooked over her arm. She lived in the flat above his, alone since the death of her mother from cancer several years before. Like him, she took the bus to an office every weekday, but out of some foreseen mutual embarrassment each always chose to go and wait at a different stop.

'Good morning, good morning,' he said rather too loudly, as if sounding a warning of his approach, and abruptly halting just above her.

She paused for breath before returning the greeting. 'Go on,' she half-articulated, half-gestured with her free hand. 'Don't let me delay you.'

To pass her was awkward, as indeed was everything about Miss Dee as far as he was concerned. He could never help glancing at her thin, paralysed foot, fixed at a painful, unnatural angle parallel now to the stairs. From her exuded a loneliness – under the neat exterior and brisk, would-be cheerful manner – which he felt he ought to assuage by an invitation to tea one weekend, all the more as he lacked any longer the excuse of an invalid mother.

'Dreadful downpour in the night, wasn't it?' he said, shuffling a further step closer.

She looked faintly puzzled and then smiled apologetically.

'I'm afraid I didn't hear anything. I'm such a sound sleeper. Still, I don't think it's wet this morning, and that's a good thing.'

She drew back against the banisters, with a resumed smile

of invitation for him to go by, and he hastened past her, muttering thanks, glad to be free of the constraint.

Outside it was grey and uncertain but, as she had said – not wet. There were not even puddles to pick a way through to his own bus stop.

That evening when he returned home and placed his rolled umbrella in the stand, he experienced a sense of relief stronger than usual. The hall was empty of letters. He felt tired, understandably enough, but it was Friday. The weekend routine waited for him almost as palpably as did the flat, demanding nothing but to be savoured. On Saturdays he shopped and cleaned, before preparing a special supper for himself (he had no sympathy with people living alone who complained they couldn't be bothered with cooking properly). On Sunday mornings he enjoyed a walk – he thought it sensible exercise – in Battersea Park, walking fast, not pausing or looking at anything in particular. If he thought at all at such times, it was of being again in the Alps, of day-long walks he had taken or planned to take, always with his camera.

Sunday afternoon and evenings were the times he liked best, when he had leisure to go through his accounts, write any letters, re-arrange his slides or even set up a screen and project some of them. He had already started shifting the cabinets of slides previously in his bedroom into his mother's – a room he was beginning to label the workroom – but with more space he could consider more elaborate arrangements. He could improve his system of indexing the slides. He could keep a screen permanently set up.

These and other possibilities floated to him in the hall with the piquancy of a real flavour – almost like the faint odour of a meal being cooked for him by his mother in the days before she was ill. For some reason he suddenly thought of Miss Dee whom it would be so easy to invite to tea – even supper – on the Sunday, but he decided that could wait until he had finished all the re-indexing and arranging of the slides.

And by the evening of Sunday he was glad the weekend had passed as usual without any interruption. Moving the last slide cabinets had proved unexpectedly laborious. There was altogether less space than he had supposed in the room, though he was pleased by having thought to hang on the walls some of his earliest successful colour photographs, including several views of and around Lugano. The room was beginning to look at once business-like and private, professionally efficient and yet snug.

He closed the door on it feeling fatigued in a pleasant way. There were still things to do but they would provide occupation for other Sundays during the winter; and when all was completed there might be the opportunity for inviting Miss Dee.

It was just as he got into bed and turned out the bedside light, that he heard the first swishing sound of falling rain. The day had been mild and dull: too warm really for the time of year, he had thought, feeling rather clammy while working.

With the sound curiously disturbing in his ears, he got up again and went in the dark to the window. He stood there listening, irritable and shivering a little, for no reason. He hesitated about opening the window. But there could be no doubt of the gushing, steady, streaming noise, though he could distinguish nothing through the glass. It remained puzzling, unless some pipe or tap was leaking somewhere in the block of flats, and with an abrupt, half-angry gesture he threw open the window to locate the source.

The street below was quiet. A very slight sheen on the road might have come from rain but seemed only reflection from the lamps suspended overhead. He screwed up his eyes to try and detect the rain slanting against their brightness but nothing was visible. At last, cautiously and fearing that he looked ridiculous standing there in pyjamas, he extended one hand into the night, tensing the skin against an expected splash.

His hand remained dry. Perhaps he had not leant out far enough, or perhaps the noise was of water running down the side of the building. He slowly pushed his head out into the darkness, twisting to glance upwards and apprehensive of suddenly being drenched.

He could see the glow of several windows, some with curtains undrawn, and the clear edge of the pale roof against the night sky. No rain was falling and there was no sign of a burst or overflowing pipe. The building looked tranquil enough, though insubstantial – like a piece of cardboard with cut-out holes for windows. The air was crisp, almost chilly, and the night seemed touched with a vague suggestion of approaching Christmas.

Mr Carter withdrew his head sharply, trembling at the thought of some other tenant noticing his peering out at such an odd late hour. Yet when he had shut the window he found he was trembling more violently. He recalled those other recent occasions when he had been convinced he heard it raining. He saw again Miss Dee's somewhat surprised face on the stairs and the dry road outside, and now it seemed to him that he had without thinking said something about the wet weather to a colleague at the office who appeared equally surprised. Yet he knew he had heard rain falling.

He had to rest his head on the sill, and the slight pain from pressing his forehead against the woodwork was a welcome, almost reassuring sensation. His whole organism grew concentrated in an act of not hearing. For a few seconds it seemed to have succeeded. As if terrified of jogging into motion some precariously balanced inner machinery, he crept slowly towards the bed and slid between the sheets. Then, as he lay there rigid, the rain very softly began again. Momentarily, he could have wept at the sound.

But it was important not to call it rain. It was merely a recurrent noise, he tried to calm himself by saying. It might be caused by something to do with his ears. It might be some unwelcome though not dangerous form of singing in the head, which a doctor could surely deal with. Nothing wrong with my ears before, he could envisage declaring to a doctor. No history of headaches, he would add firmly. Perhaps it was a mild manifestation of high or even low blood pressure; a course of pills would soon correct it. And though even when he folded the pillow around his head the noise persisted, he felt less frightened.

On the Monday morning he was still bewildered. His be-

haviour seemed slightly absurd, as did the intention to see a
doctor. By the time he joined the incipient queue of one man
at the bus stop he thought he had dismissed the occurrence of
the previous night and of the other nights as well. He wondered
if it wasn't caused by lying in bed at a certain angle, or more
probably by the faint catarrh which he always suffered from
in the winter months.

He could almost smile as the bus arrived and the West
Indian conductor leant from it singing, 'Lovely morning, all you
lovely people. First two only, *please*. There's another one just
behind.' But he felt much less patience at the office when Mrs
Neale began to describe how a rain storm had spoilt her niece's
country wedding on the Saturday; he cut her short so abruptly
that she flounced offendedly out of the room.

He began to notice a new dislike for the topic of the weather.
At work he seemed surrounded by people who spoke of little
else. Without admitting it to himself he had started to avoid
noticing the forecast, and though a week went by undisturbed
by any noise during the nights he felt he had passed hours lying
in bed awake half-listening or trying not to listen. Even his
return to the flat was spoilt now by moments of apprehension.
One evening he came in and began his normal routine of
changing into slippers when he heard unmistakably the sound
of rain – heavy, beating rain – on the window he had just
curtained. He sat there unwilling to move, afraid, and made
weary by his fear. It was like the recurrence of some illness, he
thought, when at last he dragged himself across the room. The
drumming on the glass behind the velveteen curtain was almost
human in its peremptoriness, as if commanding his attention.
It was more than any noise in the head, he knew with a sick
inevitability, and it would never leave him.

To draw back the curtains and discover that it was actually
raining outside had the impact of a magical event. The spat-
tered glass and the glistening rods of rain falling steadily in the
radiance of the street lamps made a beautiful, blessed sight.
Yet the overwhelming sense of relief frightened him by its
intensity. He realized how close he had been to utter despair,

and what lingered was the nagging awareness that not until he
looked out had he been able to judge whether the rain was real.

Every so often that night he woke with a start. The noise of
the downpour would penetrate his sleep, and he had to remind
himself as it hissed around him that this time it was a reality.
All the while he dreaded the next time, remembering the night
he had bowed his face to the window sill close to the dry pane,
tremblingly trying to exclude the sound that crept insidiously
into the room and into his head. By morning he was exhausted.
He felt too listless to look out and see if in fact it was still raining.

To leave the flat had become an impossibility. He had a duty
to remain there, it suddenly seemed, to protect it and to protect himself. Quite calmly he took up the telephone : he had a
slightly feverish cold, he was telling the maddeningy slow
receptionist at the office. 'You sound a bit under the weather,
Mr Carter,' she said cheerfully. 'I do hope you'll feel better
over the weekend.'

Learning it was Friday was somehow a shock. For once, the
promise of his weekend routine had no appeal. He knew instinctively that he would not go shopping on the Saturday, nor
take his Sunday-morning walk. There was plenty of tinned food
in the flat – enough to last for several days, if necessary. And,
besides, he lacked any appetite. After trying to eat an egg for
breakfast, he just sat in his dressing-gown in the kitchen, hearing the unaccustomed sounds of weekday activity in the block
but listening for the approach of that threatened other sound
which was bound to come.

From the landing outside came a chink of bottles. The milk-
man was going his rounds which meant that it was getting late
in the morning. Miss Dee would long ago have made her painful descent of the stairs. At the office there would certainly be
some mild surprise, since he was so seldom ill.

The thought of illness made him abruptly active. He had a
plan. If he kept all the windows not only tightly shut but curtained, he need not bother about the weather outside or torment
himself by uncertainty if and when he once more heard the

rain starting. With a sense of establishing a permanent retreat, he went round his few rooms, drawing the curtains and switching on lights. Only at the workroom did he pause; it hardly seemed worthwhile going in there since he felt he would not be using it for some time. It would be enough to lock the door.

When he had finished he stood in the hall and considered the front door. It seemed best to lock that as well, though first he hastily darted on to the landing and brought in his pint of milk. Haste was making him nervous. The bottle nearly slipped from his hand as he carried it into the kitchen. Before he put it away he remembered the wooden device hanging there and rarely used with its dial that signalled so many pints of milk and had a space reading 'O until further notice'. He reopened the front door and placed it outside.

He walked very quietly back into the bedroom, straining to detect the faintest sound but there was total silence. Without quite relaxing, he was soothed by his precautions. He switched off the light and lay down. After a while he dozed. Occasionally there filtered through noises of traffic or some loud conversation on the stairs, but these too faded as he lay there. Time is passing, he thought, and nothing is happening. But then the sound usually came at night; that was when he must be most alert for it, and he guessed he had dozed only into the afternoon.

He got up, oddly hungry. He made himself some toast and then, after a pause, opened a tin of beans and cooked them as well. Normally he despised such meals, unless it was in an emergency – and perhaps this occasion was. He felt increasingly pleased, almost excited, at his own state of readiness, though unclear beyond this feeling. As long as he preserved his attitude, it seemed, nothing could reach him. He need see no one or hear anything.

By keeping the curtains drawn he had cheated time, but after finding himself unwillingly glancing at his watch – it read half past four – he realized that that posed a threat. For a moment he contemplated smashing it. Of course such an act would be wrong, he knew. He unstrapped it from his wrist and went out and carefully put it still ticking in a drawer of his desk.

The electric light struck his eyes as harsh, hardly required. He knew his way around the flat well enough, and it was altogether easier to concentrate in the dark. He turned off the lights as he went along to the bedroom. This time he got into bed. He slept, although he had not meant to, and woke knowing he had slept soundly. In the darkness he sat up alert, tilting his head, listening. There was silence. Now he saw the process as a cure; it might take days to achieve, but it was working. What was essential was darkness, complete concentration, the restriction of his own movements. That was the routine he must follow.

Whenever he woke now, he tried to begin with a period of listening. Then he would shuffle slowly down the corridor and grope his way into the bathroom or the kitchen. Once or twice he was disconcerted to find how bright it appeared. The blind in the bathroom fitted poorly and did not entirely exclude the daylight. The plastic curtains in the kitchen were thin and partly transparent; as he stepped in there he was vaguely puzzled by its unexpectedly grubby state, with the bread-bin half open and a pile of unwashed cups and glasses littering the sink. Later, he must attend to that. Meanwhile he fumbled for some biscuits and carried them back to the warmth of his bed.

It still happened occasionally that he woke with a start, or perhaps was not sleeping as deeply as before. Yet only silence awaited him. He could not gauge the intervals between sleeping and waking, but that did not matter since both seemed tranquil enough if blurred. Outside it could even have snowed, he thought once, but he felt no urge to check. The silence accumulating around the flat was much more important and reassuring. At some point he believed the telephone might have rung, or perhaps he dreamt it. It came from so far away that it did not disturb him. He had stopped the conscious act of listening. Nothing reached his ears.

And then he was bumped painfully awake, with his heart beating wildly. It had begun again, he knew immediately, even before the sound itself impinged on him. He shifted in the gritty, limp sheets, desperate to locate its whereabouts. At first it was a mere trickle of rain, not close at hand, but as he strained to hear it he realized with horror that this time it was falling inside the flat. Unthinking he tried to jump out of bed, encumbered by the dressing-gown which he had forgotten to take off.

This must stop, he wanted to shout – or was shouting. After all his precautions, the silence and the cure had been broken. Now he was more furious than frightened. He ran into the corridor, but paused before putting on the light. He had taken such care to exclude the noise, and as he recollected his new routine it occurred to him that after all he might easily have left a tap dripping somewhere in the darkness.

Yet while he stood there the noise was increasing in vehemence, no longer a trickle but a savage, thunderous roar of driving rain. It came from behind the workroom door. He rushed towards it, thinking angrily of an open window or a burst cistern (Miss Dee's in the flat above). He could hear the splash and cascade of water pouring down the walls where his photographs hung. Everything would be ruined. The room must already be awash, he was sure, as he wrenched and pulled at the door. It would not open. His fingers slipped on the handle, as if that too was wet. He leant breathlessly against the door and heard through it the endless drenching sound of the rain rebounding on the surface of his cabinets of slides.

'It's no good,' he whispered to himself, feeling his face damp where it touched the woodwork, and still tugging at the handle but now without real force. 'It's no good.'

Inside, the deluge seemed diminishing, though drops of water continued slowly to fall. He found he was kneeling, huddled beside the door. He made no further attempt to open it. He wanted to get up, learn what time it was, what day it was, but he could not move. Silence had returned, except for the harsh, tearing sound of his own breathing. He went on holding the doorhandle in a convulsive grip.

As he knelt, a new sensation began to pervade him. Water was seeping steadily from under the door, fearfully chill on his legs through the pyjamas. Only then did he realize the futility of fighting despair. When the door swung open, he swung with it, aware of the pool he was pitching into. His fingers slid from the handle, and his body fell with fatal heaviness on the dry floor beyond.

STEVE STERN

Rudolph Finkl's Apprenticeship

Rudolph Finkl in more innocent days used to rough-house with his father. Wearing a yellow terrycloth bathrobe, several sizes large, he would climb over an unconscious mother and into the groaning double bed. He would crawl among the ashes and bits of salami that garnished his father's half of the mattress. Then, frowning at the Sunday paper behind which Mr Finkl was hidden, he would burst headlong through the Cold War and Eisenhower's smile.

'Mildred!' shouted Mr Finkl, trying to salvage the funnies, 'Call the cops, your son's trying to kill me!'

A subway would rumble somewhere underneath them, and the bed, galloping as it had not since Rudolph's conception, move to the centre of the room. A framed ancestor, in peasant smock leading bullock, might fall from the sallow plaster. And Mr Finkl, offering no more than a token resistance, would suffer his son to swarm over his hairless, speckled scalp. He let Rudolph trounce the risen dough of his belly, where it debouched from striped pyjamas, and pin an elbow against the small of his back; until, thoroughly vanquished, the father would cry,

'Uncle already. Enough!'

Then came a Sunday when – battered, trounced, and pinned – Mr Finkl did not say 'uncle'. Instead, he rent his pyjamas and fought savagely for air. Saucer-eyed, Rudolph wondered at the invisible opponent with whom his father was finally wrestling in earnest. He was sorry that the old man was, as usual, losing and that their last match should have gone unresolved.

Beside Rudolph, his mother, still sodden with sleep, half-opened her eyes to a dream. On a beach a great fish lay gasping. Sitting erect, she blinked and screamed this at her son:

'Murderer!'

Later, trying on the word, Rudolph found it, like his bathrobe, several sizes large. In time – who knows – he might grow into it. Meanwhile he thought it more discreet to stay a little afraid of everything.

In the mortuary chapel Rudolph approached a steel-grey casket on a bier of flowers. On tiptoe he unfolded the doilies in which his father's face was wrapped: he loved me, he loved me not. Though Mr Finkl, powdered and rouged, looked almost confectionery in repose, Rudolph was inclined to give him no quarter.

'Say "uncle",' he urged. ' "Uncle"!' he repeated, trying to put words in his father's mouth which belonged now, by bequest, in his own.

The queue of relations on the opposite side of the casket worried that the boy might be overwrought. An uncle, Lep by name (if not by nature), came forward to offer his services. With his carrot toupee on back-to-front, he wore tropical colours in foulard and raw silk. 'Like a rainbow over Miami Beach,' thought Rudolph, recalling a distant family vacation.

'Whasa mater, boychik?' asked the rainbow.

Shading his eyes, Rudolph squinted beyond the uncle and saw, standing with his baggage of a mother, the bully, Bloody Norman Mendelman, fiercest of Rudolph's peers. He was grinning at Rudolph fondly if lopsidedly over his father's dead body.

Then he was shoving himself between Rudolph and Uncle Lep who, thus obscured, nearly toppled from the dais.

'I come to pay my condolences,' announced the bully, as if

he'd come to pay a fine; and unofficially, 'Don't worry, kid, I'll look out for you. Am I not my brother's keeper?'

Rudolph, not wishing to argue the point, replied with all due respect, 'Who rattled your cage?'

The explanation came in time: how Norman had pilfered half the inventory of Mr Finkl's deli and, observed to have swollen by several dimensions in the regions of his pockets and paunch, fled the shop with the genuinely portly proprietor on his heels. How, lightening his load, he'd left Mr Finkl a trail of halvah, horseradish, lox, and wurst to follow, leading him into a blind alley where Norman, trapped and having dropped everything else, had climbed a fire escape and dropped his trousers. So that when Mr Finkl came puffing round the corner, he was greeted by Norman's bared contempt hung upon a railing; and attacked simultaneously from within by his heart.

'Just like the poet in him,' reflected Rudolph years later, 'to be stricken at the sight of a full moon.'

At any rate, Norman had beat it, leaving the tallow-faced old man to pick himself up out of death. A week, maybe two, and he'd fallen back in again; a wreath in the delicatessen window like the mockery of a life preserver.

So there was Norman, come to claim complicity in an assassination for which Rudolph wished to hold himself alone accountable. Guilt, resignation, sorrow – the gifts of his father's estate, he would not have parted with at any price. But what about this unforeseen gift, this Bloody Norman, which he could never even hope to give away?

Thus Rudolph found himself the victim of a friendship for which he had not asked. Denied responsibility for the demise of the father, Bloody Norman assumed responsibility for the welfare and preservation of the son.

For example: a month or so after the funeral a bunch of apprentice hoodlums dragged Rudolph into an alley for the purpose of administering to him what they called a Polish

Steve Stern

enema. They were punishing him because he would not fight back, a peculiarity which was already making him infamous in the neighbourhood around Henry Street.

They hauled him without resistance to a water hydrant beneath which they had attempted to baptize him the previous week. On that occasion he'd disgusted his inquisitors by the ease with which he was prepared to surrender his faith.

'Call me Mathew or Peter,' he'd suggested, not wishing to be difficult.

But the ceremony had been interrupted then as it was interrupted now, by a sound in the distance like a celestial breaking of wind. It came just as they were attaching a black garden hose to the hydrant, inserting the other end into Rudolph's dungarees. The hoodlums were apparently sold on the idea of trial by water.

They did not, however, hang around for the phenomenon to which the sound was fanfare. Some still had their keepsakes from the previous week's encounter – mulberry eyes and split lips, broken big brothers who had come off the stoops to defend them. Today they scattered. Consequently, when Bloody Norman, vendor of retribution, arrived in the alley, with his torch-like hair and his narrow green eyes that penetrated a blizzard of freckles, there was nobody left to whom he might distribute the bouquets of his fists and feet.

'Toad-faced pishers!' he shouted nevertheless. 'Teach you to pick on an orphan.' And taking from his back pocket a toy bugle, he chased them home with a flourish of strident notes.

'Why orphan?' asked the frail voice behind him.

Norman turned around to where Rudolph sat, still connected by a rubber umbilical cord to the wall of a derelict theatre. He considered, placing his implacable face within whispering distance of Rudolph's habitually crestfallen one.

'Because your papa is dead and your mama is as good as,' he explained.

'Oh,' Rudolph nodded his endorsement. For had not Mrs Finkl, since Mr Finkl's passage, begun to chase her thorazine with vodka and talk to the television set? But Norman dis-

134

approved of the readiness with which Rudolph dismissed his own mother.

'You only-child kids make me sick.'

'I had a baby brother,' Rudolph volunteered, wistfully, 'but he was carried off by birds.'

'*Nebech*,' hissed Norman, and turned to the hydrant whose handle he revolved several times. Then, cuffing him about the ears for good measure, he abandoned Rudolph to sink or swim in the rising reservoir of his baggy pants.

'There must be easier fates,' reflected Rudolph, turning blue, 'than to be adopted by Bloody Norman.'

He would bring round his boxing gloves and stand on the pavement, tooting his challenge on a red plastic bugle. In his bedroom Rudolph would wince and slowly emerge from his books. A tumulus, comprised of Rudyard Kipling, Rider Haggard, Edgar Rice Burroughs and Homer, would crumble, and Rudolph would crawl from beneath it to the window, sighing aloud.

'That you, Gabriel?'

'Come out or I'm coming in after you,' called Norman, a virtuoso of the ultimatum.

Then Rudolph would shamble reluctantly out on to the steps next door to the boarded-up delicatessen.

'It's time for your lesson in self-defence,' Norman would announce, presenting Rudolph with a pair of puce gloves as big as his head, causing him to flinch in anticipation of the fists that would momentarily fill them.

'Put 'em on or I'll beat the snot out of you.'

Thus prompted Rudolph would put on the gloves and Norman beat the snot out of him. The shopkeepers, children and crippled dogs of Henry Street would look on with smug approval. In the neighbourhood they now had a name for Rudolph, originated by the kosher butcher: *tsaylem kop*, meaning death's head.

After the cartilage in his nose was initially shattered, Rudolph didn't mind the punches so much. Besides, a splayed shnoz lent character to his otherwise dark and delicate features. He thought of Michelangelo and Marlon Brando. As for his eyes, insomnia had already done the work of discolouring them; Norman's jabs could only improve them with highlights.

Eventually Norman would grow bored with bludgeoning his passive protégé.

'My shadow puts up a better fight than you.'

Rudolph was the first to admit that he had nothing on shadows, except – touching a mutilated lip – the ability to bleed.

'You finished sitting *shiva* for your papa, and now you're sitting *shiva* for yourself.'

This was the accusation which Norman had been levelling at Rudolph at least once a week for the more than three years that Mr Finkl had lain mouldering in the grave. And each time he heard it, Rudolph buried himself a little deeper in his books and morbid daydreams. Therefore Norman had to dig through jungles and lost cities, past fantasies of heartless women and pages of men doomed to wandering, in order to disinter Rudolph. Then collaring him by the nape of his scrawny neck, urgently lest Rudolph should be late for his own adolescence, Norman would say,

'I'm taking you to see real life.'

It had become a game of hide-and-seek played to the death, or so Rudolph must have seen it. A day came when Rudolph locked his bedroom door and nailed it shut. Because he would not come out to see it, Norman, meaning to raise his spirits, brought real life around to Rudolph. This he managed in the shape of Fineberg, an older boy who had once been the unchallenged rogue Jew of Henry Street. Knocking Fineberg down between parked cars, Norman propped his arm against the curb and trod on it, thus inverting the angle of his elbow. Then, for an encore, Norman took on Fineberg's father, who came running from behind fruit scales with his apron still on. Looking down from his bedroom window at the Finebergs that were stacked in the gutter, Rudolph was touched, then overcome with nostalgia for the intimacy between father and son.

Then Rudolph drew the blinds. For three days he languished in bed, as one languishes on a pallet of straw. He marked the passage of time on a wall with black crayon, each slash grown a little fainter. He felt pity for the peeled husks of himself, retired from experience: his moth-eaten grey parka, his shadow, his discount wing-tipped shoes which he was using for bed-pans. Only two things disturbed him in his confinement: that the occasional blasts from a toy bugle should penetrate the thick, perspiring walls of his Château d'If; and that the fire department should break down his door. Mrs Finkl, who was a little confused as to whether her son were alive any more, had summoned them. She'd been hounded into action by Bloody Norman. Burst in upon, Rudolph sat up with eyes blinking and scarlet, his face half-eclipsed in new black stubble. He stared at the assembly, armed with axes, who stared back like villagers who had broken into the tomb of a vampire.

He was brought before the doctor whose sedation of his mother, graduated since Mr Finkl's death, had made of her life a dream; who was also, incidentally, the physician responsible for ripping the infant Rudolph untimely from his mother's womb. The Caesarean assumed a hostile stance.

'You got me into this!' he barked, apportioning blame.

'Pardon?'

'Nothing.'

Benign in his bifocals, the doctor suggested that Rudolph spend a few weeks on Long Island; there was a sanatorium near Stonybrook which specialized in the treatment of the incorrigibly sad. Foreseeing injections of cephalic tincture, keepers with porpoise-hide whips, aristocrats visiting on Sundays, Rudolph conceded it was a tempting prospect, albeit he would have to decline.

'The sadness on Henry Street is good enough for me,' he said, falling back on tradition.

The doctor shrugged as if that were that. He muttered something into an intercom and began to stoke his pipe. Through arabesque draperies of smoke, Mrs Finkl sleepwalked into the office. She approached the doctor's desk as she might have the throne of Solomon.

'Your son is still not well,' said the doctor, *ex cathedra*. 'What he needs is a little rest.'

'You know best, doctor,' replied Mrs Finkl. Then, turning to Rudolph, she demonstrated what a rude awakening were his sins. She pressed the flat of her palms to her fevered cheeks, intending – Rudolph could almost believe – to uproot her head and hurl it at him. The lacquered crest of her silver hair threatened like an angry wave.

'What have I done to deserve such *tsores*? What! What! What!' she bawled.

Appealing to the doctor to please place his mother under a stronger spell, Rudolph showed himself prepared to do anything, go anywhere, if only to get out of earshot.

In the sprawling sanatorium Rudolph looked out of high windows on to meadows full of grazing sheep and nuns. Luxuriating in a warm blue bath of self-pity, he dreamed. On a boat he was transporting his father's corpse to heaven, floating swiftly with the current, sailing by way of the Mississippi River which spilled into the Rhine which spilled into the Bramaputra which drained into jungle swamp and the sewers beneath lost cities. Awake, it occurred to him that he might have been sailing in the wrong direction, that paradise is usually upstream. No matter; by the look of things it was not an uncommon mistake. Seated about the sun-flooded dayroom, the other inmates, if not in the same boat, were perhaps in a similar which had foundered some time ago. And Rudolph consoled himself that, washed up upon this reef of melancholy, he was finally castaway among his own kind.

He admired them for their bloodless complexions and their unfathomable eyes. Cats might be drowned in their eyes and coins tossed with never a splash. Of his own (bloodshot, mauve-circled) he took a sounding in a mirror, and found them wanting in the depth of their unhappiness. They seemed paddling pools by comparison. Moreover, the other inmates – tranquil in their wicker-backed wheelchairs, unperturbed before their stale toast and powdered eggs – appeared to be looking at something which Rudolph, grateful to his myopia, was not certain that he wanted to see. On the strength of these observations, he was forced to conclude himself an impostor, the only uninitiated in a fraternity of ghosts. Humbled and a little relieved, he began to indulge in serious second thoughts.

'So how was I to know,' Rudolph asked himself, 'that they would put me on a ward with the crew of the original Flying Dutchman?'

But restlessness was new to him, and he dismissed it as due to the temporary effects of seasonal stimuli, to the sound of rain on the lead eaves and the smell of late honeysuckle invading the sleeping ward, spoiling nightmares with happy endings. He paid scant attention to the hootings of owls or to the toy bugle which blew so persistently on some evenings that it might have been outside the walls of Jericho.

When Norman finally did appear – wrestling with a pair of white-jacketed myrmidons in the vestibule before the dayroom – Rudolph was almost glad to see him. But the gladness had worn thin when, some days later, tenacious and mottled in moonlight, Norman tapped with a hacksaw on the iron cage over a second-storey window. The ward was a carpenter's workshop of stertorous snoring. Rudolph, however, was vigilant, the sleeping capsule under his pillow like a variation on the princess and the pea. He'd been expecting something like this.

'Must be the sandman,' he said, distinguishing the growl of a hacksaw from the rest of the noise, going to the window and raising it.

'What're you guys rehearsing to be, a graveyard?' asked Norman, rasping away at the iron grate in sync with the chorus of log-sawyers. Rudolph tried to explain that he didn't need rescuing, that he now had his walking privileges and could stroll unsupervised about the grounds; he could go home on weekends if he wanted.

Steve Stern

'So why don't you just get out of my life,' he said, making a gesture that should have released a dove. 'My life,' echoing himself faintly, as Norman broke away a casement-sized square of the grating and pitched it with the hacksaw into the shrubbery below. Then he thrust with his left hand, the fingers of which wrapped themselves tentacular about Rudolph's throat; he jerked his skinny friend in his pyjamas and bathrobe, which were somewhat tattered in the process, through the cage and out on to the ledge; saying,

'What life?'

Together they leapt into the darkness which was just tolling midnight.

'Where are you taking me?' Rudolph asked for the last time again. His bathrobe – seedy, yellow, several sizes small – flapped wildly about him in the September wind; his slippers slapped the interminable asphalt road.

'Nowhere,' said Norman, weary of the question. 'You're free, *shmendrick*; the world is your oyster.'

'I am the unfortunate victim of a kidnapping,' insisted Rudolph. 'You are the kidnapper; the world is *your* oyster.' And taking from his bathrobe pocket a well-thumbed copy of *The Count of Monte Cristo*: 'The book is my oyster,' he declared, prying its shell apart.

Norman, disgusted, confiscated the book and flung it into the eastern sky which, now that morning was happening, was the colour of mother-of-pearl.

They boarded an early morning train to Manhattan and, ticketless, hid behind a newspaper. Hidden behind newspapers all along the seats were commuters, visible only as a pair of legs. Passing down the aisle collecting tickets, a conductor with a predatory face paused curiously in front of the only edition of *The Times* beneath which were two pairs of legs, one pyjama'd.

'Ahem and ahem,' he said to no avail, and so was forced to assert his authority. Tugging at the paper, he flushed them out – Rudolph from Help Wanted and Norman from an advert concerning a film in which mutants emerge from the sewers.

140

'This ain't no sleeping car,' said the conductor to Rudolph, who exchanged with Norman a bewildered glance. 'Where are your tickets?'

Sensing Norman's bristling hostility, Rudolph fished in his empty pockets by way of distraction. 'Foolish me, I must have left them in my suit,' he offered, and when the conductor remained unappeased, 'the one with the houndstooth check.'

Norman's approach was, as usual, less subtle. Fixing the conductor with gimlet eye, he delivered one of his famous ultimata:

'Get out of my sight or I'll kill you.'

The conductor, recoiling, expelled an ill wind, redolent of an unnourishing diet. To protect themselves from the vapours, Rudolph and Norman took up their newspaper again. In the moment before the conductor wrenched it away from them, Rudolph stole a brief reverie. Outside the window Long Island, house and garden, blew past as in a gale. The wheels of the train clacked an insinuation which Rudolph could not help but take personally : *meshuggeneh meshuggeneh meshuggeneh.* Sadly he recalled – as the paper was cloven and dashed from their hands – how in bygone days he had used to burst through the wall of words that separated him from his father. Even now he half-expected to see, in place of the decimated *Times*, his own childhood self, rather than this strange substitution of gold watch fob, brass buttons, and lobster complexion flecked with pea-green foam.

They did not wait for the conductor to erupt, spewing threats. Instead they bolted to either side of him and ran down the length of the car, and the next and the next, past the seats full of two-legged newspapers.

The train barrelled into Grand Central Station and Rudolph and Norman alit, still running. Over their shoulders they saw the conductor hopping on to the platform a few cars back, howling for constabulary and the letter of the law. They did not turn around again. Sprinting through the crowded station, they ducked beneath shafts of sunlight which leaned against the tall windows like so many Jacob's ladders. Rudolph wondered if they were incurring bad luck. Without stopping to consider, he followed Bloody Norman, who dove underground, who vaulted a turnstile and tunnelled under a river and surfaced in Brooklyn around Borough Hall.

'Some kidnapper, you,' complained Rudolph, breathlessly malcontent, as they turned a corner into the old Henry Street neighbourhood. Abduction implied illegal transportation across foreign borders, into mountain fastnesses, et cetera. Of this he apprised Bloody Norman, concluding, 'So why have you brought me home?'

Choosing not to dignify Rudolph's question with an answer, Norman presented him with an I-wash-my-hands-of-you scowl. This being insufficient :

'I wash my hands of you,' said Norman, whose hands were as unwashable as Lady Macbeth's with Rudolph. In fact, Norman could no more ignore the would-be hostage than could the cop on the opposite pavement, who was beckoning with cobra-like forefinger.

'What's he want?' asked Rudolph, always the last to know. Norman, by way of a gentle reminder, pulled at the sleeve of his bathrobe which came promptly apart at the shoulder.

'He wants the address of your tailor.'

As Norman was still impatient with a truant momentum and Rudolph still attached to Norman's coat-tails, they fled. A few blocks on into Fulton Street, and the momentum could no longer carry Rudolph, who begged for respite. Norman led him tottering up some steps before a squat, red-brick building with a large copper dome and through the first open doors in sight.

The years turned back. They were in the parquetted foyer of the Jochanan ben Zakkai synagogue, whose threshold Rudolph had not been across since the day of his forgotten *bar mitzvah*, nor Norman since the tender year of his expulsion for iconoclasm. (He had done to a painting of Moses on Sinai what Moses had done to the tablets of the Law.) The voice of a cantor was resonating from beyond the doors to the *shul*; Rudolph and Norman pricked up their ears like Lucifers eavesdropping on seraphim.

'Why,' wondered Rudolph, 'are there services on Monday?'

'Shmuck,' said Norman, who had studied his morning paper, 'where've you been?' Savouring the disclosure, 'Today is *Yom Kippur*.'

'The Day of Atonement,' Rudolph mused, as if recalling the name of a sunken continent. Interested, he stepped towards the panelled doors and peeked in.

'This place offends my virility,' said Norman, feeling reverent, the more so since the officer of recent memory was passing in the street, whistling, his nightstick dancing in the manner of a hanged man.

Propelled by a foot at his rump, Rudolph lurched into the sanctuary, where he was ambushed by the perennially familiar : by stained glass and organ pipes, lit menorah and the lurid red everlasting light, dangling as it might have in front of the brothels of heaven. Beaded daveners swayed beneath the gallery of women, and the ancient Rabbi Fisker, face like a parchment of Dead Sea scroll, presided. The choir was singing, '*Kadosh, kadosh, kadosh . . .*'

Norman shoved Rudolph into a seat at the rear of the congregation, for which Rudolph tendered his gratitude. Apprehended, they might have been subject to the fate of the trespasser, upon which Rudolph had begun giddily to speculate until Norman brandished a fist.

But Rudolph could not keep still. Having risen from bed and travelled thus far in his nightclothes, he was assuming the licence of a veteran somnambulist (second generation and apologies to Mama). He was on high holiday from his quotidian sorrow. Excited, he managed to hold his tongue throughout the responsive readings; but during the recital from Torah, experimental with mischief, he began to propound a theory.

'I believe that Rabbi Fisker is God,' he asserted to Norman who, exasperated that after all these years this should be Rudolph's idea of a good time, told him to shut-up.

'I mean,' pursued Rudolph, undiscouraged, 'he has the look of an authentic Jehovah and he's easily as old.'

Some of the worshippers in Rudolph's vicinity were disturbed enough to turn around in their seats. They were appalled at the sight of two boys, both *sans* skullcaps, one most improperly apparelled. There was a muttering and a general commotion. Rabbi Fisker, meanwhile, with his back to the congregation, was returning the Torah to its latticed ark. This operation completed, he flung his head backwards in the attitude of one who is receiving a confidence from the Lord. He rotated towards the assembly.

His eyes and nostrils were those of a dilapidated dragon, and his mouth was working to spit sparks out of the ashes of his beard. With a forefinger that trembled from wrath and arthritis, he pointed to the back of the sanctuary. Bolt upright Rudolph invited the lightning which did not appear. So what? With no faith ventured, he had none to lose.

'Rudolph Finkl,' the rabbi intoned, managing smoky breath, 'your father would be ashamed.'

If short of the miraculous, it was still admonition enough to puncture Rudolph. He shrank to his customary stature, impressed that the old man should remember his name, that his name should be called from the pulpit where the only names read are the ones which are inscribed in the memorial book, to whom the flowers on the altar are dedicated.

He was sullen for the remainder of the service, wondering idly if any of the prayers were for him. Exhausted, he slumped in his pew, but his eyes would not close, and he worried that this time Bloody Norman had led him too far; they were obviously lost somewhere on the wrong side of sleep. Then came a sound for which even Rudolph had to sit up: the *shofar* was blowing its unearthly reveille.

The ceremony ended with a benediction. '*Leshana tova tikosevu,*' said the rabbi and, responding in kind, the congregation departed the *shul*.

Expecting him to take his usual charge of their destinies, Rudolph looked to Norman, whom he found flushed and agi-

tated on the edge of his seat. His square jaw was poised as if
his honour had been called into question. 'Oh yeah?' he was
saying to no one in particular, like a heavy who loses his mind
in a low-budget film.

'Oh yeah?' fumbling about at his waist and producing his
red plastic bugle, battle-scarred but somehow intact after a
decade or so of abuse. Standing, he blew a *tekiot* of his own
composition. The notes limped out like stupid children, dwarfed
by the serious echoes that had not finished ringing beneath the
synagogue dome. Though Norman's chest swelled to bursting
as he inhaled defiance, his bugle merely exhaled retreat. Mortified, he tucked the toy back into the belt of his trousers, withdrew it again, and discarded it in scorn.

Far be it from Rudolph, moving aside to let him exit, to come
between Norman and his tilting with windmills. On the con-
trary, he was happily excluded, relieved to have been abandoned. Scarcely did he hear himself say under his breath, 'Wait
for Sancho Finkl.' But Bloody Norman was already halfway
down the centre aisle of the empty sanctuary; he was disappearing through a narrow door to the side of the altar, re-
appearing in the choir loft, balanced upon the balcony above a
burning candelabrum with a ram's horn pressed to his lips.

At the first fresh blasts of the *shofar*, the rabbi hobbled back
into the *shul*; he rent his garments and pulled tufts from his
beard at the sight which he encountered. For Rudolph Finkl
in his fluttering bathrobe was charging down the aisle like a
scarecrow just escaped from crossed staves. He was careering
toward the altar upon which his father stood waiting. Mr Finkl,
looking weary and in need of a shave, was still blessed with his
venerable paunch. He was smiling his forlorn smile. In his
convict-striped pyjamas and his pair of magnificent alabaster
wings, with their chasing of shadows, he was a fugitive from
kingdom come. Outstretching his arms, he welcomed his son
who rushed furiously into his embrace. As they locked into
combat – the angel's strength versus the speed of the boy –
Rudolph grinned from ear to ear like a savage.

'Say "uncle" !' he wailed.

'Uncle, ncle, cle,' the dome resounded, filling Rudolph's body up with light.

The rabbi fell to his brittle knees and Norman, always one to enjoy a good fight, leaned over the ark and yelled at the top of his lungs,

'Murder him !'

CELIA DALE

Moon Daisy

We kept no end of state at Brettenham (pronounced Bretham by those in the know). There must be more than twenty indoor servants and heaven knows how many on the estate, not counting the home farm. In the autumn, when they have house parties for the shooting and each guest brings his own servants, the place must be like a medieval court; and if the Prince and Princess of Wales graciously consent to drive over from Sandringham for a day's sport – my word, what splendour!

Mind you, I've not seen this myself – I heard of it from Miss Tiffen, the Family's seamstress. She used to be the children's nurse, but now they are all grown up and away – the girls well married, the boys serving the Empire at various far-flung out-posts – she sits all day in one of the tower rooms, mending and altering and stitching, a little bent old woman with eyes as bright as a robin's. She knows everything about the Family; but she tells only what redounds to their glory and credit. The bad things she keeps silent about – as I found in the end.

I spent a fair bit of time with Miss Tiffen. She, like myself, had no fixed place in the household, she by reason of age and long intimacy with the Family which made her now more than a servant but of course much less than a friend, and I because although I am as gently bred as Lord Brettenham himself (probably more so, for he is only the third baron whereas my father could trace our line back to at least the seventeenth century, yeomen gentry who threw up scholars from time to time but lacked the venality to make their way in the world) I was at Brettenham only as an employee, filling the three summer months by cataloguing Lord Brettenham's library and family papers. And glad indeed to do so, for funds were exceedingly low until September, when I was to take up an appointment as junior master in a school for the sons of clergymen in Blackheath.

The cataloguing was tedious: the Family's interests seem, for their short but swift rise from mercantile obscurity, to have been almost entirely political and sporting, their papers accounts and meticulously kept game-books, their library political and theological. I worked each day alone in the libary, my luncheon brought to me by the under-parlourmaid. Breakfast I took alone in the old schoolroom, tea usually with Miss Tiffen, once I discovered her existence. Dinner again alone in the schoolroom – unless, ah unless! the Family found themselves a gentleman short at the dinner table, in which case, by means of a note brought to me by a footman, I would be bidden to make up the requisite number; to take in, it might be, the spinster sister of the Rector (themselves invited merely to fill the lower reaches of the table well below the salt) or some tongue-tied daughter of a local squire invited to soften his reluctance to have his crops trampled by being shot over even by Royal Highnesses.

On these occasions, arrayed in the formal black and white which had been my father's, I would make my way down the many staircases into the great hall with its fireplaces banked with potted plants, to the drawing room, its floor a hazardous ice-rink beneath costly rugs, its chandeliers a-twinkle despite the evening sun – the better, perhaps, to display the satins and brocades, the jewelled dog-collars, tiaras, parures, earrings as large, it seemed, as the chandeliers themselves, that glittered on the ladies of the swells therein assembled.

'Ah, Mr Fisher,' his lordship would drawl agreeably if he happened to notice my arrival, 'how's the work progressing, heh? Mr Fisher's our bookworm, heh?' to whoever stood nearest us.

'Very well, sir, I think.'

'Capital, capital,' and that would be the end of it. Before dinner was announced my lady would glide up to me, a-rustle with taffeta, a-twinkle with gems. Tapping me on the arm with her fan, she would instruct me as to which hapless lady I was to take in and waft me to her side. She, poor creature, seldom knew who I was, and I not often she. Throughout the interminable meal we would try and make conversation of a kind.

When the ladies left us and the port circulated I was in limbo. I did my best, but my neighbours soon gave me up as a bad job. Politics, racing and *risqué* stories did not interest me, cigars make me feel ill, and I do not care for drink or drunkards; and when blessed release came I did not go with the others to join the ladies but made my way out through the billiard room on to the terrace, to breathe in the purity and silence of the night. No one would miss me; my function had been solely to fill an empty place.

Brettenham is very beautiful, especially on a fine summer night. The house stands four-square, rather grey and bleak, on a platform backed by ancient trees. Behind the trees, beyond the park, lie the heath and woodlands over which the Family shoot, but facing down a gentle slope of parkland (beyond which, many miles away, lies the sea) the mansion seems to survey limitless tranquillity, a harmony of grassland, trees and lake.

It is the lake which gives the grace and focus to the landscape, tree-edged in places, at others fringed with reeds, and in the day constantly a-shimmer with duck and wildfowl of all kinds, clucking and preening, rising with a sharp rustle of wings as though a hundred umbrellas were suddenly opened, descending again with a long splashing wake to resettle wing and breast feathers – which feathers bestrew the grass and small beaches of the lakeside like confetti. It was my delight sometimes to gather them up into airy posies, as many different kinds as I could find, and take them to Miss Tiffen.

But at night the lake seemed spellbound. Dark in the darkness, utterly still between its reeded banks – and yet never still, always stealthily alive with wind sounds, water sounds, the small movements of water rat and vole, the stirring, breathing of birds that only seemed to sleep, muttering, chuckling, preening in the darkness, making their own silence in the secrecy of the night.

I came out on to the side terrace nearest the lake that evening of the dinner, my lungs sour with cigar smoke, my ears with the blare and blather of the swells, my heart filled with bitter loneliness and – yes – self-pity. What was I doing here, ignored or patronized by these moneyed boobies? I was a scholar. That was why I was here, recommended by my father's friend and lawyer when it was found my father had left nothing. That same recommendation would start me as a schoolmaster in two months' time, a prospect I dreaded, for although I am a scholar, it is as a writer that I wish to make my name. Was this to be my life? At twenty-two, was I already doomed to drudgery and subservience?

From the open windows of the mansion behind me I could hear music, a woman singing, the tepid clatter of gloved applause. I went down the steps and across the grass to the lakeside.

It was a still, clear night, a new moon steadfast in the sky. Sunk in my doleful thoughts I wandered with bent head along the bank; the music fell away behind me, the blessed silence enshrouded me, calmed me. And then, pale in the starlight, I saw a girl standing at the edge of the reeds.

My heart gave a thump, for she looked like a ghost standing there quite still by the water's edge, swathed in some pale material, gazing away from me down the far side of the lake. Then I realized that the paleness came from a bibbed, encompassing apron, her hair (pale in itself) partly covered by a frilled white cap. My heart resumed its normal beating and I said jokingly, 'I took you for a ghost.'

She gave a start and turned her face towards me. 'I didn't hear you, sir.'

'Did I frighten you?'

'No. I don't frighten easy.' Her voice was soft, with a faint Norfolk twang.

'It's a fine night.'

'Aye.' She turned to look down the lake again, indifferent to me. Piqued, I stayed where I was.

'Are you from the house?'

'Aye.' She faced me again. It was a pale, composed face, the mouth firm, the eyes steady. The wide starched bands on the shoulders of her apron seemed to reflect light. 'I'm one of the housemaids.'

'I've not seen you about.'

'You wouldn't.'

Her lack of 'sir' stung me. 'I'm from the house too,' I said grandly.

'Aye, you must be else you wouldn't be here.' A faint smile touched her mouth. She was like no servant I had met yet – perhaps because we were out here in the night alone, away from the rigid hierarchy of the mansion.

On impulse I asked, 'What's your name?'

'Daisy.'

'Daisy. A moon daisy.'

'If you like. Sir.' She was definitely smiling now, a soft teasing smile.

'Do you often come here in the dark?'

'Sometimes. When there's time.'

'I also. I shall look for you again.'

'Likely you will.' She began to move away, the reeds hazing the pale glimmer of her garments.

I called, 'Yes, you may be sure of it.'

Her voice had laughter in it. 'Sleep well. Sir.' And she was gone.

She must have known I would not sleep well – her voice had promise of it. But it was sleeplessness with pleasure in it. She haunted me. I kept seeing the glimmer of her face and figure, hearing the cool teasing of her voice. Her lack of servility piqued me; she knew I was a gentleman from my speech and manner. I had been dressed in evening togs too; and, as she had said, how else would I be there, strolling at ease by Brettenham's lake of a summer evening after a grand dinner party? Where in the house did she work, I wondered, why had I never seen her? But there were dozens of servants I never saw in that huge establishment; they were expertly trained to be invisible.

I tried Miss Tiffen, roundabout. 'It's such a grand household, ma'am, I've never seen the like. How many indoor servants would there be? – how many housemaids, say?'

'What's it to you, Mr Fisher?'

'Nothing. Curiosity. I thought I heard someone calling for "Daisy" in the upstairs corridor this morning, that's all.'

She gave me a sharp look. 'Daisy? No Daisy here, you can depend on that. And there should be no calling in the passages of Brettenham House. What impudence!' Well, she was old and seldom left her attic rooms; she would hardly know the names of all the staff.

Each evening if it were fine – and that summer it mostly was – I took to sauntering down to the lakeside after my dinner. I soon grew used to the darkness, and in any case the moon was waxing. I wandered round the lake, my eyes searching for the girl's pale figure, but for some nights I did not find her. Then, there she was, standing in the same reeded place, looking away down the lake.

'Daisy?'

She turned. 'Ah, 'tis you, sir.'

'Yes.'

'I thought that might be.'

I was disconcerted. 'You did, did you? Why was that?'

'That'd be telling. Let's say, because you wanted to.'

'And you?'

She laughed, and I felt not only my blood but my heart begin to pound.

'I'm only a servant,' she said. 'That don't matter what I want.'

'And what do you want?'

152

'Oh . . .' She let the word hang in the silence for a moment. 'I want to be like them.' She nodded towards the house, where lights blazed from every window. 'I want to wear fine clothes and a jewel or so and have someone else to do my washing and make my bed. I want to see London and look at the Queen.'

'London's not much of a place.'

Her voice sharpened. 'You shouldn't say that. That's not what they say. You should say 'tis a fine place and you'll take me there. You should say if I go with you to London you'll give me fine clothes and a carriage and make me a lady.'

'I can't say that. It wouldn't be true.'

'Yes you must, 'tis what they all say. You're no different.' She began to move away.

'I am, Daisy. I am different.'

'You're a gentleman, aren't you, from the house?'

'Yes, but . . .'

'Won't you take me to London, then?' She was still leaving me, her voice teasing yet plaintive.

'Yes, yes if I can. If you want . . . but why?'

'That's right. That's what you must say. That's the way of it. Sir.'

She was gone.

Even now, I cannot understand what madness seized me. I was distracted. I no longer knew whether I stood on my head or my heels. I seemed to have gone mad, to have become possessed by a girl I did not know, could never know save in impurity, a servant I had not even touched, a country girl of unknown background, shameless, unscrupulous – but magical, magnetic, all-pervading. My dreams were full of her – hot, shameful, exhausting dreams; my day thoughts turned again and again to her from the dry cataloguing of the Family's effects. I know now that I was in fact bewitched, but then it merely seemed to me that I had at last found, in that barren waste of condescension and indifference, someone who spoke and responded to me on equal terms – more, a lovely being who

treated me as a woman treats a man, teasing, promising, tender.
Yet not quite as an equal; impudent though she was, she spoke
to me as to a man of power and breeding, a swell who could
take her up on a whim and translate this country wanton into a
town dolly. I, who had no influence, no wealth, no home! It
was this that turned my head, as though I were indeed a lord,
her master. I was drunk with the power of it – and with her
strange, pale beauty, the provocation that weighted her voice
and her words.

I slipped out every evening down to the lake to see if she
were there. The weather had turned, the trees stirred and
threshed in the wind, the moon was obscured by cloud. She did
not come. I walked through the quaggy edge of the lakeside
where the reeds were as high as my shoulders, but she was not
there. In ten days' time my employment would be over, the
archives and the library in order, listed in heavy leather tomes
that no one, I judged, would ever glance at. I should be paid
my fee by the steward: perhaps her ladyship might condescend
to wish me farewell and his lordship to express satisfaction and
the promise of a reference should any of his acquaintances re-
quire my services. And I should be driven to the station in the
dogcart with my portmanteau and return to London and some
dreary lodging, to sweat out the August heat before setting
forth again to that unknown school whose general dogsbody
I would be.

No! In a ruthless world why should I not be ruthless too?
Why should I not do as Daisy urged, take her with me and
enjoy if only for a time the solace of her charms? If she was so
reckless as to trust herself to a man she hardlly knew, I would
be mad enough to accept that trust. London she wanted and
London she should have!

Calm, rich nights came again, the winds blown out. As I
kept my vigil I heard only the secret stir of lakeside life. The
moon, now full and tinged with gold, sailed huge in the huge
sky.

She was there. Her head was bare tonight, the pale hair
shining in two smooth wings either side of her face, caught

back in an old-fashioned knot, a few tendrils escaping by her ears, infinitely seductive.

She turned when I spoke her name. 'Ah, 'tis you. I knew you'd come.'

'I've looked for you each night.'

'Aye. That's full moon now. Sweethearts' time.'

'Daisy.' I took a step towards her along the narrow path. 'I leave next week. Back to London.'

Her eyes glittered. 'You'll take me?'

'Yes.'

'Ah!' She drew in her breath and smiled, not at me but up into the glow of the moon. 'You want me bad, eh? You'll take me up and set me up, like all the gentlemen say? But you'll not get nothing till we're safe in London. I'm not to be tumbled under the trees and then left to watch you drive off in your carriage and pair. London's my price, my fine gentleman – nothing before!'

Her words shocked me; and yet, in their challenging impudence I sensed a desperate fear. Despite the harshness of her manner, the provocation of her movements as she swayed a step or two away from me, there seemed terror and, yes, innocence. The face she turned to me as she moved was that of a child – a knowing child but one moved by bravado; fearful, uncertain, yet determined.

I took a step or two after her, the path squelching beneath my feet. 'Daisy,' I said, 'it's not like that.'

'London's my price,' she said, her voice like steel. 'You'll not see or touch before you've bought the goods. I'll have no gentleman's tricks from you.'

She had retreated further among the reeds and I followed her. 'It's not like that,' I said again. 'I'm not what you think. I'm not a swell, I'm not a guest up at the house.'

'You're a gentleman,' she repeated.

'Yes. But not as you mean. I'm not rich. I've no money save what I earn and that's little enough, and I'm only a sort of a lackey up at the house, at work in the library. I'm not one of the Family's set, I'm no one.'

'You must be.' Her voice was uncertain now. You're up at the house, in fine clothes and all, dining with all the nobs. You speak soft and fine and you're hot for a servant girl, like all of them is.'

'Daisy, no! You're mistaken, gravely mistaken. I'm not a nob, I'm no one. I'll take you to London and if you stay with me I'll treat you with all the respect I can. But there's no carriage and no fine clothes – only an honest heart and no lies between us.'

I went further towards her, for I wanted to take her by the hand and let her see in my face that I spoke the truth; that we'd go together, I'd keep my word, but as comrades, lovers I hoped in time, but without falsehood.

But she shrank away before me, her face bewildered. 'No!' she cried, 'that's not how 'tis. You're a gentleman, rich, and you want your will of me now, like a slut in a barn. That's all lies about going to London, you want me now and leave me, ruin me here and nothing to pay! That's how 'tis, that's how it always is!'

'Daisy, no! I'll not touch you. I'm not what you think. I'm poor, Daisy, like you . . .' I thrust nearer to her, though the reeds closed in on me and I felt the mud oozing up through my thin shoes. The reeds rustled around me and small sounds came from creatures disturbed by our presence. As I plunged towards her she threw out her hands as though to fend me off and her face, retreating before me, was whiter than ever in the steadfast beam of the moon.

'No, no!' she cried. 'Go back! That's wrong – that's all mazed and wrong! You're not the one it should be – you're like my Jed, my darling . . .' Then she raised her face and her arms to the sky and cried in a voice so raw with loss and anguish that my heart went cold, 'They hung my darling! They hung my Jed! Go back, you're not the one – go back, go back . . .'

I felt the lake water rise above my ankles, calves, knees. I blundered towards her but she seemed always to recede before me, gliding backwards through the reeds that scratched and tore at my face and hands, her face a mask of fear and, it seemed, pity, her pale hands waving me back, back, as she fled, faded, hung above the water like a shimmering mist as I tripped and fell face downward in the knotted weeds and reeds and quagmire of the lakeside, felt the water close over me, tasted the mud in my mouth, heard her voice echoing, 'Go back, go back – you're not the one . . .'

A woodman found me as he went to work soon after the sun rose. I was lying in the mud at the lake's edge, half submerged but with my face and head somehow pulled clear of the water. I was unconscious and they got a hurdle and carried me back to the house, where I gather my condition caused something of a stir. Vaguely I was aware of bustle around my bedside, voices, even her ladyship's, and someone saying with great emphasis, 'This is the third, I tell you!' I drifted and dozed, at last returning to myself at evening, the curtains drawn, a lamp shaded on the dressing table, and old Miss Tiffen seated at my bedside, her gnarled hands in her lap, her eyes shut.

I stirred and at once her lids were open and her bright old eyes regarded me. 'Ah,' she said, 'you return to us. How do you feel?'

'Very hot.'

'Naturally. You have three blankets and a coverlet and a hot brick at your feet. I will remove that now, but you have suffered a severe chill, lying out all night in the lake.' She rose and darted her arm under the bedclothes at my feet to extract the flannel-wrapped warmer. She placed it on the floor, reseated herself, and told me how I had been discovered, the reeds trampled down around me as though I had struggled to drag myself out of the lake. When she had done she folded her hands in her lap and studied me intently.

'And now,' she said, 'I should like to inquire how you got there?'

I told her. Shameful in many ways though my story was, I kept nothing back. Weakened alike by exposure and by emotion, I let the whole short but overwhelming record of my encounters with Daisy flood out of me, trying to convey to Miss

157

Tiffen the strange magnetism of that moonlit creature and the bitter loneliness in myself which caused my, as I saw it now, incredible response.

Miss Tiffen listened in silence, nodding her lace-capped head now and then. When I had done she nodded again. 'Yes,' she said, 'it is as I thought.'

After a moment I said, 'I wish no harm to come to Daisy. She was not to blame.'

'No,' she said. 'It is the world that is to blame. Lust and ambition and the power of high personages are to blame.' She nodded twice. 'She should not be blamed for wanting to better herself.'

'She'll not be dismissed?'

She gave me a queer look. 'Young man,' she said, 'I will tell you, for no one else in this house will, they fear the scandal. Daisy Hunter was murdered down by the lake some sixty years ago.' As I gasped she laid a hand firmly on mine. 'Stay still. I was the under-nurserymaid then, newly in service, fourteen years of age. We were friends of a sort. His lordship's father was the lord then. Daisy had a sweetheart, Jed Barber, a gamekeeper. She loved him, I'm sure, but she was eager to better herself and him, hot in the flesh as country girls are, not wise in the head. One of the old lord's friends caught sight of her, a foreign Highness, she took his fancy and she led him on. She was found drowned at the lakeside one full moon with marks on her throat, and it was Jed that found her and Jed they hanged for it.'

She was silent for a moment, her eyes looking into the past. Then she gave my hand a little pat again. 'There were another two found there over the years – gentlemen, friends of his lordship. Drowned in the mud at full moon, no one knew how or why. Their deaths were hushed up, of course. They could find no scapegoat for them as they had for Daisy's murder. *He* didn't hang, you see, it was all covered up by the Family. Wealth can do that. Poor Jed got the blame and was hanged for it. Yes, that's the way it was.'

'But – the others?'

'I think,' she said, and her voice was almost tender, 'I think poor Daisy's wanted revenge. It was Jed she loved, despite her grand ideas – we were bits of girls together, I knew her mind. She's had revenge and no one's lived to say how. But you've lived.'

'Why? Why me?'

She drew a handkerchief out from the pocket she kept hung under her skirt and blew her nose. Her eyes were brighter than ever, I thought, with tears.

'She saw that you weren't a villain but just a silly young man. Not a lord of creation like those others had been, to take what you like and the rest of us all keep silence, but a simple, silly young person like herself – and Jed. You touched her heart, even though she's dead.' She blew her nose again and stuffed the handkerchief back under her skirts. 'Pity wipes out revenge. Daisy's gone now, I think.'

'Amen,' I said.

She covered my hand with hers. 'Amen. God rest their souls.'

And mine, I should have echoed; for the loss and loveliness haunt me to this day.

JAMES ALDRIDGE

The Black Ghost of St Helen

The black ghost of St Helen (a small country town in Victoria, Australia) was given to the town by my father in a court of law, and though the original case, in which he was the defence lawyer, was tried over forty years ago, I heard only the other day that the ghost was still active in the town, still being seen and still frightening those who wanted to be frightened, or thrilling those who wanted to be thrilled.

Given my father's short temper and his unceasing intention, as an Englishman, to show Australians where they were going wrong, I suppose the end result of the case was bound to be the exposure of a spiritual side-slip in the town's easy callousness towards one of its true indigenes. In any case it was inevitable that my father should appear for the defence when the issue came to law because no one else was fool enough, or maybe arrogant or English enough to think that he could defend what was obviously a straightforward case of murder, even though the prosecution couldn't produce a body.

It didn't matter, because the one qualification my father always looked for in a case was its 'inner logic'. Once he had found this 'inner logic' he was always able, with his own legal logic, to build a stirring defence for his client which was usually very difficult for the prosecution to disrupt. In the case of the black ghost of St Helen his use of its 'inner logic' was particularly satisfying to him because it gave him a chance to teach the town a lesson, not only about its spiritual failings, but about the very nature of being Australian, which was really the one passion of his English, legal struggle with the town.

But enough of this anticipation and enough of my father for the time being. I shall tell the story as it happened in its own sequence, which means that I must start with Bob.

Bob was our local aborigine, 'Bob the blackfeller', and he worked as a stockman for Gil Sullivan, one of our local horse-breeders and stock drovers. Together Gil and Bob were a popular pair, not only because they were wonderful horsemen, but because they were both quiet and gentle types who yet managed, as drovers, some of the biggest herds of beef that were ever driven into the town stockyards. Bob was particularly popular because he was a smiling, obliging man who didn't mind digging a patch of garden or carrying a load for someone, simply as a favour, which was a real concession from a stock-man, even though he was an aborigine. In fact Bob was a colourful figure in his white doeskin jodhpurs, ankle boots and a wide-brimmed hat. It was the uniform then of all black stockmen. Bob also carried a stockwhip, and his prowess with it was well known. He could safely flick a cigarette from Gil Sullivan's mouth at ten yards and crack the whip loudly at the same time.

When he and Gil were not droving cattle into the town from one of the surrounding stations, Bob looked after Gil's thoroughbreds and lived in a little hut to one side of the stables. It always smelled of horse manure when we visited him, but Bob was happy with it.

'Good air!' he would say and sniff deep of the horse.

In summer Bob would often join us (boys and girls of the town) at our swimming hole in a bend of the Murray River, and he was as popular among the youth as he was among the adults. Bob never really swam. He would simply 'bob' in and out of the water, disappearing below the surface for up to two minutes, and some people said that was how he got his name 'Bob'. He loved to disappear like that and no matter where we watched for him to reappear, his smiling black face would bob up from some unlikely spot.

'How do you do it, Bob?' we always wanted to know. 'How do you stay under so long?'

'I just take a deep breath,' Bob would say simply.

In fact I know now that Bob would use a technique developed by expert snorklers many years later. He would expel every ounce of air from his lungs with a dozen quick breaths, thus venting out all the carbon dioxide, and then he would take one big pure breath and simply disappear, using as little effort as possible while under water.

Bob also knew when and where the best places were to catch fish, and if you took his advice and fished at a certain spot he would often squat beside you and simply wait, saying nothing until you caught a fish. Then he would give a little grunt and say:

'Two more there somewhere.'

And more often than not he was right. You would catch two more fish and that was that.

I suppose the real story begins with Bob's brother, or rather someone we thought of as his brother, although we didn't know for sure. We called him, in our Australian passion for the echoic, 'Job'. And Job was as different from Bob as Bob was from us. Though everybody in town knew Bob and talked to him, nobody really knew Job and nobody in town ever talked to him. He never came into town.

Job lived across the river on Pental Island, and the view most of us had of Job was a rather typical one – not of the 'civilized' aborigine like Bob, but of the native in his habitat. Sometimes when we were swimming in the river Job would stand on the bank farther down watching us. He would stand the way the aborigines stood in the bush, with one bare foot drawn up to rest against the side of the other leg, so that he looked like a stork standing on one leg.

'There's Job,' someone would shout.

Mostly we ignored him, but if some of the boys felt like a little fun they would begin to call out to him:

'Come on, Job. Come and show us how you walk on one leg.'

Job was reported to live in a *willawa* (a leaf hut) in a patch of bush on the island across the river and he hunted for his food with a spear, club and boomerang, although nobody ever saw him doing it. But we knew he did it because there was no other way he could survive.

'He lives like a fox,' we would tell each other.

And, like a fox, he would disappear the moment you approached him. We had given up making a sport of trying to catch him when he watched us from the river bank. He could outrun all of us. He was over six feet tall, was very thin, and wore nothing more than a pair of torn cotton trousers summer and winter. But he never uttered a word.

Sometimes when we went across the river to the bush where he lived we would hunt for Job, trying to catch him unaware. But though we hunted every day for his *willawa* we never found it, and if we ever did chase him it was because he showed himself and seemed to invite it. But again, we could never catch him. He would simply disappear before our eyes.

'He lives in the trees,' we said.

'No. It's a big hole in the ground, like a rabbit.'

'He's got an underwater cave, and just dives in.'

In fact the only person who had any real contact with him was Bob, who would sometimes swim the river and join Job and they would walk off together into the bush, not side by side but with Bob ten yards behind, as if that was as near as he was allowed. Often Job would rush at Bob as if he was going to spear him. Or he would dance around Bob and threaten him with a boomerang. Once I saw him hit Bob very hard with the side of his spear. But no matter what Job did, Bob would never retaliate. He would wait patiently for the threats to pass and then follow Job into the bush. I never heard it myself, but plenty of people in the town had heard shouting and screaming from the bush on moonlit nights, and they always said it was Bob beating up Job, or Job beating up Bob. Nobody knew which it was. Sometimes Bob took a sugar bag of food (we assumed it was food) with him, and in the winter when the river was too high and fast to swim Bob would ride the long way around by the bridge and stay with Job for a couple of days and then return.

But there was one thing that Bob wouldn't tolerate. If we asked him any questions about his brother, Job, he became furious.

'Mind your own bloody business,' he would say fiercely, which seemed quite out of character.

Once or twice when some of the boys teased him about Job, singing a crude rhyme which went 'Job-job, blob-blob', Bob again changed character and lashed the boys with his bullwhip, cutting one of them severely on the leg. He chased the boys when they ran away in terror, swearing at them and threatening death if they ever did that again.

'He went crazy,' Jack Johnson, one of the boys, said. 'He kept shouting at us, "Don't even talk to me. Don't say anything." '

Bob was equally fierce with any adult who inquired about Job, and when two ladies from a local Baptist organization took a bundle of clothes to Bob for his 'brother', Bob threw a spadeful of horse manure at them and shouted, 'Leave me alone!' and chased them down the street.

So the town learned not to mention the subject of his brother, and then general consensus was that Bob was embarrassed and resentful because his brother was a little touched. In fact anybody who had seen Job knew that he was crazy.

That was how it remained until the next summer, when Job disappeared. Or rather he was not seen any more. At first we didn't notice Job's absence when we began our summer pleasures in the swimming hole. But then someone commented on it, and we began to miss that stork-like figure watching us at play.

'Somebody ought to ask Bob what's happened to him,' Clive Sandiford suggested.

'Don't be stupid,' one of the girls said. 'Bob'd use his whip on you.'

'Well, what do you think's happened to Job?'

We didn't know. Job didn't show himself when we went into his patch of bush, and Bob no longer swam the river with a sugar bag full of food. It was obvious that Job had gone.

But where to?

It took a little while for Job's disappearance to penetrate the rest of the town, but when it did there was sufficient interest in the fate of Job for the police to begin to ask questions, and at this point the real problem began.

When Sergeant Joe Collins of the local police called on Bob to ask him what had happened to his brother, Bob became indignant.

'What brother?' he said. 'I haven't got a brother.'

'Well, whoever he was,' Sergeant Collins said. 'That black-feller across the river on Pental Island.'

'There wasn't any blackfeller across the river on Pental Island,' Bob said. 'I don't know what you're talking about. Not a thing.'

'Come off it, Bob. Everybody knows you had some mate or brother or relative over the other side of the river, so what's happened to him?'

'Happened to who?' Bob said stubbornly. 'I didn't know anybody across the river. I never saw anybody over there. So what are you talking about?'

Bob was adamant. There was nobody across the river. There never had been. There was no Job. Job had never existed.

The curious thing is that if Bob had simply said that Job had gone away, or fallen into the river and drowned, the police would probably have believed him and left it at that. But when Bob firmly refused to admit that there ever had been another man, whether it was his brother or not, the police became suspicious. One Saturday morning three policemen were seen scouring the bush on Pental Island, and a few days later Bob was taken to the police station and asked more questions.

'Nobody over there,' Bob insisted again. 'Never was, I tell you.'

It was too much, and when Bob finally became angry and shouted and insulted the police and denied again Job's existence, the police decided that Bob had murdered his brother and he was charged and locked up in the local jail while the police went on searching for the body.

I suppose it was a ridiculous charge from the outset, and if Bob had been a white man the police would probably have thought twice before charging him. But Bob was a blackfeller, and everybody knew that blackfellers didn't think the way we did, or accept the same rules of behaviour as the rest of the community. Aborigines in the Northern Territory were always being charged with curious, casual murders, so it was an easy sort of Australian callousness that assumed Bob to have murdered the mysterious Job. What else would explain his curious and ridiculous pretence that Job had never existed at all?

It didn't take long for the magistrate to commit Bob for trial, and already the town was divided about his guilt or innocence. A lot of people thought it very funny, others were sure that Bob had killed Job with an axe, a spear, a boomerang. A rumour went around the town that Job's body had been found farther down the river, horribly mutilated. But it proved untrue, and a dozen other rumours also came to nothing. There was still no body to prove the point conclusively when Gil Sullivan called at our house one night and asked my father to defend Bob.

'I'll pay your fee, Mr Quayle,' Gil said. 'I'm selling a thoroughbred next week, and I'll have some cash. I know Bob, and I know he wouldn't murder anybody.'

'Then why on earth does he deny the existence of his brother?' my father asked, since, like the rest of the town, he knew the story.

'I don't know, Mr Quayle,' Gil said. 'I just don't know.'

'Have you asked him why he insists there wasn't anybody across the river, when everybody has known for years that there was?'

'He won't talk about it. He just refuses.'

'If he won't talk about it, how can I defend him?' my father said.

'I don't know that either,' Gil said. 'It's pretty hopeless.'

Gil had unwittingly said the right thing; he had given my father a challenge.

'All right,' my father said. 'I'll look into it and let you know.'

My father's method of 'looking into' a case was to search for its inner logic. There had to be 'sense in defence', and though the prosecution case had very little sense in it, Bob's situation was bad so long as he insisted that there never had been another man across the river. It was tantamount to a childish (aborigine) way of trying to hide his guilt. That was the argument anyway.

My father talked to Bob, and he told me many years later that all he could do was to point out to Bob that by remaining silent he was risking his life, because he could very easily be found guilty by a local jury, and murder then was punished by hanging. But Bob still refused to say or do anything that would admit the existence of Job.

'So it was obviously something very powerful that was at work on Bob,' my father said. And because this seemed to be the clue to the 'inner logic' of the case, he set about finding out what it was.

My father had a good library and I saw him consulting some anthropological books on aborigines. There was also one other aborigine in our town, or rather she would appear in the town from time to time selling colourful, crown-like headpieces made of pink cockatoo feathers. She was Queen Aggie, and she lived as a 'guest' on the Riverside Station on the New South Wales side of the Murray, occasionally walking eight miles into town to sit on the Post Office corner selling her beautifully made headpieces. I knew that my father had long talks with Aggie because one day I saw him talking to her on the street corner, and another time she came to our house and squatted under the walnut tree and talked to my father for half an hour.

A day or two my father spent eating silently, staring deter-

minedly ahead, walking unseeing to his office and then he told
Gil Sullivan he would take the case. He had obviously found
the inner logic of the case, although he didn't tell us what it
was. He would save that for the court.

In fact the case itself was little more than a straightforward
argument between two advocates, one for the prosecution and
one for the defence. There was no real evidence, and the
premise of the prosecution was an inexplicable disappearance
which could only be explained by one man doing away with
another.

That was the case made out by the plump J. C. Strapp for
the prosecution. The facts were well known, he said. He could
produce fifty witnesses to prove that there had been another
aborigine living across the river, and that Bob had been seen
with him year after year, and that this other aborigine, known
in the town as Job, was sometimes seen to threaten Bob. Crying
and shouting had been heard across the river time and time
again, evidence of quarrels and fights over many years between
the two men.

'A *corpus delicti*, a body, isn't necessary to justify a charge
of murder,' Strapp said, waving his plump fingers at my father,
'so I hope the defence will not waste time on that aspect of the
case. There are too many precedents in English law to have the
case thrown out for lack of a body. The real point is that the
defendant has tried to hide his guilt by pretending there never
was another man, which is not only ridiculous but is obviously
the device of a very naive and primitive mind trying to deny one
fact, murder, by denying another fact, the existence of the man
he did to death. Only a simple mind would defend himself in
this way, and it is well known that the aborigines in general
have very simple minds and that death is often an easy solution
to their tribal and personal quarrels. Which doesn't make
the crime any less under our law. All that the accused has to
do is to deny what he is accused of and explain what has happened to his brother, or whoever that other man was. That's
all that is asked of him, but that is what he refuses to do. A
damning piece of evidence by itself.'

Strapp went on generalizing, while Bob sat in the box staring ahead, refusing to listen to any of it. When Strapp had finished his argument my father waited some time before beginning his defence. He knew very well that everybody in that court (except Bob) was curious to know what his argument would be. There were one or two obvious alternatives. He could ask the jury to bring in a verdict of manslaughter rather than murder, since malice aforethought or even the motive was absent. Or he could easily have argued the shallowness of the prosecution's case, the lack of evidence or proof of any kind. He was a clever advocate and he could easily have made an excellent case of either argument.

But they were too easy for my father. Moreover both arguments failed to satisfy the internal sense he insisted on.

'The point at issue in this case,' he began when he had allowed his hesitation to take effect, 'is whether or not another man actually lived across the river – the man Bob is supposed to have killed. Well . . . it is my intention to prove that there never was another man, that he never existed at all, so that Bob could not have killed him.'

There was a moment's silence, then the whole courtroom burst into laughter, including J. C. Strapp, the police and as far as he would allow himself – the judge (Campbell, L. C.).

My father was used to being laughed at in court; in fact, he would deliberately provoke it whenever he anticipated having the last laugh himself. He waited patiently for the laughter to subside, and he ignored J. C. Strapp's *sotto voce* remark : 'Now he's going to play Houdini . . .' Then he began his defence.

'The word *aborigine*,' he said in the instructive sort of voice he often used annoyingly to juries, 'is a Greek word which means a native of a place, a true indigene, a person who has the right to call a locale his own. Now, gentlemen, with this definition in mind you will note that we, sitting white and pure in this courtroom, do not call ourselves the aborigines of Australia. Oh no ! We would never do that. Instead we use that word, sometimes as an insult, for black men like Bob, black men who had been here on this very spot for millennia before we ever arrived.'

He paused again as if waiting for that much to sink in, as if waiting for the rhythm of his argument to take hold. 'So what you have to consider when you look at Bob's behaviour,' he went on, 'is that he is the true native of this place, and belongs to a totally different culture from the one which brought us here. No matter what way you look at it, we are the strangers here, and we have no right to forget it. In other words, this is really Bob's country . . .'

My father raised one of his short stubby fingers and pointed casually in Bob's direction so that everybody looked at the black figure in his jodhpurs sitting behind the wooden barrier with his fingers entwined across his chest. I suppose everybody in that courtroom expected Bob to show some response or interest, but Bob remained impassive and uninterested in anything that was going on, and the judge noticed it.

'I don't know if you are trying to impress your client or the court, Mr Quayle,' he said, 'but I hope there is some relevance to this little history lesson we are getting.'

'There is, m'lud,' my father said, 'and if I may point out it isn't a history lesson. I am simply stating a fact which lies at the root of this case.'

'Very well, but please get to the point so that we know why we have to listen to all this.'

'The point will soon become obvious, m'lud,' my father said rather irritably, as if he had had enough of this interruption. 'In fact the point I want to make here is that the culture and religion and beliefs of Bob and his people explain what this case is all about.'

'Really, m'lud, I must protest . . .' Strapp began.

'Oh let him finish, Mr Strapp,' the judge said. 'We may actually learn something about Australia from Mr Quayle, even if he isn't relevant, and I feel like learning something today. So proceed.'

'Thank you, m'lud,' my father said, 'and I hope you do learn something today because if the police or the prosecution had taken the trouble to look into the reasons for Bob's behaviour they would never have brought this case to trial in the first place.'

'Then do get on with it, Mr Quayle.'

'It's really very simple,' my father said, and for the first time directly addressed the jury. 'You see, gentlemen, all aborigine culture is ghost-ridden. They believe that everything has a spirit, even a tree, and that man himself is no more than the spirit of those who have gone before him. As a result there are ten thousand ghosts all around all aborigines at all times – in the air, the grass, the river, the trees, the animals, the men, the women. What is real and what is ghostly is often very difficult to separate, and often there is serious confusion.

'But there is one ghost that all aborigines are sure is a ghost – or a spirit if you like. And that is anyone who is touched in the head or is epileptic or mad. If the prosecution had taken the trouble to investigate they would have discovered that mad people do not really exist for the normal aborigine. They are treated as spirits. It is taboo to talk to them, talk about them, touch them or even look at them. If you destroy these taboos you can be stricken yourself with the same misfortune and turned into a ghost in an instant. Such people are left to fend for themselves although, like the Chinese who put rice bowls on the graves of the dead, it is permissible to leave food for the ghost if you wish. In fact it is considered an act of self-protection and propitiation . . .'

By now the courtroom was genuinely interested, even fascinated, and my father paused here to let his revelations have their effect.

'Now it is obvious what has happened in Bob's case,' he went on. 'Bob was dealing with a ghost across the river, not a man. That is why he always became furious whenever anyone asked him questions or tried to help. It was taboo for Bob even to talk about the one we call Job. It is quite true that there were very odd sounds heard across the river on some nights when the moon was full, but this was ritual chanting in propitiation, not quarrelling. It was Bob appealing to his totem for protection.

'Finally, gentlemen, when one of these ghosts departs, he doesn't die in the real sense, he simply replaces himself with a tree or a fox or something unknown. It is then absolutely vital that the ghost, the dead body if you like, is hidden so well that nobody can find it, and no trace is left of any kind. Nor can it ever be mentioned or talked about. If this taboo is broken it can mean death.'

Again my father interrupted himself, shuffling some papers, pushing his hands into his hip pockets and looking at the ceiling. He knew what he was doing because there wasn't a sound in that courtroom. He went on looking at the ceiling even as he addressed the jury.

'So you can see, gentlemen, why I am asking you to accept the truth of Bob's belief that nobody lived across the river, that he had no brother, never saw anybody over there and cannot explain or deny any accusations about him. He could never have killed the ghost, because the taboos in Bob's culture about touching or hurting ghosts are even stronger in Bob's eyes than murder is in ours. So, gentlemen, I ask you to judge this case by the laws and beliefs of the true natives of this country, and accept the fact that there never was anybody across the river, and that Bob was telling the truth when he denied all knowledge of anything that happened across the river. Because nothing happened. Nothing at all. A ghost simply departed, and that is the truth of the matter ...'

Again there was silence, but what was more important nobody laughed. In fact it took the jury no more than fifteen minutes to reach their verdict, and it is anyone's guess why they did reach their verdict. Was it my father's advocacy that convinced them? Was it their instinct for natural justice? Or was it the inexplicable Australian sense of humour which persuaded them to declare Bob 'not guilty'. Most likely it was the latter. In any case my father was sure of the verdict before it came in because he knew his countrymen very well, however English he thought he was.

In the years that passed my father considered the case to be one of those that were hardly worth remembering. It had been too easy. But the town was left with its curious legacy. A few weeks after the case was over a blacksmith named Peter Wallace was fishing one moonlit night in the patch of bush across the river and he came back in a panic to his wife and neighbours swearing that he had seen a ghost over there, the ghost of Job the blackfeller.

The town took it in good spirit and it was something of a joke at first. But a few months later two schoolboys camping by the river said they had seen a black man, a ghostly figure in war paint, running along the river bank. Then the ghost moved into town and Job was seen by two teenage girls coming home late one night from a party. He had leapt (floated, they said) from a big peppercorn tree in a dark corner of the town. He was seen again, dancing madly, by an old woman who lived alone in a tumble-down shack by the railway station. And, as the years passed, Job was seen regularly once or twice a year by someone or other until he became known as an old familiar, as the highly reputable ghost of St Helen.

But one thing always puzzled me. About ten years ago I asked my father exactly who had told him about madmen being ghosts, taboo to touch or recognition in aborigine beliefs.

'Well,' he said, 'I knew that all aboriginal culture was ghost-ridden. That's a fact, and old Queen Aggie confirmed it. I also knew that Job was probably mad. So it seemed logical that Bob's behaviour was based on a taboo of ghosts and madness of some sort.'

'But you didn't really know.

'Nonetheless it was the only explanation because it made sense. It was the inner logic of the case.'

So my father had really invented the whole story of the ghostly taboo, however logical he said it was. What threw further doubt on it for me was the fact that a couple of weeks after the case Bob turned up at our back door one night with a spear and a throwing stick and a boomerang. He said, 'These are for you, Mr Quayle,' and left without saying anything more.

I knew they were Job's, and I knew that if my father's story had been true Bob would have buried the weapons with the ghost, since they were sure to be as taboo as Job himself. Those old weapons hung in our hall for many years and I don't know what happened to them. I don't even know what eventually happened to Bob. In fact the only memory that remains to this day is the memory of Job himself – the black ghost of St Helen, who will go on haunting the town long after the rest of us are dead and buried and ghostless in our graves.

GILES GORDON

Mask

He put on the mask.

> She said : I recognized you.
>
> He said : You did?
>
> She said : I recognized you.

Spoken in the present tense as well as in the past, the two in one, combined. An eternity of meaning, the future held as well. A future.

With his hands, he'd placed the mask in front of his face. Mask, hands, face.

He'd found it on a cushion on the couch in the living room for what purpose he knew not, nor for whom. It wasn't his mask, hadn't – as far as he knew – been made for him, his face, to fit his face, to go in front of it. Wasn't a likeness he recognized. The features on the mask – eyes, nose, mouth and so on – did not relate to his life. Certainly not a mirror image, or anything approaching one, nor a face he knew or could remember or was attracted by. If a face at all, with the eyes being black holes, holes seen through black, and the mouth likewise, and no nostrils in the nose shape, where the nose should have been. Little chance of the mask surviving, as a face. Little flesh and blood there, in its two-dimensional form.

Idly he'd picked it up, off the cushion on the couch in the living room.

Stood there, looking at it.

O oracle, he thought. Could you change my life?

His mind, his thoughts, dreamed, faded away, time went slow, slower, slowest, slowly and slowly. Which is to say: time went fast and he was not conscious of it. It overtook his watch, his daily relationship with the hours, minutes, seconds.

The mask was on his face.

What?

He'd placed it there, himself.

Did it change him, transform him? He felt no different; not that he knew what he felt before or after, or at the time. Did people know what they felt as opposed to others – psychiatrists, psychologists, relatives, friends, lovers – telling them what they felt, what they should feel? When asked, which he as everyone sometimes was: How are you? he would think: I am; and beyond that not know.

How are you?

I am.

Sometimes he wasn't even sure that he was, beyond the organism, the standing, wasting body. If he were to hold a loaded pistol to his head, near to the eye, the edge of the head, the side of the face, the brain, and fire, the bullet entering the brain from such close proximity to the outside world and the end of the barrel of the weapon, he doubted whether his life would be altered at all, one way or another, beyond his having to wipe the gunpowder dust from his skull, around where the bullet entered and passed through, made a hole in his flesh.

Was he more real or less real with the mask on?

I must look in the mirror, he thought. See if I can see myself. Find myself in the room, behind the mask. And he remembered on which wall the mirror was, and thought he would walk over to it.

A voice. She said: I recognize you.

She began to walk towards him – no, was already walking towards him – wearing an immaculate gown, whether of the evening or the night he didn't know but it was not of the morning, nor of the afternoon. Grey satin, from the shoulders to the ground, pearls round the neck, hanging down in an arc, almost a circle, a string of them. She looked . . . radiant, serene, exotic. Words such as those. She was unattainable but real, from the real world, therefore attainable.

She said : I recognized you.

You did? he said, expressing satisfaction as much as surprise; and she smiled.

He knew the face, yes, he'd seen it, hers, but did he recognize her, know her? Was it that they'd been in the same room now for four seconds, five seconds, since she'd said to him : I recognized you, and he'd replied : You did? Maybe they'd been in the same room for much longer but he had not seen her until she'd spoken. He'd heard her before he'd seen her, too.

I recognized you, she said.

You did? he replied.

Had they been lovers? he wondered. Was that possible? Otherwise how would she have known his features through the mask, the face beyond? Had she seen him put on the mask, his face move into it? Had she been in the room before him, observing from behind a substantial piece of furniture, substantial enough to have allowed her to stand behind it, at the side of it, to see and observe without herself being seen and observed? She might not even have found that necessary, he thought, thinking that he hadn't looked around the room when he'd walked into it. He hadn't expected to find her there, of course he hadn't. He hadn't searched the room for malingerers or aliens, mice or rats under a couch or chair or table, let alone his nearest and dearest. Anyone, anybody; woman or man; and she was indubitably woman.

She walked towards him, three or four steps she took, gestured a little with her hands, a slight sense of movement, of the fingers of the hands having lives of their own, yet an affirmation of her physical identity rather than merely a vague fluttering of fingers.

I recognized you, she said.

He wondered if she had recognized his face, the mask, or him below and behind the mask, the body beneath. Did the mask change the proportions and identity of the body? How strange if it did, he thought.

You did? he said, smiling slightly, a little fear behind the smile, wondering why, why she had said that, that she had recognized him. Had she mistaken him for another? He wasn't aware that he was in disguise, hiding either from himself or from her. He happened to have seen the mask lying on the couch and he'd placed it in front of his face. Mask, hands, face.

It was, in a way, an unusual mask in that its features weren't especially grotesque, there was no element of caricature – no big hooked nose, nor giant bulbous lips, nor gaping eyes, nor wild frizzy hair. It was just a mask, a different face, perhaps a little older than his own but he occasionally wondered whether his face was or seemed older or younger than his body was, and his mind; whether the features of his face, the aspect of him the world saw, seemed younger or older than the years he had lived, the years he had lived through, the years of his life.

She came towards him, in the living room.

I recognized you, she said.

Maybe she had put the mask there, on the cushion on the couch for him to discover, and that was how she had recognized him, from the mask and not from the face beneath. She'd known that he would put it on, that no one else could or would if there were others in the house at the time. There were no other echoes, no other voices that he could hear. Maybe she had laid a kind of trap. But why could that be, why should she want to do that to him?

I recognized you, she said.

You did? he said, either in reply to her or spontaneously, because he wanted to say what he did.

They walked towards each other. She first, she had been walking as she spoke. Then he walked as he spoke but she had begun before him, speaking and walking, hers the initial physical approach.

The thought occurred to him: Could she be wearing a mask? Was that her game, was that the idea? But why should she be doing that? Did she want him to think of a new person, or remind him of an old? Did she want him to think her a different age from what she was? Younger presumably but not necessarily, children played games with masks but nothing about her looked childlike. Her face was familiar, known, but he felt that he hadn't looked at it properly, that it wasn't possible to look at it properly.

When do you know a face? Hers was reminiscent of another face that had once been properly looked at, once had been more familiar to him, touched, yes, that he had touched with skin of his, flesh of his.

What? he thought. Steady on. You don't touch masks, not intentionally, not the way he was thinking, remembering, trying to recollect. The feel of a mask is not the same as the feel of a face, however soft the mask, however weather-blasted the face.

I recognized you, she said.

You did? he said, and there was little space in the room between them, little floor and carpet.

Suddenly something changed, shifted, altered. He was afraid. Had fear. She had recognized him, and he knew what she was going to do, what she was doing. She was coming towards him, was little distance from him and was not stopping, was not slowing down although she was moving at an even, regular, reasonable pace, not rushing like a whirlpool. And he was approaching her. He was not stopping either, or preparing to do so.

He knew what she was going to do.

She was going to walk through him.

Through him? How could that be? He was solid, wasn't he? Flesh and blood and a lot of bones, components that put together in a particular order contribute towards the making of a man. And he, he realized, was having difficulty in stopping, he was walking towards her and he would walk into her if she didn't stop. There was little distance between them, three or four feet. She kept on coming and so did he, towards her. Why didn't it occur to him to stop, he wondered half-consciously. Then: not that it should occur to him to stop but that he should stop; that no thought should have to be taken. The stopping before the bodies met each other, struck, should be obvious, instinctive, a matter of self-preservation on each of their parts.

Was she drawing him to her? Was that it? No, it wasn't possible. He was a free agent. Was he drawing her towards him? He dismissed the idea.

I recognized you, she said.

But I'm not wearing my own face, he said. I'm wearing another face.

He began to explain, that he'd found the mask on the couch, that he had not known how it had got there, that he'd tried it on, and was looking for the mirror to see how it looked, how the mask changed him, when he'd become aware of her, heard her voice; but not, he realized but didn't say, her feet, not even the rustle of her dress, the movement of the magnificent grey, or the pearls round her neck, or her body beneath and within the finery.

Then they froze, each stopped simultaneously. They held the positions they were in, or were held.

She said : Another face? questioning his remark or reinforcing it; by repeating what he had said endorsing its validity.

Had he two faces? In that sense : was she wearing another face? An intriguing thought, to him if not to her, although he didn't feel particularly intrigued by it.

She said, the words coming out but her lips not being seen by him to move :

If you're wearing another face –

He interjected, snappily :

– A mask, and there was frustration, anxiety in his voice, as if the events or event in which he was participating had nothing to do with him, were beyond his control and responsibility.

She went on, not appearing to have registered his interruption :

If you're wearing another face, does it mean that you don't recognize those you know when wearing your other face?

Mask

He was puzzled, didn't understand, even wondered if she meant him to understand. Was she deliberately trying to confuse him, unsettle him?

She said: You don't know me, do you?

How could he say, how could he answer that? How could he try to explain, that he did and he didn't, that now that he knew what she looked like he couldn't tell how he'd known her in the past – if he had – that he'd put on the mask to try to escape from . . . but that must have been rationalization after the event, during the event, in the act of putting the mask on.

Mask, brain, hands, face.

He hadn't known the mask would be there, hadn't thought of it, imagined it into existence. It was not something he'd ever thought about, wanted to escape or vanish into.

Know you? he said.

And added in his mind: I know you. I can see you. We're here together in this room at the same time. That is all we can be certain of. That is all I can be certain of. He thought this in his mind but said, simply:

Know you?

As if anyone could ever know anyone, which he believed or didn't believe depending upon the person, the other person and himself. Her dress was very beautiful, at any rate.

She was coming towards him and he couldn't, didn't stop, he couldn't stop going towards her, and all this, all this, happened in a very few seconds, in real time and out of time, the clock stopped – an eternity between each second – and continued, advanced, unable to be put back, deflected.

And they knew each other.

(I recognized you.

You did?)

Must have done because her face was at his, close to his, their lips were together, their lips had met and they must have recognized, and they grunted, groaned and made erotic, satisfied sounds, and down below whimpered within like babies in their sleep, floating messages to the conscious world, and sometimes muttering special words: Darling; and: I love you;

and they'd known each other for ever, for as long as life was to each of them, and she said:

I recognized you; and he said:

You did?

And they parted, their lives gone, their lips and their bodies, and she walked away, as she had come, she walked away from him and he hadn't seen or heard her turn, didn't hear her moving away from him, leave the room, and he looked at her to speak again, to say something more, to explain and discover but she was not there, not that he could see, he couldn't find her. Maybe, he thought, she's hiding behind a piece of furniture. A game. A trick. She's good at those. I think.

He couldn't see her any more. Worse still, he couldn't remember, a second or two after he lost her, what she looked like although he'd held her, no, she had held him, they had held, been held. He couldn't discover her in the room, from where he stood, and he looked about the room with his eyes, and he knew there hadn't been time for her to go, space in which she could have left, removed her physical presence from the room and from him. No one had gone out of the door.

I recognized you, she said, had said.

He knew, he'd heard it, and her body had come to his, her face, her lips, and she had gone through him. And he had known that she had recognized him and he said, he had said:

You did?

But he didn't know if she had, or if he had recognized her.

He looked down at his hands and lifted them to his face to remove the mask, yes, that was what his hands were doing, what his mind, his brain was telling them to do, told them, and his body was co-ordinated, the hands were lifting themselves up to the face to remove the mask, his hands to his face. He knew that, understood as much.

To remove the – what? There was no mask there, just the feel of his face but it wasn't precisely as he remembered it, the feel of his face, and he stumbled to the mirror, he found the mirror, had no difficulty in locating the area of wall on which it hung and he looked at the glass and the glass was there and it wasn't a window, he didn't see through to the other side, to the beyond and another life, the lives of others. He looked in the mirror and saw, understood that it wasn't a mask, no, it wasn't a mask, it was his face, a flesh face but it was not his, not his face on his face, oh God he'd lost that, it was the mask, the face of the mask he had been wearing but this was no mask, it was the face that had been on the mask, that had been the mask and now was his face, surmounting his body and she had known, recognized, it was the face she had desired and he had to find it before finding her and having found it he had to find her to discover who or what he was or had become, for him to realize himself, and all this had happened, and he ran screaming, screaming from the room, a great shiver of fear in the hollow of his stomach.

Fear that he wouldn't be able to find her again.

And a greater fear that he would.

On a cushion on the couch in the living room otherwise empty of people was a mask.

It bore his face. The features that had been his.

SARAH LAWSON

Springtime at Kraznau

At the University of Kraznau the spring comes late but beautifully. The climate in the foothills around Kraznau seems to hold its breath during March and April, as though willing time to stand still. If it snowed in February, then why not in March? If in March, then why not in April? If in April, then why not in May? Eventually this stasis has to stop, and usually in late May spring gains the upper hand. During the year I spent at Kraznau the sheer freshness of the spring lasted all through June, at the latter end of which the students took their exams.

As a visiting lecturer in English philology, I administered exams to my small group of students in one of the dingy rooms allocated to the English Department, but students in the larger departments took their final exams in the Rectorial Hall. The Rectorial Hall was a magnificently baroque room with chandeliers; mounted on the walls were the coats of arms of the noble students at the University of Kraznau (founded 1609), the largest of which was that of Crown Prince Karel, who matriculated in 1694. (The last coat of arms belonged to the Duke of Willemar, who left without a degree in 1927.) The Rectorial Hall was at the top of a flight of stone steps leading up from the principal quadrangle, the Rectors' Court. The broad flight of stairs was crowded with apprehensive students during much of June, but at other times it was almost deserted.

The steps led only to the Hall, and except for exams the Hall was used only for grand University occasions, like the reception of some dignitary, or a lecture by a new professor in classics, or graduation ceremonies. Whatever the great Rectorial Hall had been built for, it was now the ironically grand setting for a month-long scene of anxiety as the students struggled to introduce some kind of coherence into their new knowledge.

I think most undergraduates feel a thrill of nervousness when the doors of the examination room open and they must enter, find a seat, then learn the worst and begin constructing their answers. Most undergraduates can cope with the anxiety and nervousness; some find it a considerable ordeal; a very few cannot tolerate the strain. My own students that year at Kraznau bore up to my exams with good humour. I assured them that there would be no alarming surprises among the questions. I advised my advanced class to have a particular understanding of strong verbs, the Great Vowel Shift, and Verner's Law. Most of them took this sound advice and did well in their examinations – or 'completed high' as they would say.

The English Department staff was fairly evenly divided between men and women – a refreshing change from my home university, which I represent on the council of the British Union of University Women. I got on fairly well with all the staff, but Ludmilla became a special friend, and we always had lunch together in the refectory. One day over tea with some dried lemon peel in it she was telling me about another lecturer, Vaclav, who was about to have a monograph published on *Piers Plowman*. Then she said that for the next week she would have to help invigilate examinations in the Rectorial Hall. As a visiting lecturer I was not expected to take part in these duties, but Ludmilla had to do her stint, even during examinations in other subjects.

'There is a table on a raised platform, but it is rather bad form to sit there, or any other place, while an examination is in progress,' she said. 'I have received several pages of instructions about it, and we are to keep moving about slowly among the rows of students. In fact, it is allowed to stand, rather than always to walk, but that is the ideal, you know. Can you meet me at the Rectorial Hall at lunchtime? I shall have to stay there until shortly after one o'clock in order to sign a statement saying that nothing untoward has occurred during the examin- ation and that those who are to take up the examination scripts have arrived and have taken charge of the Rectorial Hall. Or, if something untoward *has* happened . . .'

I saw that Ludmilla was becoming enmeshed in a para- graph of some subsection of her instructions. I agreed to meet her at the Rectorial Hall during the next week.

When I first arrived at Kraznau the instructors in English had welcomed me warmly, if slightly defensively. I suppose they were afraid I would ferret out any little lapses in syntax and expose them to ridicule. In fact, I was inclined to be impressed by their fluency and general command of colloquial English. But Ludmilla, at our first meeting, had taken me warmly by the hand and had said, 'I am so happy to meet you!' And then she had taken me on a tour of most of the university. We passed a clock tower which she told me had been the gift of a certain nobleman in the 1630s. It was also she who pointed out the coats of arms in the Rectorial Hall of Crown Prince Karel and the Duke of Willemar. She said then that she had taken her turn as an invigilator of examinations there for the past three years.

'It is very draughty,' she had told me. 'The windows do not fit very well against the frames. The lighting is quite good, at any rate, because then all the chandeliers are turned on. Almost 500 students can take their examinations here at one time. I have invigilated examinations in law, philosophy and science. It is preferred that invigilators be taken from faculties other than the ones in which the examinations are. In that way the invigi- lators remain disinterested and there is no chance that they might help a student unfairly.'

On Monday of that week I met Ludmilla at the door of the Rectorial Hall. Most of the students had left, the Examinations Committee had arrived with envelopes, string, and sealing wax to take possession of the exam books, and Ludmilla had signed a statement along with the other seven invigilators saying that the exam had been orderly and routine. She came forward from the clump of officials and greeted me with a cordial smile. 'I am ready for lunch!' she announced emphatically. She was a solid but not stout person; she ate well, but she also fenced, swam and played squash. Calories came and went without pause. At the refectory she had large helpings of potatoes, stew and bread. As always at lunch, we chatted about how we had spent our morning. I told her I had been marking some papers for my one class in literature.

'There were medical students today,' she said. 'I have never had medical students before. It was so warm in the Hall that we had to open some of the windows.'

'Did you have to report that?' I asked.

'No,' she said, 'that doesn't count as an unusual incident. The eight of us agreed that it was not necessary to mention it.' Ludmilla took a bite of bread. In a moment she said, 'But, you know, there was one odd thing. A student asked to move to another seat, and since there was an empty seat near by, I moved him to it. He seemed satisfied with the second seat, but I cannot imagine what was wrong with the first one. It looked like all the other seats. The bench was not loose; the desk was not uneven or difficult to write on. I didn't mention that on the statement at the end of the period.'

I could see she was a little worried about it. I thought it was nothing to worry about. The trivial bureaucracy at the University of Kraznau has to be experienced to be believed.

'No, of course not,' I said. 'I shouldn't think a thing like that would be worth mentioning. Students can be hypersensitive at exam time. He may have just felt like sitting somewhere else.' I shrugged to show how inconsequential it probably was.

'The student did not tell me exactly why he wanted to move, but he seemed quite anxious to change his seat.'

'Well,' I said, 'as long as he was marked present on the

attendance sheet, the actual place where he sat probably doesn't matter.'

'Oh yes,' Ludmilla said, finally smiling, 'I had just taken the attendance on my side of the room – seats 1 to 248 – and therefore his seat did not really matter. I don't think it really mattered.'

'No,' I said.

'He seemed very worried,' she said a moment later. 'Quite *worried*, in an odd way, as though he were afraid I might not allow him to move – as though it were of very great importance to him.'

Just at that moment Dr Bielsky joined us. He was the University librarian and another particular friend of mine, because he was interested in improving the library's collection of English-language books and wanted me to advise him on acquisitions. Dr Bielsky was ordinarily a very cheerful person, and today he was even more cheerful, because he had scored some sort of obscure coup in the context of the library; perhaps he had found another table for the reading room. He asked how Ludmilla was and how I was and how our colleague, Wenzel, was. Ludmilla mentioned her invigilating duties in the Rectorial Hall for the anatomy exam that morning, and Dr Bielsky's interest seemed out of all proportion. I wondered if he rather fancied Ludmilla. He was enthralled by the information about the windows, spellbound by the narrative of the student who wished to move.

I met Ludmilla again on Tuesday, and as we walked towards the refectory she told me that on the previous afternoon another student, and that this morning a third student, had asked to move. The third time it had happened she had realized that all three students had been sitting in the same seat.

That morning she had looked carefully at the seat to see what could be wrong with it. The desk and bench looked exactly like all the others. As she stooped down to look under the desk she rested her hand on top of it. It was surprisingly cold to her touch. She felt the desk next to it and found it warm by comparison. There was no noticeable air current near this desk, in spite of the draughtiness of other parts of the room. Thoroughly puzzled by this piece of furniture, Ludmilla sat down on the bench and rested her elbows on the desk.

'I felt terribly cold and . . . nervous – rather anxious. I felt a kind of dread – and always this inexplicable coldness,' Ludmilla said.

We had by now reached the refectory, where we took our place in the queue. Ludmilla took her duties seriously, but I could scarcely imagine her being really anxious or afraid. I had sometimes even been struck by her casual fearlessness. For example, there was the night of the storm. It was raining stair rods and a gale was blowing. We were sheltering in a doorway of the Arts Faculty quadrangle waiting for it to clear up enough for us to walk home. There was a loud crash from a lamp standard which had blown over. Just when I was deciding to spend the night in my room, Ludmilla laughed. 'What are we waiting for?' she said. 'We can only get wet, and we won't blow away – or not far. We'll always be stopped at the frontier!' She laughed merrily and strode out into the rain and wind. In the circumstances there was nothing I could do but follow her. It took us almost an hour to get home, and I was thoroughly exhausted at the end of it. We couldn't even talk because of the wind. When we reached my door she just squeezed my hand and then went on to her own house. The next day there was no wind at all.

We had scarcely taken our trays and found a seat when Dr Bielsky appeared. He sat down beside Ludmilla and asked how the morning had gone in the Rectorial Hall. He kindly spoke in English for my benefit. Ludmilla told him about the strange bench and desk.

'I cannot explain how unpleasant it was,' she said. 'I had a terrible feeling – I felt as though something horrible were about to happen. I felt as though the ceiling were going to fall on me or as though the floor were going to give way under me. I jumped up from the desk immediately. No wonder those three students wanted to move! I know I should report this, but I don't know what to say. How can I explain it?'

'I should like to see this desk and to touch it,' said Dr Bielsky. 'May I come to the Rectorial Hall this afternoon?'

'Yes,' said Ludmilla, 'but you must leave when the examination begins.'

We finished our stew and then we all three returned to the Rectorial Hall. It was unlocked and Ludmilla took us in, switching on the electric chandeliers at our end of the Hall. The seats had been laid for the afternoon's exams with a grey answer book and a sheet of blotting paper on each desk. Ludmilla took Dr Bielsky and me to a desk marked with the figures 187 on the top. It was four or five rows in from the centre aisle and one or two seats in from the back wall of the Hall and the great double doors by which we had entered. Just as Ludmilla had told us, it looked exactly like the adjoining seats 186 and 188, and to each side, 176 and 197. Dr Bielsky placed the flat of his hand on seat 187, looked at it expectantly and then looked away. He touched the next desk with the fingertips of his other hand. I also put one hand on 187 and the other on 176. I couldn't feel any difference in temperature. Even when we assured her that we could feel no difference, Ludmilla still declined to touch the desk again. When Dr Bielsky sat down on the bench of 187, Ludmilla turned away.

'You don't feel anything unusual,' she asked.

'No,' said Dr Bielsky.

'Nor do I,' I admitted.

Ludmilla seemed relieved but slightly annoyed. She naturally wanted us to understand what she had experienced. I even sat down at the desk, half hoping to have some peculiar sensation, but even auto-suggestion could not make me feel any change in temperature. The other invigilators were arriving and the rest of the lights were being turned on. In another few minutes the students would be allowed in.

'The examination this afternoon is in endocrinology,' Ludmilla said, as Dr Bielsky looked round the room, studying the windows and pillars, the floor and the other seats.

When the students came in there was a rush of low talking and footsteps. The expression on Dr Bielsky's face changed so

...enly that I instinctively looked round to where he seemed
be looking, but I could see nothing. He uttered an exclama-
tion and said, 'The desk is growing cold!'

Ludmilla and I both touched it, and it *was* colder than
before, colder than the surrounding desks. Dr Bielsky looked
thunderstruck. A student then approached to where we three
were leaning upon her desk, as though engaged in an impromptu
séance. She stopped a few feet away and we slowly backed off
from the desk. Before Ludmilla could say anything the student
sat down and began to arrange her pens and a ruler in the
groove at the top of the desk. She suddenly stopped and looked
up, frowning. Ludmilla stepped forward and asked, 'Would you
like to change to another seat?'

Instead of answering, the student sprang up, swept her pens
off the desk and moved to the seat Ludmilla indicated. Dr
Bielsky then tentatively sat down at the desk. He stayed there
for almost a minute while Ludmilla and I watched. Then
he quite deliberately got up.

By this time most of the students had taken their places, the
seal on the question papers had been broken, and the invigilators were laying the papers on each desk, face down. 'You
must leave now,' Ludmilla whispered to us. We left through
the double doors just as the chocks were being taken away and
the doors were about to swing shut.

Outside on the marble landing I wanted to ask Dr Bielsky
about the desk. Before I could, he said, 'Let us talk about this
affair of the desk. I want to show you something. Come to my
office in the library.'

As we walked through interconnecting courtyards to the
library Dr Bielsky told me about a manuscript he had cata-
logued. 'It was in the estate of a former student who died last
year, leaving his books to the university library. God knows
where he got it. It was a diary of a student who matriculated
here in 1721. I have been trying to find out more about him,
off and on, for much of this spring. His name was Bruno von
Hrady.'

Dr Bielsky's office was a cramped little room reached by

marble stairs which steadily became less magnificent as we neared the upper floors. Here he showed me a well-preserved leather-bound book full of neat but unreadable handwriting. 'It is an excellent example of a fluent early-eighteenth-century hand,' Dr Bielsky said. 'This student, von Hrady, may have been a great, great, great, great grandfather or uncle of the man who bequested the diary to us. Probably more "greats"; I don't know how many. What interests me is this . . .' and he flipped through the pages. 'June of 1723,' he said under his breath. 'June . . . June. Here it is. Now. Now.' He was skimming the strange handwriting and slowly turning a few pages. 'Yes. The twenty-eighth of June. You see, von Hrady was still in Kražnau although he was not taking examinations. Most of the other students had left for the summer, but von Hrady had not yet gone home for various reasons. He seems to have ordered some books which had not yet come and also he had become ena-moured of a young woman in the town and was not eager to leave Kražnau on that account. Now, so,' Dr Bielsky paused. 'The medical examinations were under progress. Bruno von Hrady hears from his friend Wilhelm . . . yes, here :

I spoke to the Prussian, Wilhelm, this evening in 'The Little Goat' and he told me a strange tale. This afternoon during his examination in *materia medica* in the Rectorial Hall a student ran out before anyone could stop him, right in the middle of the examination! He shouted something in English and was out of his seat and through the doors in a moment. Wilhelm says it was someone called Tschadouik in the English Nation. I said I didn't know that there was an English Nation at Kražnau he said it was very small and that they are all in the Medical Faculty. So this Tschadouik ran from the room screaming. A second later they heard a clatter on the Great Staircase and then some muffled talking. Later they learned that Tschadouik had fallen down the stairs and broken his neck. He was as dead as a foot-stool. Wilhelm says he was a clumsy fool and probably tripped over his sword, which he insisted on wearing. By the time the others left the Rectorial Hall the body had been taken away and there wasn't even any blood. Old Klinger apparently says that this kind of thing is not uncommon and in his time there have been three suicides from the bell tower. *'Brüder, laßt uns lustig sein, weil der Früling währet!'* I will tell Maria this story; it will give her a good *frisson*. Again no books today. The devil take the bookseller!

'Now,' said Dr Bielsky, 'I have an intuition that these events are related. In about 1725 most Medical Faculty examinations were transferred from the Rectorial Hall back to the Medical Faculty. It is only quite recently that we have begun to use the Rectorial Hall again. I have been unable to discover why the examinations were moved in 1725, but it might have been because the Hall had a kind of . . .' – he searched for a word – 'a *Geist*, you know, a spirit of some sort. When I sat in that seat a most indescribable feeling came upon me – a feeling of fear and dread and *Angst* and great apprehension. I suspect it happens only when a medical examination is under progress. That is why the desk felt cold only when the students began to come in. There is something very strange about seat number 187.'

Dr Bielsky's manner was very reasoned and persuasive. I was inclined to think there might be something in what he said. The whole thing gave me a very eerie feeling for the rest of the day. I thought of the young English student, Chadwick, in 1723 falling down the Great Staircase and breaking his neck. He would have lain in a horrible twisted heap at the bottom until someone had come and bundled the body off somewhere. And now perhaps a presence of some sort lingered about the scene of this event. I was inexpressibly glad that I was not invigilating exams in the Rectorial Hall.

I was writing a few personal letters in my office when Ludmilla came in after the afternoon exams. She had a teapot in her hand, very full and very hot, I gathered from the way she held it. I got out some cups and saucers. 'Well, my friend,' she said, 'I shall be very happy when these examinations are finished.' She stirred some sugar into her tea and sat back in my easy chair. *'Very* happy.'

I passed on to her the story Dr Bielsky had told me. She

shuddered when I had finished and said, 'I would not be surprised if that was true. There is something very unusual about
that seat – number 187 – and this afternoon I thought the
whole vicinity of it was rather sinister. I walked past it a few
times in the course of my duties, and I found it quite unpleasant. I had little bumps on my skin – little bumps of
apprehension.'

'Goose pimples,' I said.

'Ah yes, "goose pimples",' Ludmilla said. 'Each time I
passed that seat.'

We drank our tea in silence for a while. 'Which exam is it
tomorrow morning?' I asked her.

'*Materia medica*,' she said.

'That's the one the English student was taking when he ran
out,' I said.

'Yes, I know.'

The next morning I unlocked my office door with the intention of parcelling up some of my books to send back to
England. I began taking some of the books off the shelves, but
I kept thinking about the *materia medica* examination in the
Rectorial Hall. Very soon I found myself locking the door
again and making my way toward the Rectors' Court. I stood
at the entrance of it, looking across to the Great Staircase. As I
glanced at the other sides of the quadrangle, who should I see
in the entrance at right angles to mine but Dr Bielsky! He saw
me at the same moment and I waved to him. We hurried towards each other and met midway on the old flagstones diagon-
ally opposite the Great Staircase.

'Dr Bielsky,' I said, 'you know that the examination this
morning is in *materia medica*?'

'Yes,' he said, 'I do. I'm afraid I suffer from great curiosity.
I felt compelled to come to the Rectors' Court, although I do
not think I would like to go into the Rectorial Hall.'

I was about to tell him that it was against the rules anyway,
when there was a loud noise as of a door slamming somewhere
near us. We both looked round, but could see nothing. The
sound seemed to be coming from the Staircase or the Hall,

but the big double doors were motionless. Again the sound came and again we could see nothing. Now the slamming was continuous, as though a heavy door was blowing violently to and fro in the wind. In a moment one of the big doors of the Rectorial Hall creaked open and an angry invigilator stepped out.

'Stop that!' the invigilator shouted at us and at the otherwise deserted quadrangle. He looked round sharply and stared at us. He smiled slightly and nodded, as though to exclude us from his angry outburst. He was still standing in the doorway holding one of the double doors slightly ajar when the door was thrown open violently and the invigilator pitched forward on to the stair landing. As he lay there, the second door opened wide and we heard the sound of running feet. They seemed to be scuffing over stone, taking short, quick steps. Then I heard an unusual sound – one I had not heard for many months. It was another English voice without a foreign accent.

'I can't do it! I cannot! I cannot! Oh God, I can't do it!' it said. The agony in the voice was indescribable. 'I can't do it! Oh God, I can't!'

The invigilator was lying curled up at the top of the steps with his arms round his head. He slowly slid down two or three steps and then clung to one of the massive stone balusters at the side of the Great Staircase. While the voice was still uttering its repeated cries, Dr Bielsky and I heard something soft bumping down the steps, interspersed with a metallic clatter. We looked at each other; it was Chadwick and his sword! The wail gradually died away, but the bumping continued, with its strange mixture of softness and clattering. In a moment it too died away and we felt a cold wind sweep through the Rectors' Court. In another moment there was an absolute silence, not even broken by the sound of breathing.

Dr Bielsky and I gingerly approached the Great Staircase and edged up to where the invigilator was still lying. He looked up and saw us and loosened his grip on the baluster. After staring at us blankly for another moment, he said, 'Something tried to push me down the steps. Something knocked me down and tried to push me down the steps!' He very slowly gathered his feet under him and stood up.

Ludmilla stepped out of the Rectorial Hall and came toward us. She asked what happened and we tried to tell her. The other invigilator was rubbing his back between the shoulder blades. Ludmilla nodded at everything we told her.

'I think,' she said, 'it is like a thunderstorm which is over. I notice that seat number 187 is of a normal temperature. I think it is finished – for this year.' And then, almost in the same breath, she turned to the young invigilator and added, 'We will have to write a report about this.'

MICHAEL VESTEY

An Apple for Miss Stevenson

They knew January was a bad month to go house-hunting but they had no alternative. They had already sold their own house. Kent looked more like the backyard than the *garden* of England. Still, the Sheldons reasoned, it was the same bleak landscape in all the Home Counties and it wouldn't put them off living in the country.

Phillip Sheldon and his wife Elizabeth were both Londoners but they had made their decision to move out, like so many young couples before them. They now felt strangers in the city, and they disliked the noise, the discomfort, the poor schooling, and the growing shabbiness. Besides, there were the children to think of, or, rather, their one child, a little girl of five called Emma. Far better for her to grow up in the country than the town.

That is how they came to be standing at the lichen-cloaked gate to Rose Cottage on the edge of a village in the heart of the Kentish hop fields. Phillip shivered in the coldness of the New Year. The sky was the colour of the wood-smoke that spurted from chimney pots in the village. The trees in the rambling garden were bent like arthritics in the sharp wind. Gamekeeper's weather, thought Phillip. He wondered if he would miss their warm, centrally heated, purpose-built town-house in the suburbs.

Elizabeth looked up at her husband and smiled. 'Well, it's big,' she said.

Phillip frowned. 'Yes . . . are you sure we've got the right place?' There was no For Sale sign evident. 'It seems too big for a cottage.'

Without knowing what the inside was like, Phillip felt instinctively that the house was a bargain. He looked down at the estate agents' particulars on a sheet of white paper flapping in his cold hands.

Elizabeth said: 'I'm amazed it hasn't gone before now. It must be awful inside.'

'Right, let's go in and see the dreadful truth,' he said, opening the gate and walking up the drive. Elizabeth was about to follow him when she felt her arm jerked backwards. It was Emma. The little girl stood firmly the other side of the gate. Her pale face could just be seen peeping through the hood of her black duffle coat and the thickly entwined scarf.

'No,' cried Emma. 'No.'

Phillip was halfway up the drive, unaware of his daughter's reluctance to follow him, when he suddenly realized he was alone. He turned, a tall, thin, pin-striped figure, wisps of dark hair blowing across his spectacles. 'Well, come on then,' he yelled, stamping his feet. 'It's chilly out here.'

'It's Emma,' his wife replied. 'She won't come.'

'Oh God! What a time to throw a tantrum,' muttered Phillip. She'd been so good on the journey down and even at the previous house they had viewed. He could see that Emma clearly did not want to budge. What he could see of her tiny white face was set hard with determination, an expression both he and Elizabeth had learned to identify. The last time she had behaved in this way was on her first day at school.

Elizabeth crouched and put her face close to Emma's. 'Darling, we won't be long, this is the last house we'll see today. And then we can all go and have tea somewhere. Won't that be nice?'

Emma's chin trembled and her face began to crumple. She started to cry.

Phillip became impatient. 'Can't she play in the garden while we're inside?' he shouted.

'No,' replied Elizabeth. 'If she's going to live here, then she must see it first.'

'Oh well, I'm going on. You join me later.' Phillip strode up towards the house which sat on a small hill at the highest point of the garden. Weeds sprouted through the worn gravel and scattered shingle of the neglected drive. 'The garden was once a feature of the house,' he said to himself, repeating the words in the brochure. 'Not any more it isn't.' He glanced at the thick bushes, matted together like uncombed animal fur, the deep-pile lawn which would take several mowings to recover its health, and the brambles snaking across what had once clearly been a vegetable patch. The summer would be an energetic time!

A few yards from the house he stood with hands on hips and looked it over. It was timber-framed and clad in white-painted weatherboarding, some of which was peeling. The window and door frames were painted black to provide a sharp contrast. Unpruned climbing plants covered the downstairs windows, making it impossible to see inside. There were solid brick chimneys at both ends of the house, between which the sand-coloured tiled roof gently undulated.

He turned the key in the lock and with some difficulty pushed open the front door. Inside it felt damp and almost colder than it was outside. He could smell the decay caused by the moisture in the floorboards and plaster. It came as no surprise to him. After all, the agents had made it clear the house had been empty for two years.

After passing through a small lobby he found himself in what appeared to be the main sitting room. It had wide, oak floorboards in reasonably good condition, and a huge inglenook fireplace, high enough for a man his height, six feet, to stand up in without bumping his head.

'Isn't it lovely?' said a voice behind him. Elizabeth stood in the doorway holding Emma by the arm. Neither parent noticed that Emma's face had turned a sickly grey.

'I don't know what's the matter with her. I had to promise all sorts of bribes to get her up here. There, Emma!' she said, tugging at the little girl's arm. 'What do you think?'

Emma stared with deep curiosity in the direction of the inglenook fireplace. She said nothing. Her parents shrugged, and moved towards the kitchen which turned out to be a high-ceilinged room with black-painted oak beams running from end to end. One side of the ceiling sloped downwards to follow the line of the cat's slide roof at the rear of the house.

Upstairs there were five bedrooms, including a small room in the roof. Elizabeth was attracted by the character of the house with its oak floors and beams; Phillip by the size of the rooms and the feeling of space in a house three hundred years old. An additional bonus was that he had bumped his head only once – on a low door frame.

'Yes,' Elizabeth murmured. 'We must have this.'

'Subject to survey and contract,' said Phillip, who, as a solicitor, was not going to allow sentiment to overwhelm him entirely. They both laughed. 'Come on, then,' said Phillip. 'Let's go back and make an offer.'

When they reached the front door they realized that Emma was not with them any more. They called out and listened. Not a sound, apart from the wind. Phillip became aware of how quiet it would be living there and he wondered, fleetingly, if he would be able to cope after the city.

'I'll go and find her,' said Elizabeth, moving towards the room with the inglenook. There she spotted Emma seated in the gloom of the fireplace engrossed in something, she couldn't see what.

'Oh, there you are, darling. Come on, we're off.'

Emma seemed startled. She glanced up at her mother, and in the poor light Elizabeth noticed a familiar expression of guilt on Emma's face. However, Elizabeth was anxious to return to the estate agents'. She held out a hand. Emma nodded, smiled and then skipped towards the front door. Surprised but also pleased at the sudden change of attitude in her daughter, Elizabeth said: 'That's better.'

At the estate agents', the senior partner Mr Wilcox showed little enthusiasm when the Sheldons told him they wanted to buy Rose Cottage. 'You *liked* it then?' he asked cautiously, seated behind his leather-topped desk.

Phillip nodded. 'It's got more than enough for a growing family, and bags of character, of course.'

'Yes, it's certainly roomy,' replied Mr Wilcox, unscrewing the top of his fountain pen. 'It was once a school, you know.'

'A school!' both exclaimed in unison. 'It's not that big, surely?' questioned Phillip.

'No, but it was big enough to be a small prep school. It was called St Anne's.' He smiled. 'Occasionally, the local vet and the supermarket manager stop and stare over the garden gate with nostalgic looks on their faces.'

Elizabeth and Phillip gave Mr Wilcox their full attention as he gave them a brief history of the house. It was a farmhouse until the turn of the century when it was bought by a wealthy widow who lived there until the outbreak of the Second World War. She sold it to two middle-aged sisters, Amy and Charlotte Stevenson, both spinsters who ran a prep school in Dover. Rather than risk the bombs, the sisters searched inland for suitable premises to house their school. That's how they found Rose Cottage, explained Mr Wilcox, though it wasn't called that then. Because of its size the school could cater only for about twenty-five to thirty pupils with a few boarders. In their spare time the sisters, both amateur horticulturists, transformed the garden from an ordinary patch of lawn and shrubbery into what Mr Wilcox fondly recalled as a 'scented paradise' of rare flowers and plants. 'It was lovely then,' he sighed.

'Pretty red roses,' said Emma suddenly.

Mr Wilcox glanced across at Emma who was sitting on a chair by the window. He seemed surprised. 'Yes, that's right, young lady. Miss Amy Stevenson's roses were famous in this area, especially the red ones.'

'I didn't see any roses,' said Phillip. Elizabeth shook her head.

Mr Wilcox laughed. 'All roses are red to children,' he said

with a chuckle. But when he had spoken the cheerfulness gave way to a frown.

'By the way,' said Elizabeth. 'What happened to the old ladies?'

'Ah, yes.' Mr Wilcox clasped his hands together on the desk-top, pursed his lips and squinted slightly through his spectacles. 'Well, they both passed on. Rather sad really; St Anne's became too much for them. In the last years they could manage only elocution lessons. That's when the school ceased and they called it Rose Cottage instead. First Miss Charlotte went, in hospital, and then Miss Amy, about a year later, I think. The house has been empty since then, as you could see from its neglect.'

'I'm surprised you haven't been able to sell it before now; it's not in that bad condition,' said Phillip.

Mr Wilcox agreed. After an initial hesitation he gave a short nervous laugh. 'Well, the fact is . . . I mean, I don't personally believe in these things myself but . . . well, some say the house is well, haunted.'

They both laughed. 'Haunted! I've always wanted to live in a haunted house,' cried Elizabeth, clapping her hands together with amusement.

'You didn't notice anything then?' Mr Wilcox asked almost timidly.

Phillip answered : 'Such as?'

'Well, I don't know. Some people who have been round it say the house has a definite atmosphere. In fact, to be quite frank with you, I showed a young couple like yourselves round it recently and afterwards they told me, and I quote, that it gave them the creeps. Couldn't see it myself but there we are. Before you decide you ought to talk to a neighbour, a retired doctor called Hadley, he's – '

'Well I don't think I'll bother with that, thank you,' Phillip interrupted sharply. 'Like you, I don't believe all that stuff.' He looked at his watch and said it was time they returned to London. He made an offer for Rose Cottage which was con-siderably less than the asking price. Even Phillip was sur-

prised when Mr Wilcox replied instantly and without thought :
'Accepted.'

'Don't you want to consult the vendor?' asked Phillip.

'No, it's an executors' sale. They've left it to me. Glad to get
it off the books, if you really want to know.'

As they drove back to London they said little, working out
in their minds their respective plans for Rose Cottage. As they
approached the yellow street lighting of the outer suburbs
Emma spoke for the first time on the journey. 'Some of the little
children brought red roses for the school and Miss Stevenson
put them in pots and they grew again in the garden. That's why
she had such lovely roses.'

'Oh really,' answered Elizabeth, preoccupied with wallpapers
for the upstairs bedrooms. 'Is that what Mr Wilcox told you?
What a nice story.' Her thoughts returned to the problem of
the main bedroom. It might have to be painted white, paper
might not go with oak beams . . .

As they slowed for traffic lights Phillip wondered what sort
of mortgage he would succeed in raising on such an old house.

The Sheldons were an efficient couple. As a solicitor he was
able to carry out his own conveyancing on the house. In the
meantime, she was responsible for organizing builders. She
made several trips to the house to supervise the work which was
duly completed a mere two weeks after the target date. After
staying with friends for a few weeks, they moved into Rose
Cottage.

This time, Emma displayed no reluctance to return to the
house; if anything, she seemed to look forward to it. She also
started at the village school.

About a fortnight later, on a cold morning in spring, over
breakfast in the warm kitchen, Emma said : 'Don't want to go
to school today.'

Phillip continued reading his newspaper, while Elizabeth
sewed a name-tag into Emma's coat. Emma sat at the table
pouting. Her rust-coloured hair that fell to her shoulders
gleamed in the weak sunlight from the kitchen window. She
repeated herself and finally elicited a response.

'Why not?' asked her mother, continuing to sew.

'Miss Stevenson told me not to,' came the brief reply.

'Who is Miss Stevenson?' asked Elizabeth, biting the thread with her teeth and wrenching away the loose end. 'There! That's another one done.' She held up the coat and admired her handiwork.

'Miss Stevenson lives *here*,' replied Emma impatiently. 'You know.'

'What on earth are you talking about, child?' said Elizabeth, taking an interest for the first time. 'A Miss Stevenson used to live here but she's, well, she went to heaven, didn't she?'

'No she didn't,' Emma shouted. Her face began to match the colour of her hair. She was normally quite pale. 'She didn't, she didn't, she's here!'

At last, Phillip lowered his newspaper. 'What's the matter with her now?'

Elizabeth put her arm around Emma's shoulders. 'Now, darling, you are going to school today, and that's that. I don't want to hear any more nonsense about Miss Stevenson. Has someone at school been telling you stories about her?'

A look of panic crossed Emma's face. She gulped, as if for air, jumped off her chair and ran towards the stairs.

'How extraordinary,' said Phillip, looking at his wife. 'Has she ever done that before?'

'No, not since her first day at that other school. What are we going to do?'

'Send her to school, of course. There's nothing wrong with her.'

Elizabeth thought for a moment. 'The trouble is, Phillip, she does seem to have a thing about this Miss Stevenson. I've heard her holding conversations with someone in her room, and sometimes by the fireplace in the sitting room.'

'Oh, all children do that,' said Philip scornfully.

'Yes, that's what I thought. But something's odd. She recited her two-times table the other day in her room. She didn't know I was listening the other side of the door. And she knows her alphabet, and I know for certain that she hasn't got round to these things yet at school.'

Philip wasn't convinced. 'It's play-acting,' he said, standing up. 'She just doesn't want to go to school. We'd better put a stop to it now.' He started to walk upstairs, beckoning Elizabeth to follow him.

The white-painted door to Emma's room was closed. Phillip was about to turn the handle when he heard a child's voice. He listened carefully.

Emma was saying: 'They told me I *had* to go to school.'

There was a long pause. Phillip and Elizabeth held their heads against the door as closely as possible without making a noise.

Emma began speaking again: 'No, I won't. I promise.'

Her parents heard a chair scraping across the floorboards, and then Emma spoke again: 'Once two is two, two twos are four, three twos are six, four twos are eight ...'

Phillip turned the handle and pushed his way into the room. Emma was sitting on the bed surrounded by exercise books. She held a pen in her hand. No one else was in the room. Emma smiled innocently. 'Hallo, Daddy, I'm just doing my tables.'

'Yes, so I can see. Now put your coat on and Mummy will take you to school.'

'But I'm doing my lessons,' replied Emma with a frightened look on her face.

Phillip advanced towards the bed, reached down and smacked Emma on the leg. 'You'll do as you're told.'

Emma began crying. 'Miss Stevenson said I wasn't to.' She put a hand up to her face as if to staunch the flow of tears.

Phillip knelt by the bed and said firmly: 'There is no Miss Stevenson any more, do you understand, Emma?'

Emma pointed to a chair by the window. 'That's Miss Stevenson,' she said, quietly sobbing. 'She teaches me things.'

Phillip got up and walked over to the chair. He swept an arm across the seat. 'There, you see, nothing. There is no one there. It's just pretend. Now do you believe us?'

Emma's eyes widened. 'She is there, she is,' she repeated.

Phillip was becoming exasperated. He looked at his watch. 'Damn! I've missed my train.' He wagged a finger at Emma. 'You are going to school if I have to drag you there.'

Emma stared fearfully at the chair by the window. She seemed for a moment to be filled with terror. She began gasping for breath, her tiny chest heaving as she fought for air. The whites of her normally grey-blue eyes bulged slightly and the colour drained from her face. To her parents' astonishment she began to convulse.

'Christ, she's having a fit,' yelled Phillip. He urged Elizabeth to run down the lane to fetch their neighbour, Dr Hadley. Meanwhile, Phillip tried to loosen Emma's jersey. She had successively gone white, yellow and purple. Now she was grey. Suddenly, he was pushed aside by a scruffily dressed man who stood over Emma and felt her pulse. She was still shaking but not so violently. Dr Hadley pulled a blanket over Emma, turned and said: 'I'll be downstairs to see you in a moment.'

Phillip and Elizabeth took the hint and went downstairs to the sitting room. After what seemed an inordinately long time – though it was only ten minutes – Dr Hadley joined them. He was wearing a worn tweed jacket, rough trousers and mud-stained boots. He was almost bald but had a pleasant weatherbeaten face and a friendly manner.

'You caught me gardening,' he said, as if reading their thoughts. 'She's all right now. She's asleep. Has she had fits for long?'

'Never,' replied Elizabeth.

'Any history of epilepsy?'

'Good heavens no!' exclaimed Phillip. 'Nothing like that.'

'We had a little chat before she went off to sleep,' said Dr Hadley.

'Did she mention how it all started?' asked Phillip.

Dr Hadley nodded. 'Very interesting, very interesting.'

'You don't believe all this nonsense, do you? Surely it's absurd to think this house is haunted by Miss Stevenson?' Phillip now seemed angry.

Dr Hadley smiled. 'Maybe, but I tend to keep an open mind.'

An Apple for Miss Stevenson

Phillip failed to notice this subtle rebuke and might have been rude had not Dr Hadley continued: 'You see, I knew Miss Stevenson well. She was a very strong-willed woman. If the house is haunted I can't say I'm surprised that it's her and not her sister. There are several people in the village who say they've felt her presence though no one has ever seen her – until now.'

Phillip was startled. 'So you do believe her?'

'I'm not saying that, but your daughter tells me she is here and that she gives her lessons. And there are one or two things she told me about the sisters that could only have come from them.'

'Such as, Doctor?' Elizabeth wanted to know.

'Well, Emma told me that there had once been a little girl at the school just like her, with red hair and even the same colour eyes. Indeed there was. I remember the girl quite well, I once gave her a jab for something or other. There's a quite astonishing likeness. Now, only Miss Stevenson could have told her that. She also mentioned a little boy who kept climbing the hop poles in the next field and how the farmer chased him away. Now that happened twenty years ago. Did you know any of that?'

Phillip was shocked for a moment. He glanced at Elizabeth who said: 'There was that story about the red roses, Phillip. Do you remember, in the car on our way back to London after we'd bought the house? I didn't think anything of it at the time but thinking back, how on earth could she have known about the roses?'

'The roses the children brought and which Miss Stevenson quickly re-potted and later planted in the garden?' asked Dr Hadley.

'Yes,' Elizabeth answered.

'They were famous for miles around, those roses. They came from the children of a local rose grower. Miss Stevenson couldn't afford to buy his roses herself, so she used the cuttings the children brought. She was no fool.'

Phillip now felt less certain about it all. He had never

believed in ghosts, and still didn't, but he was no longer quite so confident in his scepticism. 'If all this is true,' he said slowly, 'then Emma must have first met Miss Stevenson the day we saw over the house.'

'It does explain a lot of things we were too busy to notice at the time,' said Elizabeth.

After a pause, Dr Hadley asked: 'What are you going to do? These fits are no good for her at all.'

'Well, it seems to me,' replied Phillip thoughtfully, 'that we have three alternatives: we can move house; we can take her to a psychiatrist, or,' he paused for a moment, 'or, we can bring in an exorcist.'

Rather than uproot themselves again they decided to take Emma to see a psychiatrist in London. She spent three sessions with him, all of which failed to remove the notion of Miss Stevenson inhabiting Rose Cottage as a ghost. The psychiatrist said helplessly that he had never before met a child with such fixed ideas, and that perhaps Rose Cottage was haunted after all. He recommended an exorcist.

This led the Sheldons to their local vicar, a man brimming with sympathy, but offering little hope. 'I knew Miss Stevenson well,' he told them. 'A dear old soul. I can't believe she haunts the place, though I have heard tales, gossip, you know.'

When they persisted he agreed to ask a clergyman in another parish who specialized in exorcism. 'A clear case of possession by an evil spirit must be proved, though,' he warned. 'He'll also have to get the permission of the bishop.'

After the late, cold spring, summer eventually arrived. Phillip worked in the garden at weekends and evenings clearing the undergrowth, digging the vegetable patch and uncovering the famous roses. Phillip had to admit that in full bloom there were some magnificent specimens, Emma helped him sometimes as best she could. She had not been to school for two months. Illness had been the excuse. Now that it was summer she spent many days in a wild part of the garden that she called her own.

She had demanded that this area should be left untouched. The wild meadow grass grew high there and Emma could play in her secret garden without being overlooked.

Although Emma had not been to school she was still receiving an education. She allowed her mother to teach her at home but only those subjects not covered by Miss Stevenson.

Reluctantly her parents went along with this, fearful of another scene like that in the spring. But they found they were no longer sleeping as soundly as they did once. Elizabeth needed sleeping tablets for the first time in her life, and Phillip's work began to suffer.

On warm days Emma took her lessons with Miss Stevenson hidden from view in her own patch of the garden. This she would do punctually at nine with a break for lunch at twelve-thirty, returning to lessons at two until four o'clock. Sometimes Emma would take Miss Stevenson a small gift like an apple.

One morning, as Phillip was about to leave for the station, a letter arrived from the local vicar. He regretted that the bishop had refused permission for an exorcism as it was not felt that the little girl or the house were in any way possessed. Instead, he advised medical treatment.

Phillip slumped into an armchair. 'Well, that's it then,' he said dejectedly. 'We'll have to move again.'

Elizabeth agreed, and without Emma realizing, arrangements were made to put the house on the market. Two days later, Mr Wilcox arrived unexpectedly to view the house. They were surprised to see him as the intention had been to hide the visit from Emma. Mr Wilcox strode into the sitting room and gazed around him admiringly.

'You have done a lot to the old place,' he said with a broad smile. 'Country life too dull for you, eh?'

Before they could answer, Emma appeared at the doorway from the kitchen. Mr Wilcox grinned at her. 'Hello, little girl, I can't remember your name but I remember you very well. With that lovely red hair of yours.'

'Emma, say hello to Mr Wilcox,' said Elizabeth wearily, at the same time wondering how her daughter would react.

Emma said nothing but glared at Mr Wilcox who seemed taken aback by such obvious hostility. Phillip decided to tell the truth. 'Emma, you remember Mr Wilcox don't you? He sold us Rose Cottage. Well, now we've decided to move again, probably back to London. It will be fun to see your old friends again won't it?'

But there was no conviction in his face and Emma could see through it. After staring at nothing in particular in front of her for a few moments she turned on her heels and rushed from the room. They could hear her clumping upstairs.

Mr Wilcox tried to reassure. 'Moving always unsettles them at that age,' he said hastily. 'Now let's get down to –'

He was interrupted by a piercing scream from above, a cry that seemed far too loud and penetrating for a child of five.

'Emma!' shouted Elizabeth, and ran towards the stairs, followed by Phillip and Mr Wilcox. They found Emma screaming hysterically on the bed, turning and twisting her frail little body as if trying to wriggle free from some awful bondage.

'Oh God!' said Phillip, running a hand through his hair .'Get Dr Hadley.'

Mr Wilcox disappeared, and returned a few minutes later with the retired doctor who gripped Emma's shoulders and shouted : 'It's all right, you're not leaving here. Understand? You're not going away. You can stay with Miss Stevenson.'

Emma seemed, through her hysterics, to comprehend. Slowly, her body ceased its feverish activity; apart from an occasional twitch, she seemed to calm. Her eyes opened and to her parents, relief she managed a weak smile. She began sucking her thumb and turned over on her side. Within seconds she was asleep.

All four looked at each other. Mr Wilcox stood rooted to the spot, his face dripping with perspiration. They left Emma sleeping and crept downstairs. In the sitting room Dr Hadley apologized. 'I'm afraid it was the only quick way I could think of getting her to stop. I must confess I was surprised that it worked so rapidly.'

'But does that mean we can't move now?' asked Phillip, with a note of desperation in his voice.

'I'd leave it for a bit if I were you,' advised Dr Hadley. 'She might grow out of it, you never know.'

A day later, after much discussion, the Sheldons abandoned the idea of leaving Rose Cottage. They resigned themselves to their predicament. They would have to compromise. After breakfast, Elizabeth stood up, looked at her watch and said: 'Come on, Emma, you're late for your lessons. Miss Stevenson will be cross.'

GRAHAM LORD

A Child is Born at the Inn

Friday 19 April 1889

Finally entered Austria from Germany late yesterday, Thursday, crossing the border on the River Inn and taking a room here in the little Austrian town of Braunau-am-Inn at the guesthouse Gasthof zum Pommer.

Room comfortable enough, though hardly comparable with my room in Munich, and surprisingly chilly considering it is spring. Last night I swear the temperature dropped below freezing. I woke shivering and trembling in the middle of the night.

Also heard the sound of rats above my head. Tails slithering.

In addition, the human noise from the rooms above is a constant irritation; continual comings and goings; voices; activity; footsteps creaking and thudding across my ceiling even before dawn. A family of four appears to live permanently in the rooms above (a Customs officer, his wife, two young children) and I understand the wife is about to be delivered of another child very soon. In addition, their resident maid also lives upstairs, so no doubt the disturbances are unavoidable. I have asked the hotelier to move me to another room but it appears that there is none available, no further room at the inn. Indeed, the hotelier has made it exceedingly obvious that he considers me to be decidedly fortunate to find any lodging whatever since today is the first day of the Christian Easter celebration, Good Friday, and the town is filled with Christian revellers and relatives and natives who have returned to Braunau for the holiday. The hotelier (who is obviously no great lover of Jews) went so far as to stress that as a Jew I should be exceedingly grateful to find any lodging at all during this particular Christian festival.

I took his remark to be a warning and have decided to spend the day indoors. The Christian Good Friday is certainly not a good Friday for a Jew to venture out in a Christian community since so many Christians even now consider us Jews to be individually responsible for the crucifixion of their wretched Jesus-*bar*-Joseph more than 1800 years ago. They tend to overlook the fact that their wretched Jesus-*bar*-Joseph was Jewish himself, but I am not the man to remind them of the fact, especially on their Good Friday. They are quite illogical in their religious superstition : after all, is it not positively absurd of them to give the name 'Good' Friday to the day on which their god was killed? How can you reason with such people? I shall stay in my room to write up this diary, read, think, plan the next stage of my journey towards Linz and Vienna.

Later. A tedious day. I am restless and bored confined in this room, with nothing to do but scribble in this diary. Is it really necessary to hibernate thus, even in spring, or am I merely being over-sensitive and cowardly? I confess it is decidedly irritating to be recognized so constantly and so swiftly as being Jewish. Only too often Christian strangers appear to be immediately wary and suspicious of me as soon as they meet me without knowing anything of me whatever. They react like a cat smelling a dog. At times I have been tempted to announce loudly that although I have been cursed with an Hebraic nose (for which there can be no imaginable cure save for some fantastical surgical butchery) it is years since I entered a synagogue or attended to the mumbo-jumbo rituals of my fathers. Tonight, for instance, on the night of the Christian Good Friday and the eve of the Jewish Passover Sabbath, a *good* Jew would refuse even to write in his diary! As for the Christians, if their wretched Jesus returns again to earth (as they keep threatening he will) he had better ensure that he returns as something other than a Jewish carpenter on Good Friday. His followers would probably lynch any Jewish carpenter with hammer and nails in his hands on Good Friday.

It seems decidedly malicious of our mutual God that the most important annual festivals for both his religions should fall at the same time and yet inspire such irreligious hatreds and prejudices. Some Christians in Eastern Europe still suspect that during Passover/Easter Jews secretly re-enact the crucifixion of their wretched Jesus by kidnapping and killing Christian infants as a Passover sacrifice to Jehovah! Would you believe it! In this modern age, in 1889! Even in this very Austro-Hungarian Empire, no more than seven or eight years ago, some unfortunate Jew in Hungary was actually *prosecuted* for the ritual Passover murder of a Christian child. Tislár, I think his name was, or Tiszaeszlár, something like that. Eventually he was acquitted, of course, but his Christian tormentors still went as far as to torture a 'confession' out of the poor devil. And that was only seven or eight years ago, in Hungary. In the nineteenth century! It is scarcely credible! The whole ludicrous charade reeks of the Middle Ages, when they forced Jews to wear distinctive yellow badges.

Things are not that bad nowadays, of course, and Hungary is hardly comparable with this part of Bavarian Austria, but I still intend to hibernate in my room here for the whole day. If Christians wish to believe that I personally hammered the nails into their wretched Jesus-*bar*-Joseph more than 1800 years ago then they are welcome to their superstitious delusion. Despite the tedium, I shall remain in my room and write and read for as long as I am allowed by the dreadful racket going on upstairs, where the wife of the Customs officer is about to give birth not only to yet another child but probably, by the sound of it, to a whole cavalry regiment of the Austro-Hungarian Empire thundering across my ceiling. The racket they make upstairs rivals that of Pharaoh's horsemen or camel corps pursuing Moses and the Israelites as they escaped across the Red Sea!

Evening. A wearisome day, drawing at last to a close, praise be.

A curious coincidence: the Customs officer who lives in the rooms above me is the very Customs officer who examined my baggage yesterday at the Austro-Hungarian Customs post on the German side of the border before I crossed the river and entered Braunau. A self-important man aged about fifty, he seemed yesterday at his Customs post, probably easily angered and somewhat pompous and dictatorial, in his middle years and his ludicrous Imperial uniform of white breeches and plumed hat. I wanted to laugh aloud when I saw his bushy whiskers, for they are obviously modelled most meticulously on the whiskers of his stupid old Emperor Franz-Josef, and he carries himself as though he were a minor local celebrity. He was not, however, at all anti-Semitic in his treatment of me and his manner was perfectly proper and efficient if a trifle tetchy, even dogmatic (as you might expect in a man who is quite obviously of peasant stock but has managed to make his way in the world by his own efforts to a bureaucratic position of some local importance in a small town like Braunau). At least he treated me in a civil (if brusque) fashion, for which I should be grateful. Perhaps it takes a few years for fashionable Vienna opinions to reach such a far-flung outpost of the Austro-Hungarian Empire as Braunau. Indeed, the Customs officer even nodded at me in a curtly polite fashion when later we passed each other on the stairs last night (unlike the anti-Semitic hotelier who ignores me as much as possible and makes it plain that he considers he has done me a great favour by allowing me room at his inn at Easter).

I do wish, though, that the Customs officer were equally unprejudiced about the thundering feet of his family above my head. I slept badly last night and required a brief nap this afternoon.

A Child is Born at the Inn

It is late, almost midnight. At last I am weary enough for sleep.

At least the family upstairs is silent at last.

Uncannily so.

A moment ago I thought I heard a rat again above my head. I must brace myself to speak to the hotelier about it.

A distinct sound of a tail slithering across my ceiling.

Saturday 20 April 1889

A splendid day: so much so that I have decided to stay on here in Braunau for another couple of nights. I revelled in freedom after my self-imposed confinement. Perhaps the true appreciation of freedom requires some previous enslavement. I was even so bold this morning as to mention the possibility of rats to the anti-Semitic hotelier, who was not only civil enough to grunt that there were no rodents in *his* establishment but who even condescended to point out to me his three lean and hungry cats.

I must have heard something else trailing across my ceiling.

To start this splendid day I had an excellent night's sleep, even though my room was still startlingly cold for this time of year. Oddly enough the rest of the guesthouse appears quite warm and the chill affects only my own room. To enter it is to receive an icy blast. Curious, though there must of course be some scientific explanation. Perhaps my window faces north. Or perhaps it is affected by cold breezes off the lake. But at least the silence from the rooms above was long and deep throughout the night (almost uncanny, if I were of a super-stitious turn of mind, as though something important were about to happen) and I slept for nine hours and woke refreshed and full of energy.

The weather has been very fine and I ventured out with confidence and pleasure. It has been a delightful spring day, this Sabbath, and the Christians are much more relaxed on their Easter Saturday. After all, they expect their wretched Jesus to rise again from the dead tomorrow, so yesterday's grim mourning has given way to optimism and a mood of holiday cheerfulness. I did, however, take care to behave modestly and unobtrusively in public (with a nose like mine I certainly took great care to carry neither hammer nor nails!).

Braunau is a pretty little town on the edge of a small lake and I walked for hours. There are a surprising number of interesting sixteenth- and seventeenth-century houses and I entered two Gothic churches without hindrance (St Stefan's and the Spitalkirche). The town also boasts no fewer than *two* monuments commemorating the martyrdom in 1806 of the German nationalist Johann Palm, the Nuremburg bookseller who was shot by Bonaparte's French soldiers for selling patriotic German literature. Palm has become a local hero and a symbol of our growing sense of German unity and nationalism. I confess that as I stood before the larger of the two memorials I felt a tingle of German pride down my German spine to think that a humble Nuremburg bookseller should be prepared to defy the French dictator and his invaders and die for his proud belief in his own people and race. I too (like a steadily increasing number of German patriots) also dream of the day when the Fatherland will gather together into one glorious German Reich all the undoubtedly German peoples and provinces that are still at present ruled by foreigners (including this most Bavarian part of Austria). This ramshackle Austro-Hungarian Empire of Franz-Josef's must surely collapse one day soon, and with justice the twentieth century (how inspiring *that* sounds) will see the great work of Bismarck brought to its full conclusion, with a greater Germany rightly acknowledged in the forefront of the great united nations of the world.

Fortunately I was out and about the town for so long that I thankfully missed the greatest possible commotion in my room in the early evening. The noise there then must have been unbearable, for on my return to the guesthouse I discovered that at six-thirty this evening the wife of the Customs officer gave birth at last to her child in the room above mine. What a galloping about my ceiling there must have been! What a thundering of human hooves! What cries of pain and panic, the first wailings of the infant and the screechings of women!

A Child is Born at the Inn

I was so thankful to have been spared such torture that I repaired instantly to the tavern for a glass of wine. The tavern's atmosphere could hardly compare with the jollity of a Munich *Bierkeller* but still it was cheerful enough, for the Customs officer was there (amid a throng of admiring cronies) celebrating the birth of his child, a son, only an hour earlier. Gone was the choleric stiffness he had earlier displayed at his Customs post. Now his Imperial Franz-Josef whiskers positively *twitched* with homely pride, and his eyes gleamed with paternal exuberance. In his moment of pleasure I warmed to his simple humanity. Here was merely another man, despite his religion and his nationality. Already the wine had reddened his cheeks and his face gleamed in the glow of the gas-lamps and the crackling fire, and in his expansive mood I could see that he was popular among his intimates despite his earlier pride in his official position and his irritable peasant sense of inflated dignity.

'A boy!' cried one of his cronies. 'And on Easter Saturday too, Alois. It must be a good omen.'

Alois: there was something warming even about his name, and their merry mood infected me with pagan benevolence. Yes, I thought: a good omen, indeed; a Christian child born above the room of a wandering Jew at the Christian Easter and on the Jewish Sabbath; a pagan as well as a religious omen; a token of resurrection, a new rising, a rebirth. Indeed, there is symbolism everywhere if only one cares to seek it out. Tonight, for instance, is the first full moon of spring, the beginning of another cycle of seasons and hope. That, to me, is the real significance of Passover/Easter: they are both married to the gloriously pagan first full moon of spring. And even the name of Braunau the town itself derives from the word *Brunnenau*, 'a place with many springs'. Above my head, as I write these very words, there slumbers a child only a few hours old who symbolizes human hope, perhaps even a new tolerance between Christians and Jews. My room itself almost seems a little warmer than it has been for the last two nights.

Nonsense, of course. Ha! It must be the wine that has warmed me and made me so fanciful and sentimental. I confess I drank a little too much of it tonight, caught up in the celebrations of the Customs officer and his cronies. He spotted me soon after I entered the tavern.

'Ah!' he cried jubilantly. 'The Wandering Jew!'

But he meant it jocularly, without a sneer, simply a slightly tactless alcoholic jest, and I managed to laugh with him and he could not have been more civil.

'You shall drink with me!' he cried. 'Wine for my friend, Hans!'

'You are most kind,' I said, 'Herr – ?'

'Alois,' he said. 'Call me Alois. I have become a father again.'

'Many congratulations,' I said.

I hardly spoke to him again all evening, for he was surrounded by noisy friends and an interloper such as myself could not but feel somewhat excluded from such intimate merry-making. But later I purchased them all a bottle of wine to contribute to the celebration and he raised his glass at me and smiled and the warmth and jollity of the occasion, though hardly comparable with that of a Munich *Bierkeller*, still kept me far too long in the tavern no less than the prospect of returning alone to my chilly, empty room with the inevitable disturbances from above of a wailing new-born infant and the bustling feet of anxious women.

Instead I fell into conversation in the corner of the tavern with an elderly gentleman who seemed to pity my isolation and invited me to sit at his table.

'Forgive my presumption,' he ventured, after our first glass of wine together, 'but I trust you took no exception to Alois's little jest about the Wandering Jew.'

'None whatever,' I returned, silently admiring his perspicacity.

'I am pleased to hear it,' said the old gentleman. 'There are many of your faith who would have been quite rightly offended by such a thoughtless remark, but I assure you that Alois was simply attempting to be friendly.'

'Oh, certainly. Some of my fellow Jews are far too sensitive about such minor matters.'

A Child is Born at the Inn

'I commend your tolerance,' said the old man, 'though undoubtedly many of your race would be amply justified in taking offence at such a remark. It would be quite excusable considering the constant persecution of your people even in recent years. Indeed, it can scarcely be more than seven or eight years since the Russian riots and pogroms and the iniquitous legislation against Russian Jews.'

I did not welcome so serious a discussion in so cheerful an atmosphere, so I laughed dismissively and replied: 'The pogroms are over, sir. They were a dreadful aberration that will never be repeated. After all, the twentieth century is almost upon us. No civilized nation will surely ever again descend to such barbaric medieval persecution of the Jews.'

He stared at me with an expression that disturbed and then irritated me. 'I pray you may be right,' he said, 'but even here in Austria, and in Germany, I detect an undercurrent of increasing anti-Semitic prejudice, particularly among those groups of Germans who dream of building a greater German Reich.'

'I have not noticed it,' I lied, wishing to change the subject, 'and I too, despite being a Jew, am also a German patriot who believes in the great future destiny of the German Reich and people. Now tell me, sir . . .'

'I suppose you are too young to remember the Austrian stock-market collapse of 1873. Of course you are! It was sixteen years ago! Sixteen years! It seems like yesterday.'

He sighed, an old man with memories, conscious of the swiftly passing years, an old man who was born when Bonaparte was still alive.

'In the Depression that followed the collapse of the stock market,' he said, 'there was a sinister general tendency to blame the Jews for what had happened. *Gründungsfieber*, they called it: a fever of speculation; and the Jews were blamed.'

'Sixteen years ago,' I said. 'Old history.'

'Ah,' he said.

He sighed again.

'Yes,' he said, 'old history. But could it not happen again?

With another collapse of the stock market, perhaps? Another Depression?'

'People learn,' I said smugly. 'Now . . .'

'Do they?'

His expression troubled me, and my good humour began to evaporate.

'Man is constantly educating and improving himself,' I said. 'Why, even here in Austria now your workers are forbidden by law to toil for more than eleven hours a day, and they are given every Sunday for a day of rest. Fifty years hence, in 1939 (Lord, how fantastical *that* sounds), in 1939 they will be amazed that we in our ignorance could even think of discriminating against a man simply on account of his race or beliefs. Do you really imagine that mankind could remain so debased so far into the twentieth century that there could still be anti-Jewish prejudice and pogroms in 1939? Come, sir. You will be telling me next that Jews will again be forced to wear yellow badges, as they were in the Middle Ages!'

The old man smiled sadly. 'I am boring you,' he said.

'Never,' I said. 'But we must have more wine and speak of happier matters. I am fascinated by your town. Now tell me . . .'

And he did. The evening regained its former gaiety in the glow of his gossip and reminiscence. While Alois the Customs officer and his cronies laughed and slapped backs and discussed not only music but also (of all things!) the finer points of bee-keeping, the old gentleman kept me constantly entertained with stories of most of them, some of them hilarious, some quite scandalous!

The old man claimed (but with a twinkle, without any malice) that Alois was even rumoured to be half-Jewish himself! Not only that, but born illegitimate too! What fun there is in small-town gossip! There, drinking no more than a few metres away with his cronies, was a man I first assumed in his uniform and Customs post to be pompous, dogmatic and humourless; yet it transpires that his story is far more amusing and eccentric than that of most of us. Apparently Alois's mother was a peasant girl from the remote Waldviertel country district who bore him out of wedlock, causing a village scandal, and his father was rumoured to be Jewish! It seems that even until he was middle-aged Alois still called himself by his mother's bastard maiden name, until he changed it to that of his foster-father not long before he came here to Braunau about seven or eight years ago. And there is more! Those apparently pompous, dignified Imperial whiskers and starched uniform conceal a decidedly passionate nature! According to the old gentleman, Alois's present wife is his third, and this child she has borne this evening is no less than his fifth by various women! Sadly the last two children have died in infancy: but the older two who live in the rooms upstairs (a seven-year-old boy and a six-year-old girl) were the fruit of his last marriage; and the first was born illegitimate, and the second only three months after the wedding!

How we misjudge people! According to the old man, Alois's present wife is so much younger than he (more than twenty years younger) that after four years of marriage and three children she still calls him not 'husband' but 'uncle'! There is even a scandalous rumour attached to *that* story: it is whispered that Alois *is* her uncle, or at least her cousin! And to top it all, it appears that despite his fifty or more years and his three wives and five children, our dignified Customs officer still has an eye for the ladies, especially young serving girls! Perhaps *that* explains the thundering of feet across my ceiling every night: no doubt it is the sound of the Customs officer pursuing the latest resident maid!

I was so diverted by such scandalous but kindly gossip that I sent across yet another bottle of wine for Alois and his group of cheerful friends. I must have been mad or drunk (or both!) but it was worth it. I shall count the cost tomorrow, of course, but it was good at the time to see their smiles and to disprove so effectively the slander that all Jews are mean. Alois raised his glass again and called that I must join them all tomorrow in his rooms at the top of the inn to view the new child. I shall surely accept. I felt among friends. There is something symbolic about an obvious Jew being invited to a view a Christian infant at Passover, on their Easter Sunday. How good the world can be.

It is almost Sunday already; a few minutes before midnight. My brain and hand are tired. Why do I write so much? The wine, I suppose, and a certain euphoria; a feeling of acceptance by my fellow man, by strangers, even though I am a Jew. And something more : an inkling that there is something important about this night, this Easter Sabbath eve, with the bright full moon beyond my window, the first full moon of spring in this town of springs; and above my head, slumbering in absolute silence, with not the slightest sound of footsteps or pain or sorrow, a happy man with his young wife contented and fulfilled, and their new-born babe wrapped in swaddling clothes lying in a crib and sleeping in bliss and comfort, just five hours old.

I pray for that infant; not to Jehovah or to any identifiable god but simply to the pagan Spirit of the Universe. It is too long since I prayed. I feel a curious sense of religion tonight : a presence of something greater than myself. I pray that the boy-child in the crib in the room above will grow firm and straight and strong and loving; that unlike Alois' last two infants he may survive to sturdy manhood to enjoy the jollity of a Munich *Bierkeller*; that he may be blessed with a world of peace, prosperity and harmony, and love.

It must be the wine. Too much wine, and noise, and talk; but at least the old gentleman was made happy to have someone to talk to, and I was the cause. A good feeling.

How curious : I never asked the old gentleman his name. I must sleep. I shall sleep as well as the babe above.

All in all a splendid day : one of the happiest I can remember; as though it marked a new beginning.

My room is strangely filled with the most delicious smell of meat cooking. Perhaps the hotelier's wife is already preparing tomorrow's meal, a special Easter Sunday repast. A curious hour to be cooking, but then she *is* a Christian. And an Austrian ! Perhaps the late hour has some special religious significance. It certainly smells delicious. Lamb ?

A Child is Born at the Inn

Perhaps the Lamb of God!

Sunday 21 April 1889

Two hours later.

I have hardly slept at all.

It is two o'clock in the morning.

The room is ice-cold; but it stinks of burned flesh. Apprehensive of fire, I have just descended the stairs to investigate, but the inn is dark and silent, the kitchen is cold and empty. Whence, then, this smell of charred meat?

My fingers are weary from all the writing of only two hours ago, and my head throbs most painfully: perhaps from the wine; perhaps from the nightmares; perhaps from the sounds from the room above.

The full spring moon is hidden behind a cloud. It is dark, and bitterly cold, and the world seems dead.

I have not the strength to write much, and my fingers are frozen; but I must do something to banish the sounds and the darkness.

My lamp flickers.

Like a child I dread the shadows.

Writing of my fear may dispel it; and in any case I can no longer simply lie in my bed listening to the sounds.

Briefly: I had barely crept into my bed after completing my diary entry for yesterday, just before midnight, when I heard above my head, in the room above, the distinctive sound of a horse (or some other hooved creature) stepping across my ceiling, across the floor of the room above.

Simultaneously I distinctly heard again the slithering sound of a rat's tail above my head.

Rats do not bother me. They are older than Man, and far more terrified of us than we are of them; and we have allies in all those cats.

But a *horse*? On the top floor of an Austrian guesthouse?

I did not believe my ears at first.

I believe them now.

The hooves have been stepping regularly across my ceiling

for the past two hours, as though patrolling the room above. They make little noise. They are quiet; almost gentle. Their very delicacy disturbs me. Does a horse (or even a goat) step quite so daintily? At times I have to strain my ears to catch the sound, it is so faint. But it always returns, always the echo of light hooves stepping across the room above, fastidiously, and the sinuous slithering rasp of a rat's tail.

On and off during the past two hours, between the sounds (and fitfully), I have dozed and dreamed dreadful dreams.

I can only imagine that they have derived in my wine-weakened mind from my conversation earlier with the old gentleman in the tavern, for the nightmares are obviously inspired by images of the recent Russian pogroms and the sufferings there of my fellow Jews.

In my nightmares I have seen millions of Jews dying: tortured; burning; suffocating; starving; beseeching Jehovah.

Many were naked.

Their gaunt bones and their swollen eyes haunt me.

Their breasts and genitals were shrivelled, as though they were no longer animals, let alone humans; and shrunken infants were torn from their mothers' arms and slaughtered.

And there were millions of them.

Four million?

Five?

Six million?

They seemed to stretch beyond every horizon, standing accusingly but helpless and silent behind sharp wire fences.

And they go to their deaths silently, these nightmare Jews, uncomplaining: to their deaths in small chambers; pens; beside long trenches and huge communal graves.

I smell gas, and acid.

I hear a voice bellowing and ranting.

It is a high-pitched German voice, hysterical.

It excites me even though I fear it.

There is a terrifying sanity in the voice as well as a terrifying madness; in the way that genius so often also borders on lunacy.

Lunacy: I feel it close.

A Child is Born at the Inn

Perhaps it is I who is going mad.

I cannot write much more. My fingers tremble with the cold and my wrist aches.

Among those millions queueing for death I saw always an old man I knew must be me. His eyes were haunted, as though he remembered with bitterness some great lost opportunity many years before.

Why have I written so much tonight? Lord knows why, but it seems important. I shall laugh at this entry in the morning, when the spring sunshine splashes this icy little room with its yellow, like a badge of optimism. I shall read these words in the morning and scoff at my own superstitious fears: no better than some ignorant rustic Austrian rabbi supervising the unleavened kosher Passover bread.

It is bitterly cold. The first full moon of spring still skulks behind a cloud.

There!

Again.

Above my head.

Hooves. Lightly. Across the ceiling. Like a lady stepping delicately from her carriage.

I would welcome now the thundering human sound of the Customs officer and his family and his maid stampeding above my head.

The world seems quiet and dead, as though something of vital moment has occurred and still the world does not realize it.

And now (there, above my head, behind the hooves), following the hooves: the sound of the tail of the rat.

Now, above this little desk.

It slides: sinuous; revolting; immediately above this little desk as I write.

Even my lamp seems to catch its breath and gutter.

Too many words. I can write no more.

But a rat? Upstairs? It must be close to the new-born babe. I should warn them, wake Alois the Customs officer, tell him of the rat.

I shall do it. Now.

Rats have (heaven forbid) been known to attack and kill new-born infants.

I must wake him; warn him.

I should never forgive myself if anything happened to that new-born child through my negligence.

Monday 22 April 1889

Thank God.

I have escaped that sinister inn at Braunau.

I am writing now in Linz in the home of a friend of my father.

I fear I may be going mad.

I fear that the wrath of the Lord is upon me.

Briefly: I awakened the Customs officer, Alois. I mentioned the possibility of a rat near the babe's crib. He was tetchy again (no doubt the choleric effect of too much wine) and exceedingly annoyed to be disturbed when there was no sign whatever of any rat in his rooms. We searched together. Nothing at all. Not a trace. I dared not also mention the sound of hooves.

'You are drunk,' he said.

'I heard it. The sound of a rat's tail.'

He swore.

His young wife lay in the bed, not yet thirty, attractive, frightened. The old gentleman in the tavern said she is a churchgoer, a good mother to her stepchildren.

'It is nothing, Klara,' Alois said, 'just a drunken Wandering Jew.'

Then I saw the babe lying in the crib.

I wanted to kill it.

As soon as I saw the infant I was grasped by dread: an overpowering sense of evil. I wanted to seize it (God forgive me; spare me, O Lord) and I wanted to dash out its brains against the wall.

I can write little more.

For a moment I was alone with the child as Alois stamped

grumpily back to his room, and I wanted to kill it just as the Christians say all Jews plot the secret ritual blood-sacrifice of Christian infants during Passover.

The pallid infant lay on its back.

Its eyes were tight-closed; but in my madness I believed it stared at me with hatred.

Its eyes were tight-closed but somehow I knew that its eyes were protruding; and blue. They hypnotized me: and I heard again in my mind the ranting nightmare German voice and saw again the millions of naked emaciated Jews shuffling forward, queueing for death.

Beside the crib I distinctly heard the sound of two gentle hooves, and a rat's tail slithered like a cynical chuckle.

I fear I am going mad.

How could I hate a babe just eight hours old?

Perhaps at last the God of my fathers is punishing me for my ungodliness with a plague of madness.

I could scarcely resist the impulse to kill that infant. It was so strong that I could barely keep my fingers from its tiny, frail throat.

During Passover.

In the early hours of their Easter Day, before dawn: the Christian day of resurrection.

Lord forgive me.

As I stood over its crib, momentarily alone, the infant was sick, spewing milk and mucus over its mouth and Aryan nostrils like an obscene little white moustache. It coughed, and began to choke.

I wanted it to suffocate on its own vomit.

God forgive me.

Spare me, Lord.

I rejoiced that the infant might die in its own spew.

The hooves clipped and clopped beyond the cot. The tail slithered, revolting me. I was appalled by my lack of reason.

'Alois!' I called. 'The child is choking!'

The mother was at my side in a moment (taller than I expected), wiping the child's face, turning it, crooning to it.

The infant coughed again, and wailed, a sound like a frail siren, a sound that chilled me to the bone.

The father grunted. 'We are grateful to you,' he said. 'Without your concern the child might have . . . we have lost two infants already, Klara and I. Neither survived its second year.'

'I am sorry,' I said.

I clenched my eyes to control my nausea and saw again the face of the old naked emaciated me, queueing bitterly for death, haunted by the memory of a great long-lost opportunity many years before.

The mother had begun to weep. I imagined her naked too and the fantasy excited me, God forgive me, her child torn from her arms just like the women in my nightmare, her bones and eyes staring, her breasts obscenely shrunk.

'We thank you,' said Alois.

I left the Gasthof zum Pommer as soon as possible after dawn.

I had to escape.

I must see a rabbi tomorrow.

I fear my own madness, the wrath of the Lord.

I must make a new covenant with the Lord.

My father's friend here in Linz has promised to introduce me tomorrow to a good local rabbi.

I must see him.

'What will you name the child?' I asked Alois as I left his rooms.

'Adolf,' he said. 'It sounds good, no? A fine name. Adolf Hitler.'

God grant me the courage to return to the faith of my fathers. The Lord will save me. But I must ask the rabbi about the Sabbath, God's day of rest, the day the child was born.

I must ask him if God perhaps sleeps on his day of rest and leaves the world to fend for itself.

The rabbi comes from a little town, north-east of here, called Auschwitz.

ESME DODDERIDGE

The Villa Inglese

We noticed the villa the very first time we did the laborious climb up to Due Ponti to do our shopping.

The road to Montecastello dei Due Ponti, to give it its full title, swept upwards in a series of dizzying hairpin bends across the face of the hillside and the villa rested comfortably in one of these bends as in the crook of an elbow. From the road it looked forbidding with its severe wrought-iron gateway flanked on either side by a couple of tall male cypresses and, at the top of the overgrown driveway, a pair of the dark, squat female trees framing the doorway.

It was known, we were told, as the Villa Inglese.

Why, we asked the *verduraia* in the market square, why the Villa Inglese? Who owned it? It was obviously untenanted, neglected. Why was that?

'*Cara signora*,' she said, her eyes on the scales as she weighed out my kilo of zucchini. '*Non si sa* – no one knows. They say it belongs to some English people, but they don't come any more.'

'What a shame! How long is it since the English last came?'
She shrugged dismissively: 'Oh, a long, long time ago.'

'But it isn't as overgrown as all that. Surely someone must have been looking after it some of the time?'

She bent down behind the stall to find a bag for my vege-tables and busied herself putting them into it as she said, 'Oh, there have been people here sometimes – for short periods – you know, in *villegiatura.*'

On our way down the hill again, we found we could see the hinterland of the villa from above. This quite dispelled the first sinister impression it had made on us. Its sun-drenched vine terraces and its little olive grove spilled down the hillside with an effect of lovely and slightly careless disarray that was wholly enchanting, the more so perhaps by contrast with the neighbouring vineyards. These were newly planted by the look of them and the rows of white concrete supports at first glance had the chilling appearance of the stark crosses in a military cemetery.

We realized that the sense of almost cornucopian profusion and lushness which it gave was due to neglect, and we felt a trifle guilty at finding ourselves with such a strong preference for its enticing little glades and alleyways of foliage dappled with sunlight rather than for the prim, well-pruned, severely coiffed correctness of its neighbours.

On our next visit to Due Ponti we sought more information from the *verduraia.*

'The Villa Inglese – is it to let as a holiday villa? Who is the agent?'

'I've no idea,' she replied. 'No one from round here, anyway.'

'That's odd. I wonder how we could find out? It's such a lovely-looking house, I'd love to rent it one summer if we could afford it.'

'Ah – it wouldn't suit you at all, *signora.* It's not a convenient house. It's cold and damp, and it hasn't been lived in for such a long time that – well – the air's bad, they say.'

'The air's bad!' I repeated incredulously. 'What do you mean?'

Her voice was hurried and agitated as she replied. 'Well, that's what they say, *signora.* I don't know anything about it. You must excuse me.' And as she turned away, I saw that she was making the sign of the 'horns' to ward off the evil eye.

Of course, we were more intrigued than ever, but none of our casual inquiries from townspeople elicited any more con-

crete information: everyone was vague and evasive, professing
to know nothing, which seemed highly unlikely in a town like
Due Ponti, where everyone knew everyone and moreover knew
everybody else's business even better than their own. However
there was really no point in pursuing the matter for, delightful as
our daydreams had been, they had no basis in reality. How
lovely it would be, we thought, if in some unspecified way we
suddenly found ourselves with enough money to buy the villa
and come and live in this delightful place. We should restore it to
working order and live a life of rustic simplicity and solid
worth, tilling the good earth, producing our own olives and
grapes. In the evening, after a day of healthy toil, we should sit
on the terrace under the vine trellis and sip our very own wine.
Even though we laughed at our absurdly romantic fantasy,
somehow it cheered our spirits after the return to the realities
of London office life and the rush-hour commuter trains.

We had fallen in love with Due Ponti, absolutely, totally, from
the noble medieval piazza on the crest of the hill down to the
V-shaped confluence of waters embracing its foot. Here, span-
ning either arm of the 'V', were the two narrow, hump-backed
bridges that gave the town its name. With its battlements and
great bastioned wall, the little town seemed to emerge from the
hill like some natural formation: rocky outcrop and man-made
fortress seemed equally part of a natural untamed landscape.

Moreover it was no museum piece: the ordinary people of
the town lived and worked in its castellated palaces, now converted into flats and shops, offices and workshops, where once its
soldier princes had lived and ruled. It had a bustling, animated
life of its own that delighted us. On weekdays, the square was
full of people going about their business, stopping to argue or
gossip, except for the afternoon siesta time when shops shut,
shutters came down and the square was left to the ubiquitous
pigeons and the lone passer-by. But if it was animated and
full during the week, on Saturdays it seemed to burst its con-
fines: rivers of people and cars poured down its steep, narrow
streets and settled in seething colonies on every visible surface.
The cars moved forward at walking pace, seeming to nudge the

pedestrians gently in the behind with their bonnets to force a way through. In the piazza, groups of men and women shouted and gesticulated at one another to beat the surrounding din.

At the far end of the main piazza stood the cathedral. Its majestic frontage formed the boundary of the square at that end; set laterally to it, like the short arms of a 'T', were two smaller squares. Here one Saturday we happened across a concourse of men, sombrely dressed in what looked like their funeral-going suits, talking furtively in groups. Some of them wore long black cloaks and every now and again, we could tell that something was being secretively drawn out and displayed to a small tightly knit group of two or three. Here the voices were muted, no more than an indistinct conspiratorial mumble.

The groups broke and re-formed, broke and re-formed like some complicated formal ballet designed to illustrate the theme of conspiracy, until one such movement momentarily revealed to us that the sinister merchandise on display was in fact samples of corn : the farmers from the outlying farms for many miles around had brought specimens of their grain-crops to show the factors : quality and price were being discussed and bargains struck as farmers and factors circulated with sample and offer until finally two and two, they came to some mutually satisfactory arrangement.

This and everything else about the place delighted us. As I say, we were in love with it, and with a lover's infatuation, we translated everything about it into a new enchantment. The slight mystery about the empty villa only drew us to gaze on it more lovingly.

That winter we became more determined than ever to return the next summer, and somehow or other for a longer period than a miserable three weeks, even if it meant lying or taking unpaid leave to do so. And in the end this is what we did, fabricating a story about the loan of a villa for six weeks in return for doing the caretaking while the owners were on holiday.

The moment we sighted the Villa Inglese on our first day's excursion we knew it was no longer uninhabited. We had a sudden view of the house from below before we expected to because the high overgrown hedge had been cut back, revealing the upper portion of the house. We felt an absurd sense of loss and resentment, as though some prized and personal possession had been casually taken by a passing stranger. When we had climbed high enough to look back and see the whole house and its vineyard we could see the figure of a man seated in front of an easel on the terrace at the rear of the house. We could see too that a lot had already been done to reduce the place to order, but without in any way spoiling any of its charm.

When we reached the top we went into the little tobacconist's to buy the local paper. The woman remembered us from the previous year and greeted us warmly. It gave us a pleasing sense of homecoming.

We asked immediately about the Villa Inglese, and this time there was no hesitation about the reply. Yes, it had been taken by an English couple once again. Very nice people they were, both of them. '*Simpaticissimi*,' she said.

The *verduraia* too was informative. They intended to live there all the year round. Nice young people they seemed, poor things.

'Why poor things?' I said. '*Lucky* things to be able to come and live here in that lovely house.'

'It's early days yet,' she said obliquely. 'One must hope for the best.'

Before I could reply to this lugubrious remark, the *verduraia* turned to greet a newcomer, a pleasant, smiling young woman of about my own age.

'Here is the *Signora* Wilson now,' she said to me, and to the newcomer 'This *signora* also is English!'

'Hello,' said young Mrs Wilson. 'I'm Patricia Wilson. Do you live in Due Ponti too?'

'Janet Sedley,' I said. 'No, I'm afraid not. I wish we did. We're only here on holiday. Forgive my asking, but from what the *signora* said I gather you are the people who've taken the Villa Inglese.'

'Why yes, that's right.'

'I can't help being horribly envious,' I said. 'We were here on holiday last year and we thought it was one of the most lovely places we'd ever seen.'

'You must come and see it properly. My husband and I would be very pleased to show you over it.'

At this point John came up and my new acquaintance pressed us to finish our shopping and go back with her for a cup of coffee. We demurred, but she insisted that Dick, her husband, would welcome the interruption. He was going through a difficult patch with his painting and this depressed him. New company would cheer him up, she was sure.

Dick was a very tall, thin, finely drawn young man whose face looked surprisingly tired and colourless for one who must have been spending quite a lot of time out of doors. Patricia, on the other hand, was magnificently bronzed and full of vitality.

Dick greeted us warmly and his melancholy face broke into a smile of considerable charm. He certainly seemed pleased, almost relieved one would have said, at the interruption, and quietly set out chairs for us on the terrace.

'Let's have coffee first,' said Patricia, 'and we'll show you round afterwards. Don't expect too much, will you. We're only slowly getting it into shape.' And off she went.

'I'm amazed that you managed to get hold of the place,' John said. 'Last year when we asked about it people were so extraordinarily cagey that we couldn't find out anything at all about it.'

'Well, actually, we saw it advertised in the English papers,' said Dick. 'The executors of some estate wanted to get rid of it and really they were asking such a ridiculously low price that we could hardly believe it. We gathered from them that the local people have some silly superstition about the place. That's really why they were asking so little for it, I suppose. There was actually a murder here some years ago, and the local people believe it's haunted.'

'No – really? A real live ghost? Who is it – the murderer or the murderee?'

'Neither, actually. It's supposed to be haunted by a dog.'

'A *dog*? Oh, no! I can't believe it. A sort of Hound of the Baskervilles or something? How hilarious!'

Dick smiled, a little thinly I thought, and I felt rather silly at my frivolous response. But really, who could help laughing at the idea?

'Do tell us about it,' said John. 'If you don't mind, that is.'

'Mind?' said Dick, again a trifle tetchily I thought. 'Why should I mind? Well, the story's quite absurd, of course, but the murder seems to have caused a lot of bad blood locally. Apparently an English couple inherited the place through some complicated Anglo-Italian marriages in, I think, the wife's family. Anyway, they decided to come and live here. Well, the *contadini* who'd been cultivating the land had got used to having all the grapes and olives and things to themselves since the previous people hardly ever came. They'd begun to regard it really as their own and were furious when the English couple simply walked in and tried to take over.'

'Mm –' said John, 'I can imagine it. Not very tactful of the English lot.'

'No, it was a stupid thing to do and of course there was the most God Almighty row.'

'And the *contadino* did for the English chap, I suppose?' said John.

'No – it was a most bizarre thing actually. The *contadino*, it appears, had a very savage German Shepherd dog – a great big brute of a thing – and he used to set it on the English couple whenever he saw them – used to send it down into the vineyard to chase them out. Attacked the chap several times, apparently, though it never harmed the girl. Anyway the Englishman naturally got pretty mad about this, so he bought a gun and the next time the dog appeared on his land, he shot it.'

'I can't say I blame him, but I suppose that hardly did him any good locally,' said John.

'Well, of course. The *contadino* threatened to kill him in retaliation, and the chap got so scared, they say, that when he locked up at night he used to bar and bolt every door and shutter.'

Dick paused for so long that I thought he had come to the end of the story, and said in some disappointment, 'Is that all that happened? And the dog's supposed to haunt the place?'

'Well, no, it isn't – all that actually happened, I mean. One night a party of local lads were coming back up the hill very late after the grape-harvest celebrations in Basso, and they heard terrible screams and shouts from the house and then several shots. Probably if they'd all been sober they'd simply have legged it off home, but they'd had quite a lot to drink, of course, and had more courage than usual. So they went and banged on the door of the villa and tried to get in, when suddenly the door burst open and the chap staggered out babbling away in English and pointing inside. They went in – and they found the girl full of gunshot wounds, dead on the bedroom floor, and the gun on the bed.'

'Good Lord – what a horrible thing! What happened – I mean, what on earth did they do then?'

'Well, the long and the short of it was that the chap maintained that he was woken up in the middle of the night by terrible screams. He saw a huge dog savaging something on the floor and realized it was his wife. He seized his gun, which he always kept loaded by the bed, and shot the dog, but when he managed to get a light there was no dog – only his wife's body there on the floor, riddled with shot.'

'How ghastly! Was he mad, d'you think, or what?'

'God knows. At the trial when the prosecutor pointed out that the room *must* have been too dark for him to see, if in fact it was shuttered and locked up as he maintained it had been, he simply said he *did* see the dog because it was outlined by a faint glow – like phosphorescence, I suppose. So, of course, the local people reckoned the dog was a ghost come for its revenge. But the girl's body hadn't been savaged in any way: the only wounds were those from the gunshot.'

'What an eerie story! What happened to the chap in the end?' I asked. 'Was he hanged?'

'No, he hanged himself in his cell, poor devil. Of course, the prosecution made out that it was a *crime passionnel* and that he'd shot his wife in a fit of jealousy. Apparently the *contadino* bloke whose dog was shot was known as a bit of a Don Juan about the place.'

'Sounds more likely than a doggy ghost, anyway,' commented John.

By this time Patricia had returned and we were drinking our coffee.

'Is anyone else ever supposed to have seen this ghost creature?' I asked.

'Oh, of course, the local people talk a lot of rubbish about it,' said Dick. 'I wish to God,' he added with surprising venom, 'they'd control their real dogs instead of blithering on about ghostly ones. There's a bloody animal somewhere that howls like a demented spirit whenever there's a full moon.'

'Come on, Dick. Stop getting so steamed up about it,' protested Patricia. 'It's only happened very occasionally. As a matter of fact, I saw it one night. I looked out of the window and it was sitting up on that knoll on the other side of the river and baying – very melodiously as it happens. It looked a gorgeous creature.'

'Gorgeous creature indeed!' snorted Dick. 'I'd be tempted to take a pot-shot at the thing if I had a gun.'

'Stop being so beastly about it, Dick,' said Patricia vehemently. 'Even if you don't mean it, it's a horrid thing to say.'

'I *do* mean it,' growled Dick.

'Who does it belong to?' I asked.

'Oh – you know how it is round here. You can never get anything definite out of people if they think you're going to complain. They just look very shifty and say they don't know anything about any dog. The whole thing's ridiculous. I expect it belongs to some poacher fellow whom they all know, and he'd be in trouble if we could prove that it was his dog that was always prowling round our land, the bloody animal.'

'Don't be silly, Dick. Always prowling round our land – that's rubbish!' said Patricia hotly.

John and I were beginning to feel slightly uncomfortable over this altercation between them about the dog, and John cut in quickly with an invitation to them to come out and have supper with us at one of the town's *trattorie*.

And so, little by little, our acquaintanceship with them progressed : the occasional meal out together, a drink or a coffee in the little bar in the piazza, the borrowing and exchange of such books as we had. The relationship was never a very close one, however; it remained casual and on the surface. Dick was still strained and edgy, dissatisfied with his old style of painting but unable to forge a new and individual style for himself. Patricia, on the other hand, seemed filled with an almost electric vitality that drove her for long walks in the country while Dick struggled with paint and canvas. She expressed interest and concern about his work when we were together, but somehow I felt her real attention was elsewhere : there was something in her manner of one who humours a child with pretended interest, but whose real, adult concerns are quite other.

One night John and I were sitting out late watching the flickering dance of the fireflies in the Bianchi's orchard. It was as though a myriad of silent searchers were switching minuscule torches on and off between the trees. I had never seen such a sight before. Suddenly we heard, far off, the howling of a dog. It was unmistakable although so muted by distance. It is always an eerie and upsetting sound, and with one accord we got up to go into the house and close our ears against it.

A couple of days later we came upon Dick sitting morosely drinking by himself in the bar in Due Ponti. We could not do other than join him, though I could see with a sinking heart that he had already drunk more than was good for him.

'Hello, Dick, old lad. How's tricks?' said John fatuously, unable to think of anything else to say.

'Tricky – that's how tricks are – tricky,' said Dick thickly.

'Patricia here, too?' I asked stupidly, though I could see clearly she was not.

'No – no – not here. Bloody dog, that's what. Shoot it if I had a gun.'

'Yes, we heard it howling the other night too. It's a disturbing noise, I agree.'

'Disturbing? Disturbing? Downright disgustin's what I call it. Roving around the hillside that time of night in a nightgown.'

'In a nightgown?' I repeated disbelievingly. 'What on earth d'you mean?'

'Yes, she did. Went off to find that dog – just in her nightie. 'Sgustin' I told her. Came back bloody pleased with herself. But I'll put a stop to that, I can tell you.'

'Do you mean Patricia went out alone at that time of night to find the dog? What a crazy thing to do! It might have bitten her – could have killed her come to that.'

'That's what *you* think. She said it came and – came and – licked her foot.' He spat the words out with loathing. 'Licked her foot – filthy beast. I'd put a bullet through it if I got the chance. She's mad – mad as a hatter if you ask me.'

We got him to sober up with some strong black coffee and then walked back to the villa with him in silence. Patricia was not there and Dick did not ask us in, but dismissed us as quickly as he decently could. We went home in some disquiet, but still reluctant to get mixed up in this strange quarrel between husband and wife.

A couple of days later again Patricia came to see us. She was anxious and worried because Dick had now bought a shotgun and had sworn that he would shoot the dog.

'He'll get involved in some dreadful vendetta or something if he does. After all, it must belong to *someone* and it's such a lovely animal – it must be quite valuable.'

'Then you really have seen it!' I exclaimed.

'Of course I have,' she said calmly. 'It's the gentlest creature – honey-coloured and *so* beautiful. Nothing odd or mysterious about it at all – just that it seems to sense that Dick doesn't like it and slips away the moment he appears. I've seen it in our olive grove several times, but now I don't mention it to Dick, because he really has become almost deranged about it.'

Neither of us wanted to be dragged into this affair, but we agreed in the end to try to dissuade Dick if the opportunity presented itself.

A few days went by before we found Dick alone. Again, it was in the bar in Due Ponti. His appearance shocked us: he was unshaven and looked somehow disturbingly gone to seed. It was rather horrible to have witnessed the deterioration, almost the disintegration, of a person in such a short space of time.

He looked at us sullenly as we approached his table, barely acknowledging our greeting. The moment we sat down he leaned forward and said, 'You know what? She's in love with that bloody dog. In love with a bloody dog. Wha' d'you think of that then, eh?'

'Oh come on, Dick, don't be absurd!'

'Don't you "come on" me,' he cut in dangerously. 'She's trying to stop me shooting that son of a bitch . . .' He stopped abruptly and began to laugh. 'That's good, that is – that's rich – that son of a bitch. Did you hear what I said? That son of a bitch! Good, isn't it?'

'Yes,' agreed John, 'a very appropriate epithet. But look, Dick, of course she doesn't want you to shoot the animal; she thinks the owner would start some vendetta thing against you. And that's really only too likely, you know. The creature doesn't seem to do any harm, after all, so why not leave it alone?'

'Leave it alone? Leave it alone? And have my wife making assin – assinations – tha's right – assinations with it?'

'You can't make assignations with a dog, Dick,' I said fatuously.

'Perhaps I couldn't and you couldn't, but *she* can. She has assinations with it all over the place. But I'll put a stop to it, I promise you. She thinks she's going to go and meet it when I'm asleep, but she's not, you know. Because I'm going to lock and padlock all the doors and windows and keep the keys where she won't find them. It can howl its head off out there and she won't be able to go to it.'

'He's horribly crazy,' I said to John when eventually we

were alone again. 'I think he's dreadfully sick in his head. Patricia ought to take him back to England to see a doctor.'

But Patricia, when we saw her, was much less anxious than she had been previously.

'Go back to England? Now?' she exclaimed at this suggestion. 'Oh no, I couldn't. We both love it here. I've never been so happy in my life.'

'But Dick's not at all well, Patricia. Really. He's in a very strange state, you know he is.'

'No, really he's much better now. He did have a silly fixation about the dog for a while, but he's quite got over it now.'

'Well, I hope you're right, but he didn't seem to have done the other day.'

'Yes, but he was a bit pissed then, wasn't he? He's all right when he's sober. He's been a bit silly – drinking too much lately, but he says he's going to keep off it for a bit.'

'To hell with the pair of them,' said John when she had gone. 'I wish we'd never met them. They've really begun to bugger up our holiday. Let's go off somewhere on our own for a while and get them out of our system.'

We enjoyed our days away and by the time we came back we felt we could put the whole thing into perspective. Even so, we did not intend to invite an encounter and we did not go up to Due Ponti for several days.

Then one night we heard again the howling of the dog. The distant ululations, charged with a savage grief, rose and fell, rose and fell on the night air, and I lay disturbed and shaking in my bed, glad of John beside me and the reassurance of the touch of him. Again and again came the anguished howling. Finally John got up and shut the window to try to keep out the sound.

It was two or three days before we made up our minds to go over to Due Ponti. As we approached the Villa Inglese, catching our first glimpse of its upper floor from below, we saw that all its windows were shuttered – surprising at that time of the morning. As we rounded the bend and looked up to the entrance, we saw a group of people standing uncertainly round the gate. One was the postman and there were one or two people from the nearer houses and cottages on the other side of the road. They greeted us with a kind of eager relief and asked if we had news of the *signori* from the villa.

No, we hadn't, we said in some surprise. We'd been away and hadn't seen them for nearly two weeks. Was something wrong?

Well, said the postman, the postbox on the gate hadn't been emptied for two or three days. Moreover, said the neighbouring *contadini*, no one had seen the *signori* for at least three days and the windows had remained shuttered.

'Perhaps,' I said hesitantly to John, 'they've gone to England. Do you think that Patricia had enough sense to take him home after all?' But inside myself I did not believe this.

A little group of us went up the drive and knocked at the door. I don't think anyone had expected an answer and none came. We stood around uncertainly and then John and I walked round to the back of the house. All the doors and windows were tightly secured, but the furniture was still out on the terrace and Patricia's gardening tools were propped up against the wall of the little flower garden she had planted just below the terrace. It was extremely unlikely that they would have gone leaving these things lying about.

Someone went off to fetch the police, but I knew long before they came and broke down the door what they would find there: the two bodies – Patricia lying on her back on the floor in a pool of dried blood, shot through the heart, and Dick on the bed, the shotgun beside him. But what I had not foreseen was the savage mauling of Dick's body. At the inquest it was established that the terrible lacerations of his throat had been the immediate cause of death. These and other wounds on his body seemed explicable only in terms of savaging by some ferocious animal. But . . . every door and window was locked and barred. There was no evidence of entry or exit, no evidence anywhere of any presence, except these otherwise inexplicable wounds.

These irreconcilable facts manifested themselves to all of us in that room on that dreadful morning. We could not meet one another's eyes and our fear was a palpable presence. As the police unshuttered the windows and allowed the morning light to stream in, I saw a huge honey-coloured dog standing under the big vine below the terrace. For one moment its eyes looked deeply into mine with an intense searching look before my voice came back and I heard myself cry out: 'Oh my God – he's there – in the garden. Look!'

John sprang to the window and looked out.

Then he spun round, staring at me with a frightened, questioning look.

'Jan?' he said, 'Jan? But there's nothing there.'

He seized me by the arm and shook me urgently.

'There's nothing there, Jan,' he repeated, 'nothing at all.'

JANICE ELLIOT

Reflections

'The new waiter?'

'Yes?'

'I have the impression he wears a wig. And yet it is white.'

'That is nothing to me,' says the proprietor. 'He is efficient. He is working his way up.'

'Also, he rubs his upper lip as though he were missing a moustache.'

The restaurant on the Avenida is, as it has ever been, the sober-sided refuge of the middle classes who prefer things to be as they have ever been, and there is nothing wrong with that. All around there is change and mostly decay – what with the junkies and the muggers and the takeaway Chinese – but the moment you close the door of the restaurant behind you and walk through the bead curtain, what solace there is in the brown and muted decency. New paper tablecloths every morning, on each table the Martini ashtray, a single carnation that wilts through the week from Saturday to Friday and the carafe of water, though most clients prefer mineral water or the light fizzy beer of the country. (There is little demand for wine : the local white is over-sweet and the red rusty to the teeth – the copper, or some other mineral in the soil, one says, enters the vine from the root; the French does not travel well or, having travelled, sickens; besides, one would wake from one's siesta with vinous gravel in the mouth or rage in the head. There is

251

work to be done. Now, more than ever, work must be seen to be done.)

There has always been the electric fan, the walls have always been brown, the mirrors reflect everything that goes on in the restaurant on the Avenida. A famous poet came here once, and he was reflected, also his harlot. No dogs are allowed and therefore they are not reflected, though there is the old actress who brings her cat and feeds it raw *biftek* on a fondue fork. She was once a belle and in those days when she came in for an after-theatre supper the mirrors reflected her beauty, but they do not remember it. Mirrors are unforgiving.

There is a writer, also, everyone respects and no one reads (myself), but he dresses like a doctor or a solicitor (to confuse the mirrors?). A painter comes here too, a lemony fellow who draws murderously on the paper tablecloths. But neither the actress nor the writer nor the painter is representative of the clientele who are solid accountants and store-owners or managers and dentists and actuaries and civil servants. Their reflections are irreproachable. In the middle of the day they wag their heads over the newspapers. In the evening many call in for a beer or a *fine* at the stainless steel bar with the Cappucino machine and on Fridays they buy a lottery ticket. Sometimes they bring their wives and families here for dinner (hardly ever their mistresses, because of the reflections).

There is a recess across which curtains may be drawn for private parties but mostly it is the staff who eat here, about three o'clock and also at midnight.

Gruber's feet do not seem too good but, as the proprietor says, he will rise. At first he never had much to say but he is the hardest worker I have ever seen. By seven in the morning he is sweeping out the restaurant and he is still there at midnight. Where he sleeps is a wonder. He might be the loneliest man I have ever seen.

Gruber looks a little like Chaplin in his last years, but more vigorous. He wears a white jacket, black trousers, a little black tie, and he takes particular pleasure in polishing the mirrors: he works away with leather and vinegar water like a window cleaner – you might almost believe there was a view beyond to be revealed.

Thus, one day at three-forty the restaurant on the Avenida is empty, but for Gruber, who wrings out his leather and vinegar for the last time and brings me a *fine* on a tray, in a glass, on a paper mat on a saucer.

'You work very hard, Gruber. Yourself?'

'Thank you, sir. A beer.'

'If you will join me. You are rising, Gruber.'

'I believe so, sir. My step-brother was in the same trade, but he did not rise. You can imagine my age, sir? I am eighty-nine.'

'Eighty-nine is a great age for anyone and for a waiter working his way up it is miraculous. For most people. For the majority.'

'The majority represents not only ignorance but cowardice. The majority can never replace the man.'

'Indeed.'

Rubbing his upper lip in the familiar gesture, Gruber appears to weigh me (for the first time I notice his extraordinarily piercing eyes – normally lowered as he goes about his duties). Satisfied, he speaks confidentially. His voice is a little harsh. He has an air of authority and I guess this is not the first time in his life he has been on the rise. I wonder if he has been a schoolmaster or even a captain of industry. One does not ask Gruber such questions. As he talks he rearranges the table to his satisfaction: the salt cellar is apparently a little out of line, the water carafe must be centred, exactly so.

'This place, for instance, is anarchic. I intend to initiate some reforms. You are startled, sir, I can see that. But my propositions will be acceptable to the proprietor. I have persuaded him that the kitchen staff – not to mention those who wait upon table – will welcome a firm hand. The psyche of the broad masses is accessible only to what is strong and uncompromising. That has been my experience.'

'You have considerable experience of catering, Mr Gruber?'

'Not of catering, sir; but of human nature, yes.'

*

After this first interview Gruber and I have many such chats (this appears to be his only weakness – the need for a confidant). In fact, it is he who tends to initiate the conversations and – I realize – set the subject. I am amazed by the old waiter's grasp of politics, history, music, art, architecture.

The proprietor falls ill and gives Gruber leave to carry through his programme of reforms. The service improves, the food no longer arrives tepid at the table. Gruber no longer sweeps out in the morning or washes the mirrors – he has underlings to do this now. There is a spring in his step, he looks younger, he snaps his fingers for service and begins to spend more time with the customers. With the staff he becomes positively tyrannical, and, overhearing his way with a sloppy cook, a waiter whose paper cuffs are not fresh that morning, the fish chef who has been caught spitting in the *bouillabaisse* and sacked without notice, I ask Gruber how it is that he appears to inspire and retain unusual loyalty? What I mean is – and I think he understands – the serving classes will not put up nowadays with autocracy.

'Then,' he says, with a smile almost sly, 'they may go elsewhere for a job.'

'But there are no jobs to be had.'

'Exactly.'

Another time.

'You're a monster, Gruber. You're working them to death.'

'The masses are scarcely conscious of the fact that their freedom as human beings is abused. They feel very little shame at being terrorized intellectually. You would agree these are bad times?'

(Who could deny that?)

'I have history on my side. They will do as they are told. And my customers? Have you heard any complaints that the omelettes are light and the plates are hot?'

The proprietor dies. Gruber takes over the restaurant. He puts on weight and it turns out that he is not, after all, alone in the world. At half past three or at midnight, he dines with a crony in the staff recess. We do not have so many talks nowadays. It is autumn, then it is winter. The leaves fall from the trees in the Avenida, awnings are taken in, and pavement tables; a cold wolf of a wind blows from the *sierra*, the old actress dies and will never more be reflected. Her little cat is found in the alley behind the restaurant, its neck broken. I do not sleep so well and at midnight wrap up, push my flask into my pocket and pace the Retiro Park and the Avenida. I think of flying out, but there are hijackings almost every day and a strike at the airport, broken up by the militia – but there is still no one to fly the planes. And then the militia strike. There are riots: pointless when there is no militia to put them down. This is a bad season for everyone but Gruber, who flourishes. He buys up the restaurant across the Avenida, then a couple more in the city. I hear that these deals are not altogether straight, that Gruber has brought pressure to bear, that he has connections with some organization that is not entirely legal (though who it to say, nowadays, what is and is not legal?). Gruber puts up his prices. Some of the old customers disappear. One day they are there, the next they are not. The painter, I notice, has been moved from his corner table to one by the serving door and he no longer draws on the tablecloths. I still retain my place (by grace perhaps of the many interesting chats I have had with Gruber on all kinds of subjects) and so can still see, when the curtain is not drawn, the recess where the staff used to eat about three o'clock and midnight, reflected in a mirror on the opposite wall: but the staff no longer eat there – instead Gruber holds court for an increasing number of intimates (I had no idea he had so many friends in this city). For these cronies nothing apparently is too good: fantastical ice creams, the whole roast head of a pig, lobster out of season, wines imported by air, black-market Cuban cigars, oysters, *ortolan*. Well, Gruber deserves it – he has risen.

He still spares a little time for me, for the sake of the good talks we have had. In spite of the company he keeps, the servant turned master still strikes me as a lonely soul.

'I am a self-educated man,' he says. 'This is not the first time I have risen. But I must tell you, my friend, at my age it becomes tiring to work one's way up.'

'You're healthier than I am, Gruber.'

'Ah, that cough. Might I prescribe rum and lemon? With a little honey?'

Gruber is right about the cough. For a few weeks I am away from the restaurant then resume my insomniac night walks, though I am probably not fit to go out. A slight fever keeps me warm, I sit in the park, then around the middle of the night find myself shivering in the Avenida. I take my accustomed table in the empty restaurant and, waiting for the barman to bring me a *café filtre* and a cognac, I look up and see reflected in the mirror, dining in the recess, a jolly party: Adolf Hitler, Goebbels, Bormann, Goering, Himmler, the six Goebbels children – Hela, Hilda, Helmut, Holde, Hedda and Heide (who should be in bed by now) – and Adolf's dog the great Alsatian, Blondi – the first dog ever to be reflected in the restaurant on the Avenida. It's bitter out, there is snow in the wind. Nearly Christmas. The conifers on the *sierra* will have had their first frosting and the air will be very clear and bright. I gulp my cognac and run home.

Of course, it is absurd: some waking dream or hallucination. Still, I keep away from the restaurant in the Avenida, nurse my cough and take my exercise in the Retiro Park. Even in winter it is a pleasant place: a few nurses still bring their charges here to play, there are the pink-stockinged flamingoes on the lake and cheerful ducks. I carry bread for the ducks and nuts for the squirrels.

One afternoon just before Christmas I find the gaunt painter from the restaurant in the Avenida sketching the Retiro flamingoes. He's a dry fellow with whom, in all the years at the restaurant, I have never exchanged more than a nod, but on an impulse I take a place next to him on the bench. We sit in silence for a while.

'Tell me, how are our friends in the Avenida?'

'I no longer go there. It is not a happy place – except, of course, for Gruber and his pals.'

He explains: from his table by the serving door he overheard the so-correct Gruber shouting at the kitchen staff. Prices went up, the quality of the food went down. As for himself – it was made clear that he was no longer welcome. First the table by the serving door, then a dirty tablecloth, a cockroach in his soup. Finally he was told that no table was available, even by the serving door.

The next day we meet again. We take a *café-cognac* at the small bar in the Retiro Park, standing at the counter. My new friend, etiolated, could be a flamingo himself, roosting on one leg. He wears mittens to sketch outdoors in winter. He tells me there are rumours that Gruber is running a protection racket. He also tells me that for many years when they were younger, he was the lover of the actress with the cat – though she had no cat then (extraordinary, these unlooked-for connections one discovers by chance, like secret passages in a house).

He talks of painting, I of books.

'I wonder, did you ever read a story by Isaac Bashevis Singer – or someone – about seeing Hitler and his buddies dining in a New York restaurant?'

'No, I never read that story.'

A few days later, sitting on our bench on a raw, grey afternoon, I think again of the conifers on the *sierra*, of decorated trees and childhood.

'What will you be doing for Christmas?'

My friend snaps his sketchbook shut. His coat, I think, though once good, is too thin for this weather.

'I do not regard Christmas. I am a Jew.'

Previously alien in this Catholic, southern hemisphere, Santa has somehow got a work permit and drives his sleigh down the Avenida chuckling 'ho ho ho'. Some desperation has seized the

city and in these bad times he has more customers than the
Virgin or her sweetly scented crèche in the porch of the cathedral. The shops are brilliant, everyone throws their money away
like dirt, which it nearly is. This is old Claus's Christmas and he
rides through the town like Bacchus, frightening children. There
are drunks around Christmas Eve; with the crowds still in the
streets at eleven and the electronic Christmas peal of bells from
Flores, the big store on the Avenida, there is an air of terrible
carnival. There is a firemen's strike and at midnight the restaurant on the Avenida is burned to the ground. Someone with
a grudge. Maybe that fish chef who was sacked for spitting in
the *bouillabaisse*. It must have been someone with inside knowledge, to pick a time when only Gruber would be there, with his
friends. No one survives. The militia break in with axes and
shatter all the mirrors, every one.

Spring in the Retiro, a light like gauze, soft air, children with
balloons and pets, nurses in tow. The local currency, too, is
buoyant again and at the Retiro bar old belles gossip over their
cream pastries; there is a new restaurant in the Avenida but I
prefer to share my lunch with the ducks and drowse and hear
the nurses call.

A big dog nearly topples me and is called off by one of the
children. I don't mind. I like dogs.

'What's his name?'

'Blondi.'

And I hear the nurses call after the children: 'Hela, come
here! Hilda, Helmut, Holde! Hedda! Heide!'

KIERAN PRENDIVILLE

The Spirit of the Game

Love, so legend had it, was easy to come by at the licensed premises we know as the Black Horse. That's my local, by the way, the Black Horse in Hammersmith. Mind you, when I say *was* easy to come by, I mean a hundred years ago. As it happens, love isn't too hard to come by even now because of the nurses' home around the corner. Indeed, so strong were the recent links between many of our regulars and these angels of mercy that their matron in charge was moved to describe the Black Horse in the local rag as a 'brothel' – announcing at the same time that her chargelings would no longer be allowed to dispense their exquisite medicine among us.

But of course my local is no such thing as a brothel. A market place perhaps, where favours are traded and sweaty bargains struck – a house not so much of ill-repute as one with just a slight temperature.

The matron had put her finger on it, though. It was just that she was a century out of date. The Black Horse had indeed *been* a brothel and a rather seamy place it sounded too, dealing as it did almost exclusively in very young girls for the benefit and amusement of Mayfair's wealthy, talented and titled. Mayfair, of course, had its fair share of brothels too, but the Black Horse had something extra. For while these unpleasant 'gentlemen' lounged around waiting for their particular twelve-year-old fancies, the management provided them with the facilities to play cards. In particular, a game recently arrived from America, very popular in the western parts of that continent: poker.

And that's really what I was doing there a hundred years on. I was a regular drinker there anyway, but I was also a trusted and accepted regular and member of the Black Horse poker school: Prop. Seamus the landlord, players Nick the Greek, Mathew the plumber, Saudi Roche (actually he was from Dublin but had worked on gas pipelines in Saudi Arabia) and Maltese Johnny. All of them had colourful backgrounds known variously to the police, their bookmakers, a handful of credit agencies and, in some cases, their parish priests.

So there we were again – Friday night, the last bell gone, the last comatose drunk poured out on to the pavement and, despite matron's ruling: exit a group of student nurses – anaesthetized by alcohol and their number swollen by a visiting rugby 'B' team whose losing run looked very likely to change.

Now there are various unwritten rules in poker and principal among them is that, if you're going to play, you shouldn't drink. Quite right, too. And we all solemnly agreed as Mathew the plumber ordered a round. Clearly, Mathew said, if we were all pissed, we all played badly and no one suffered an unfair advantage. Seamus the landlord just smiled. And well he might. If he could handle his evil Irish poison from the top shelf, there was no way another couple of drinks were going to bother him.

Curiously, though, we'd been playing now for a number of years and one thing was for sure: Seamus lost and won just like the rest of us. None of us really lost a wad nor won one. (Actually I was down maybe fifty pounds over the previous two years but I was damned if I was going to admit it.)

Maltese Johnny pulled out a table into the middle of the saloon under the main light and proceeded to arrange chairs around it.

'Right,' he said. 'Who's sitting where?'

We drifted over as casually as possible without showing the urgency that, week after week, ensured we all sat in exactly the same places. It mattered to me, for instance, that I sat on the left of Seamus the landlord. He was a good player but a wild one, which gave me a chance to stack my hand before venturing out with my own bet. As it happens, I'm a cautious player but good enough to vary my play so they can't always guess what I am holding.

Mathew the plumber never cared much where he sat. A quiet player, he was also a brave one and kept a very close eye on the game. It assured him of steady pots throughout any session. Saudi Roche was a cowboy who ought to lose every week and indeed did most weeks. It was simply that every fifth or sixth week, he won a stack which brought him back his losses of the previous ones. Most weeks he was legless with drink – then he'd sober up and play a cracker. (You were fairly safe in our school. Each of us had so many deficiencies ranging from recklessness to drunkenness it all seemed to even out.) Roche sat on Mathew's left, Nick the Greek on his left and Maltese Johnny on his.

Now Nick the Greek was a curious fellow. The only thing he really had in common with that sun-kissed land of myths and legends was that he was a bit of a tragedy. He had once attempted to revisit the country of his ancestors but, after spending three days at Luton Airport waiting for his plane to take off, he decided instead to head back down the motorway to London and a gambling club where he unloaded every penny of his holiday money in three hours. Nick was gambling mad : horses, cards, roulette, it made no difference to Nick, and his fortunes went up and down like a yo-yo.

As for Maltese Johnny – well, like Nick he was olive-skinned, but unlike Nick, who was a fairly gentle fellow, Maltese Johnny was capable of great ferocity. We all agreed it was only a matter of time before we saw his name in the New Year's Honours List as 'Maltese Johnny GBH'. Johnny was a one-man industry, a positive godsend to the Post Office over the years, due to the prodigious number of mailbags with which he had provided them, albeit reluctantly. The reason he spent so much time sewing mailbags was because he spent so much time trying to knock off Post Office vans. And the reason he looked so ferocious was because of the scars and bruises on his face – legacies of those times when, quite understandably, Post Office van drivers decided they'd rather not stop to pass the time of day with Johnny . . . and drove right through him.

Unfortunately for Johnny, his glowering 'boat-race' and complete lack of repentance only ensured he drew a longer stretch than he might otherwise have done. On those rare occasions when he walked free, Johnny would join us at the card table on a Friday night where we would all be extremely careful not to unbalance his sensitivities any more than they clearly already were. For all that, Johnny appeared to feel at home with us.

Seamus the landlord wasn't flattered that Maltese Johnny felt at home with us because of the fact that his presence would occasionally attract visits from the neighbourhood constabulary. This was embarrassing less for Seamus than for the *other* members of the local constabulary who were frequently to be found at the bar after closing time themselves, doubtless working on the hypothesis that to understand your villains you have to drink deep into the night with them. Happily this was not the case tonight.

Now the game at the Black Horse was five-card draw poker. Each player is dealt five cards. If someone opens the game with a bet, the rest of the table decides to play with him or fold. If they're playing, they can draw more cards – but in our game, no more than three. Nick the Greek shuffled the cards with a dexterity that was rarely matched by our play : a bit theatrical maybe, but good to watch.

Nick began the deal but, just as the first cards came whizzing off the deck, there was a tapping at the window.

'Bloody stroll on,' said Seamus. 'Who the hell is that at this time of night?' He went to the door and shouted through the letter-box. 'What do you want?'

'I'd rather like to buy some cigarettes,' said this extremely cultured voice.

'I'd rather you pushed off,' said Seamus, which wasn't that funny but got a laugh. 'We're closed.'

'Please,' said the voice, 'this is the fifth pub I've tried.'

Well, Seamus wasn't a bad skin really, so he unbolted the door and let the man in. Saudi Roche was the first one to burst out laughing. It wasn't very hospitable, but you could see why.

The visitor was a tall man, six feet probably, wearing a stovepipe hat, a long frock-coat, a ruffled dinner shirt and carrying a silver-knobbed cane. He had these massive whiskers that took a sharp right-angled turn across a face, reddened by good living, to form a moustache. He had a rather superior look about him, but I put that down to the clothes.

He smiled benevolently at our laughter: 'Oh yes – I'm on my way to a fancy-dress ball.'

Then he saw the card table and stood silently for a second or two, his eyes seeming to turn rather sad.

'What kind of cigarettes do you want?' said Seamus. The visitor broke out of his glaze and waved a white-gloved hand airily in a gesture of unconcern. Seamus lifted his eyes heavenward and pulled out a packet of Number 6 tipped, which I thought not only inappropriate but a little shabby.

The visitor looked again at the table and said, 'May I inquire, gentlemen, what game it is you're playing?'

Seamus's face perked up as he walked over from the bar with the visitor's cigarettes. 'Five-card draw poker,' he replied and, cautiously, 'Do you . . . play?'

'In the past I have,' the visitor said dreamily and then, hopefully, 'I don't suppose you gentlemen could accommodate a rather rusty hand at the table?'

'You're not one of those huckin' fustlers, are you?' asked Seamus, grinning, which was a bit of a cheek considering that Seamus and one or two others around the table reckoned we might have a mark here. Then Seamus nodded, and the visitor joined us at the table.

We played for a time, the visitor playing a tight game, rarely going with a bet, apologizing the while for his caution, his reason being that he hadn't played for a while. No one tried very hard to find out too much about him; in the circles that many of our regulars moved in, it was not always considered wise or healthy to do so. But our man was polite and charming and even bought a round of drinks which made us all feel a bit more comfortable.

'Weren't you going to a fancy dress ball?' I asked after an hour or so.

He regarded me briefly (almost patronizingly, I thought with irritation), and he said, 'All the time in the world.'

It was my deal. I took the cards, having just dropped twenty pounds by backing my three queens against Johnny's flush. The one thing you could say about Johnny was that he took his winning like a gentleman. After dealing I looked at my hand. Absolutely nothing. I reckoned I'd stack but see what the rest were doing first.

Mathew the plumber threw in his cards right away. 'Rubbish,' he said.

Saudi Roche followed with: 'I can't open.' Nick shook his head.

Johnny started the ball rolling with a pound in the pot. Our visitor matched his bet. Seamus considered briefly, shook his head and backed out. I went with Seamus. Roche followed suit. That took it back to Nick the Greek who decided to venture a bet as well.

'So it's a three-horse race,' I said unnecessarily. 'How many cards do you want, Nick?'

Nick asked for one which probably meant he was chasing a straight or a flush. If he had two pairs he would have opened the game when he had the chance.

'Johnny?' I asked.

He grinned smugly. 'I'll smoke,' he said.

Aa-hah! Now that was interesting. Johnny looked like he had a pat hand. 'Smoking' meant he didn't want any cards, so he was probably already holding a straight, possibly a flush, and, who knows, maybe a full house? Of course, he could have been pulling a fast one by holding just a pair, maybe two, and creating the impression of holding a stronger hand by not buying anything. Still, a good game so far and Nick could yet have him beaten.

'How many cards?' I asked our visitor.

'I'll keep the game honest,' he said, smiling.

I dealt him three cards. Buying 'honest' in our game meant you took three cards, declaring pretty obviously that all you had was a pair.

I put the deck down on the table, lit a cigarette and said, 'Down to you, Johnny.'

As the opener, Johnny was first to bet. He had a quick and pointless squint at his hand – he hadn't taken any fresh cards – and took out his wallet, counting out ten one-pound notes.

'It'll cost you a tenner to look at me,' he said confidently.

Our visitor looked appreciatively at the bet and then fanned his fresh cards slowly before his eyes. He frowned almost imperceptibly but, in my opinion, deliberately – a frown that was meant to be seen. The man was a better card player than he'd shown up to now. Don't ask me how I knew that. I mightn't be the greatest myself but a gut feeling told me Johnny was about to get caned.

The visitor looked back at Johnny. 'Ten pounds, you say?'

'Ten pounds,' replied Johnny happily, and by now I almost felt sorry for him. Our visitor had pulled something in the draw, I was sure of it.

'Your ten pounds and a raise of . . . let's see now . . . yes, another ten.'

Nick was the first to react by promptly stacking his hand. He obviously hadn't drawn whatever he was after and seemed almost relieved. It was a high betting game by our standards.

So that took the bet back to Johnny who took yet another look at his hand and, for the first time, began to consider what our visitor might be holding. Might be holding? The permutations of three fresh cards were so great that there wasn't a lot Johnny could do anyway. Did he have a full house? Fours even? Johnny made his mind up. Whatever the visitor had, Johnny was going to play the strength of his own hand.

'Your ten and up another ten.'

Our visitor smiled kindly at Johnny. 'It must be good,' he said.

By this time Johnny, who was pretty humourless anyway,

wasn't in the mood for chat and just said, 'You seeing me or what?'

The visitor said, 'I think not.' Johnny reached for the pot but it wasn't over yet because our visitor came right back with : 'I'm raising *you* twenty pounds.'

Johnny pulled his hand away from the kitty slowly. And now he began to consider the obvious. He'd been suckered. By appearing to deliberate over the strength of his hand, our visitor had created the impression that he didn't have a great deal. Well, there was nearly a hundred pounds in the pot now – a lot to play for. At the same time, was it worth another twenty pounds?

Johnny looked at our visitor who smiled blandly back. 'Take your time,' he said.

Johnny took his time. For a full thirty seconds he stared at his hand, put it down, looked inside his wallet, made a quick calculation and said, 'It's yours. I fold.'

'I reckon you did the right thing there, Johnny,' I said with all the wisdom and insight of someone who hadn't a clue but had a fifty per cent chance of being right.

'What did you have, Johnny?' asked Nick.

'Ace high flush,' said Johnny miserably, 'but I reckon there was a full house going up against me.'

Our visitor raked in his winnings, probably the highest pot we'd ever seen in our game.

Johnny couldn't resist it and I couldn't blame him. 'What did you have?' he asked the visitor.

'Come now,' he replied, 'the asking price was twenty pounds.'

'Oh, be fair,' said Johnny. 'The pot's yours anyway.'

'Sorry,' said the visitor. 'It's not in my interests to let you know, is it? I don't want to let you know how I bet.'

Seamus interrupted. 'The man's right. Forget it.'

But it was all too much for Johnny and he made a grab for the visitor's cards just before they went back into the desk. Turning them over, Johnny choked. 'You bastard,' he said, his voice strangled. And there they were. Five cards, the total value of which was sweet sod all. Highest card he held was a queen. A perfect scam. But our visitor was not amused.

'Young man,' he said coldly, 'I am not, as you describe me, a bastard. I am a poker player and a substantially better one than you. You on the other hand are pathetic. If you're going to bet you should see it through and not back out half-way. It shows lack of character. Looking at my hand, however, is a flagrant abuse of the rules of the game and I should be obliged if you would remove yourself from the table – or, to use your probable vernacular, why don't you just "piss off"?'

Now, telling Johnny to piss off was normally about as foolish as Daniel crawling into the lion's den, sticking his head between the animal's gaping jaws and deciding to renege on a belief in the Almighty. Personally I applauded our visitor's bravery but felt his judgement in this matter was severely lacking.

'What did you say?' said Johnny in disbelief.

'Take it easy,' said Seamus. 'You were out of order looking at his hand.' Seamus turned to the visitor. 'This is my game. I decide who goes and who stays. You're leaving.'

The visitor regarded Seamus contemptuously. 'This isn't a game of cards. It's more like the music hall.' So saying, the man got to his feet and made for the door. Johnny rose too and blocked his path.

'No one tells me to piss off,' he spluttered.

'My dear fellow,' responded the visitor, 'I just have, unused as I am to such vulgarity.'

Johnny's knee came up sharply with a view to impressing upon our visitor the folly of his attitude. But this wasn't Johnny's night. Instead of striking home, Johnny's knee came into sharp and painful contact with the blunt end of a silver-knobbed cane. He roared with pain and outrage and made a lunge with his fist for the visitor's nose.

A quick sidestep and this time the cane came down sharply on Johnny's knuckles. As Johnny drew back, the visitor rammed the cane into his stomach. Johnny doubled up with pain only to have the cane crash down on to the back of his neck, leaving him gasping on the floor.

I doubt if any of us had too much sympathy for Johnny who

had got what he asked for, but Seamus stood up to the visitor and said, 'All right, pal, that'll do. Away with you now. On your bike.'

The visitor shrugged calmly and made for the door again. But this time he wasn't quick enough. Johnny grabbed an empty beer bottle and, his face contorted with rage, smashed it over the card table and thrust the jagged end into the visitor's chest. The visitor lurched back with the impact but, astonishingly, stayed on his feet. A long wicked-looking piece of glass that had broken from the bottle protruded from his heart. We stood like idiots, dumbstruck.

And then, unbelievably, the visitor extracted the glass from his chest, let it drop to the floor and said to Johnny so softly we could hardly hear him, 'You cannot know, young man, how good that makes me feel.'

Seamus, half smiling and shaking his head, looked at him almost with recognition. 'So you really do exist,' he said.

The rest of us sat immobile, horrified. Who was this man that he could take a piece of glass in the heart and still speak afterwards?

The visitor spoke again. 'Divide the money, my friends. Tonight you have given me what I have been seeking for a very long time. Now I can sleep.'

With that he walked slowly to the door, let himself out and disappeared into the night. Seamus walked over to Johnny who seemed to have gone into a trance. He poured Johnny a whisky: 'Drink that and go home.' There was a silence.

I looked at Seamus. 'What did you mean – "so you exist" – what was all that about?'

Seamus took a large draught from his poison. 'How long have I been here, in this pub?' he asked in return. We looked at each other.

'Ten years?' guessed Mathew the plumber.

'Yes, I suppose it's about that,' said Seamus. 'Well, just before I got this place, I was having a chat with the brewery personnel man about, you know, what kind of place was it and so on.'

'What's that got to do with anything?' Nick asked, irritated.

'Just listen,' said Seamus. 'Now, you know, back about a hundred years, this place used to be a brothel and that?'

Mathew said, 'You told us that ages ago. I didn't believe you, though.'

'It's true,' said Seamus, 'and listen to this. The story I was told by the brewery man was that one night there's about five or six of these gents from up west come in for the crack. So, while they're waiting, they're having a game of cards like always. Now one of them is a certain Lord Wilcox. A big man, six feet tall, a lot of whiskers and a bit of a dandy too. Natty dresser and a very sharp tongue on him. Anyway, they're playing five-card draw, would you believe, and Wilcox is dealt a pat flush. He weighs in heavy but in the end he's bluffed out of the kitty by another player holding absolutely nothing.

'Well, Wilcox doesn't like that, does he? There's a bit of a barney and before you know where you are, out comes this silver swordstick and the poor old sod is skewered where he's sitting.'

'Who's skewered?' I asked puzzled. 'Wilcox or the other guy?'

'The other guy,' said Seamus. 'Well, old Lord Wilcox isn't hanging around for the executioner (if you'll forgive my pun), so he's off a bit sharpish, isn't he? Only what happens is, he's barely out the door when he runs straight into a hansom cab. Wallop! Down he goes. Well, you'd think that would be the end of it, wouldn't you? Rough justice and all that.'

'Was it?' asked Nick.

'Well, they closed the brothel after that and turned the place into the respectable house it is now,' said Seamus with a smile. 'I forgot all about that story until, about five years ago when we all went over to Dublin for the Rugby international . . .'

'Don't remember much about *that*,' said Mathew, rolling his eyes.

'You wouldn't, you alcoholic,' said Seamus. 'Anyway, the relief manager had a little game of his own when we were away and apparently this guy comes in about one o'clock looking for cigarettes. And guess what he looked like? Your friend and mine from tonight. Said he was going to a fancy-dress ball, he'd tried five other pubs for cigarettes, couldn't the manager make an exception? And of course he gets himself invited to sit down with the lads and play a few hands of cards.

'Now in one game he pulls off a lovely bluff against little Mike Hogan – you know Mike, don't you, Nick?'

'Sure,' answered Nick. 'Nice lad.'

'Well, here's the really strange thing. He starts to accuse little Mike of thinking he's a cheat. I mean, can you imagine anyone accusing someone of *thinking* he's cheating? Well, Mike, who wouldn't say boo to a goose, just says, "I never called you a cheat – you won fair." Only this guy keeps on at him, really trying to provoke him. He's saying stuff like : "I can tell what you're thinking. You reckon I'm a cheat, you bastard." Well, poor old Mike doesn't know what to do so he gets up and goes home. And this guy just sits there all pale and grey, then apologizes to the lads and says : "One day I will be back. Don't you understand? I haven't paid for it yet." And then he's off too.'

Responding to a story like that wasn't easy but Maltese Johnny's shock was briefly lived : 'Load of cobblers,' he said. 'I'm off.'

He'd just gone out the door when I said to Seamus, 'What did you say happened to Lord Wilcox when he'd just done this guy in?'

Seamus said, 'Got run over by a hansom cab . . .'

From outside there was a screaming of skidding tyres mingled with a shrieking human voice. A loud thump came a split second later. Seamus dashed into the street.

'A cab?' I shouted after him.

Seamus stuck his head back into the pub. 'A Post Office van.'

H. H. WASHBROOK

Keep It in the Family

I murdered my wife on a brisk morning in early January.

We had just made love. It was quite pleasant. I looked at the curve of her white neck as we lay together in bed in the eaves of the narrow-shanked building in the German town where I worked.

I was a teacher. It was quite pleasant.

I fondled the tawny hair at the nape of her neck. I stroked her buttocks. I tickled the blade of her right shoulder. Then I took the pillow, rammed it down hard over her face and suffocated her. She made little noise. A grunt here. A grunt there. And then she was dead.

I got out of our bed and made my way barefooted to the cupboard in our living room. I had a pistol there. I checked that it was loaded. I released the safety catch. I placed the barrel inside my mouth. I pressed the trigger. I felt the bullet thuck into my flesh. I heard the splintering of bone. I smelled charred skin and the sweetness of gore.

And then I looked at myself in the mirror.

Not a blemish had come to my face. It had not changed one jot since the bullet had torn into it and sent blood and flesh and brains splattering on the walls behind me.

Curious, I thought.

Five hours later at seven o'clock I looked at myself again. No change to my face. Still the same crooked nose, and the same green eyes tinged with hazel, the same sparse blond beard and the sticky-out ears.

I ate a leisurely breakfast of grey bread, thin butter and the damson jam presented to me by one of my pupils the week before. The jam had a sour tinge, but was most palatable none the less.

I returned to our bedroom and dressed. My wife lay dead in our bed. I looked at the crooked purple scar on her belly and the marks of my nails on her hips.

Then I put on my raincoat and left.

I met the janitor of our apartment on the stairs. He was returning from a walk in the park with his Schipperke. Perky little dog. I liked it.

'Good morning, Herr Leitner,' I said. He looked at me hard. I bent down to pat the dog on its coal-black head. It growled.

'Mm,' I said. 'Doesn't like me this morning.'

The janitor pushed his corduroy cap to the back of his head and stared at me in silence for a moment.

'No?' he said. 'No?'

The tram was daffodil yellow. Lovely colour for a tram. I stood on the platform behind the driver. He had a cluster of warts on the back of his neck and the right elbow of his uniform topcoat was patched with leather. He worked the brass brake handle with gusto.

That I liked.

At the toll bar a few metres outside the town gates he climbed down from the tram and changed the points with a steel-tipped ebony stick. He heaved and he grunted and his breath curdled the clear frosty air. He winked to me as he resumed his station on the platform and commenced to hum to himself.

That I liked, too.

The school occupied two storeys above an agricultural bank.

I entered the lobby and looked at myself in the mirror. Still the same face. No change.

'Excuse me, sir.' It was the receptionist, Fräulein Brimminger. A pleasant lady, Fräulein Brimminger. Her father bred albino canaries.

'Good morning, Fräulein Brimminger. Sharp day,' I said, and made for the entrance to the staff room.

'Excuse me, sir, but you are not allowed to enter that door,' she said.

'I beg your pardon, Fräulein Brimminger?'

'That entrance is for members of staff only. If you are a new student, you must first deposit your registration papers with me, and then I shall direct you to the student common room.'

'I beg your pardon?'

'You are new here, sir. We have our rules.'

I looked at her slowly.

Fräulein Brimminger as always. Insipid hair in an apologetic bun. Damp spots on her chin. Podgy thumbs with square-cut nails. I smiled.

'It's me, Fräulein Brimminger,' I said. 'Herr Mercer.'

'Herr Mercer?' she said.

'Yes.'

'Herr Morgan Mercer?'

'Of course.'

'One minute, please.'

She placed her slim rolled-gold propelling pencil on the table in front of her. She turned to a dark green metal filing cabinet beside her. She opened a drawer, took out a file and from it extracted a photograph. She examined it closely. She examined my face closely. Then without speaking she handed me the photograph.

The same familiar face. Crooked nose, green eyes tinged with hazel, sparse blond beard and sticky-out ears, open-necked flannel shirt my wife had bought on her last trip to Wuppertal.

'Well then?' said Fräulein Brimminger.

'It's me,' I said. 'Morgan Mercer.'

A certain look came to her eyes. I felt an icy bite of terror scutter over my nerve-ends. I began to back towards the door.

'I have known Herr Mercer for this past nineteen months,' said Fräulein Brimminger.

'Yes,' I said. 'Of course.'

And I fumbled, both hands behind my back, for the handle of the door.

'He is a quiet man. He is a gentle man, a polite man. He is a man of honour.'

'Yes,' I said. 'Of course.'

My right hand felt the slim porcelain handle of the door. I clasped it.

'You, sir,' she said, 'you, sir, are not Herr Morgan Mercer.'

I spun round on my heels, threw back the door, raced down the stairs and went out into the narrow street, sly with winter.

I stood in the park. In the spring and the summer and the lazy autumn I had met my wife there every lunchtime.

Wicker prams purring with babies, pattering ducks on a paunchy lake, sandpits brazen with toddlers, nuthatches scittering, fat sausages sizzling, a plump, wastrel sun – sights, sounds and smells of past happiness.

Now the park was sparse. Bleak-veined trees, creaking ice, dull crows hooded with cold – a frieze of bleakness. I shivered in my summer raincoat.

My feet crackled on the gravel as I hurried down the main path and left the park to its winter pain. I crossed the road and entered the bar with its ochre tiles and the smug bottles of *Korn* behind the bar.

We drank there every evening, my wife and myself. She would be waiting for me, when I finished work. Often I would stand silently in the door and pleasure myself with the sight of her tawny hair resting softly on the whiteness of her neck. I would wait there, and eventually she would turn to me, and her dark brown eyes would splinter with joy and the laughter lines at the crook of her mouth would crease and crinkle. Now the fat stove rumbled, and it was warm.

I made my way to the *Stammtisch* and sat down.

Heinzl, the barman, was on the phone. He had his back to me. Fat Heinzl from Munich. What fun we'd had. A coach trip to Frankfurt to see SV Hamburg and Uwe Seeler. A trip to Aachen on the footplate of a fat locomotive with his brother, fat Alois. A trip to Colgne to Rosenmontag with his fiancée, fat Traudl.

With fat and slumbering slippers he slouched to my table.

'Heinzl, *grüss Gott, servus,*' I said. 'The same as always, if you please.'

'Sir?'

'The same as always, you fat old slug,' I said.

He squared his shoulders and began to rub the backs of his hands. I had seen him do that before on nights when Canadian squaddies slobbered their beer.

'I beg your pardon, sir,' he said, 'but the *Stammtisch* is only for regular customers who have been invited to sit there.'

'What?'

'It is the custom of the house, sir,' he said. 'It is the custom of every house, as you must well know.'

'Heinzl?' I said. 'Heinzl, what's going on?'

He placed his hands on his hips and began to rock on his heels.

'I do not know you, sir,' he said, and a barren hardness came to his voice. I had heard that tone before.

'It's me, Heinzl,' I said. 'Morgan Mercer. Good God alive, man, you know me. I drink here every night. With my wife. I'm always here. We've been on trips together. To Frankfurt. You remember? We saw Uwe Seeler head that brilliant goal. We got pissed on the . . . Good God alive, man, you know me.'

He placed his two hands firmly on the rim of the table. He crunched his head into his squat shoulders. A certain look came to his eyes. I fled.

Darkness had come to the town.

The river was in spate. It boomed under the lank bridge. It hissed as it raced between its snarling stony banks.

I went into the tobacconist's. Familiar smells. Familiar sights and familiar sounds.

'Frau Glockner,' I said.

A diffident lady with dark spectacles and wizened rings to her fingers looked up.

'Yes?' she said.

In the cabinet behind her I saw the packets of pipe tobacco she had ordered especially for me. Danish tobacco; dark, tacky and aromatic.

'Herr Mercer,' she had said to me one rumbling summer's afternoon, 'the scents of your tobacco bring to me great joy and great comfort.'

I looked at her closely now as she took off her dark spectacles and rubbed them nervously on the sleeve of her nigger-brown woollen dress.

I caught a glimpse of myself in the mirror at the back of the counter. Same familiar face. Same crooked nose, green eyes tinged with hazel, sparse blond hair and sticky-out ears.

'Frau Glockner, you must answer me very truthfully,' I said. 'Do you know the name of the brand of the tobacco I smoke?'

She dropped the spectacles on the counter and began to sidle towards the stock room door.

'For Jesus, Joseph and Mary's sake, Frau Glockner,' I shouted. 'It's me. Herr Mercer.' I reached out to grab her wrist.

She spun away and my hand crashed into the heavy brass cigar lighter with its pale blue flickering flame. My belly lurched into the glass counter, scattering the basket of book matches and the bowl of dried anemones.

'Please, please,' she whimpered. 'I do not know who you are. I am an old woman. If it is money you need, you may take it from the till. But, please, please, go at once. Please.'

A certain look came to her eyes. I fled.

A strange bar in a strange part of town. I had never been there before.

Why was I here? How had I got here?

I remembered passing the tram sheds and the old barracks with the crumbling stone walls and the pocks of ancient bullet marks on the iron-clad doors. I remembered crossing an unfamiliar bridge, skulking down unfamiliar streets, pausing for a moment in an unfamiliar square with a stone trough and a blind man cursing his dog.

Why? Why was I staring at my face in the greasy, steaming mirror behind the bar? Not a single change to a single feature. Why?

'Toni. Sorry I'm late.'

A woman touched me on the shoulder and sat down on the high stool beside me. Rough fingers rasped on the collar of my summer raincoat. She had coarse carroty hair, black at the roots. Her cheeks were rouged. Her teeth were filmed with green. She wore a black satin blouse that bulged. She placed her hand on my thigh and squeezed it.

'Yes, please, Matti,' she said to the barman, and at once he placed a small glass of rum in front of her. She downed it in a single gulp and offered it for re-filling. She was obliged.

'Okay, Toni, so tell me all about your day,' she said, and she twined her foot about my ankle.

'My day?'

She laughed. I smelled stale nicotine and stale rum. I saw a tongue streaked with yellow, and when she tossed back her head, I saw powder caked in the crevices and pot holes of her neck.

'You're tired, my pet. As usual,' she said, and she wrapped her arm around my waist and rested her head on my shoulder. 'Okay, Toni, I'll tell you about my day.'

Who in hell was she? Never in all my life had I seen her before. Never in all my life would I have wanted to.

'. . . and, of course, the tram was full and no pig of a man would stand and my feet were killing me and this Canadian squaddie was pressing himself up to me and feeling my arse with the palm of his hand so I turned to him and I . . .'

Cheap perfume. Harsh soap. Porcine eyes. I looked around

me. Market men embroiled in their beer. Scrawny women with black velvet bands around scrawny necks. Shifty men shifty with their schnapps.

'. . . so, of course, he orders me into the stock room and don't think I didn't know what he was up to and sure enough as soon as he locks the door he starts pawing me, fondling me, slavering over me, stalking me into a corner, undoing his buttons and . . .'

Juke-box retching, heaving out great gollops of fetid sound. Scrawny women dancing with each other. Stockings sagging round ankles. Pinched bottoms heaving. Shifty men, staring shiftily above the rims of shifty glasses.

'. . . . and then, of course, the old bag launches into this story about her daughter-in-law in Brazil who's just had her womb removed and I tell her I don't give a bollock about her poxy daughter-in-law, I've got enough troubles of my own what with my brother and that poxy wife of his in Dresden and that son of mine in . . .'

'Who are you?'

Her mouth dropped open. Rum dribbled down her chin. 'What?'

'Who the hell are you?'

'You what?'

The voice, shrill and strident, silenced the noise in the bar. Faces turned to me.

'What the hell are you saying to me, Toni Becker?'

'Toni Becker?' I said.

'Dear God. Dear God.'

The eyes flashed.

She pushed me in the chest, and I had to cling to the bar to keep my balance.

'I knew it. I knew it,' she screamed, and her fists beat at my chest. I scrambled off the stool and began to retreat towards the door. Hair awry, black satin blouse bulging and heaving, the woman waded in after me.

'I knew your game all along,' she screamed.

No music now. Hostile faces. Exit to the door blocked by two shovel-fisted market men in plaid hunting jackets and leather trousers.

'Another woman, isn't it, Toni Becker?'

'What are you talking about? I don't know what you mean. My name is . . .'

'Your name is Toni Becker and you are a pig.'

She flung herself at my throat, and her podgy fingers clawed at my flesh. I grappled with her, smelled the rum and the nicotine on her breath, heard the rasp of her pumping lungs. She pinned me against the wall.

'It's another woman, you swine,' she screamed, and she drew up her knee and rammed it hard into my groin. I covered my head with my arms to ward off the blows of her fists.

'And I know her name,' she screamed. 'Helen Mercer.'

'What?' I cried. 'What?'

'Don't look so innocent. Don't look so surprised. She's an Englishwoman. She's married to some poxy teacher. You've been having it off with her for months. Where were you last night? Overtime in the mill? Don't make me laugh. Don't make me vomit. You were in her house, having it off with her, while I was . . .'

She flung herself at me once more, biting, scratching and thrashing out with her feet.

'Pig,' she screamed. 'Poxy pig.'

The two market men lifted me up by the scruff of the neck, thrust me through the door and hurled me out into the street, rampant with winter.

An hour later.

Cold sweat pouring down my chest and my thighs, I turned into the street where I lived. Police vans outside our house. Lights flashing, crunch of boots on snow, neighbours thronging the sidewalk.

My God, they've found her body.

Flee. Get out of it. Run for it, Morgan Mercer. No.

Something drew me on towards the house, some force I could not control.

I would be recognized by the neighbours. The janitor would point me out to the police. Flee. Now. But, no, I could not draw back.

I elbowed my way into the crowd of neighbours.

Frau Dorfner, Herr and Frau Langer, Fräulein Schneeblum with the cast in her right eye – not a flicker of recognition from them.

'What's happened?' I whispered hoarsely.

'Someone has been murdered,' said Fräulein Schneeblum, and she giggled nervously. I could not move. Transfixed I stood as three policemen came out through the front door, holding the elbows of a figure covered by a blanket.

And then the blanket fell away and I saw the face of my wife. At once she saw me. At once she cried out.

'Toni. Toni Becker.'

I shrank back.

'Don't go, Toni. Don't run. I need you. They say I've murdered Morgan. Tell them it isn't true. Tell them, Toni. Tell them you and I were together in my bed for the whole of last night.'

A certain look came to her eyes. I fled.

MICHAEL GILBERT

Camford Cottage

'Then I know it,' said Miss Symondson, 'I'm certain I know it. It's at the top of a cliff. Hardly a cliff, more a headland. It's in a little garden of its own, with fields all round it. And there's a long flight of steps leading down from it to a private landing stage.'

'The same place, without doubt,' said Miss Melchior. 'It's some distance from any village. How did you come to be familiar with it?'

'I'd hardly call it familiar, since I had tea there, once only. But it was an exceptionally fine tea. That was thirty years ago. I cannot have been more than five or six at the time.'

'It must have been in the days of "Prince" Camford, the artist. He had no use for architects, you know. The house, we were told, was built by local builders from a sketch he made on the back of a drawing pad. And very well built, too, in local brick.'

'I didn't realize, of course, that he was a famous artist. To me he was just a funny man with a beard. He'd come on my older brother and sister and me, playing some game in the bushes at the top of the headland, Pirates or Indians. We were dressed in holiday rags and he got us to pose for nearly an hour while he made sketches of us. Then he took us down to the house for tea. Cornish butter and cream, on scones baked by his wife, a dumpy little woman with grey hair.'

'Also an artist,' said Miss Melchior. 'A water-colourist. You can still see her Cornish seascapes in the galleries.' Miss Melchior was a woman who knew things like that. 'They are both dead now. My brother bought the cottage – it had some other name – I forget it – but he named it "Camford Cottage" after its famous builder and owner. He and Patricia spent their honeymoon there. They were the only people who ever lived in it.'

'What a tragedy,' said Miss Symondson. She was not thinking of the honeymoon, but of what had happened at Camford Cottage some years later. A tragedy which had been widely reported.

Frank Melchior and his wife were keen sailors; Frank possibly a little keener than Patricia, who was apt to be sick if the sea was rough. They had set out one evening intending to sail down to the south-west, with a favouring wind, spend the night at sea, round the point of Land's End, and finish up by beating up to Fowey, where they had friends. It was a trip they had made many times before. On this occasion they ran into rougher weather than they had catered for. Their boat lost its mast, the auxiliary engine failed, and they were driven on to the Pen-Gallion Shoals. Fishermen, who had observed their plight in the early dawn, picked up Frank; Patricia's body was never recovered.

'He shut the cottage up for years after that. No one was allowed into it. He wouldn't listen to any suggestion of selling it. Not that he had to bother about the financial side of it. Patricia was a Dupont, and her money went to him. Poor compensation for a broken heart, but on top of what he was earning already, it left him free to get on with his writing.'

'I read his last one a few weeks ago, when I was in bed. The nursing home got it for me out of the public library. I can't afford to pay nearly four pounds for a detective story.'

'I don't believe anyone can,' said Miss Melchior. 'Have you met my brother?'

'Yes, once, when he came to give a talk at the school. We were all introduced. I thought him rather formidable.'

'It changed him, of course.'

'Has the cottage been closed ever since – ever since it happened?'

'No. In the end I persuaded him that he was being selfish.' Miss Melchior spoke with the firmness of an elder sister. 'We took some of his nephews and nieces, and I went down with him. I told him, "You'll find no ghosts in Camford Cottage. It's a happy place." The holiday was a great success. Pol-en-Perro is a wonderful place for children.'

'I certainly remember it as such,' said Miss Symondson wistfully. 'I suppose that development has spoilt it now.'

'Not a bit. The land round the cottage is farmland, and very good farmland too, I believe. No one can touch it. And, of course, when the weather was fine the children enjoyed the tiny private beach at the bottom of the steps, and the boating. Frank was nervous about letting them use the boat at all, but I told him, "Forget the past, live in the present." '

It had sometimes occurred to Miss Symondson that the reason Miss Melchior, who was handsome and well endowed, was not married might be on account of her firmness with everyone. She was one of the governors of the school where Miss Symondson taught, and ruled the Chairman and other governors with a rod of iron. Nevertheless, she could be kind. She had been very kind to her, when a bout of influenza, coming on top of an exceptionally hard term's work, had nearly carried her away. It was Miss Melchior who had whisked her out of her lodgings and into a private nursing home; and it was Miss Melchior who had dragooned the doctors into taking her case seriously. Now she was proposing a further kindness.

'A week will do you all the good in the world. It will quite set you up for the coming term. I'll order a stack of logs for the sitting-room fire. The cooking is all done by bottled gas. I'll have two cylinders delivered. They'll be outside the front door. I'm afraid you'll have to do your own cleaning. Local people won't go into the cottage – not since the tragedy.'

'Oh, why?'

'They think it's haunted,' said Miss Melchior, in the robust voice in which common-sense people speak of ghosts. 'I'm sure you're not one of these people who believe in ghosts.'

'If there was one, it should be haunting the Pen-Gallion Shoals, not Camford Cottage.'

'*Exactly* what I told my brother. And I can assure you that when we all went down there, there were no psychic manifestations.'

'But on previous occasions,' said Miss Symondson, 'it's only the family who have used the cottage? Are you sure your brother won't mind? Oughtn't we to ask him?'

'To the best of my knowledge, my brother is in Tangiers, gathering material for a new book. He was uncertain of his movements, and left no address. It could take weeks to get an answer.'

'If you're sure he wouldn't mind.'

'I am ab-so-lutely sure.'

When Miss Melchior was ab-so-lutely sure, there was nothing more to be said.

For the first six days it was as agreeable as Miss Melchior had promised. Although it was still early April the summer, as sometimes happens in Cornwall, had seemed to come earlier than it did elsewhere. The days were warm enough for strolling over the headlands and through the deep lanes, already yellow with primrose and white with may-flower. The evenings were cool enough to enjoy the fire of logs which blazed in the wide brick fireplace, set squarely in the middle of the living-room wall.

The nights were a little troublesome at first. Miss Symondson put it down to sleeping in a strange bed, but she was honest enough to admit that it was more than this. She was a child of the city, born and brought up among streets of houses full of people. Holidays had been things you took, with others, in camps or hotels or hostels which were even fuller of people.

Here she was conscious of being surrounded by emptiness. On one side, the sea. On the other three sides, fields. The nearest human habitation was the farmhouse which she visited daily for milk and eggs, half a mile inland down a track which was easily negotiable at this time of year by the tradesmen's vans and by the old taxi which had brought her from Pol-en-Perro Station. It must have become difficult in winter. Her only direct connection with the world outside was a telephone line; a single umbilical cord joining her to the world of men and women.

In the times when she lay awake she comforted herself with what Miss Melchior had said. It was *not* an unhappy house. Why should it be? The tragedy had not happened here, in this snug and civilized cell, but out on the wild grey sea, in a driving wind, among mountainous waves. Sometimes she visualized the helpless boat, its mast gone, its engine useless, drifting on to the fangs of the Pen-Gallion rocks.

She had never herself been on the sea in anything smaller than a cross-Channel steamer, and it is possible that she exaggerated its perils. She looked down on it, timidly, from the edge of the cliffs, but had never even ventured to descend the steps down to the beach and the jetty. They seemed to her to be steep and dangerous. Adequate, no doubt, for nimble children in gym shoes, or for active men and women who took care to use the tarred-rope side rail.

It was on the evening of the sixth day, with the taxi ordered for nine o'clock the next morning, and she was standing at the top of these steps, when it happened.

The day had been the warmest so far, more of an autumn than a spring day, the heat no longer fresh, but turned damp and stale. As she looked out to sea, it was as though a veil, thin at first but thickening, was being drawn across her whole field of vision. The effect was so startling that she passed a hand across her eyes to wipe away what seemed to be a blurring of her sight. Then she realized what was happening. A white fog was rolling up towards the mouth of the Bristol Channel.

It came with astonishing speed. One moment she could see. The next she was blind. One moment she was warm. The next she was shivering with cold. Thank goodness, was her first thought, that I wasn't out on the cliffs, miles from home. I shouldn't have known what to do. She turned round, with great care, took six paces up the path which led from the stair-head, found the front gate, and was soon back inside the cottage.

She turned on the lights in the sitting-room, and put a match to the fire, which was neatly laid. Warmth and light soon worked their magic. The fog was outside. She was inside, safe and sound. The next few hours were pleasantly occupied with cooking and eating supper. For this last meal of the holidays she had saved a half-bottle of red wine; and, greatly daring, she drank it all, finishing the last glass with her coffee.

As she sat, pleasantly drowsy, in front of the fire, she found her thoughts going back thirty years. How odd to think that she, the very same person that she was now, changed in body but the same in essence, had sat at almost exactly the same spot that she was sitting at now. Her brother had been on her right, at the top of the tea table, piling the delicious scones with butter and cream and honey, and stuffing them into his mouth one after another. She didn't want to think too much about him. His body was in Northern France, near the spot where his fighter plane had crashed.

Her sister had been sitting beyond him, half scandalized at the amount her brother was eating, half determined not to be left behind. Married now, with children of her own.

And what of herself? If she tried hard, could she summon back the six-year-old child, with pigtails, dressed in shorts, and a grubby aertex shirt, with sandals on the end of brown, scratched legs. She had always been the thoughtful one, the one who noticed things. What had she been thinking about, what had she been looking at, on that summer afternoon, thirty years ago?

There had been a tiny golden clock on the mantelshelf. That had gone, of course, and had been replaced by two vases. To the right of the fireplace, there had been bookshelves. This worried her. Because she was certain that the bookshelf had not been a detached piece of furniture. The shelves, five or six of them, had been fitted into the alcove on the right of the chimney breast. Yes. And in the corresponding alcove on the other side had stood the old grandfather clock. She could remember thinking, how unusual to have two clocks in one room. Big clock and little clock. Grandfather and grandchild.

Why in the world, she said to herself, should anyone have bricked up those two alcoves, so that the wall now stretched, level with the front of the fire, from side to side?

As she asked the question, the room seemed to change. She was looking at it as it had been. The books were back on their shelves on the right, the gold clock winked on the mantelshelf, and old grandfather swung his pendulum solemnly from the recess on the left. She knew that if she could turn her eyes she would see her brother and sister, and their kind host at the other end of the table, but her head was held, as in a vice.

Something was happening to the lights. They were dimming. And the room had grown deadly cold. But it was now, once again, the room of the present, not the past. She was looking at the blank stretch of bricks on the left of the fireplace and at the lady standing in front of them. She felt unsurprised, and unafraid. The lady was smiling. Clearly she meant her no harm. It was not Mrs Camford. This lady was younger, slimmer, and more fashionably dressed than that grey-haired dumpy water-colourist. Surely she knew the face? She had seen it somewhere, in a fashion magazine. Of course, it was Frank Melchior's wife, Patricia.

Who was dead.

Drowned, battered to pieces, her bones washing about on the floor of the sea, under the Pen-Gallion rocks.

What was she doing here? Why was she standing, quietly, patiently. Standing like someone who had been waiting for help, and knew that help was at hand?

All at once Miss Symondson knew the terrible answer. Moreover, she knew what she had to do, and she was locked to the chair; her body shaken with uncontrollable spasms, the sweat cold on her face.

As she struggled to move, and realized that she was helpless, the spell was suddenly broken.

The telephone was ringing.

A male voice said, 'Miss Symondson?'

Scarcely able to speak she gasped out something.

'I can't hear you.'

'Yes. It's Miss Symondson.'

'My sister told me you were using the cottage. Is something wrong?'

'No. Yes.'

'What is it? You're very indistinct.'

Miss Symondson said, in tones of one stating some unimportant but incontrovertible fact. 'I have just seen your wife. She came out from the recess which used to be beside the fireplace in the sitting-room.'

During the long silence which followed, she began to realize what it was she had said. He must think her absolutely mad. Perhaps she was mad. People had sometimes told her she was psychic. Had she passed over the borderline between sanity and insanity?

'I'm sure you'll think I'm raving mad,' she said, with a pathetic attempt at lightness, 'perhaps it was the fog and the general atmosphere and knowing – knowing the story – '

When the man spoke again it was a surprise. Before, his voice, without being rude, had been cold and formal. Now it had reverted to a friendly, conversational level.

He said, 'I was interested in something you said just now. You mentioned that this – this apparition – came from the recess which used to be beside the fireplace. How did you know that there was once a recess there?'

'I came to the cottage many years ago, when I was a child. I had tea here.'

'That would have been in Prince Camford's time.'

'Yes.'

A further silence. Then, 'I don't want to alarm you, Miss Symondson, but I think you may be in some danger. I don't think you ought to spend tonight alone in the cottage.'

'But how – '

'I'm speaking from Plymouth, where I landed earlier today. Is the fog very thick?'

'Yes, very.'

'It usually clears before midnight. It will only take me a couple of hours to get to you. I'll fix a room for you at Truro. Sit tight, and, Miss Symondson – '

'Yes?'

'My advice to you is, keep out of the sitting-room. Light the stove in the kitchen. You should be safe there.'

He rang off.

She had noticed the old black stove in the kitchen, but had not dared to tamper with it. Now she got sticks and paper, and a shovel full of coal, opened the front, and set it going. It showed a tendency to smoke, but this soon cleared, and she was able to put on a few small logs on top of the coal and closed the front. The stove gave out a companionable roar.

To be doing something was a comfort. It helped to keep her mind off the problems of what danger could possibly be lurking in that front room. It helped to pass the time. And that needed help. Only forty minutes since the telephone call. If the mist stayed thick it might take Melchior hours to reach her. He might not be there until morning.

There was a basket full of logs in the front room. They would keep the stove going for an hour or so. The alternative was to fetch a fresh supply from the woodshed, but this would involve making her way out into the fog and crossing the back yard. Surely it could not be dangerous, simply to go back into that room, just for a moment?

When she opened the door she remembered that she had turned out the light, and the switch was on the far side of the room.

She said, out loud, 'Don't be such a goose. *There's nothing in the room that can hurt you.* Just walk across and turn on the light.'

The fire in the grate had burned low, but it gave enough light for her to see, and avoid the furniture. Her hand was on the switch when she stopped.

The sound was definite and unmistakeable.

Someone was coming up the front path.

By the crunch of the footsteps on the gravel it was a man. He was coming cautiously, but was unable to avoid making some sound.

Miss Symondson was so paralysed with fear that she was unable even to raise her hand to the light switch. She stood in the darkness of the sitting-room and watched the figure loom closer through the fog.

Now he was at the door. A hand came out to try the door. Very gently.

Thank God she had bolted it, top and bottom.

The man stood still for a moment, his head bowed as though he was listening. Then he turned and marched straight up to the window, and pressed his face against it.

Miss Symondson, cowering inside, recognized him at once. It was Frank Melchior.

She was filled with unimaginable terror. The first words which came into her head were, 'He's come back for his wife.'

Plymouth? That was nonsense. He must have lied about that, and lied quite deliberately.

Why had he told her to sit in the kitchen? Was it so that no light would shine out from the front room indicating to any chance passer-by that she was in the cottage?

The man was moving now, quietly, away from the window, on the path that would take him round the house and directly to the kitchen door.

Which, she realized with frozen horror, she had left unlocked.

She tiptoed across to the front door and, with fingers which seemed not to belong to her, slid back the top bolt, and stooped to open the bottom one.

At that moment she heard the sound of the kitchen door being opened, and a voice which said, 'Hello, Miss Symondson. Where are you hiding?'

The second bolt slid back. She straightened up and eased the front door open. Gently, gently.

Footsteps crossing the kitchen floor, and the voice again,

'Are you in there? I thought I told you not to go in there.'

Then she was stumbling down the front path. The front door, as she let go of it, swung shut behind her. The noise must have warned the man that she was escaping. As she reached the front gate she heard heavy footsteps on the path. She stepped off the path, just inside the gate, and cowered down like a wild beast. Like a wild beast, she had the sense to realize that if she moved the man would hear her; and if he heard her, he would catch her.

The footsteps crunched past. The man outside the gate now. His steps were moving away, casting uncertainly, to right and left; lunging into the fog at some supposed shadow.

A sudden scratching of nails, on rock. A wild scream, and a series of horrible bumping noises. Then silence.

Miss Symondson got to her feet, and edged her way out of the gate until she felt the ruts of the track which led to the road. Down it she stumbled for an eternity of time, blinded by fog, her heart hammering, choking, kept going only by fear of what might be behind her.

As she reached the main road a light showed through the mist; there was a squeal of brakes and a car slid to a halt almost on top of her. The Cornish voice of Police Constable Greig said, 'Why the hell can't you look where you're going?' And then, 'Why, Miss Symondson. What's to do here?'

'A killer,' said Superintendent Assher to the Chief Constable of Cornwall. 'A careful killer, and a killer for money.'

They were standing in bright sunshine outside the door of the cottage, watching the workmen finish the demolition of the brick wall which concealed the recess behind the fireplace; a recess from which a skeleton, already identified as Patricia Melchior, had been removed and carried to the mortuary.

'You said, a careful killer?'

'Very careful. He must have been planning it for at least a year. He built that little summerhouse with his own hands.' He pointed to a neat construction, in the same brick as the house, which stood at the end of the lawn. 'He ordered a few hundred more bricks than he needed. And he taught himself, carefully and slowly, how to lay them. I expect his wife watched him, and admired his increasing skill. When the time was ripe, he strangled her, put her body inside, and bricked her up. To balance things, and make the wall look natural, he bricked up the other recess as well.'

'Why not just bury her somewhere outside?'

'He was a writer of detective stories, sir. He knew that digging in farmland leaves traces. And if the body was recovered from the sea, the pathologist would know she'd been strangled. Safer to keep her in the house. No one had ever used it, except the two of them. No one ventured in afterwards. Maybe he spread the story of its being haunted. Later, of course, he didn't mind family parties as long as he was there to keep an eye on things. And then, by one chance in ten million, it was let, behind his back, to a woman who'd known the place as a child.'

'What do you think he'd have done to her?'

'Thrown her down the steps, no doubt. Everyone would have assumed she was out in the fog, and had slipped, and killed herself. As he did.'

The Chief Constable thought about it. He said, 'Did you believe what she told us?'

'Most of it,' said the Superintendent cautiously.

'About Mrs Melchior appearing to her.'

'I saw no reason to disbelieve that.'

'Then you believe in ghosts.'

'Certainly,' said the Superintendent with a smile. 'Good ones and bad ones. This was a good one. She'll sleep easy now, poor soul.'

He was smiling because he knew that ghosts were hard things for a stolid Devonian like the Chief Constable to credit. He himself had been born and bred west of the Tamar, and like all Cornishmen knew everything there was to know about ghosts.

STEVE WILSON

O Keep the Cat Far Hence

It was evening, towards the end of autumn. I drove through
the lanes of north Norfolk, on my way to pay an unplanned
visit to an old friend. Torn-out hedges opened up the long
vistas of the fields, and one could get the grandness of the sun-
set that the eastern county so often quietly affords : the evening,
if not quite spread out like a patient etherized upon a table,
at least flung across the sky colours whose extravagance I used
to think existed only in the sunsets that publicized Digger pipe
tobacco, until I first visited those parts.

I drove slowly, with the car window lowered, savouring the
evening. Though the scene was far from exclusively idyllic –
the ravaged hedgerows, dead elms and, from time to time, dead
creatures squashed into the surface of the road – the evening
calm glossed over these unpleasant particulars. Drop by drop,
the invisible dew permeated all, to melt and weld every feature
beneath a melancholy reflective mantle; which had yet to become the chill of nightfall itself.

In my case part of the melancholy that evening may well have
been projected. I was leaving an assignation long anticipated,
meticulously organized, and disastrously realized. For some
while the wife of an acquaintance and I had discovered a deli-

cate attraction developing between us, which circumstances had forbidden a physical expression until the previous day; when, with my acquaintance away abroad on business, his wife and I had at last contrived a rendezvous, a weekend together at an East Anglian country inn.

However, the promised bliss, pneumatic or otherwise, had failed to materialize; marred the previous night by unguessable physical complications on the lady's side, and that morning, with redemption within our grasp, by an urgent phone call from a friend announcing the comedy of the unexpectedly returning husband, which caused the precipitate departure of my companion. A quiet weekend indeed. And beneath the comedy; both of us had known as she left that something valuable and fragile had been spoiled. Thus my thoughts wove melancholy patterns in the dusk as the car whispered between the hedges, along a route I thought I had forgotten; not precisely the stages of my age and youth, but something of that.

A final hamlet, a mile of open field and then I was turning into my friend Emily's narrow drive, under an arcade of dark thorn hedge towering unkempt on either side of the cracked concrete sections of the drive. At the bottom of this dark natural alley the track ended on a small apron of concrete, where I pulled up next to Emily's Morris Traveller, its green bodywork splotched with brown rust. Across the little lawn ahead of me, dotted with rose bushes, lay the cottage; a bequest from her late parents and as a weekend retreat from her working life teaching the piano in Cambridge, a great comfort to her mostly solitary existence; a single woman, whose only remaining family consisted of a married sister who lived in the south and visited infrequently.

I got out, closing the car door quietly, and with the stillness that such places communicate, stood for a long moment, in the dusk, in the almost palpable descent of the dew. Far away across the fields a church bell rang, and ceased. I gazed at the cottage; beneath a pink-washed, pebble-dash exterior and the pantiled roof characteristic of the region, lay a basic two-up, two-down structure over three hundred years old; but with larger cheap modern windows, and the recent additions of a porch, and an extension at the rear, which had been more ambitiously conceived than executed.

Wood smoke curled from the chimney; Emily was home. I reached inside the car and pocketed a somewhat depleted bottle of Teacher's whisky; no unexpected visitor should appear empty-handed. Walking towards the cottage my feet slipped and skidded on wet dead leaves and a profusion of rotting fruit from the overhanging apple trees, which littered the path and the little lawn to either side of it. The air was heavy with the over-sweet smell of blown roses, those petals still unshed now turning a curling brown at the edges. The effect on me of this over-ripeness, and Emily's necessarily intermittent efforts in the garden, was a familiar but forgotten depression; and I asked myself why I was paying this call. Alone, myself, getting no younger, and, the events of the previous night insinuated, no longer attractive, perhaps I was approaching that time in life when more and more the friends one seeks out are those previously neglected or dismissed, the isolated, the eccentric, the slightly twisted – because only with people of that sort will you feel at ease, they alone will welcome you as you wish – as you sidle, perhaps, towards their ranks yourself.

As I approached the cottage I also kept a weather eye out for animals. I had first known Emily while we were both up at the university, and even then she had had a reputation as the keeper of a series of particularly ill-starred pets and foundlings; and the more than two decades that had elapsed since then had done nothing but confirm and amplify this unfortunate tendency in her. Untrainably wild and incontinent dogs, supposedly neutered cats of a startling fecundity, cannibal rabbits and gerbils, hysterically insomniac dormice, broken-winged birds that could still contrive to aviate unpredictably and spray Emily's rooms with droppings, before dashing themselves against her window panes or expiring, lingeringly and malodorously, in the shoe boxes she had provided for their recovery – these had been some of Emily's companions over the years, and some of the crosses that friends and visitors had had to bear;

creatures whose only common factor had been their accelerated mortality.

But by the time I reached the porch there was no evidence of any fresh candidate for extinction. The cottage lacked a doorbell or knocker, so I rapped once on the door and pushed my way into the porch and thence into the sitting-room, intending a pleasant surprise should Emily not have seen the car.

She was, as I had half-expected, kneeling by the fire; and surprised enough to see me, though scarcely pleasantly. She scrambled to her feet and backed away to the wall, her normally flushed face drained of colour, and one hand extended as if in a warding gesture.

There was a long moment of silence, and then she said:

'James, I'm sorry, I thought you were . . .' and then we were both talking at once, I apologizing for my unannounced arrival, she for her dramatic reaction to it. I noticed that she was actually trembling, and approaching her with comforting sounds, swept an arm round her in an avuncular way. For there had been no suggestion of a physical relationship between us since the early, occasional advance on my part, while inebriated, during or after long-ago college parties. Fruitless attempts, and it had soon become clear to me that Emily's needs and desires were at once extremely discriminating, particular and fastidious, and also inchoate to the point of universality – her position, subsequently stated, was that only the development of one's immortal part escaped the meaningless; and obviously a partner in love had to at least appear to cooperate in this field of endeavour. There could be no casual encounters. Advances such as mine, however well meant, could hardly hope to succeed; and indeed it was only briefly that even drink caused me to lose sight of the fact that such advances to Emily, with her intense if muddled spirituality, were as inappropriate as they were unkind; and remained so whether or not one subscribed to the conventional view that her spiritual longings were no more than a result of physical repression.

So I contented myself now with a hug and a squeeze of comfort, glancing down at her the while. Yes, the face told the story; round face, and almost round, very dark brown eyes, liquid, brimming with unshed tears; the rather doll-like features framed above the fastened neck of a fussy, fluffy pale blue sweater; features frozen in an expression of appeal and expectation appropriate to youth, to the threshold of life. But it was an appeal which the world had ignored; though it was perhaps Emily's fear of the world which had caused this to be so. It was only her pets and foundlings which had provided her with something of an emotional outlet, and they had never lasted long. Thus at her age her appearance seemed to me poignant, and also pathetically but unavoidably irritating, exasperating even. Why didn't she pull herself together . . . And I noticed with a certain alarm that her eyes were now wider, the appeal more desperate, than I had remembered.

This was no time for irritation, then; apart from her life situation, something specific was quite obviously upsetting her tonight. The bottle of whisky in my overcoat bumped between us; with a flourish I produced it, found glasses conveniently to hand, made drinks, made conversation. For here was my chance to play the bluff, worldly good fellow, the drinking man and *bon viveur*; to represent in fact, for Emily at least, that life force of which, if truth be told, in these middle years I felt myself to be in increasingly short supply.

Seated by the fire in an elderly overstuffed armchair with faded floral covers, drink in hand, gaze taking in the pleasantly untidy little room, the massive central beam hung with bunches of herbs from the garden to dry, the evening coming down outside the windows, I prepared to listen; analyst, father confessor and part-time friend. Once launched, Emily was far from reticent, I knew. My guesses about what I was to hear ran to: an ailment, psychosomatic or otherwise; the death of a pet; or some crisis involving her work – the advent of the comprehensive system had been a sore trial to her. Emily sat on the floor by the fire and began to talk, I sat in the armchair and drank and listened. It was all as I now remembered countless previous occasions, only mildly irritating, and at any rate,

I told myself selfishly, preferable to the empty flat which awaited me in town. For what followed I was totally unprepared.

The last time I had seen her had been just over a year previously. Three months after that, she had been driving the wintry roads southwards to London on an urgent errand, to pick up a Cambridge friend who had just completed a long and painful attendance at her mother's death bed, and was too broken down by the experience to get herself home. An adult waif and stray; Emily, being Emily, sped to the rescue. But turning the corner of a wet and lonely stretch of road she was first on the scene of an accident so terrible that others, arriving some time later, could only vomit. Soon one man was dying in her arms; one, on the other arm, said only, again and again:

'May God forgive me, I was the driver.'

When the ambulances came at last, Emily drove on to her waiting friend with blood on her hands. But not alone; on the back seat of one wrecked car, between its two passengers, one dead, one dying, she had discovered a wicker carrying box, and inside, a young and sickly black cat. Somnambulistically, she had put the basket in her own car and now drove down to her friend with bloody hands and the cat beside her.

Emily, recalling the day, gazed at the fire, I prompted gently. 'And your friend?'

'It was Elizabeth Pruham, you remember?'

Inwardly I groaned; if anything was more disastrous than Emily's animal familiars, it was her human ones, her friends. Elizabeth I had indeed met; I had been told she had forsaken a convent during the later stages of her novitiate as an Anglo-Catholic nun, and I had found her a rather repelling mixture of the rigid and the sentimental.

When Emily arrived, the two overwrought women fell on each other. Listening to Emily recount the horrible events of the crash, Elizabeth immediately seized on certain elements of the events. '. . . *May God forgive me* . . .' They discovered that they shared a belief in the forces of good and evil; they quickly convinced themselves that Emily's arrival at the death scene so soon after Elizabeth's ordeal with her mother went beyond coincidence. Death and evil stalked together; care and faith must oppose them. Illuminated by their shock and exhaustion, every detail became significant, and above all the cat which Emily had carried away.

The little creature proved to be ill; very weak, and septically infected. Elizabeth's husband and child had gone to stay with his parents while she was attending her mother, and Elizabeth insisted that they should remain there now. For two days and nights, in the Pruhams' large, empty Victorian house, she and Emily sat up, backs aching, nerves jumping with terminal exhaustion, while the cat hovered on the edge of extinction. Evil must not prevail, they prayed; the little thing must live.

On the third morning, the cat began visibly to improve. The two friends decided it should stay where it was and live with Elizabeth. I could imagine what it must have cost Emily with her love of pets, but couldn't help thinking that the creature, which they had identified as a tom and christened Daniel, would have had a better chance of survival away from her. Though perhaps, I speculated, given Emily's present distress, it had eventually succumbed?

Emily continued her story with the return of Elizabeth's husband, Edward Pruham, and her six-year-old son Mortimer. And again I shuddered inwardly; I knew them both.

Edward Pruham was an Anglican priest who held the post of chaplain at a large minor public school outside Cambridge. As such, he had fallen on his feet. He was one of those priests who recognize, but refuse to admit, his faith's inadequacy when confronted with the nexus of real problems in the late twentieth century, and had retreated from that recognition and despair into a rigid endorsement of a social system which his charges and many of his colleagues were noisily or unobtrusively in the process of dismantling. He was a ferocious snob, stood politically somewhere to the right of Ghengis Khan, recalled his own schooldays with fondness, and endorsed, domestically and professionally, what he referred to as 'the public school discipline'.

I must confess prejudice here; as an ex-participant in the

five-year chastening of the sons of the rich and titled, the rituals of dominance and submission, scorn and sentimental attachment, that seem to find their natural expression in beating and buggery, it has consistently eluded me how anyone but a sick man could recall those years as the happiest days of his life. For what, one must surely ask, does that say about the quality of the rest of his days?

And Edward Pruham took the least pleasant aspects of a thoroughly unpleasant experience, the discipline, and made of it an article of faith. Approaching fifty, he was, necessarily and quite palpably, a split man : a tall Christian, muscular to the point of apoplexy, whose veined hands one could equally imagine clenching the edges of a pulpit or busy beneath his own capacious mackintosh in the audience of a blue movie show in Soho; or, as had been rumoured, rummaging under the cassocks of the younger and more cherubic of his choirboys. The murmurs of gossip along the latter lines at the school threatened increasingly to come to a head in actual accusations against him, and this constituted a further source of strain on his domestic situation.

It should come as no surprise that the offspring of such clergy, especially growing up in gloomy Cambridge, would probably turn out somewhat neurotic, but the Pruhams' son Mortimer was a genuinely disturbing case. What trauma his conception and his birth had involved for an ex-novice, one can only guess; but from the start it seemed he had not felt at home in the world, and in his mother's arms. A difficult baby; a fretful, howling infant; and as he grew, his father's authoritarian tendencies had seen to the rest, I suppose.

I had seen him only once, at the cottage, when Edward and Elizabeth had brought him with them to visit Emily the previous summer. Emily's married sister had also been staying there with her two-year-old daughter. Mortimer, then five, had seemed to take to the little girl and the adults left them sitting on the steps playing. A minute later we heard screams, and looking from the window I had seen Mortimer flailing the child with a broom handle and at the same time stamping hard on her dangling legs. I had heard Emily remonstrating with him as gently as she was able.

'But you could have hurt her, Mortimer.'

I had heard the boy's reply :

'Good.'

His tone was chilling; to my untutored ear it seemed to go beyond childish spite, far beyond. Emily had told me how later that day, after I had left, in the evening she had gone outside and, finding a disgraced and sulking Mortimer, had suggested a game to divert him. One can imagine a certain frantic edge to the game of hide-and-seek that followed. At all events, Emily was running away when suddenly the child went totally rigid and fell into a fit. It was minutes before he revived, screaming the blame at Emily whom he insisted be punished; anxious to avoid attracting the attention of Edward and Elizabeth, she ended up standing in the dark in the holly hedge, with Mortimer piping that he was glad, she'd be cold and want to go to the toilet, wet herself and get into trouble. He knew.

'Yes,' he said, 'my father is a great locker-up.'

At last Emily was allowed to come out, and she and the boy stood for a moment in the still of the evening as night fell.

'Isn't it quiet?' she had said.

'Yes,' said the boy, 'it is an apprehensive time. At night, I am a man of blood.'

This was the home which the cat Daniel had entered.

Daily life with Mortimer, with his food-hurling, his fits, his strange pronouncements and his undoubted cruelty, resembled nothing so much as a non-stop dress rehearsal for *The Exorcist*. But under the circumstances Elizabeth and Emily's pre-occupation with *metaphysical* evil seemed ironic. As in a film with a cunning director, their gaze had been concentrated away from the direction from which the shock, the true horror, comes. Or perhaps the pattern of what was to follow did suggest some malign impulse, some destiny.

Following the healing of the cat, Emily went home to her flat and was ill herself, and after that, catching up with her backlog of work meant that several weeks had elapsed before one evening she had visited the Pruhams. The cat was outside when she arrived, and as an honorary aunt to Mortimer she was allowed to read him his bedtime story while downstairs Elizabeth made them coffee. As she read she looked at his head on the pillow, his pale, flawless child's face, calm grey eyes and fine dark hair. Perhaps it was the contrast with what she knew of him (and to her alone would his mother confide some of the boy's worst excesses), or perhaps some sense of the injustice of a child carrying so much history of unhappiness; but Emily found the moment painfully touching, and began to sob gently as she read. At first Mortimer would not believe she was crying; because, it transpired, amazingly in that tortured household, he had never seen a grown-up shed tears. Neither did he know how to touch her to comfort her, but eventually attempted to do so by silently pressing two drawings that he had done into her hand. Then his mood changed and suddenly he was screaming that they were his, that everything in the room was his, that she get out.

Shaken, Emily left his room; and there at the end of the passage was the cat. Daniel looked well, had put on some weight and filled out under a now sleek black coat, but as she went towards him, unable to run from her due to the closed doors along the corridor, he spat and shrank, cringing in the corner. Thinking him simply nervous, Emily bent to stroke him; claws flashed and she screamed, the blood running down her fingers where the cat had deeply raked the back of her hand. Hearing her cry out, Mortimer in his room laughed aloud.

Yes, said Elizabeth almost censoriously, Daniel was understandably a very sensitive creature and one had to exercise a reasonable prudence approaching him. Though he and Mortimer were often alone together.

Perhaps Emily might have discounted this incident, but soon, from pupils at her school, over the following months she had begun to hear disquieting tales. Even the Pruhams' detached residence and respectability finally were unable to conceal from the neighbours either their child's abuse of the pet, or the father's treatment of the child; though being England it was the former that finally caused the first complaints. A particularly formidable elderly lady, ironically a retired missionary, from her house next door had seen Mortimer tormenting the cat mercilessly with a pair of compasses after partially immobilizing it with string; and before too long, tales of Edward Pruham's frequent resorts to corporal punishment together with his 'locking-up' capabilities, with Mortimer shut in dark rooms for hours at a time, began to circulate. There were complaints about the cat itself as well. Daniel had grown rapidly; he could be seen prowling the area in a fighting crouch, ears flat to his skull. He terrorized the neighbourhood pets, savaging other cats, eating their food – he entered and fouled other houses at will – putting one or two fairly large dogs to flight in the process.

The complaints had the effect of an unfortunate vicious circle, however, in that Edward was led to vent his icy rage on his son as the cause of this public embarrassment, and Mortimer no doubt extracted his revenge on the cat, who continued to wreak havoc locally. The cat's aberrations were treated by the Pruhams in the same day as the child's: the pretence was now maintained, rigidly, that they did not exist. Indeed when Emily finally, and tentatively, broached the subject in private with Elizabeth, she was rebuffed with a sharpness that indicated the tense, unremitting self-deception that was evidently necessary to prevent the situation in their household falling apart altogether.

For Edward was by now conceiving his relationship with his son exclusively as a battle of wills. If charity begins at home, so in this case did the public school discipline, and Mortimer was a permanent affront to it: wild and cunning, by turns dependent and resentful, exuberant and depressed – above all, unpredictable, undisciplined. The punishments and confinements became more and more frequent and severe.

I interrupted Emily's talk at this point to reach for the bottle and offer her another drink. She declined, but I poured one for myself, a generous one; I was not enjoying this story and not relishing hearing its outcome. Outside, I realized, night had come. The room, lit only by the flickering fire, contracted;

above, from the corner of my eye, again I glimpsed the bunches of herbs hanging from the black beam, but in the indistinct light now they could have been dolls, fetishes, instruments of some wise woman's purpose. Emily's voice continued, an unbroken flow, rising and falling, gentle, supplicating, hypnotic. I gulped at my drink. My whisky, my bluffness, seemed a fragile protective barrier now in a world where such things could happen.

The climax had come the week before. Elizabeth Pruham had rung and, quite collectedly, asked if she could drop round to Emily's flat the same evening and see her; but from this unusual request itself Emily had guessed everything was far from well. (She was correct : Elizabeth was to unburden herself on the subject of Edward's unmusical activities with the younger members of the choir at his school, over which an official accusation was in the offing.) On the phone, however, she merely mentioned that it was Edward's night to dine at his old college, but that a babysitter had been arranged.

In the event, Elizabeth had already left for Emily's when the babysitter telephoned Edward to say that her younger brother had just been diagnosed as a case of measles. Had Mortimer had them? He had not; so she felt, as a possible carrier, that she had better not come that evening.

Edward hung up, seething. There were no alternative sitters to be had at that hour, and these gaudy nights were very precious to him, one of the few occasions remaining for him to act the man he wished he was. He padded upstairs to Mortimer's room; perhaps the child was asleep and could be left, at least until he could phone Elizabeth at Emily's and recall her? All was silence until he was outside the bedroom door; then, sickeningly, the child's preternaturally sharp hearing seemed to detect his approach and he set up a wail of complaint and reproach.

Edward entered the room, sat on the bed; the child was no calmer. Ignoring his din, Edward began to talk, man to man, gravely and calmly, asking whether such a big boy would not mind being left alone in the house for a few minutes. Mortimer ignored him and screamed. Edward hastily reached out his hand to stroke his head and soothe him; Mortimer bit it. Edward cuffed the boy instinctively, but the small head turned, the blow landed obliquely and Mortimer's nose began to bleed, big stars of blood dropping on the starched cotton sheets. He began to howl in earnest. Panicking, mindful of the neighbours, Edward seized a handkerchief and stuffed it in the child's mouth, securing this makeshift gag with the boy's school tie; while he was doing this, Mortimer, hysterical, scratched, kicked and bit him to some effect.

Edward felt the voluptuary rush of control deserting him, of letting go. Snatching the child from his bed he carried him out into the hall, shaking him continuously and shouting at the top of his voice,

'You're a disgrace to this house, damn you, and it's time you were taught a lesson!' – perhaps repeating the rubric preceding some long-forgotten humiliation by flogging of his own at the school he now idealized in hindsight. Tearing off his belt he secured the boy's wrists roughly to the banisters, immobilizing him temporarily while he plunged downstairs to the kitchen for some rope.

Returning, he tied the boy up with a thoroughness and expertise which when subsequently discovered suggested both enthusiasm for the work and practice; securing him by both wrists, still gagged and silent, in the appearance of submission, in a forced crouch at the foot of the banisters.

Then he switched off the landing light and left the house to dine at high table. What old school songs, what martial music pounded in his head as, heels ringing, he strode through the streets to college? Music insistent enough, evidently, to obliterate his awareness of the appalling risks, from fire perhaps or suffocation, aside from the mental anguish, in which he had left his son.

It cannot have been long after the echoes of the slammed front door died away in the dark house that Mortimer, alone and helpless, heard the first scampering footfall of the cat.

The screams, when they came, mercifully alerted the ex-missionary neighbour, the only one in the road who chose not to possess a television and so could hear them clearly. She could not gain entry to the house but, fearing fire or worse, was sufficiently alarmed to summon a younger and more agile neighbour, who broke a window. As they climbed the stairs towards the source of the ceaseless shrieking, the cat slipped past them into the darkened hallway.

Emily and Elizabeth had decided to return together; they arrived as the ambulance sped from the drive. Explanation and abuse were mingled as the neighbours collected in the drive, told them what had happened. Elizabeth drove after the ambulance, leaving Emily to contact Edward at the college. After she had done so, she listened to the neighbours speculating on how Mortimer's gag had been displaced sufficiently for him to cry for help. Some said it had simply slipped, but others, more ingenious, and having caught a glimpse of the child's head as he was carried out to the ambulance, guessed that the gag had been ripped off by the cat as it savaged its helpless tormentor's blood-streaked face.

Emily was unable to speak to Edward when he returned; angry neighbours had summoned the police, and he was taken immediately to the station for questioning, as a result of which he was charged and remanded in custody.

Elizabeth was driven home later that night in a state of shock. At the hospital she had been told that although her son would live, he now had a further handicap to add to those of his parentage and his disturbed temperament; the loss of sight in both of his maimed eyes.

'Oh my God.'

I heard my words drop, hollow, in the silence of the dark room and the horror which we now shared. A silence which stretched, agonizingly, as we sat on, Emily and I, silence interrupted only by the hissing, the sudden crack and flare of dry elm wood on the fire.

At last I said :

'They put the cat down, I suppose?'

There was no answer.

'Or did it run away?'

Still Emily sat in silence; but she turned her head to look at me, and the pools of her black-brown eyes seemed to enlarge in anguished supplication as she gazed up at me.

'Emily,' I said, 'what happened to that cat?'

Then, my eyes still locked on hers, I felt the hairs on my nape rise and my heart freeze; as from the dark behind me came a single, growling purr.

DOMINIC COOPER

Will Stringer

I found them quite easily not long after the boy from the upper farm had turned back. I caught sight of their fire out on the edge of the moors. By then the sun had been down a while, yet there remained a haze of half-light in the sunken path which I was following through the top of the wood. The day had been warm and still with the hours full of the insistent calling of cuckoos and the drumming of snipe. But I was tired for it had been before noon when I left Owmby and my leg had not stood up well to the journey. I had tried asking Robert for the use of the old donkey we had but he had refused me, saying that he might be needing it himself – though this, I think, can only have been out of some perverseness or resentment towards me for, God knows, he has not left the village in months and in any case the poor creature could never have borne his weight.

Although I lost sight of the fire for a while once I had left the wood and was out in the scrub of furze and juniper, I knew from the boy that I had only to keep on along the path until I came to a drystone pen and that I would then find them a short way further on, higher up on the hillside. And indeed, in the very moment that I reached the pen, I caught the drift of smoke from their fire, heavy with the smells of resin and juniper and rosemary. I was fairly sure that I would know one or two of them by sight from the market days in Owmby; yet, all the same, as I climbed the last few hundred paces up towards where the glow shone in the thickets, I felt nervous about how they would receive me.

There were five men and a young lad seated round the fire. But before any of them noticed me, I found myself surrounded by their dogs – low, dark streaks patched with white, crossing the arms of firelight and leaping up at me with hot breath and the sour tang of sheep, or stalking my progress, head down and poised.

' 'Evening!' I said as I came up to the fire.

They had all turned and were looking stolidly at me. One of the dogs was snuffling at my legs though all the others had settled back into the shadows. I bent down and patted it and its throat filled with a tremor of muted wariness.

'Come here!' growled one of the shepherds to it.

The dog slipped away. A place was made in the circle and I sat down, stretching out my aching legs in front of me. Some more wood was thrown on to the fire and the twigs and smaller branches went up with a noise like spitting fat and sent a column of sparks spiralling into the enormous darkness above. In this sudden upsurge of flamelight, I glanced round at the shepherds. They were watching me.

For a long time we sat there in silence and the fire had burned quite low before one of them leaned over and offered me a large piece of bread soaked in mutton dripping.

'It's Owmby you're from, isn't it?' he said, watching me eat. 'I've seen you there...'

I nodded, swallowing a mouthful of bread.

'That's right,' I said. 'My name's Gilbert.'

'Ah... You'll be with the priest then...'

'Yes. I am. I'm clerk to Robert of Owmby.'

Peter Colfox, the oldest of the shepherds, I knew by sight from the last Michaelmas fair. Tall and angular, with glassy blue eyes and vast, knotlike hands, he had been pointed out to me as a man who, in his youth, had had three wives in almost the same number of years after which he had never married again. Like most of the others around the fire, he was dressed in a long sheepskin jacket and wore a skull-cap of soft leather. As

I ate, he sat there eyeing me surreptitiously and munching ceaselessly with his gums so that the silvery stubble on his face glistened in the firelight.

I knew two of the other shepherds as well. One was Bob Rigmaiden, a taciturn, wizened man with a broken nose who had a reputation in the parish for his skill with animals. The other was Alan Sugg whose round face and curly hair suggested an easy-going and benevolent nature but who I happened to know was in fact a sharp-tongued and difficult man. Perhaps he recalled my name from the case in which his family had been involved concerning the land that surrounded the chapel at Sowenford; for when, a short while later, he looked up from the fire and spoke, there was a coldness in his voice.

'Don't often see priests' clerks up this way,' he said flatly.

'No,' I replied, ignoring his tone. 'I suppose not. There'll not be much up here . . .'

'Just the sheep,' he said. 'And us.'

I looked at him but he dropped his eyes to the fire.

'I suppose it'll be some way over the moors to the next farm,' I said.

'Old Tunn's place is the nearest,' put in Peter Colfox, 'though you couldn't rightly call it a farm. And that'll be the best part of half a day's walk away . . . wouldn't you say so, Nick?'

'Aye, it's a good walk,' said the small man to whom he had turned. 'And Stephen here,' he went on, gesturing to a swarthy youth on his left, 'will tell you that it's no place to get caught in bad weather. We went over that way in March. Just before the snow came. And cold and wet as you may be, old Jack Tunn's not one to make you feel welcome . . .'

The shepherds laughed. But before the gentleness of the sound had dissolved into the night air, Alan Sugg spoke again.

'Is that where you're headed for then? Across the moors?' he asked, slipping me a curious, sideways look.

I shrugged.

'No,' I said, stretching casually. 'No, I don't think so. I'm looking for the stringer.'

It was just as I had expected. Immediately, a stark silence settled over us. For a moment, I caught Bob Rigmaiden's eye, puzzled and aggressive, before he too turned away and looked at the ground. Peter Colfox, who was leaning back on his elbows, remained motionless staring up at the stars.

For a long while we sat like that, held rigid by the strain of the silence that had grown between us. From time to time a drop of sap at the edge of the fire would hiss and bubble greasily or the bleating of a lamb would come to us from over the moor : but otherwise there was nothing to disturb the passing of the night hours while we sat there and gazed blindly at the fire being gradually hollowed out by the heat.

Later, much later, when my head was beginning to sag with exhaustion, Peter Colfox suddenly spoke.

'He's dead, you know,' he said quietly, still staring upwards. 'Didn't you hear in Owmby? It was early last winter that it happened . . .'

'Well, perhaps that's what we heard. But you hear a lot of things if you care to listen to people talking.' I paused before going on. 'He must've been a strange man . . .'

'Who? Will Stringer?' said Peter Colfox, sitting up. 'A strange man? Yes, perhaps . . . I don't know. I'd say most folk are strange. But death . . . well, there's not much strange about that, is there? I mean, when it comes, it comes. And that's all there is to it . . .'

'It sounds simple enough like that,' I said laughing.

'Well, isn't it?' broke in Alan Sugg with a sneer. 'As Peter's said, the stringer died. It's quite simple . . . What more do you want?'

'To see him,' I answered quickly, turning on the man.

'See him? What are you talking about? What stupid ideas has that suspicious fool of a priest been giving you?' he said and spat.

'That "suspicious fool" as you call him wants his church records kept up to date. And that's my job. So there are certain things which I need to know . . .'

'Like what?' asked Bob Rigmaiden sharply.

'Like, for instance, how he died.'

'It's not known,' said Peter Colfox quickly.

I looked across the fire at the old man and found the same peremptoriness in his harsh blue eyes.

'Well now,' I continued, 'that's odd . . . The priest led me to believe that he had been found by a shepherd . . . from Attlegarth.'

The fire crackled. Nobody spoke. I determined to persevere.

'So I'd imagined that it was one of you . . .'

Again nobody spoke.

'Well,' I insisted, 'was it?'

'Yes,' said Peter Colfox fiercely. 'It was Stephen here that found him.'

I turned to the rough youth.

His eyes flickered away towards the old shepherd before he looked back at me and nodded.

'Was he already dead when you found him?'

The smallest dip of the head was all the answer I got.

'And where was it you found him then?'

Stephen glanced quickly round at the others and then gestured vaguely towards the moors.

'Well now,' I said patiently, 'just you tell me what you can about it . . .'

'That's won't be much,' put in Bob Rigmaiden, picking his nose as he spoke.

I looked quizzically at Stephen. With a shrug and a sheepish grin, the youth opened wide his mouth and waggled the pink, useless stump of his tongue. As I turned away in horror, I noticed the wry smile on Peter Colfox's face.

'Well anyway,' I pursued, my anger beginning to rise, 'what became of his body? Just tell me that, will you? Where was he buried?'

'That's not known either,' said Peter Colfox defiantly.

'What do you mean?' I retorted.

But once again my question was received by a sullen silence in which I could sense the strength of the shepherds' resentment. Robert had warned me that it might be so and had told me that

I must at all costs be patient and employ guile and subtlety rather than any kind of threats.

'Look,' I said as gently as possible. 'I am not here to make trouble. That I promise you. All I want are a few details so that I can go back to Owmby and complete the records. That's all.' I paused, hoping to give their animosity time to settle. 'Was nobody with Stephen when he found the stringer's body?'

'Aye,' said the small man Nick after a moment's silence. 'I was. At least I was and I wasn't . . . We'd come up together from Attlegarth you see. On our way over to Sowenford, we were. Stephen went on ahead to have a look at one of the traps. I'd a yearling on my shoulders so I was just following along in my own time. . . .'

For a brief moment, he stopped talking and waited as if with his ear cocked. I heard nothing. Then he cleared his throat and went on.

'Well, as I was saying, there I was, coming along, when all of a sudden I saw Stephen running back. All excited, he was – waving his arms and trying to tell me something. Anyway, once he'd calmed down a bit I understood easily enough that he'd found a dead man . . . the stringer. Well, we went back to the spot where he'd found him, at the foot of a rock-fall above the beck but . . . but there was nothing, no sign of him. He'd . . . that is, he'd gone, as it were . . . Isn't that how it was, eh, Stephen?'

Sitting there with his mouth half-open and his eyes fixed on Nick, the young man nodded brusquely and swallowed.

'And I suppose nobody's ever seen him again?' I said sardonically.

Nick stared me full in the face for a moment.

'No,' he said and pursed his lips.

'He's dead,' said Alan Sugg. 'We've told you.'

I nodded slowly and poked at one of the flaming logs. Peter Colfox took a small pipe out of his jacket and began to play. It was a gay, jerky tune that leaped about to the accompaniment of the fire and which seemed to me, in my mood of frustration, to be played for my benefit alone. For a while I kept my eyes

down, pretending to be engrossed in my thoughts but in fact
penetrated by the music, obsessed and mortified by the sheer
spirit of it. At last I could bear it no longer. I looked up. All of
them, even Peter Colfox as he played, were watching me. It was
almost as if they were expecting something, though what I
could scarcely have ventured to say. I bit my tongue and looked
down again. Yet as time passed and the music continued on
its relentless, energetic course, the anger gradually went out of
me so that I began to hear the pipe-tune in a different way. By
now, Stephen, Nick and Alan Sugg had stretched themselves
out and were dozing. Seeing them, I suddenly knew that I
too must sleep. As I lay down by the fire, I asked Bob Rigmaiden where the lad had got to.

'Lad? What lad?'

'There was a lad, a dark-haired boy, with you when I
arrived.'

Bob Rigmaiden frowned and very slowly shook his head. I
looked across at Peter Colfox whose playing had taken on a long,
sinuous rhythm that matched the dying force of the fire. And
even as he played, he gave me a soft, fervent smile. I lay back
and closed my eyes. The fire's heat seeped along my side. The
night hung above me, filled with smoke and starlight. And the
pipe played on and on.

The fluting sound was no more. From behind the hill came
distant laughter and cries, broken by the steady singing of
children. And in amongst all this were also the pinched and
bearded voices of goats, the crowing of cocks and a sound like
the belling of a stag. The smells that drifted on the air were
those of strong, new sweat and of smoke, of ale and dung and
bread and blood. And all the while the first light was lapping at
the high, night clouds and the force was pounding at the chill
pool below the moorland's edge.

> *The turning wheel masters all.*
> *Even ending, it begins beginning.*
> *Takes you where you cannot go,*

Back before beginning's ending,
Out beyond the end's beginning.
The turning wheel masters all.

When I awoke, the shepherds had gone. The sun still lay down below the higher land to the east but above the morning haze the sky was bright. I got to my feet and shook my head clear of the weight of sleep. As I bent down to pick up my sack, I saw the little wooden pipe that Peter Colfox had been playing the night before. It was lying in the cold ashes, snapped in two. I turned away and set off quickly back down the track towards where the hamlet of Attlegarth lay in the shadows.

'Well, I say it's a disgrace, I do, a downright disgrace! I mean just look at her! She ought to be ashamed of herself, sitting out there in the sun like that, preening herself and showing off that great belly of hers for all the world as if the wretched child was going to have a lawful father. Her man didn't die until October it's true – but she doesn't fool me! Not for a moment! No, that brat was started a good while after her Adam went down under the elm tree . . . Oh yes! And anyway you can tell that that little fellow's not planning to spring into the world for a while yet. No, you wait and see – it'll be all of eleven months after her man's death that she's brought to bed. The young hussy!'

Sarah Pyett was very much as Robert had described her. Old and toothless, she constantly looked about her like a wild animal sniffing the air. Her wrinkled face, collapsed by age, was rough and weathered by the years of grime and sun but her eyes were polished and clear with the sharpness of perception.

Following the woodsman's directions and coming down the path, I had caught sight of her out at the back of her house feeding her hens in the early morning sunlight. I had approached her casually and started talking, speaking of this and that but always of petty things while she peered at me suspiciously and gave me gruff replies. At last, in a sudden lull in our conversation, she asked me where I was on my way to. And so, as

I had planned, it finally came out that I was clerk to Robert of Owmby and that I had come to Attlegarth on business. She hummed and ha'd for a while and then, in a roundabout yet transparent way, she inquired what this business might be. I told her bluntly that I was wanting to discover a few things about Will Stringer.

For the briefest of moments, those eyes of hers swept the steep slope of the wood behind me.

'You'll not find many around here who'll speak to you of him,' she said.

'And why's that?' I asked innocently.

'Why? Because they're afraid, that's why,' she said with an edge of bitterness to her voice.

'Whatever of, when the man's been dead six month or more?'

She looked at me with something that was neither quite a sneer nor a smile.

'A bowl of fresh milk would do you good,' she said and turned away before I had time to answer.

I followed her round the side of the house and ducked in below the thatch. She was waiting for me in the shadows and as I came in she stepped behind me and peered out of the door-way.

'There she is again,' she said, tutting. 'That Kate!'

And off she went into her explosion of reproach over the young woman whom I could see sitting on the grass not far away. When she had finished, I said by way of calming her.

'Well, I suppose the father of the child will marry her in due course . . .'

Sarah Pyett looked up at me and her face twisted with scorn.

'Marry her! What children you men are! Did he marry Mary Bless or Ann, the mason's daughter from Overhouse? Did he? Or Maggie Kellet for that matter . . . though she died with the child, poor girl . . . And the others . . . oh yes, there've been others all right these three years past. But nobody'll ever say anything . . . or do anything to put a stop to it. Perhaps now at least it'll be different,' she went on just as I was opening my mouth to ask her who she was talking about. 'If the priest's sent you then perhaps it's because he's heard of the goings-on and is thinking of doing something about it.'

For a moment I was so taken aback by the old woman's outburst that when she finally paused I was not sure what to say. And perhaps too there was some instinct in me which told me to keep quiet. For I just stood there gawking and waited, caught in that dark hovel of a room while out in the brilliant sunshine a cuckoo called over and over again. The old woman was staring at me though I had the feeling it was not really me she was looking at. At length the cuckoo must have passed up into the wood for its calling grew fainter and fainter and then ceased altogether. And only then did she speak.

'You'll know how it was with the stringer, I'm thinking. You'll have heard about it from the priest.'

'No,' I replied in all honesty, 'he told me very little.'

'Not about what happened here that summer, three years ago?'

'But no,' I protested, 'I've heard nothing. I've only been with him since Lammas last.'

'Well now . . . ' she said thoughtfully, 'then perhaps after all . . . You see, it was like this . . . Three summers ago, at the time of the new moon after Whitsuntide, that priest of yours rode over from Owmby. Aye, once again he came with his grumbling about the lesser tithe. Said we were late in paying or something, I don't know . . . Well, maybe there was a bit of truth in what he said . . . Anyway, that tithe had been a sore point between him and us for years. Bah! How can we be expected to find what he demands? Oh aye, he's a real leech that man – though perhaps I shouldn't be saying so to you. And it's common knowledge just how well he does out of the parish . . . Well, in any case, when he started on at us like that we did what all sensible people do when a priest takes it into his head to come and preach to them about tithes – we just stood there and waited till he'd had his say and then went off and got on with things just as before. We weren't bothered. He could wait . . . But Will . . . well, I don't know but there'd always been something a bit strange in the stringer. Even when he was still only a lad. I remember saying to my man that he'd not turn out quite right. You see, he'd always been a terrible one for moods, the stringer. He was peaceable enough as a rule, I suppose, but from time to time he'd fly into the most violent tempers. And when the devil had got hold of him like that, one did well to avoid him for he was tall and as strong as a horse. Well, that day the priest came was one of Will's days. While we all went off as quiet as mice when the priest had finished with us, Will stayed behind and started arguing with him. Something the priest said must've angered Will for they say he suddenly started shouting, cursing him and telling him that he'd show him up for the money-grubber he was. To begin with, the priest kept his temper but in the end, well, he too was white with anger. I expect you know how he can be . . .'

'Yes,' I said wryly, 'I do.'

'Aye, well . . . All the same, we thought that that was the end of it all. But later that day Will went off with some others to shoot in the butts, over towards the woods behind his house. They say he was still a bit irritable and on edge but that he began to cheer up as he shot. I think he was pleased with some new strings he'd made or something . . . Well, at one point, late in the afternoon, they were shooting at long-distance clouts. But when they'd finished the round and had walked the ten score paces or so to the clouts, what did they find but Will's dog, lying stone-dead with an arrow through the back of its neck. Close by it, right near the centre of the clout, there was a large bone. It must've been thrown there from the bushes while they'd been walking away to the shooting line . . . Now it was well known how Will loved that dog. Aye, he was in despair, was Will, when he found it dead. And then when he got home and heard from his wife that the priest had been seen with the dog, well, you can imagine just how it was . . .'

I nodded, thinking of Robert and those hard, small eyes of his and wondering if he would really have resorted to such a petty and spiteful thing.

'But, you know, it was a queer thing,' she went on slowly, 'for after he'd shouted and stormed for a while, he suddenly fell into an odd silence. Aye and it went on too. Just sat there brooding, he did. Nobody could get a word out of him. When people went to buy bowstrings, they were dealt with by his wife, a handsome sort of woman though on the quiet side like so many of them from over Stanwick way . . . Well, it continued like that for a time and then one day, why, they just closed the door on us. No warning, no explanation, nothing. Of course, we knew they were still there. We could hear them. But a while later, about two weeks after the priest's visit in fact, we woke up one morning and found them gone. Just gone . . . Well, we never really found out why it was – I mean the row with the priest or the dog being killed or whatever – but there was no doubt about it that something that day had turned the stringer's mind. Anyway, they were gone, that was for sure . . .'

'For good?'

Sarah Pyett glanced up at me. Once again, for no precise reason, I longed to be out of the shadowy dankness of that room and back in the summer sunshine.

'Well,' she said cautiously, 'it's three years since they left, isn't it? And I've never seen either of them again.'

'Then . . .' I started to speak but she cut me short.

'Listen!' she said aggressively, thrusting her face up towards mine. 'I'm an old woman. How do you expect me to prove anything? Whatever I were to say, they'd just laugh at it and tell me to stop my nonsense. Well, maybe I am old but there's nothing wrong with my eyes or my ears . . . But if you're wanting to know more then you'd best go and ask them yourself!'

'Them?'

'Aye! That Kate, for instance,' she said with a scornful gesture, 'or any of the others for that matter . . . Just you ask them about their children. Ask where the father is. And when they lie to you and mumble some excuse or other, just ask them if they remember an occasion when they happened to be out by the edge of the wood at dusk and heard a jay shrieking. And when they look away and hesitate in answering, you ask them exactly what they did when they heard the bird. Did they recall what they'd heard tell and quickly turn back for home like any decent, Christian woman would? Or did they perhaps stay on to see what would happen? And if, by any chance, they stayed and listened to the jay as it came gradually closer through the wood, didn't those little hearts of theirs start knocking . . . ? The little fools! Aye, for once they'd stayed, it was always too late . . . Oh yes, I've seen a thing or two these last few years! It all happened so slowly to begin with . . . but once it'd started, there was no stopping it – oh blessed Lord, no! First it was the young women and then later, when they could no longer answer for themselves, they got their menfolk to go out with them too. Oh aye and I've seen them, seen them with my own eyes I have . . .'

'Where?' I asked breathlessly.

'Oh but it was a long while back,' she replied hastily. 'I don't bother myself with watching for them any more. Anyway I'll be gone soon. What'd be the point in my trying to do anything now . . . ?' She paused. 'But in those days, a year or two back, I took to walking about early on summer mornings and sometimes, just after sunrise, if I went up by the woods, I'd catch a glimpse of some of them coming down from the moors. All messed about they were, with stains and marks on them . . .'

'But where?' I insisted. 'Where was it they'd been?'

At that moment there was a slight sound out beside her house. The old woman drew in her breath sharply and turned away into the room's inner darkness.

'It's not known,' she said in a clear, flat voice. 'I tell you, it's nothing to do with me.'

'But . . .' I began indignantly.

'It's no good!' she hissed at me. 'I know nothing!'

We stood there without speaking. I glanced round and saw one of her hens strutting across the glaring brightness beyond the doorway. As it vanished out of sight, I turned back towards her.

'So you too are afraid,' I said softly.

'Perhaps . . .' she answered. She paused before going on in a suppressed but tense tone. 'Yes, well perhaps I am . . . Now just leave me be, will you? Tell that priest anything you like – but just go away and leave me alone!'

I had no desire to upset the old woman further. It was clear that she was frightened; and indeed I too now felt oddly uneasy. It was something to do with the contrast between her dark insinuations and the warm blaze of the light outside ... And yet, at the same time, my imagination was alive, kindled both by what she had told me and by the confusion of unexplained things from the night before. If I found myself still talking of Robert and the church records and the official nature of my inquiry, there was no deceit in this : yet it was no longer the whole truth for by now I felt compelled to discover more if only for my own peace of mind.

After the years of my youth in which everything had seemed so clear-cut and simple, it was now as if a tremor had shaken the order in my life. And though it brought fear and confusion to my heart, what this tremor intimated also awoke an excited curiosity in me. *'The turning wheel masters all . . .'* As I stood there, staring into the darkness, I found those words once more floating in my mind. . . .

I left shortly afterwards. Somehow I had managed to cajole old Sarah into telling me the name of the place though whether I achieved this simply by covert threats or by the effect of the very urgency in my voice, I cannot honestly say. 'Dollman's Cut,' she had breathed in my ear, her chin quivering with fear, and a moment later I had turned for the door.

After the dense, clinging warmth of the lower land, it was pleasantly cool up in the wood. I had got my directions from the same man who had pointed out the way to Sarah Pyett's house earlier in the day. On that occasion he had been friendly enough but when I met him the second time and asked him if he could tell me where Dollman's Cut was, he simply looked away as if he had not heard. Annoyed, I repeated my question. For a moment or two he went on with his work but then, seeing that I was not going to leave him without an answer, he looked up sulkily and jabbed with his thumb in the direction of a little footpath that broke away from the main track a short way further on and disappeared up into the trees. But since then I had been walking for some time and, having left him and his sour mood far behind, I had reached a point on the path where it cut across the slopes of a narrow valley.

Down below me hushed a beck, by the look of it quite a sizeable torrent in the winter months but now with little more than a trickle of water in it. The valley was wooded on both sides but the hardwoods that grew so thickly in the lower wood near Attlegarth were beginning to give way to a motley of bushes and pine trees as the soil gradually turned to that of the moors.

I limped along slowly, suddenly overcome with exhaustion. Because of the trees it was difficult to see how the path was going to take me clear of the valley which was getting narrower and steeper at every moment. And as I rose away from the main body of the wood, I felt myself coming back into the heat again. Gone were the cool noise of the beck and the great caverns of shade, the mysterious sounds of scuttling in the undergrowth and the sudden flight of pigeons exploding high overhead in the sky-pocked greenery of the trees. Now it was all dust and rock, dry peat and the snagging of contorted pine roots, while overhead the midday sky had taken on a sombre opaqueness. Slowly but surely the moors were coming into view.

In my exhaustion it began to seem to me that it was all a madness. What was I doing hauling myself up on to the sunbleak moors? What, in fact, if anything, had happened the evening before? Had it not just been a meeting with a handful of ignorant shepherds? And what indeed, I asked myself, had I heard that morning other than the distorted ideas of a solitary old woman ... ?

But even as I was thinking this, I stopped in my tracks. A hundred paces or so ahead of me, standing by itself, was a large pine tree. And fixed in the centre of its trunk was a wooden wheel. My heart was bounding. So what? I tried to tell myself. A wheel fixed to a tree. Is that so very strange? I rubbed the sweat from my eyes and looked around. The dusty blue sky was empty; the sweeping edge of the moors was merely a long, featureless line. Not a sound – no bird, no beast – nothing but the buzz of a single fly hanging in the windless heat by my head.

I walked out from the bushes and as I came on to the open hillside, I saw that beyond the tree a narrow gorge turned eastwards from the valley's head. I knew that I had reached the cut.

I went slowly up to the tree and stopped. The wheel was about five spans across and quite plain except for a number of pierced blocks of wood attached to its rim. I touched it and discovered that it was not fixed rigid to the tree but was free to turn on a heavy wooden pin that had been sunk into the trunk.

Once again I looked around. Nothing moved. The silence remained untouched. Everything was dominated by the booming of my pulse. I glanced towards the mouth of the gorge but could see nothing but a flat expanse of bare, sand-coloured rock where only the occasional wiry bush sprouted. The thoughts ground round and round in my mind. What was in the cut? What, in the past three years, had happened there? And his wife – what about her? Nobody had even mentioned what had become of her ... And why, if he was dead, did ... ? But my eye was once more caught by the wheel. It seemed to be the only certainty in my growing panic. I looked at it, considered it carefully. Was I going to do nothing after all? Just turn tail and go back to the safety of my desk in Owmby? My pride nagged angrily at me.

I gave the wheel a little push. It turned smoothly enough on its pin and then stopped. I looked nervously over my shoulder. And then, in a sudden moment of impatience with myself, I gripped the wheel's rim and swung it hard – once, twice. As it gathered speed, I jumped back for a soft fluting sound came from it which carried out over the upland silence. And almost immediately the sound was answered by a series of pulsing echoes that rose from within the cut. For a while it held and I stood there before the turning wheel, quite unable to move, feeling myself gripped by the vibrating note. And then, as the wheel slowed, the note began to fall, dragging the echo down behind it in a disconcerting conflict of sound. I bit my tongue and prayed for it to stop but on and on it went until I was ready to cry out. And then quite suddenly it was over and the silence had returned. I remained absolutely motionless, waiting . . . At that moment, from what seemed like only a few paces behind me, a cuckoo called.

The sound burst upon me. Driven by panic, I spun round and began to stumble back down the path. With my head swimming and my breath caught in my throat, I plunged into the bushes without so much as looking back. It was just as I thought myself safe in their cover that I glanced to my left and found myself face-to-face with Peter Colfox. He was sitting crosslegged on a flat rock just above the path and was looking fixedly at me. But I never so much as stopped. With a gasp of surprise, I blundered on towards the wood. It was just as I passed him and saw his smile that I heard the chatter of the jay in the trees below me. And it was as if that sound had unleashed the whole countryside for immediately all the other birds came alive. A knot of pigeons hurtled over the tree-tops and swung away across me; a scattering of crows, rising into the sky from nowhere, broke into a harsh cawing; while a whole multitude of smaller birds from blackcaps to finches and thrushes filled the air with their frenzied calling. But, mindless of all the confusion and excitement around me, I sped on, dragging my wretched leg as best I could. As I left the moors and the upper wood behind me, the noise of the birds gradually began to subside and at last, in a state of collapse, I came out on to the main track behind Attlegarth. I had never heard the jay again.

The woodsman had gone. After a short rest I pressed on and was soon down among the houses again. Of Sarah Pyett there was no sign and the door of her house was closed. But I was not concerned : I had no desire to hear any more of her madness. My one idea was to get away. I flexed my leg and set off for Owmby.

As I left the hamlet I passed the place where the woman

whom Sarah Pyett had called Kate had been sitting. She was no longer outside the little house but as I walked by something made me turn. The young woman was standing in the doorway. And as she stood there with her hand touching the side of her swollen belly, I saw that she was staring at me and that there was an unwavering smile on her face.

MARGARET A. DOODY

The Tale of Edie's Teeth

That summer, back in the fifties, I was twenty-four, an age when
you feel you know about life; as I was studying medicine, I
felt I knew more than most. After finishing the year in med.
school in Halifax, I came home to the farm at Sandford to help
with the harvests. I bounced down from Halifax in my bright
yellow second-hand Ford. It was pleasant to be going back,
although Sandford is everyone's idea of the neck of the woods.
Rather a scrawny neck, too. We have none of the rolling hills
and craggy seashore you see in postcards of Nova Scotia;
Sandford, set between the mining area and the Strait, lies in
flat scrub land, richer in blueberry barrens and tamarack trees
than in any of nature's lusher productions. Sandford is my
native village – a sprawl of a few farms, with a gas station at
the crossroads, a general store, a drugstore and two churches.
Still, there is much more general bustle of living in a place like
that than people who accidentally drive through the back of
beyond would believe.

The first night, I went out on a toot with some of the local
boys, and next morning took advantage of the homecomer's
privilege of sleeping in. After that everyone expected, including
myself, that I would get up at daybreak and be useful. I remember sauntering into the kitchen that morning; there was
a smell of coffee and baking bread. My mother was rolling

pastry, and directing Edie's activities at the washtub. Edie's presence was no surprise – she often came to do for us, as for other households. Nobody was better, people said, at chores around the house, although she was 'a bit wanting'. She was a large woman, shapelessly bulky, with a red moon-face and small head, with a kind of sub-head at the back in the form of a large tightly twisted knob of dull black hair. Edie had looked much the same when I was a child.

'Here's Dan, back from Halifax,' my mother said politely.

Edie's strangely unlined red face loomed out at me through the steam like the sun in a mist, and she gave me a close-lipped smile, like a parody of the Mona Lisa. I grinned back. Edie wasn't much on conversation, but she liked smiles. I poured myself a cup of coffee, and watched Edie's wrinkled hands carefully rubbing. She had a slow thoroughness that was restful to watch. Edie had taken to cleaning in all its branches many years ago when she was instructed by farmers' wives anxious to procure her assistance. It seemed a strange vocation for someone who lived in a tar-paper shack near the woods.

Edie lived with her mother, a child-scaring hag. Mrs Tonna was a walking bundle of rags; she had no occupation, but she had a hobby, a passion for collecting junk, not for sale but for private use and ornament. Portable objects, such as kettles and cracked cups, she carried off herself; heavier properties, such as disused bedsteads, she would persuade people to drop off at her place. The shack was a dirty museum of her finds. Sometime before the Flood she had taken a partner in life – or for a term of it; it was he who had built the shack. Whether the union had been blessed by the law no one was quite certain, nor even whether it was this union or some other which had been blessed with Edie. Even in village history there are gaps and questions. People agreed that 'good blood somewhere back' must have gone into the making of Edie, for she proved to have a taste for work. Once thoroughly impressed with the desirability of scrubbing the corners of rooms and the techniques for doing so, she saw to it that every corner was immaculate. She seemed to take pleasure in her repetitive achievements. Edie was not without self-respect, even concern for personal appearance. Once she had learned the arts of laundering, she washed and ironed her own shapeless garments at her employers' homes. Any gift of clothing, any little ornament, would be carefully tended for years.

The close-lipped smile was a manifestation of painful self-consciousness, as I had learned a few years back when I had asked my mother, 'Why has Edie taken to grinning with her mouth shut?'

Ma gave me a reproving look: 'Because, poor thing, she had to have a lot of her teeth out.'

I was just remembering this, as I bit into a fresh crust, when mother said, 'Edie's had all her teeth out this spring, haven't you, Edie?'

Edie paused and nodded, but not with embarrassment, almost with pride. She suddenly opened her mouth in a wide empty grin and flashed moist, toothless gums at me.

'No teeth now!' she said.

'And,' Ma continued, 'she's going all the way to Amherst this afternoon in Dr Turner's car to get her new dentures. You're going to have new teeth after today, aren't you, Edie?'

Edie smiled, Mona Lisa again, and nodded emphatically.

'Sure. New teeth.'

And shortly after noon, Edie, with a battered hat on and an old plastic handbag in her lap, was sitting in the front seat of Dr Turner's car. A ride in a car was a valued treat to her; the trip to Amherst would have been an occasion, even without the glory of the expected teeth. Jack Turner was the doctor of the region. He spent energy and his own money on a small hospital in Traceyville, where he dealt with births and farm accidents, uncertainly assisted by Dr Martin, who was bright but given to drink. The overworked Jack grunted at us and drove off with Edie nodding by his side.

'Poor thing,' said mother, watching the car go down the road. 'I hope she'll like her dentures when she gets them. Grandpa Holt said his were a trial – claimed the raspberry seeds always got stuck in the roof.'

'How come she's getting them at all? You have to pay, don't you?'

'Oh, that's Mr McAndrew. Such a good man. You never think of a minister noticing whether someone has a tooth in her head or not – but he saw how Edie minded losing her teeth, and gave up smiling, so he insisted she should have dentures made. He took her to Amherst for the first fitting, and I think he's paying for it all out of his own pocket. We must all try to make it up to him. Really, the Bertlesons should help – but they only care whether Mr McAndrew will make a husband for Linda.'

This explanation seemed very likely. Mark McAndrew, the United Church minister, was only about ten years older than me. In Sandford's eyes he was not particularly prepossessing; learning was at a discount, and Mark was dark and thin and wore spectacles, which naturally gave him the name of a 'book-worm' locally. He read a lot, but spent much spare time tramping around the countryside; he had an interest in plants, animals and local history. His collection of Indian arrowheads was the admiration of all boys. Some of the girls liked him too, especially the older ones. He was supposed to have had a fiancée who had died. The residents of Sandford, especially the women, did not approve of celibate clergy, or of bachelors, and he was invited to teas and suppers where daughters in starched dresses and Toni perms were set before him.

At that time I was an atheist or agnostic or something, but I liked Mark, and used to talk to him a good deal when I was at home. It was like him to think about getting teeth for Edie.

We soon had a chance to see how Edie liked her teeth. I was at the garage getting some petrol, about seven o'clock that evening, when Dr Turner and Edie arrived in the centre of the village. Jack slowed down, as Edie, waving furiously, evidently wished to communicate with me.

'Hi!' she called. 'Look! Teeth!'

She grimaced, so widely it must have hurt, and there were the new teeth, in their exact and artificial beauty, white as snow and even as piano keys.

'Gee, that's great, Edie,' I exclaimed. 'They look swell, eh?'

'Yeah,' she agreed, then, leaning her head out of the car window (which it seemed to fill), she gave Al Trent the garage man the benefit of her resurrected smile. 'Teeth!' she yelled, in case he didn't notice. 'All new!'

'Well, that's right pretty,' said Al. 'Have all the boys after you now, Edie.'

So she did; the little boys who hang around garages and drugstores had lined up beside the car and were staring.

'There's Mr "Kandrew",' said Edie – and so he was, just leaving the Trent place after visiting Great-Grandma Trent. Edie hollered and waved.

'Look, Mister! Teeth in now.'

Mr McAndrew came up, smiled, and shook the hand extended out of the car window at the end of the great arm – or rather, she shook his hand vigorously as soon as she got it, with the action of someone operating the handle of a stiff pump.

'Jump in,' said Dr Jack to Mark. 'I'm taking Edie back to her place.'

Mark got in the back seat and the car started off slowly, accompanied by the two Green boys, a tow-headed Trent, and a juvenile Bertleson, all going beside at a walking pace. On an impulse I hopped into my car and followed. Down the road we proceeded, over the little bridge, past ribbons of wayside lupin, by fields and pastures and wide-eyed cows. Edie smiled broadly and solemnly, waving her hand and bowing her head in strange imitation of the young Queen that we had seen in newsreels at the movies.

Indeed, we were very grand, going slow and stately. We could have been a funeral, which is about the grandest procession Sandford knows.

Eventually we drew up in front of Edie's place. Mrs Tonna, not doing anything in particular, not even obviously waiting, was visible in the front garden, which bore a rich crop of rusted bedsprings and broken saucepans.

' 'Lo, Ma,' said Edie, heaving out of the car. 'Look – I got me teeth!'

Mrs Tonna, chewing spruce gum rhythmically with her own natural grinders, gave Edie's choppers the once-over.

'Fine,' she said in shrill approval. 'You look good.' Then she appeared to notice the rest of us, and her face darkened.

'These guys want money? Tell them we ain't got any.'

'No, Ma, no. All free – in town. Look!' and Edie exhibited her smile again. She seemed distressed by her mother's reception of her friends and supporters. It was one of the difficulties of dealing with the Tonnas that Edie's mother, who could speak fluently when she wished, refused as a general rule to speak directly to anyone but her daughter, whereas Edie, who was sensitive to social niceties and enjoyed company, was not gifted by nature with much talent for speech.

'Now, Edie,' said Dr Jack. 'Before we go, we must plan how you're going to deal with your teeth at night.' He turned to Mrs Tonna. 'You got a glass or mug in the house?'

'You tell him nothin' in the house,' said Mrs Tonna. 'I been left with nothin'.'

'Ma,' said Edie. Then, in evident unusual defiance of her mother, she said to the doctor. 'You come in. I find it.'

Dr Jack and Mark and Edie went into the shack, and I followed – whether to give moral support or merely from curiosity I don't know. The kids had discreetly retreated. Mrs Tonna plucked at us with her frail claws, feebly, then slipped in and stood at the door, glaring at us and guarding her property. The room was a mess of old rags, broken bottles, inner tubes and unattached portions of old copies of the *Family Herald*. It also whiffed tremendously. But from an orange-crate cupboard in the corner Edie produced a wide-necked jar, and placed it on the stained table.

'Here, Edie. Every night you take your teeth out and put them in this jar of water. Just water – not pop or rum – and new water each time.' Jack poured some spring water from a cracked ewer into the jar.

'Take out – put in water,' Edie repeated, concentrating.

'Let's see if you can take them out,' said McAndrew. We

thought Edie might object, but she obediently tried, wrinkling her face and filling her mouth with fingers.

'Like this,' said Mark, and he imitated the gestures with his own mouth and fingers. 'Forward – up – out! – bottom set. Forward – down – out! – top set.'

After several tries, Edie succeeded and stood astonished with her teeth smirking at her in her hand.

'No teeth now,' she said, distressed.

'Now practise putting them back in. You can do it,' Mark encouraged. 'See! – bottom – on, like this! – back – so. Top set – on – back – swallow!'

Eagerly staring at his pantomime, Edie, after several false starts, got her smile into place again.

'Now – out again!' drilled McAndrew. 'Splendid – *and* in again!' We watched a hypnotic sequence of Edie's teeth emerging and resettling.

'I do it now,' she said happily. 'I kin take 'em out, put 'em in, any time.'

'Great,' said Dr Jack, his own lesson having been interrupted by this elementary course. 'Every night, you take them out. If you don't they'll hurt you and go bad. But before you put them in the jar, this is what you do – ' and from his pocket he proudly whipped out a toothbrush and a tin of powder. 'Special cleaning powder, Edie – for dentures. Clean them so they'll taste good and look good. Clean – like this – ' and he brushed energetically with powder and water. 'Rinse – and put them in the jar.'

'Like washing clothes,' I said, trying to be helpful. 'Only this is the way to wash new teeth.'

Edie took her teeth from the jar and popped them in again.

'I wash 'em good,' she promised. 'Every night.'

'Fine,' said Dr Jack, with relief. Edie's mother, who had been muttering to herself, now burst out in unexpectedly dramatic utterance.

'Oh God! Who'll protect a poor widow woman?'

She glared at the minister, having evidently singled him out as her chief persecutor.

We left as politely as we could. McAndrew paused and slipped something into Mrs Tonna's small indignant hand.

'What did you give her?' I asked, as we waded through the curious rusting produce outside.

'Fifty cents,' he sighed, almost apologetically. 'It was what I had on me.'

Naturally, I had my own affairs to attend to that summer, and Edie didn't occupy much place in my thoughts. But I saw a good deal of her around the village, and her perpetual white smiles. The pearly ornaments of her mouth were to her all that sables or diamonds could be to a wealthier woman. All summer she was especially fond of displaying to admiring children how fearlessly she could bite into ice cream. The last time I saw Edie – but really it was nowhere near the last – I treated her to an ice-cream cone. She bit enthusiastically into the raspberry ripple, and I left her, still eating, on the hot and dusty corner of the crossroads. It was only a ten-cent cone; I've often wished it had been a twenty-cent one. That was on the last day of August. I was to see Edie again, but never a happy Edie – except once, perhaps.

Four days later, I was up shingling the barn roof when I saw a blue dot rushing along the field path from the next farm. Eventually it resolved itself into young Betty Robinson, and I could hear what she was yelling:

'Dan! Dan! You gotta come quick! Edie's hurt – awful bad!'

I shinned down the roof and raced back with her. When I got into the Robinsons' kitchen I could see that Edie was indeed hurt 'awful bad'. She was lying, red, blotched and blistered, in the middle of the floor, groaning faintly. An overturned copper boiler and a flood of cool water told their own story – she was evidently severely scalded, and had been lying there the Lord knew how long. I tore off a lot of her clothing, gritting my teeth – face, arms, hands, breast, stomach and legs were severely affected – and applied compresses, getting Betty to help and listening to her incoherent explanations of how everyone else was out and she had been picking berries and returned to find Edie on the floor. Leaving the scared girl with the unconscious woman, I ran back for the car and brought it round. Bundling Edie in – and trying not to hurt her – was a gigantic task, but at last she was lying on the back seat, and I was sending my cheerful yellow car flying down the road like a bat out of hell.

I met Mark, walking outside the village, and took him aboard. It lost us only thirty seconds and I wanted company.

'She's in severe shock,' I told him. 'And the scalding's pretty bad. We can't afford trying for Amherst. I'm making for Jack's hospital at Traceyville.'

'You think it's serious then,' said Mark. I nodded. It seemed an age before we got her to the little hospital and to a room on her own. She looked even worse now. While Dr Jack was shooting out orders to the nurse, McAndrew and I were still standing dumbly by the bed, when Edie opened one eye about an eighth of an inch. I had thought her unconscious, but she suddenly made a hoarse murmuring sound, and seemed to try to look at Mark and me. We bent down and could just catch a few words:

'Bury me with me teeth in.'

'All right, old girl,' said Mark. 'So we will if it comes to that, but it won't, you know. This is a hospital – the place they make you better. They'll make your skin new for you.'

Edie subsided again.

'She's gone under,' said Dr Jack. 'Out you get, you two.' And we did.

The village buzzed with the news, and harsh things were said of Mrs Robinson's fecklessness in leaving 'the half-wit' by herself. There was real concern for Edie, and for Mrs Tonna. Poor Mark, accompanied by two kindly matrons, went to break the news to her. I think he had a rough time of it, and so did Mrs Bell and Mrs Buchanan. They were not able to comfort Mrs Tonna or offer company in her sorrow according to custom – she merely closed up like a clam after yelling at them to get out. The good ladies, may God reward them, would have sat with Mrs Tonna day or night in that filthy shack as if it were a parlour – had they been allowed.

This sounds as if the anxious time was a long one, but it was not. Only three afternoons later I was sent a message – verbal and roundabout, as our farm had no phone – Mark had had an urgent summons to Traceyville. His car being out of action, he had caught a lift, and would I please follow and bring a truck. The last part of the communication seemed a bit odd, but I borrowed a rattletrap farm truck and sped along, feeling anxious and low. I had never seen anyone die.

Nor was I to do so now. When I got to the hospital, I found only Mark in Edie's empty room. It looked both bare and untidy. The drip apparatus hung from the ceiling, tweezers and bandages cluttered the tables. A few of Edie's possessions were to be seen on the bedside table and on the straight-backed chair : a Bible, a cotton dress, a shell necklace, her hat, her handbag. Somebody – probably Mark – had brought them along for her in the interim. Mark looked rather dazed.

'She's gone, Dan. She was in a coma, and died soon after I came. Jack's out on an emergency call – Sam Martin was here. I don't think anything could have been done.' He sighed. 'She suffered a lot, I'm afraid. I'm glad that at the end she couldn't have known anything.' He wandered about the room. 'I'll have to tell her mother. Well, I'd better collect her things – not that there's much, poor Edie.'

He picked up the floppy Bible. 'She couldn't read, of course, but she was rather set on her Bible – used to bring it to church with her.' He put it into a large brown paper bag, then picked up dress, hat, beads, handbag, and put them in, too – and then, espying Edie's teeth in a glass, almost obscured by a fortification of bandage, he wiped them off and popped them in on top of his parcel.

'Well, Mark – hello, Dan,' Dr Martin came in, sad-faced and tired. 'If you want to see her, come along.'

We followed him through the corridors.

'Sorry to drag you in,' said Mark to me, 'but it struck me

that if she died now it would be better to take her back to Sandford before the funeral. Her mother has the right to sit up with her if she likes. Mrs Tonna would never come to the hospital. I could hardly hitch a lift with a coffin – and I thought a truck would be easier. I'll make all the other arrangements.'

'Here,' said Dr Martin, ushering us into a sort of shed that served as a mortuary. It smelled of carbolic and fresh pine, and also unmistakably and sweetly of death. On top of a low trestle table Edie lay in a new coffin. She had been dressed in something white that decently hid the torso and legs, but her exposed face was grotesque. In all my later experience, I have seen no corpse look deader. What were once red blotches were now hideously pale scars. This distorted face betrayed every bit of damage in indelible marks, like the effects of bookworm up and down a page, or beetle and woodworm in an old plank. She seemed swollen, yet eroded, and her arms and legs were horrid too, like chewed leather, like dirty lace. Adding to the strangeness was the fact that her hair, which I had never seen in anything but the tight bun, was loosed and had been arranged flowing down her neck, past her shoulders, in thick lustrous black tresses, an image of feminine beauty not known in life, and now made bizarre by its proximity with disfigurement and death.

We looked at her in silence. Dr Martin had slipped out with a promise of bringing us the certificate. I felt a bit sick. Suddenly something pinched and sunken about Edie's mouth, even in that shapeless face, caught my attention.

'Her teeth,' I whispered fiercely to Mark. 'You've got her teeth!'

He drew them out of the parcel and we looked at each other. We were both remembering her command 'Bury me with me teeth in', and each knew he did not have the courage to pry about that horrid face, to fix the shining teeth into that dead mouth. Mark extended the teeth to me, and I, budding doctor that I was, in a supreme moment of cowardice shrank away, as if pretending not to notice. Mark moved to the side of the coffin – I nodded – and he thrust the teeth down by the side of the bulky corpse, in the gap between the left elbow and the torso. The teeth were now well hidden from view, and we nodded at each other in complicity. Edie, undisturbed, lay straight and neat, arms extended by her sides, toes pointed up, cold closed eyes towards the ceiling.

Dr Martin returned, with the certificate and accompanied by a shambling individual.

'Now, Jed,' said Dr Martin. 'Nail it up.'

And Jed went to work, fitting the lid and then hammering it on with hearty strokes, taking the bright nails out of his mouth, one by one, as required.

'If you're taking it back to Sandford,' said Dr Martin, 'best to get it nailed up right quick and keep it that way. This ain't the weather yet for open coffins. Besides – the less seen of *that*' – we knew he meant the corpse – 'the better!'

We ferried our melancholy luggage back to Sandford, the coffin jouncing heavily in the back of the open truck. First we drove to the shack, but Mrs Tonna only yelled, 'Take it away! I don't want that here!' She was equally unfavourable to the idea that she should come to the manse and sit with her dead in the front parlour. However, she consented to accept the parcel of Edie's belongings, counting them over carefully. We drove back to the manse; there was nothing to be done but for Mark to keep the coffin himself.

When we got to the manse, the unlocked house was full of neighbours. We – and our load – had been sighted, and the grapevine had been busy. From that Thursday evening until the funeral on Saturday, there were relays of watchers who sat up with the coffin, while the daylight crept about the subdued parlour, or while the oil lamps (thought more respectful than electricity) winked through the long night watches over the nails in Edie's tight box. The bereaved remained obstinately in her shack, despite attempts to persuade her to come to the manse.

Edie's funeral was a particularly fine one in spite of the hurry. The packed church smelled of hot varnish and flowers.

Just before the service there was a whisper at the back, and I heard a small Bertleson say, 'Look, Ma, there's the guest of honour!' To universal surprise, Mrs Tonna, led in by Mrs Buchanan and dressed in respectable black dress and hat (patently donations), had consented to perform her function as chief mourner. She sat erect and quiet with the women in the front pew through all the prayers, Mark's short address, and the singing about Time's sons flying forgotten.

She also went decorously in a car following the hearse to the graveyard. Sandford's burying-ground is not beside either church, but outside the village, in the opposite direction from the Tonna dwelling. It is a piece of cleared land near a little fir wood, an extension of the family plot of some original settler and always called 'Parkers' graveyard', though the Parkers have long since either descended into it or left. The distance from church to cemetery being nearly three miles, a funeral procession can look impressive. Edie had a flatteringly numerous following. She would have been pleased. I remembered how she liked cars.

The interment was brief and moving; it always is moving to see a coffin lowered into the dark ground. Then the earth was heaped over it, and wreaths were laid on the mound.

'Poor thing,' said Mrs Bell. 'She was a good worker.'

Mrs Tonna turned on her. 'If Edie hadn't of worked, she wouldn't of died! Huh! Washin' in a lot of damn kitchens!' And she fell to her customary muttering. I felt even more depressed. There was something unanswerable in what she said. If the meek are going to inherit the earth, they're taking a long time about it.

The rest of the weekend was rather subdued, but life went on as usual. As Mark seemed to appreciate company, I went over to the manse on Tuesday evening. Although there was a September chilliness after sundown, it was warm enough for us to sit on the back verandah. A soft yellow light fell from the kitchen window; the dusk turned into night, but we didn't notice, as the conversation drifted along. We talked of this and that –

about the Canso Causeway, tourists, bears, the prophet Elisha, Indian reserves and Indians. Mark was just launching into one of his favourite topics when we dimly saw a small, apparently headless, human figure coming across the backyard. Our words died on our lips as the shrouded shape moved along the path and up the steps. As it came into the illuminated area we saw, to our momentary relief, that the figure was only Mrs Tonna – in all her rags again, with a gunny-sack over her head and shoulders.

'Mrs Tonna,' said Mark. 'What can we do for you? Do take a chair.'

Mrs Tonna ignored his remarks. She stood at the edge of the pool of light and in her shrill thin voice shouted, 'What have you done with my Edie?'

I had a wild impulse to answer promptly 'Buried her', as that seemed the obvious answer. Fortunately I kept quiet.

'You know,' Mark said gently, 'that Edie's dead, don't you? You were at the funeral – '

'Ah!' shrieked Mrs Tonna. 'Liar! I know what you done.'

'Well,' Mark said, trying to be patient, 'what is it that you think we have done?'

She came a step nearer.

'I seen my Edie and she told me. Don't think you can hide it from me, 'cuz she told me what you done. You buried her without her teeth in!'

Neither Mark nor I could speak for a minute. The cold seconds dragged by, with Mrs Tonna standing there, like an infernal angel in a poor state of plumage.

I found my voice. 'What do you mean, you've seen Edie?'

'What I said. My Edie – leastways her sperrit – come to me last night and told me. She's a walkin' and can't get no rest becuz her teeth ain't in.' Mrs Tonna's rags fluttered as if moved by unhealthy air from another region. I avoided looking into the shadows behind her.

'She asked you,' said Mrs Tonna. 'She begged you on her dyin' bed to see her teeth was put in and *you*,' she turned vehemently to Mark, '*you* promised partickler to do it. But

340

when the time come, you stuffed 'em down the side of the coffin. She thought the world of them teeth, Edie did.'

Mrs Tonna started trembling and wringing her hands. Suddenly her face puckered, and tears began to spill from her eyes.

'Oh, Mister, you gotta do sumpin'. Edie can't take no rest in her grave. And I can't rest, neither, I'm that frightened! I'm sceered to go home, 'cuz Edie will just keep comin' and comin' and give me no peace!' She sobbed aloud, her little bent shoulders shaking. 'Oh, please, Mister, make it right, or Edie'll haunt me to my dyin' day and I won't get a wink of sleep until the Judgement!'

It was heartbreaking to see her misery. From an eldritch messenger, Mrs Tonna had become a distressed pathetic old lady – although that didn't undo the fearful nature of her message.

Mark went over and put his arm around her. 'There – don't cry, Mrs Tonna. It's true, but it can be put right, and it will. We – I'll go to the graveyard and dig Edie up and put her teeth in. You can come if you want, and make sure it's done properly.'

He meant it, every word. I stood up. 'I'm going with you.' That moment of cowardice had to be paid for.

Mrs Tonna dried her eyes with the sacking. 'We go now?' she asked eagerly.

'Yes, now, or as soon as we can get the things we need.'

Mark collected a couple of shovels while I got his flashlight and a dark lantern from the manse. We got into my jolly-coloured car – Mrs Tonna beside me and Mark in the back – and went along, stopping only by our farm where I quietly borrowed a pickaxe, a hammer and chisel from the shed.

We drove off again, slowly. I thought of happier night drives down that road. What was I doing, in the company of a minister, a pickaxe and a madwoman, going to dig up an acquaintance who had been dead for five days? We passed a dead skunk; the choking odour invaded the car and hung darkly about us. A new moon came into view, and the northern lights were shining across the sky. The surrounding world might be shrouded, but we were naked to the pale heavens above.

Too soon we got to Parkers' graveyard. I left the car where it wouldn't be seen; we had no desire to be caught at our grisly work. Carrying the implements, we walked along the scrubby ground, bumping into gravestones. Mrs Tonna followed quietly. Edie's grave was not hard to find; the heap of flowers marked it. There was my mother's bouquet, exactly where I had placed it – but the white roses were now flabby and blackened. I scraped all the flowers away. We arranged our flashlights and the lantern so they would be useful without making us too visible. The night itself, although cool, seemed now mercilessly bright. The moon rose higher, and the aurora borealis shot across the sky, turning the multitude of stars pale in the long flickering rays into insistent searchlights.

'There is nothing hidden that shall not be revealed,' said Mark suddenly, and began to dig.

I shovelled away, too. The sandy soil was not heavy, but it was well packed, and Edie had been buried the proverbial six feet deep. Mrs Tonna stayed nearby, but kept out of our way. I saw perspiration on Mark's face, and felt myself sweating. The horrible job at the end of all this had to be done by me. I, a doctor, couldn't shirk it a second time.

At last our shovels struck the coffin. I loosened it in its bed with the pickaxe and then we could bring it to the surface. That wasn't easy, because we both had to stand in the pit and heave it up; it would have been too dark and cramped to complete the job at the bottom of the grave. When she saw the coffin arrive at the surface, Mrs Tonna clapped her hands, softly, and stared at it with expectation. Mark and I stood and looked at it also. We were streaked with dirt, and the coffin too was soil-stained. Everything smelled of earth – and of something else. I took the chisel and hammer and pried all round the lid before trying to force it off. Jed had done his work well, and this took quite a while; I didn't want to crack the wood, as I would have to replace the lid – afterwards.

At last it felt as if there were enough give for the lid to come off easily.

'I can open it now,' I said hoarsely.

Mark and Mrs Tonna stood beside me. The wind blew suddenly, as if the earth were shivering. Trying not to look, and wishing I could stop my nostrils, I moved the lid off with one violent wrench.

'Aiee–ee-e!' It was Mrs Tonna shrieking, and running for the road, screaming as she ran.

'My God!' said Mark.

I looked. There was Edie. But now her right arm lay across her chest, and the scarred skin on the back of her pale hand was newly scratched, as if abraded by contact with a hard surface. And there, firmly in her mouth, were two rows of teeth, fixed in a broad white smile that gleamed and glittered triumphantly under the northern lights.

About the Authors

JAMES ALDRIDGE was born in 1918 and spent his boyhood in Australia, but before the war he moved to London where he began his career as a journalist on the *Daily Sketch* and *Sunday Despatch*. During the Second World War he was a correspondent for the Australian Newspaper Service and later for the North American Newspaper Alliance, covering Finland, Norway, the Middle East, Greece and the USSR. He was awarded the Llewellyn Rhys Memorial Prize in 1944. His books include *The Diplomat, The Last Exile, A Sporting Proposition* (filmed by Disney), *The Marvellous Mongolian* and *Goodbye Un-America*. James Aldridge is married with two sons and lives in London.

DOMINIC COOPER was born in 1944. After working at various jobs in London until 1970, he then went to live in Iceland in order to have the time and freedom to write. He spent two years there before making his home in the Hebrides where he wrote his first novel, *The Dead of Winter*. Moving to Edinburgh in 1973, he worked for four years as a clockmaker and completed two further novels, *Sunrise* and *Men at Axlir*. In the spring term of 1978 he held the Residential Fellowship at the University of East Anglia. His home is now in London.

About the Authors

CELIA DALE is the daughter of actor James Dale and spent much of her childhood more or less backstage, much of it in Stratford-on-Avon and the United States. She worked for a time in Fleet Street, and is the widow of journalist Guy Ramsey. She now works as a publishers' adviser, and is the book reviewer in *Homes & Gardens* magazine. Her recent novels include *A Dark Corner, The Innocent Party* and *Helping with Inquiries*. Many of her stories have been read on radio or have been adapted as plays on both radio and television. She lives in Highgate, London.

PETER DICKINSON was born in 1927 in the middle of Africa, within earshot of the Victoria Falls, but has lived most of his life in England. He won a scholarship to Eton, and enjoyed a very old-fashioned education there and at Cambridge, broken by an undistinguished spell in the army. For seventeen years he was an assistant editor at *Punch*. His first books were published in 1968, and since then he has written about twenty, half of them slightly weird detective stories, and the remainder mostly children's adventure fantasies. Both kinds of work have won prizes, and have been published in ten languages. He is married, has two adult daughters and two teenage sons. He spends half his time in a small house in West London, and the other half in a decayed Victorian dower house in Hampshire. He likes to do things for himself, from plumbing to thinking.

ESME DODDERIDGE is Welsh. She grew up in North Wales and was educated there and at Bedford College, London. She has worked both in Britain and abroad as teacher, translator and lexicographer. She is married and has three children. Short stories of hers have appeared in *New Stories I* and *The Guardian*. Her first novel was published in 1979 by Taplinger Publishing Co., New York.

MARGARET A. DOODY, born in Canada, was largely educated in England. She has an Oxford BA, MA and D.Phil. From 1969 to 1976 she was a lecturer in English at Swansea University, and she is now an Associate Professor of English at the University of California. Two of her interests are ancient history and fiction. She is the author of *Aristotle Detective*.

JANICE ELLIOTT has published twelve novels of which the latest was *The Honey Tree* (Hodder & Stoughton). One of her earlier books, *The Buttercup Chain*, was filmed by Columbia. She has also written short stories that have been widely published and translated, and highly praised children's books. After reading English at St Anne's College, Oxford, she worked for some years as a full-time journalist on a number of publications, including *Harper's Bazaar* and *The Sunday Times*. Currently she reviews regularly for the *Sunday Telegraph*. Since her first novel was published in 1962 Janice Elliott has lived with her husband and son in Sussex.

PHILIP EVANS, aged 35, is employed by a publishing firm. He has written two and a half novels of adventure; some books on football; and has written about the game for several magazines and newspapers including *The Sunday Times* and the *Observer*. His favourite composer is Beethoven; his favourite cartoonist is Charles Addams; and he likes the works of Raymond Chandler.

MICHAEL GILBERT's novels are translated into a dozen languages and published all over the world. He is also well known as a writer of stage, television and radio plays and serials. In private life he is a busy and successful solicitor and still does much of his writing on the train to London every weekday. He was a founder member of both the Crime Writers' Association

About the Authors

and of the Screen Writers' Guild. He has two sons, five daughters and lives at Cobham, in Kent.

GILES GORDON has published five novels, three collections of short stories and edited a number of anthologies including *A Book of Contemporary Nightmares* and *Prevailing Spirits*, a book of Scottish ghost stories.

WILLIS HALL began his writing career during military service when he was responsible for numerous scripts for Radio Malaya. After returning to England he had his first major success in the theatre with *The Long and the Short and the Tall*, which won him the *Evening Standard* 'Best Play of the Year' award in 1959. He has since twice been associated with the same award, in collaboration with Keith Waterhouse, for their adaptations of Eduardo de Filippo's *Saturday, Sunday, Monday* (1973) and *Filumena* (1978). In addition to his work in the theatre, Willis Hall has written extensively for both the cinema and television. His TV plays include *The Villa Maroc, They Don't All Open Men's Boutiques* and *A Song at Twilight*. He has also written a number of children's books and plays including the *Kidnapped at Christmas* trilogy. He has an avid interest in sport in general and soccer in particular, and has written a number of books on sport as well as countless journalistic pieces.

SARAH LAWSON was born in Indianapolis in 1943 and graduated from Indiana University and the University of Glasgow. She has worked as a teacher, typist, amanuensis, examinations' invigilator and swimming instructor. She is now a freelance writer and lives in London. She is currently working on a children's book and a translation from the French of Christine de Pisan.

MICHAEL LEVEY is the author of several books, including biographies of Mozart and, more recently, of Walter Pater. He has also written a good deal on the visual arts. A short story of his appears in *Winter's Crimes* (1979). He is Director of the National Gallery, London.

GRAHAM LORD writes the *Sunday Express* books column. Now 36, he was born in Rhodesia, raised in Mozambique and schooled in Rhodesia and at Cambridge University, where he edited *Varsity* and worked for the *Cambridge News*. He lives with his wife and two daughters in a Berkshire village. He has written five novels: *Marshmallow Pie*; *A Roof under Your Feet*; *The Spider and the Fly*; *God and All His Angels*; and *The Nostradamus Horoscope*.

ROBERT NYE was born in London in 1939. He left grammar school when he was 16 and supported himself by odd jobs before becoming a full-time writer at the age of 21, going to live in a cottage in Wales where he worked on two collections of poems which won him a Gregory Award in 1963. His principal books of poems are *Darker Ends* (Calder & Boyars, 1969) and *Divisions on a Ground* (Carcanet Press, 1976). His novel *Falstaff* (Hamish Hamilton, 1976) won both the Hawthornden Prize and the Guardian Fiction Prize, and has been translated into several foreign languages. He has also published one collection of short stories, *Tales I Told My Mother* (Calder & Boyars, 1969), and several books for children. He is married and lives in Ireland.

KIERAN PRENDIVILLE is 31, married and has been a working journalist for eleven years, having started his career as a copy boy in a news agency in Oldham, Lancashire. After eighteen months he moved to Fleet Street where he worked for various newspapers as a general news and sports reporter based at the Fleet Street News Agency. In 1972 he joined the BBC as a researcher for the *Man Alive* documentary series. Shortly after he began work on a consumer programme called *That's Life* where he joined the presentation team after the first series. Since that time he has worked on various BBC productions including *Nationwide, Holiday Programme, The Risk Business* and – since he left *That's Life* in 1978 – *Tommorow's World*. His interests, such as poker, horse racing and Queen's Park Rangers Football Club, are probably unhealthy but one of them has got to come up some time.

AGNES SHORT was born in Yorkshire of Scots-English parents and studied English literature at Exeter University. She has worked as a teacher, secretary, research assistant and in the editorial offices of a Sunday newspaper and has lived in London, Oxford, Wiltshire and Malaya before settling in Old Aberdeen . . . in the house which inspired her story 'Intercom'. It was her inquiries into the history of this sixteenth-century house – and the Old Town – which formed the basis for her historical novels, *The Heritors* (1977) and *Clatter Vengeance* (1979) (Constable and Co. Ltd).

STEVE STERN was born in Memphis, Tennessee, in 1947, under an evil eye. For the first nineteen years of his life, he slept soundly. Then, in the late sixties – harassed by friends, baited by psychiatrists and the protagonists of certain novels, cudgelled by drugs – he awoke somewhere in north London. There on the evening of the thirteenth of April, while looking out of a window, he was happy. As a penance he returned to the States and took up residence on a dirt farm in Arkansas, a little to the south-west of history. Amid genial surroundings he engaged in such activities as sin, pot valour and animal husbandry. When memory returned, he went into the university where he devoted himself to letters and the fear of women. Here his life comes to its formal close, though he was resurrected for a while in 1977, in England, in search of lost causes.

KATHRINE TALBOT was born and raised in Germany and came to England as a refugee in the late thirties and learned English via Chesterton, Dickens and Jane Austen. By the middle of the war she had advanced as far as Henry James. She has written some novels (three published), many short stories (some published), and translated a great variety of German texts, from scientific papers on the mating habits of baboons to scholarly works on art history. She is married to the painter Kit Barker. They lived in the United States in the late forties and early fifties, moving from east to west and back again, earning their living by any job available. Back in England, they settled in a completely unhaunted Tudor cottage in Sussex where they have lived ever since, with occasional excursions to the Continent and the United States.

PETER TINNISWOOD is 42. He was born in Liverpool. He is the author of five novels (the first, the award-winning *A Touch of Daniel*). He writes comedy series for the BBC and also writes regularly for stage and radio and newspapers.

MICHAEL VESTEY is 34, and was born in London. He has been a journalist on national newspapers, and has also contributed to magazines such as *London Life*, *Newsweek* and the *New Statesman*. He is currently a reporter for BBC Radio and an occasional presenter of the *Today* programme on Radio 4.

H. H. WASHBROOK is American. He is known for his incredible beauty and his deep knowledge of cricket and lacrosse. He is a prolific writer of books of all genres and is at present working on a love story of epic proportions entitled *Shemerelda.* He lives in the West Indies.

FAY WELDON was born in England but reared in New Zealand. She has an MA in economics and psychology, and before turning to novel writing was a highly successful copywriter, spending much of her advertising career at Mather & Crowther. She has also written plays and scripts for radio and television including the first of the *Upstairs Downstairs* scripts (she formulated the characters as well), worked on a six-part television series of *Pride and Prejudice*, a black comedy entitled *Mr Director* which was staged at the Orange Tree Theatre in Richmond and a new play called *Action Replay* which was premiered in 1979 at the Birmingham Repertory Theatre. She has also written an episode of *Send in the Girls* and thought up the slogan 'Go to work on an egg'. A current member of the Arts Council's Literary Panel, she has already had six of her novels published, has another under her belt and is currently at work on the next.

STEVE WILSON was born in 1943. Educated at Harrow and Oxford, he worked and travelled throughout Europe, South America and the US West Coast; he has since taught adult classes in literature. His work includes the prize-winning story *Michael michael Motorcycle* and six others, and novels *The Lost Traveller*, *Dealer's Move* and its forthcoming sequel *Dealer's War*. He is married with two cats and lives in London.